EBB TIDE

The Nathaniel Drinkwater Novels:
An Eye of the Fleet
A King's Cutter
A Brig of War
The Bomb Vessel
The Corvette
1805
Baltic Mission
In Distant Waters
A Private Revenge
Under False Colours
The Flying Squadron
Beneath the Aurora
The Shadow of the Eagle
Ebb Tide

* * *

ALSO AVAILABLE FROM MCBOOKS PRESS
A River in Borneo
The Darkening Sea

EBB TIDE

A Nathaniel Drinkwater Novel

Richard Woodman

McBooks
Press

Essex, Connecticut

McBooks Press

An imprint of Globe Pequot, the trade division of
The Rowman & Littlefield Publishing Group, Inc.
4501 Forbes Blvd., Ste. 200
Lanham, MD 20706
www.rowman.com

Distributed by NATIONAL BOOK NETWORK

British Library Cataloguing in Publication Information available

Library of Congress Cataloging-in-Publication Data available

ISBN 9781493071791 (pbk. : alk. paper) | ISBN 9781493071807 (epub)

∞™ The paper used in this publication meets the minimum requirements
of American National Standard for Information Sciences—Permanence of
Paper for Printed Library Materials, ANSI/NISO Z39.48-1992.

For
Jane and Vernon Hite

Contents

There is a tide in the affairs of men,
Which taken at the flood leads on to fortune;
Omitted, all the voyage of their life
Is bound in shallows and in miseries.

Shakespeare, *Julius Caesar*, IV, iii

The Sunset Gun

Mr Martin Forester was growing anxious. He pulled out his watch and looked at it, then glanced up at the sky before turning his gaze impatiently towards the shoreline. It was getting late and wanted only six minutes to sunset, but an advancing overcast had obscured the setting sun to cause a premature darkness. He did not like the look of the weather. The ship, although anchored in the lee of the high land half a mile to the south of her, lifted to a low swell rolling along the coast, and the wind was strong enough, even here, to set up a mournful moan in the rigging. Beyond Bull Point to the westward the Atlantic was brewing an unseasonal gale. He felt the vessel, lying with her head to the west, snub to her cable as the flood tide surged past her hull and fought for mastery of her with the wind in her rigging. If the wind got up any more, he knew she would see-saw back and forth, her cable occasionally jumping against the whelps on the windlass gypsy with a judder, until the tide turned and she lay betwixt wind and tide, rolling to the swell. It was not going to be a pleasant night. Not for mid-July, anyway, he concluded, giving vent to his feelings.

'Damn it!' he muttered.

Sensing rather than hearing the mate's agitation, the quartermaster on the port side of the bridge above the paddle-box lowered the long watch-glass and announced helpfully, 'No sign of the boat yet, sir.'

'No,' responded Forester irritably. 'Damned nuisance.' He sighed resignedly and walked across to where Quartermaster Potts stood. 'She won't be back before sunset, so we'll make colours first. Pipe the hands to stand by.'

'Aye, aye, sir.' Potts replaced the telescope in its rack and moved to the centre of the bridge where the wheel and binnacle stood, relinquishing his post to Forester. The mate was not a bad fellow, Potts thought, but always wanted things to run smoothly, and when there was a delay, as there was this evening, he was apt to become irritable. Potts had been the victim of Mr Forester's short fuse on several occasions and had learned to live with it. He put the call to his lips and blew the piercing summons that would bring the watch on deck.

Standing out over the paddle-box, Forester took another quick glance at his watch and then, composing himself for the few minutes he had yet to wait until the obscured sun dipped below the western horizon, he looked about himself. Being the steamer's mate and a conscientious seaman, he cast an experienced eye over her from his vantage point. The paddle-box that rose over the sponson was not only high above the water but was also outside the line of the ship's rail. With his back outboard he could, in a single sweep, take in the whole ship from her bowsprit to her counter stern.

A seaman emerged from the forward companionway and walked up to stand by the jackstaff. The jack, a curious device of St George's cross quartering four ancient ships whose broadside cannon belched fire, flapped vigorously in the southwesterly breeze that came off the Devon coast, carrying with it the scent of grass and wood-smoke. The foremast yards with their close-furled sails were neatly squared to Mr Forester's exacting standards. The sails on the mainmast astern of the narrow bridge that spanned the vessel from paddle-box to paddle-box were equally tidily stowed. But rising above and dominating the whole after part of the ship was the great black column of the funnel.

Mr Forester hated that funnel. Even now a sulphurous shimmer from its top told of the banked boiler hidden down below and, if he looked across on the starboard quarter, he could see the faint but unmistakable pall of its smoke laid on the grey surface of the sea. With the boiler fires banked, the funnel was quiescent, a malevolent threat which, it seemed to Forester in his more irritable moments, possessed a secret hatred for the mate, for he was engaged in a ceaseless war with the thing. Mr Forester had been bred in a tough school and had spent most of his life under sail. He had, moreover, seen service in the Royal Navy as master's mate and had been in Codrington's flagship, the *Asia*, at Navarino. He was therefore accustomed to decks being white, not besmirched by soot and smuts. Steam, whatever its advocates might claim, seemed to Forester to

2

have introduced as many problems as it had solved. He sighed and let his gaze roll aft again. Beyond the long after deck with its saloon skylight and the glazed lights which illuminated the staterooms below, rose the huge ensign staff. A seaman stood alongside it, the halliards of the large defaced red ensign ready in his hands. Its snapping fly bore the same device as formed the jack and it was repeated yet again in the flag which stood out like a board from the mainmast truck high above his head, indicating the presence on board the steamer of an Elder Brother of the Trinity House.

Satisfied, Forester turned forward again, distracted by the noise of voices almost immediately below him on the foredeck where the crew closed up round the polished brass barrel of the short six-pounder, one of four carriage-mounted guns borne on the long deck of the Trinity House Steam Vessel *Vestal*.

'Colour party mustered, sir,' Potts reported, as the gun-captain below the bridge knelt behind his gun's breech, one hand upraised.

'Aye, aye.'

Forester withdrew his watch again. One and a half minutes. He wished the boat had returned and that he could have had the whole deck snugged down with the cutter in her davits before embarking on this ritual. If the wind veered and caught them on a lee shore, they would have to get under weigh, so he wanted to make sure the ship would be fit for the eventuality sooner rather than later.

He stared out over the leaden water with its froth of white caps and watched a fulmar cut its shallow, sweeping dive across the very surface of the waves, its wings immobile. The absolute confidence with which the bird made so close an approach to the turbulent surface never failed to amaze him. Beyond lay the high coast. Lights were appearing in the town of Ilfracombe which nestled beneath the moor in the seclusion of its rocky bay. The strong tide which flooded east offshore would be scarcely felt within the compass of those rocks, he reflected. Then he saw the boat.

It came clear of Chapel Hill, its oars moving in perfect precision, and headed out towards *Vestal*, the diminutive flag at its bow showing grey in the gathering gloom. As the coxswain cleared the land he applied his helm to offset the eastward sweep of the flood and the cutter began to crab across the tide, exposing her starboard side, though making for the steamer in a direct line, judged to a nicety.

'Damned good coxswain, that Thomas,' Forester murmured approvingly before glancing at his watch again. He nodded at Potts, turned aft, drew himself up and raised two fingers to the forecock of his hat.

The pipe shrilled its high, imperative note and Forester saw the ensign start its slow descent. Behind and below him on the boat-deck the gun-captain applied his match, and the sudden boom of the gun, with its sharp stink of burnt powder, echoed round the bay, reverberating from the cliffs and sending into the air scores of roosting auks and kittiwakes. The smoke swept past Forester as he stood immobile, atop the paddle-box, until, giving an almost imperceptible nod to Potts, the quartermaster blew the descending notes of the 'carry-on'.

Forester relaxed and walked inboard to where the bridge widened on the ship's centreline to provide the compass platform and steering position, behind which stood the handsomely varnished teak chart-house. 'Very well, Potts. Pipe the watch to stand by the boat falls.'

Potts blew the pipe yet again and both men waited as the hands turned up from below. A steam-ship provided power for hoisting the boats, so the job could be accomplished with the deck-watch alone. Now that they worked the three-watch system, it made life much easier for the seamen, though Forester, in his blacker moments, was certain all this ease was not good for any of them. He had a remorseless belief in the imperatives of duty.

'No need for another flag, Potts,' he remarked to the quartermaster, 'now that Cap'n Drew's is up.' Forester nodded at the main truck where the Elder Brother's flag still flew, unstruck at sunset since it was a command flag and remained aloft as long as the officer so honoured was on board.

'There's Drew now, sir,' said Potts as a gold-braided figure appeared on deck below.

'Come up to meet the new fellow,' Forester added conversationally, mellowing now the cutter was almost back.

'Who is 'e, sir, this new fellow?' Potts inquired.

'Captain Sir Nathaniel Drinkwater KCB,' explained Forester, who made it his business to know such things. 'Newly elected to the Court of Trinity House, but a distinguished sea-officer.'

''Ow is 'e distinguished, then, sir? Were 'e at Navarin?' asked Potts mischievously, knowing Mr Forester enjoyed reminding them of his presence at the battle.

'No, he was well-known as a frigate captain in the war. I don't think he ever commanded a ship-of-the-line, though. Spent a lot of time on special service, I believe . . . ' A cough interrupted this cosy chat and

Forester turned. 'Ah, Cap'n Poulter, sir, red cutter's approaching, Captain Drew's on deck, and the wind's tending to freshen.'

'Very well, Mr Forester. I had better go down and join Captain Drew.'

Poulter settled his hat and made for the ladder, hesitating at the top and turning his head as though sniffing the air. 'You're right about the wind, Martin,' he added informally, then disappeared to the deck below.

Captain Sir Nathaniel Drinkwater drew his boat cloak more closely round him as the cutter pulled out from the shelter of the bay. He could sense the damp in the air as it made the old wound in his shoulder ache, and there was a discouraging bite to the wind as they came out from under the shelter of the land. He cast an eye over the men at the oars. They were all kitted out in ducks and pea-jackets, long ribbons blowing in the wind from their round hats as they bent in synchronized effort to their oars. Beside him the *Vestal*'s second mate, a young man who had introduced himself as William Quier, directed the coxswain's attention to the influence of the tide.

'Mind the force of the flood now, Thomas,' he said with quiet authority, catching Drinkwater's eye, then looking hurriedly away again towards the ship. Drinkwater followed his gaze. She was an ungainly brute, he thought, her great funnel and huge, grey paddle-boxes dominating the black hull. He supposed by her two masts that she was, technically at least, a brigantine, but the presence of the funnel gave so great a spread to them that she lacked all pretence at the symmetry and elegance he thought of as characterizing the rig. He recalled the brig-rigged *Hellebore* and her handiness, and could find no indication that *Vestal* might be manoeuvred with such facility. He grunted, and Quier shot him a quick glance, to be recalled by the boom of the gun at which the young man jumped involuntarily while the men at the oars grinned.

'Sunset gun, sir,' Quier observed unnecessarily.

'Yes, indeed.'

Drinkwater smiled to himself; poor Quier seemed a rather nervous young man and he himself was a damned old fool. He had forgotten the ship ahead of them had a steam engine, even though the confounded thing proclaimed itself by that hideous black column!

'How does she handle, Mr Quier?' Drinkwater asked, nodding at the *Vestal*. 'I presume you can back one paddle and pull or', he added with a self-deprecating shrug, abandoning the metaphor familiar to men used to pulling boats, 'put it astern, eh?'

'Indeed yes, sir. She handles very well in smooth water. She can be turned in her own length.'

Drinkwater regarded the younger man. 'You can turn a brig in her own length, you know. I suppose a brigantine is not so handy.'

'Not quite, sir, but for either you need a wind.'

'Of course . . . ' The folly of old age assailed Drinkwater again and he smiled ruefully to himself. There was no point in feeling foolish; one simply had to endure it with the consolation that it would come even to this young man one day. He reassessed Quier. The young man was shy, not nervous. It occurred to Drinkwater that he might be a rather intimidating figure, sitting stiffly in the *Vestal*'s cutter.

But Quier was overcoming his diffidence and was not going to let Drinkwater escape so easily. 'Is this the first steam-ship you have been aboard, sir?'

'No, I made a short passage on the sloop *Rhadamanthus* – oh, I suppose eight or nine years ago, just after Evans brought her back across the Atlantic, but I'm afraid I don't recall how well we manoeuvred.' Drinkwater paused, recollecting something the second officer had said. 'You mentioned *Vestal* manoeuvred well in fine weather . . .'

'In a smooth sea, yes, sir. She isn't so handy when a chop is running.'

'Oh?'

'It's the paddles, d'you see,' Quier explained, his pleasant face betraying his enthusiasm. 'They function best at a particular draught; if the ship rolls heavily, the deeper paddle has greater effect than the shallower one. When steering a course the inequities tend to cancel each other out, but when manoeuvring, matters aren't so predictable.'

'I see. D'you use the sails to help?'

'You can, sir, but we don't usually have sufficient men to do all that if we are manoeuvring to lift a buoy.'

'No, of course not . . .'

'And when we set our sails to assist the steam engine, the steady heel, though more comfortable, tends to hold one paddle down all the time.'

'Yes,' Drinkwater nodded, 'yes, I comprehend that.'

'You see, it doesn't usually matter too much, sir, because we can only pick up buoys in reasonably good weather . . . '

6

'Yes, of course,' Drinkwater broke in. Then, seeing Quier's crestfallen look at the interruption, he added, 'A long time ago, Mr Quier, I myself served in the buoy-yachts.'

Quier looked at his passenger in some astonishment. The old man's face was shadowed by the collar of his cloak and the forecock of his hat, but Quier could see that the watery grey eyes were shrewd, despite one curious drooping lid with what looked like a random tattoo mark upon it. The deeply lined mouth curved into a smile, revealing by a slight asymmetry that one at least of the furrows seaming Sir Nathaniel's cheeks was due not to the passage of time, but a sword-cut.

'You are surprised, I believe.'

'Only that I supposed you had always been a naval officer, sir.'

'I was unemployed after the American War.' Drinkwater saw the young man frown. 'Not the recent affair,' he explained, referring to the war which had ended twenty-eight years earlier and during which Mr Quier might just have been born, 'the *first* American War.' He paused again, adding, 'in which the United States gained its independence.'

Quier's mouth hung open and when he realized his astonishment was as rude as it was obvious, he said hurriedly, 'I see, sir.'

'It was', Drinkwater agreed ruefully, 'a very long time ago.'

'Comin' alongside, sir,' the coxswain muttered, and, as the *Vestal* suddenly loomed huge and menacing, her stilled paddles ahead of them like the blades of an enormous water-wheel, Quier was obliged to attend to the business of hooking on to the falls.

Helped out of the boat as she swung in the falls and was griped in to the rail, and creaking with what he called 'his rheumaticks', Drinkwater retrieved his cane from Quier and acknowledged the salute of his fellow Elder Brother, Captain Richard Drew.

'Good to have you aboard, Sir Nathaniel, how was your journey?'

'Good to be aboard, Drew. I've been two days on the road from Taunton, damn it, so the ship's a welcome sight.'

'May I introduce Captain Poulter, the vessel's master . . . '

'Sir Nathaniel . . . '

'Captain Poulter, how d'ye do? I knew your father; served under him for a while after the first American War. I met him last in 'fourteen when we both served under the late king when he was, as he was pleased to term it, "Admiral of the British fleet".'

7

'It's good to have you aboard, sir.'

'I understand we're taking a look at the light at Hartland Point tomorrow if the weather serves?'

'That's right,' Drew interrupted, 'I've told Poulter we should be off the point at about half tide to gain the best conditions. There's a small breakwater at the foot of the cliffs. We shall land there.'

'All being well,' Drinkwater added, smiling, sensitive to Poulter's resentment at Drew's authoritarianism.

As if to confirm this perception, Poulter nodded. 'Quite so,' he said.

Quier arrived and informed Poulter that Sir Nathaniel's effects had been placed in the second state-cabin, whereupon the gathering on the deck broke up.

'Come and take a glass, Sir Nathaniel,' Drew invited, 'there's no need for *us* to keep the deck, eh?' and the Elder Brother led the way below chuckling.

It was now almost dark as Forester chivvied the hands about the deck, and the overcast covered the sky.

Drinkwater was floundering and he beat vainly for air as though his flailing arms could provide what he gasped for if he strove hard enough. He was curiously aware that he was drowning, yet equally convinced that he was dry, and that if he kept his arms moving he would survive. Yet the sensation filled him with terror. Somehow his subconscious mind registered the fact that this was not real, that the drowning was purely a vehicle for fear, and that it was only the fear which could touch him now.

As he grasped this and felt his heart hammer with increasing apprehension, he caught sight of something he dreaded with all the primeval fear of which his imagination was capable. She came upon him with ferocious speed, at first a faint glow in the distance, then with the velocity of recognition. Now she loomed over him and he felt the chill of her presence and her cold ethereal fist reaching for his lurching heart.

He would fain have averted his eyes, but her face, at once as beautiful as it was hideous, compelled his attention. And with her came the noise, a noise of roaring and clattering, of the scream of wind and of things – what things he did not know – tumbling in such confusion that it seemed the whole world had lost its moorings and only the ghastly white lady maintained her terrifying equilibrium, poised

8

above him. Then she descended upon him like a gigantic succubus. He felt his body submit to her in a painful yet oddly delicious sensation while his soul fought for life.

Drinkwater woke in a muck sweat, the perspiration streaming from him and his heart thundering with such violence that he thought it must burst from his body. He imagined he had screamed out in his fright, yet around him all seemed quiet as he recollected his circumstances, making out the unfamiliar shapes of the state-cabin's furniture. As his heartbeat subsided, the last images of the dream faded. He could still conjure into his mind's eye the white lady, but she was receding, like the dying image of a sunlit window on the closed eyelid, identifiable only as an afterglow of perception.

For a moment he thought he had suffered a seizure, such had been the violence of his heartbeat, but it had only been a dream, and an old, almost familiar one. He tried to recall how many times he had had the recurring dream during his long life and remembered only that it had often served as a premonition.

The thought worried him more than the dream's inherent, terrifying images. They were so contradictory as to be easily dismissed, mere eldritch phantasms inhabiting the fearful hours of the lonely night when extraordinary, illogical contradictions possessed the power to frighten. But if it were premonition, what did that signify?

He lay back and felt his mortality. He was an old man. How many summers had he seen? Eighty? Yes, that was it, eighty summers and this his eighty-first . . .

He sighed. His heart, which had hammered with such insistence, would not beat forever and he had lived longer than so many of his friends. Poor Tregembo, for instance, whom he himself had dispatched with a pistol ball fired out of mercy to end the poor man's fearful suffering; and James Quilhampton, killed in a storm of shot as his cutter, *Kestrel*, had been raked in the Vikkenfiord . . .

How he mourned Quilhampton. Better that Drinkwater himself should have died than poor James, so newly wed after so long a betrothal . . .

Drinkwater pulled himself together and shook off the last vestiges of the dream. He was no stranger to wakefulness in the night and knew its promptings were more substantial than a damned dream! Wearily he threw his legs clear of the bunk and fumbled for the jordan.

But even after relieving himself he could not sleep. The ship was rolling now, the tide having turned and the wind grown stronger. She hung in equilibrium, tethered to the sea-bed by her anchor and cable which would now be stretched out to the eastward, but with the strong wind in her top-hamper canting her round against its powerful stream.

'Some things', Drinkwater mused, thinking of *Vestal's* steam-powered sophistication, 'remain always the same.'

The rolling was persistently irritating. He was unused to the fixed mattress in the bunk and found the way his body-weight was pressed first on one side and then on the other a most disconcerting experience. He lay and thought fondly of his wife, knowing now, as he tossed irritably, that she had been correct in thinking him a fool for wanting to go back to sea.

'There is, my dear,' he could hear her saying, 'no fool quite like an old fool. Every dog has his day and surely you have had yours, but I suppose I shall let you have your way.'

It had been no good protesting that, as an Elder Brother of the Trinity House, it was his duty to ensure that the lighthouses, buoys and light-vessels around the coast were properly maintained for the benefit of mariners.

'If you had never sent in that report about the deficiencies of the lighthouse on Helgoland they would never have heard of Nathaniel Drinkwater and never have elected you to their blessed fraternity,' Elizabeth had berated him. 'Either that or they wanted your knighthood to adorn their Court . . .'

'Thank you, Lady Drinkwater,' he had said, aware that her head, for all its customary good sense, had been turned a trifle by the title. God knew, it was little enough by way of compensation for all the loneliness she had suffered over the years, but perhaps, he thought, imagining her lying abed on the opposite side of the country listening to the rising gale, he should have spared her this last anxiety.

When at last he fell asleep it was almost dawn. He stirred briefly as the ship weighed her cable and her paddle-wheels thrashed the sea until they drove her along at nine knots. Then, acknowledging that the responsibility of command was not his, he rolled over and settled himself again. It was a supreme luxury to leave matters in the hands of another.

He woke fully an hour later as *Vestal* met a particularly heavy sea and shouldered it aside, her hull shuddering with the impact. A moment later the steward appeared, deferentially producing a coffee pot and the news that they had doubled Bull Point and that he might break his fast in the saloon in half an hour.

Drinkwater rose and shaved, bracing himself against the heave of the ship with the reflection that he had never, in three score years, proceeded directly to windward like this. He sipped the strong coffee as he dressed, cursing the need to perch spectacles on his nose in order to settle his neck-linen. Though never a dandy, Drinkwater had always tied his stock with a certain fastidiousness, and the one concession he made to fashion now that in his private life he rarely wore uniform, was a neat cravat. Satisfied, he pulled on a plain blue undress coat over the white pantaloons that he habitually wore, and walked through to the saloon.

Drew looked up and half rose from the table where he was hacking at cold mutton. 'Give you good day, sir.'

'And you, Richard . . .' The two men shook hands and Drinkwater joined Drew at the table.

'Did you sleep well?'

'Well enough,' Drinkwater replied. He was at least thirty-five years Drew's senior and had no wish to arouse the younger man's impatience with tedious references to a weakening bladder and those damned rheumaticks! Instead he would test the mettle of the man, for he knew Drew had made his name and a competent fortune in the West India trade before he was forty, and had been a member of the fraternity for some years. He was, therefore, Drinkwater's senior aboard *Vestal*. 'What d'you make of the weather?'

Drew pulled a face. 'Well, it ain't ideal, to be sure, but the worst of it went through during the night and it was short-lived. The swell will soon drop away. We've a good chance of making a landing.' Drew smiled blandly and Drinkwater hid his scepticism. The situation reminded him of a terrible day ... but then so many situations reminded him of something these days. He dismissed the memory and forbore from alluding to it lest Drew consider him among those men whose present consists of boasts about their past.

'Of course,' Drew expatiated, laying down his knife and fork and sitting back as *Vestal* gave a lurch, 'if we cannot scramble ashore we shall have to steam across to Lundy and anchor in the lee until there's a moderation.'

When they had finished breakfast, they repaired to the bridge. *Vestal*'s long, elegant bow and bowsprit pointed directly into the

11

wind's eye as she rose and fell, meeting the advancing ridges of water with her powerful forward impetus. Her engine was remarkably quiet, though the splashing of her paddles as they thrashed the water and drove the ship along made a counterpoint to the wind soughing in the rigging. The decks were wet with spray and recent rain, and the sky remained heavily clouded, though there was some break in the overcast to the south-westward.

Mr Quier was studying a pair of luggers on the port bow and clearly had the watch, but Poulter too was on the bridge and crossed to greet them. 'Good morning, gentlemen.'

'Mornin' Poulter,' Drew said, acknowledging his salute.

'Good morning, Captain,' said Drinkwater. 'Not the best of 'em I fear.'

'Alas no, Sir Nathaniel . . .'

'What d'you give for our chances?'

Poulter pulled the corners of his mouth down and was about to speak when Drew interrupted him. 'Oh, we've a good chance of it. We may have to lie off in the boat and pick our moment, but we shall have a shot at it, eh Sir Nat? You're game for it, ain't you?'

Drinkwater disliked being called 'Nat' by anyone not a close friend, and Drew's overbearing familiarity was as irritating as it might be dangerous. He looked at Poulter and replied, 'Of course I'm game, Drew, though I'd not want to risk the boat's crew contrary to Captain Poulter's judgement.'

The gratitude on Poulter's face was plain and Drinkwater sensed that these men had been at odds before he came aboard. Poulter's task was no easy one and Drew's presence on board was analogous to that of a fractious admiral, for while he must carry out the wishes, instructions and orders of the members of the Trinity Board embarked, the safety of the ship and her people remained the master's responsibility. Drinkwater recalled the dilemma with startling clarity, remembering Poulter's father in the same position many years earlier when he himself had held young Quier's post.

'Yes, yes, of course,' Drew was saying testily, 'of course, we'll see. But we can prepare the boat, nonetheless,' and he stumped off across the bridge. 'Here, sir! Mr Quier, sir! The loan of your glass if you please!'

Quier spun round and offered the glass with a hasty gesture, and Drinkwater met Poulter's gaze. Propriety would keep Poulter's mouth shut as it ought to secure Drinkwater's, but he was an old man and age had its privileges. 'You have been having a difficult time I think, Captain, have you not?'

Poulter nodded resignedly. 'There is an assumption, Sir Nathaniel,' he said with ill-concealed obliquity and bending to Drinkwater's ear, 'that we know all about the lighthouse service. For myself, I'm used to it, but poor Quier has suffered rather.'

Drinkwater nodded. 'I gathered as much. He seemed a little nervous of me last evening.'

Poulter smiled. 'You come with a formidable reputation, Sir Nathaniel. Quier's a fine seaman, but unfortunately he was over-ridden in the boat at Flatholm a day or two ago . . . It serves ill in front of the men.'

'Of course. I shall endeavour to take advantage of my grey hairs, though he seems determined to have a shot at the landing.'

'Yes. The business at Flatholm was unfortunate in that Captain Drew was proved right . . .'

'And thus considers himself a greater expert than formerly, while Quier feels a touch humiliated, eh?'

Poulter nodded. 'Indeed. Quier was not at fault, merely a trifle cautious . . .'

'Because, no doubt, Captain Drew was in the boat beside him?'

'Exactly so.'

'Well, we shall have to see what we can do to moderate matters,' Drinkwater said.

'I hope you won't mistake my meaning, Sir Nathaniel, but . . .'

'Think no more of it, Poulter,' Drinkwater replied reassuringly and then, seeing Drew lower the glass and turn towards them again, he called out, 'Well, what d'you make of it?'

'It's not so bad,' Drew answered, leaning against the cant of the deck and waving the telescope at the headland that lay like a grey dragon sprawling along the southern horizon on their port bow. Its extremity dipped to the sea, and just above the declivity stood the squat lighthouse of Hartland Point, revealed in a sudden patch of brightness that banished the monotone and threw up the fissured rock, patches of vegetation and the white structure of the lighthouse and its dwellings.

'See, the sun's coming out!' Drew threw the remark out with a flourish.

A few moments later sunlight spread across the sea, transforming the grey waste into a sparkling vista of tumbling waves through which, it suddenly seemed, *Vestal*'s passage was an exuberant progress. As if to emphasize the change of atmosphere, a school of bottle-nosed dolphins appeared on the starboard bow, racing in to close the plunging steam-ship and gambol about her bow under the dipping white figurehead.

'And the wind is dropping,' added Poulter with a rueful nod.

'I believe you may be right, Captain Poulter,' Drinkwater agreed, turning to judge the matter from the snap and flutter of the flag at the masthead. 'And let us hope it continues to do so.'

They had lowered the boat in the *Vestal*'s lee. Poulter had set the fore-topsail to ease the roll of the ship as she fell off the wind, and the slowed revolution of the paddles kept a little headway on the ship, laying a trail of smooth water alongside her after hull, beneath the davits.

The boat had been skilfully lowered and they had swiftly drawn away from the ship, the men bending to their oars with a will. Once clear of the protection of the *Vestal*'s hull, both wind and sea drove at their stern as they pulled in towards the land. Hartland Point rose massive above them as they approached, and Drinkwater stared at the surge of the sea as it spent itself against the great buttress of rock. He sought the breakwater and saw a short length of hewn stone forming a small enclosure, but it seemed that the turmoil of the sea within it was no better than outside, and this was worsening.

Off the intrusion of the headland, the tide sped up and they felt the force of it oppose the wind to throw up a vicious sea, dangerous to *Vestal*'s cutter. Drinkwater could see that this sudden steepening of the waves surprised Drew. He caught his fellow Elder Brother's eye.

'There's an ebb tide in here,' Drew called, raising his voice in some wonder above the sound of the wind and the sea which was no longer making a regular, subdued hiss, but fell in a noisily slopping roar of unstable water.

'It's an eddy under the headland,' Drinkwater replied, 'it's not uncommon.'

'Sir, I think . . .' Quier began, catching Drinkwater's eye.

'I agree, Mr Quier,' he nodded and looked again at Drew, 'there's no chance of a landing. We should put about.'

Drew was clearly reluctant and turned to stare again at the towering mass of rock. They could see two lighthouse keepers and one of their wives standing on the path that wound tortuously down the cliff

14

face. One of the men was waving his arms to and fro across his breast in a gesture of warning and the apron of the woman fluttered in the wind.

'I suppose', said Drew offensively, 'you ain't as handy on your legs as you might once have been.'

'If that is put forward as a reason for abandoning our attempt, Captain Drew, I shall overlook the impropriety of the remark ...' Drinkwater retorted, aware of a sharp intake of breath from an incredulous Quier beside him. 'I prefer, however, to consider that common prudence dictates our actions.' He gave Drew a withering glance and turned to Quier. 'Put up the helm, Mr Quier, and let us return to the ship. Quier turned to the coxswain and, the relief plain on both their faces, the boat began to turn as the coxswain called, 'Put yer backs into it now, me lads!'

Drinkwater ignored Drew's spluttering protest and turned to cast one last glance at the forbidding cliffs, only to feel an imperious tap upon his knee. Drew was leaning forward. 'Sir, I am the senior!' he hissed, his face red with fury. 'I shall give the order!'

'Sir,' Drinkwater replied in a low voice, "tis seniority in a Pizzy Club, pray do not make too much of it, I beg you.'

Drew's mouth twisted with anger and he reluctantly sat upright, visibly fuming, his sensibilities outraged. Drinkwater, incredulous at the man's stupidity, turned his attention to the now distant *Vestal*. The men at the oars were going to have to work hard to regain the safety of her, for she alternately dipped into the trough of the seas so that only the trucks of her masts and the pall of her funnel smoke were visible, then rose and sat on the elevated horizon like an elaborate toy.

The boat's bow dropped into a trough and threw up a sheet of spray that whipped aft. 'God blast it!' snarled Drew. Then the stern fell while the bow climbed into the sky and breasted the tumbling wave. The men grunted unconsciously as the man at stroke oar set the pace. Drinkwater could see the oar-looms bowing with their effort.

He shivered. It had grown suddenly chilly. He looked up to see that the sun had once more disappeared behind a thickening cloud, and the joy went out of the day.

Aboard *Vestal* Forester, peering attentively through the long glass, had seen the boat turn. He lowered the large telescope and reported the fact to Poulter.

'Thank the Lord for small mercies,' Poulter said, relieved. 'D'you keep an eye upon it if you please, Mr Forester, while I run down towards them.'

'Aye, aye, sir.'

Poulter leaned over the forward rail and called to some seamen on the foredeck. 'D'you hear there! I'm running off before the wind for a few moments. Hands to the braces and square the foreyards!'

The hail of acknowledgement came back to them as Poulter rang for half speed ahead on the telegraph, ordered Potts to put the helm up, and watched as *Vestal* paid off before the wind.

Forester's glass described a slow traverse as the ship swung and then he was staring ahead. A moment later Poulter called, 'Very well, Mr Forester, I can see the boat perfectly now, thank you.' Forester lowered the glass and glanced forward as the men on the foredeck belayed the swung braces.

'Harrison!' he shouted. 'Pass word for the hands to stand by the boat falls!'

'Usual drill, Mr Forester.' Poulter's tone was abstracted as he concentrated on closing the cutter.

'Aye, aye, sir.' The *Vestal*'s mate shipped the telescope on its rack. Casting a final look at the boat ahead, he dropped smartly down the port ladder to the main deck to muster the men at the boat falls and supervise her recovery.

Drinkwater saw *Vestal* swing and head towards them. Here was a real facility, he thought admiringly, the quick response of the steam propulsion to the will of the vessel's commander; a minimum of effort, hardly a hand disturbed in the process, and while his hypothetical brig could as easily have swung and run downwind, it could not have been accomplished without the co-ordinated presence of at least a score of men. Drinkwater, who had hitherto considered the new-fangled steam engine best left to young men, felt a faint, inquiring interest in the thing. Perhaps, he thought, he ought to have a proper look round the engine-room. There was a Mr Jones on board who rejoiced in the rank of 'first engineer' and who was to be infrequently glimpsed on deck in his overalls, like an old-fashioned gunner in a man-of-war whose felt slippers and pallid complexion betrayed his normal habitat far below in the powder magazine.

Captain Poulter watched the boat breast a wave and dive into the trough where he lost sight of it for a moment. *Vestal* was running before the wind, her paddles thrashing as her hull scended to the succession of seas passing under her, yawing slightly in her course.

'Watch your helm now, Quartermaster,' he said, and Potts mumbled the automatic 'Aye, aye' as he struggled to hold the ship steady on her course.

Poulter stood watching the boat and the sea, gauging the shortening distance. In a few moments he would turn *Vestal* smartly to starboard, reversing the starboard paddle and bringing the ship round to a heading of south-south-east, off the wind but not quite across it, to reduce the rolling effect of the seas. He was aware that as the ship moved closer inshore, the state of the sea worsened, for the cumulative effect of the presence of the land, throwing back the advancing waves which met their inward-bound successors, created a nasty chop.

If he judged the matter to a nicety, he could tuck the plunging boat neatly under his lee and almost pluck her out of the water. Forester and his men were well practised at hooking on the falls, while Quier and Coxswain Thomas were a competent pair. All in all, it ought to impress the objectionable Captain Richard Drew! As for poor Sir Nathaniel, Poulter marvelled at the old man's pluck.

He looked at the foredeck. Forester, being the good mate he was, had a few hands on the foredeck ready to tend the topsail braces as the ship was brought to. Poulter looked again at the boat, missed her, then saw her much closer and right ahead.

He moved smartly to the engine telegraph and rang for the paddles to be stopped. The jangle of bells seemed oddly short, as though First Engineer Jones had had his hand on the thing. Perhaps he had, Poulter thought, pleased with his ship and her personnel. A man could take pride in such things. He took two steps to the bridge rail and peered over the dodger. He had lost sight of the boat again, then she appeared almost under the bow and Poulter's self-satisfaction vanished. *Vestal's* paddles were still thrashing round, the wash of them now hideously loud in Poulter's receptive ears. His mouth was dry and his heart hammered painfully as he jumped for the telegraph and swung the handle in the violent double-ring of an emergency order. The heavy brass lever offered him no resistance. Instantly Poulter knew what had gone wrong: the long chain connecting the bridge instrument with the repeater in the engine-room had broken somewhere in the narrow pipe that connected him with the first engineer down below.

17

Just as the realization struck him, Poulter heard the cry of alarm from the foredeck.

'Hard a-starboard!' he roared at the quartermaster, then rushed to the rail. The two men posted forward to handle the braces were pointing and shouting, looking back up at the bridge, their faces white with alarm.

'Oh, my God!'

It was then that Poulter realized he had compounded matters, that he was in part author of the disaster he was now powerless to avert. In his moment's inattention, Poulter had not noticed the ship slew to port, nor observed Potts' frantic attempt to counter the violent skewing effect of a large sea which had run up under *Vestal*'s port quarter with fatal timing. As a result, as the ship's head had fallen off to port, she had brought the boat across to her starboard bow. Poulter's attempt to throw her unstoppable bulk away from the boat consequently resulted in the exact contrary.

Even as he watched, too late to do anything, Poulter's ship ran down her own boat.

Drinkwater had seen *Vestal*'s head fall to port and thought the sheer deliberate, perhaps the first indication of a turn. But the sudden steadying of her aspect, growing in apparent size with the speed of her approach, turned her from a welcome haven to a terrifying threat. For a few seconds those in the stern staring forward processed the implications of the evidence before their eyes. Drinkwater heard Quier swear under his breath, joined by the coxswain in a louder tone.

'Bloody hell!'

Drew's cry completed this crescendo of comprehension while his look of stark fear caused the oarsmen to break stroke as each man jerked round to stare over their shoulders. Quier leant for the tiller even as Thomas hauled it over. But it was too late, and in those last few attenuated seconds men thought only of themselves and began to dive over the port side of the boat in a terrified attempt to escape the huge, dark mass approaching them.

Only Drinkwater sat immobile. In that second of understanding and nervous reaction, as the combined weight of all those in the boat moving to escape destruction from that terrible, overwhelming bow caused her to capsize, he knew the meaning of his dream. The presentiment of death was confirmed, for he saw above him, in the pallid shape of the *Vestal's* figurehead, the white lady of his recurrent nightmare. Hers was not the petrifying face of Medusa, nor the fearsome image of a terrifying harpy; she bore instead the implacable expression of indifference.

As he was pitched out of the boat into the sudden, shocking chill of the sea, Drinkwater felt the utter numbness of the inevitable. For a ghastly moment of piteous regret, he thought of his wife. He heard her cry and then a figure loomed briefly near him, open-mouthed in a rictus of terror, and was as suddenly gone. He glimpsed the sky, pitiless in its lowering overcast, as his body was swept aside by the moving mass of the ship. As suddenly he was tugged back again. The ship's black side with its copper sheathing rushed past him.

Suddenly loud in his ears, he heard the familiar clanking of the dream, a crescendo of noise which filled him with fear and abruptly resolved itself into the thrash of the great starboard paddle-wheel and the adjusting of its floats by the eccentric drive rods radiating from its centre.

Then he was trampled beneath it.

It battered him.

It shoved him down until his whole head ached from the pressure and he bled from the lacerations of its indifferent mechanism.

Finally, it hurled him astern, three fathoms below the surface of the sea, as his bursting lungs reacted and his terrified mind thought that he would never see Elizabeth again.

PART ONE

Flood Tide

It is commonly held, though upon what authority I am uncertain, that a drowning man clutches at a straw, that he rises three times before the fatal immersion and that his life passes before him in a flash.

Elizabeth

It was end of November 1781 when His Britannic Majesty's frigate *Cyclops* rejoined the Grand Fleet at Spithead. In the grey half-light of a squally winter afternoon her cable rumbled through the hawse and she brought up to her anchor amidst the huge assembly of ships and vessels. Since frigates were constantly coming and going, her return from the Carolinas was unremarkable, but Captain Hope called upon Rear-Admiral Kempenfelt with some misgivings, for *Cyclops*'s mission had been unsuccessful.

Having seen Hope down into his gig, Acting Lieutenant Nathaniel Drinkwater, a captured French sword at his hip, crossed the quarter-deck to where Lieutenant Devaux was levelling a telescope on the flagship. Kempenfelt commanded the rear division of the Grand Fleet from which Hope's frigate had been detached for special service some months earlier, flying his flag in the huge first-rate *Royal George* which lay some three miles away.

Drinkwater halted at the first lieutenant's elbow, coughed discreetly and said, 'Captain's compliments, sir, but would you be good enough to ensure no boats come alongside until he returns.'

Devaux lowered the glass a little and turned his gaze on the steel-grey waters of Spithead which were being churned by the vicious breeze into a nasty chop.

'D'you see any boats, Mr Drinkwater?'

'Er, no sir.'

'Er,' Devaux mimicked, replacing the telescope to his eye, 'no sir. Neither do I.'

'Except for the Captain's gig, that is, sir.'

'But no boats containing pedlars, usurers, tailors, cobblers, whores or whoremasters, eh?'

'None whatsoever, sir.'

'Then, Mr Drinkwater,' said Devaux with an ironic smile, turning his hazel eyes on the younger man, 'do you ensure that not one of them gets alongside. We must keep all manner of wickedness away from our fair ship, don't you know.' Devaux allowed a crease to furrow his equable brow and asked conversationally, 'Now, Nathaniel, do you suppose this sudden concern for the moral welfare of our people has anything to do with the fact that Rear-Admiral Richard Kempenfelt is a religious man?'

'I suppose it might, sir.'

'I suppose it might, too,' responded the first lieutenant with a heavily exaggerated smile, replacing the telescope to his eye and returning his attention to Kempenfelt's flagship.

Drinkwater smiled to himself. Lieutenant the Honourable John Devaux was a man whom Drinkwater both admired and liked. He cautiously hoped that Devaux held Drinkwater himself in some esteem, for the nineteen-year-old enjoyed no patronage beyond the initial recommendation of his parish priest. Although this had secured him a midshipman's berth aboard *Cyclops*, nothing more could be expected from it. His acting rank was merely a convenient expedient for the ship, detached on special service as she had been. He expected to be returned to the midshipmen's mephitic berth in the next few days, as soon as a replacement could be found from the admiral's numerous *élèves* who inhabited this vast concourse of ships. Drinkwater sighed as he thought of his consignment to the orlop. His previous experiences of it had been far from happy. Hearing the sigh, Devaux turned upon him, lowering the glass and closing it with a sharp snick.

'Well, sir? How the deuce d'you intend to shoo the damned bumboats off our side if you just stand there sniffing like an impregnated milkmaid?'

'I'm sorry, sir.' Drinkwater was about to turn away, aware that he had tested the first lieutenant's patience, when Devaux, staring around the ship, said with an ironic smile, 'Ah, but I see you *have* seen them all off.'

'I haven't seen a single one throughout the anchorage.'

'No, no one in his right mind would be out in a boat on an afternoon like this unless they had to be. 'Tis almost cold enough for snow, don't you think, or is it just because we hail from warmer climes?'

'Well, 'tis certainly chilly enough.'

'And I suppose you're concerned about your future, eh?'

'A little, I must confess.'

'You damned hypocrite, Nathaniel!' Devaux laughed. 'But don't expect a thing, cully. There'll be enough young gentlemen here-abouts', he went on, waving a hand expansively round the crowded anchorage, dark as it was with the masts of the fleet, 'to ensure we aren't without warm admirers. When word gets about that we've a berth empty in the gunroom, they'll all be writing to Howe or Kempenfelt or . . .'

'But there isn't an empty berth in the gunroom,' Drinkwater pro-tested.

'A prophet is never credited in his own land, is he, eh?' Devaux remarked ironically. 'Resign yourself to the fact that by nightfall you will be back in the orlop.'

'I already have, but I cannot say I relish the prospect.'

Devaux looked seriously at Drinkwater. 'I shouldn't be surprised, Nathaniel, if we were not to be here for some time. If you would profit from my advice, I should recommend you to seek examination at the Trinity House and secure for yourself a warrant as master. You cannot afford to kick your heels in a midshipmite's mess until someone notices you. Unless I am completely out of tune with the times, there will be fewer opportunities to make your name as this war drags to its unhappy conclusion. At least with a master's warrant, your chances of finding some employment in a peace are much enhanced.'

'I shall mind what you say, sir, and thank you for your advice.'

''Tis no matter. I should not entirely like to see your abilities wasted, though my own influence is too small to afford you any advantage.'

'I had not meant . . .' Drinkwater protested, but Devaux cut him short with a brief, barked laugh.

'You've no need to be ashamed of either ambition or the need to make your way in the world.'

'But I had not meant to solicit interest, sir. I think, however, that I want experience to be considered for examination.'

'Don't be so damned modest.' Devaux turned away and raised the glass again.

Drinkwater had relinquished the deck when Hope returned. A cold and windy night had set in, with the great ships tugging at their

25

cables, their officers anxious that they should not drag their anchors. The chill struck the gunroom, and those officers not on duty were considering the benefit to be derived from the blankets of their cots when Midshipman White's head peeped round the door.

'Mr Drinkwater,' he called, 'Mr Devaux's compliments and would you join him in the captain's cabin, sir.'

Ignoring the taunts of the other officers, Drinkwater pulled on his coat, picked up his hat and made for the companionway to the gundeck. He halted outside the captain's cabin, ran a finger round his stock, tucked his hat neatly under his arm and, as the marine sentry stood to attention, knocked upon the door.

'Come!'

Captain Hope clasped a steaming tankard of rum flip, his shivering body hunched in the attitude of a man chilled half to death as he sat in his chair while his servant chafed his stockinged feet. The flickering candles showed his gaunt face pale with the cold and his eyes reddened by the wind. Devaux sat, elegantly cross-legged, on the settee that ran athwart the ship under the stern windows over which the sashes had been drawn, so the glass reflected the light of the candelabra.

'Ah, Drinkwater, my boy. I have some news for you.'

'Sir?'

'We are to have a new third lieutenant, I'm afraid.'

Drinkwater looked for a second at Devaux, but the first lieutenant's attention was elsewhere. 'I understand, sir . . .'

'No you don't,' said Hope so sharply that Drinkwater coloured, thinking himself impertinent. 'Lieutenant Wallace will join tomorrow,' Hope went on, 'but since the establishment of the ship has been increased by one lieutenant, I have persuaded the Admiral to allow you to retain your acting commission.'

'I am much obliged to you, sir.' Drinkwater shot a second glance at Devaux and saw the merest flicker of a smile pass across his face.

'I have recommended that your commission be confirmed without further examination. I can make no pledges on Admiral Kempenfelt's behalf, but he has promised to consider the matter.'

'That is most kind of you, sir.'

'Well, well. We shall see. That is all.'

In the succeeding weeks *Cyclops* languished at Spithead, turning to the tide every six hours, but otherwise idle. Her people were active enough, hoisting in stores, water, powder and shot, and in due course other transactions began to take place. Though unpaid, since the present commission was of less than four years' standing, the frigate's people had received their accumulated prize money. Hardly had this been doled out by Captain Hope's prize agent's clerk than *Cyclops* was surrounded by bum-boats and invaded by a colourful and noisy mob whose trades and skills could provide both officers and ratings with their every want. A host of tricksters, fortune-tellers, tooth-pullers, pedlars, cobblers, vendors of every manner of knick-nack, traders' runners (advertising the expertise of their principals as sword-cutlers, tailors, pawn-brokers and portrait artists), Jewish usurers, gypsy-fiddlers and two score or so of whores infested the ship.

Amid this babel, the routine duties of the ship went on. Captain Hope absented himself for three weeks and Lieutenant Devaux took a fortnight's furlough. The ship underwent a superficial survey by the master shipwright of the dockyard, and her upper masts and yards were lowered and new standing rigging set up and rattled down. Five spars were renewed and Midshipman White spent three miserable days in the launch towing out replacements from the mast-pond in Portsmouth Dockyard.

Lieutenant Wallace arrived and was revealed as a protégé of the Elliot family to whom he was distantly related. His claim on their favour was small, it seemed, and it was acknowledged that he could have been a great deal worse. Life in the gunroom was thus tolerable enough. Drinkwater enjoyed the society of his fellow-officers, particularly the amusing banter between Devaux, when he was present, and the serious-minded but pleasant Lieutenant Wheeler of the marines. The sonorous gravity of the surgeon, Mr Appleby, often verged on the pompous, but his lengthy perorations could fill the gloom of an otherwise tedious evening with amusing targets for what passed for wit. Drinkwater exercised regularly with foils, and Wheeler and he recruited White and three other midshipmen into their *salle d'escrime*, as Wheeler, with light-hearted pretentiousness, insisted on calling the starboard gangway. As the junior lieutenant, Drinkwater was responsible for training the hands in the use of small arms, holding regular cutlass drills and target practices when, in the wake of the marines, they would shoot at bottles slung at the main yardarm.

In the midst of this activity Drinkwater received a letter, an answer to one he had sent off almost as soon as *Cyclops* had dropped her anchor, and he was soon afterwards anxious to obtain a few days' leave himself. The letter was from Miss Elizabeth Bower, whom he had met when last in England and to whom he had formed a strong attachment. She, it seemed, felt similarly attracted to him and they had exchanged correspondence, but he was uncertain of her whereabouts since her widowed father, with whom she lived, had moved from the Cornish parish of which he had briefly been inter-regnant. Now, having hardly dared hope that his letter would reach her, for he had sent it by way of the Bishop of Winchester, he found that her father had been inducted as incumbent in the parish of Warnford, which lay in the upper valley of the Meon, not many miles north of Portsmouth.

... It is so Comforting to hear from You, Elizabeth had written, *for Poor Father Exhausts himself in his Exertions to help the Unfortunate and Deserving Poor hereabouts ... We have a Pleasant House with more Chambers than we can Sensibly use and Father joins me in Extending a Warm Invitation to you for Christmas, should You be Fortunate to Gain Your Freedom ...*

Keen both to justify Hope's faith in him and to oblige Devaux in the hope that in due course the first lieutenant would indulge his request for leave, Drinkwater penned a cautious note of acceptance hedged about by riders explaining his predicament, then threw himself into his duties. Occasionally these took him out of the ship, as when he acted for Hope on some business with the captain's prize agent, carrying papers ashore to the lawyer's chambers at Southsea. On this occasion, and in confident anticipation of his request being granted, Drinkwater spent two guineas of his prize money on a present for Elizabeth and was in high good humour as he returned from his expedition.

At the Sally Port he hired a wherry to take him back to the ship. It was a fine, cold winter's afternoon, with a brisk wind out of the northeast. A low sun laid a sparkling path upon the sea and threw long, complex shadows from the spars of the fleet. The wherryman set a scrap of lugsail as the boat cleared Southsea beach and they swooped and ducked over the choppy water in the lively but remarkably dry little craft as it fought the contrary tide. The panoply of naval might lay all about them in the brilliant sunshine. Curiously Drinkwater regarded each of the great ships as they lay with their heads to the westward, stemming the flood tide but canted slightly athwart its stream by the brisk wind. As they passed each of the ships-of-the-line, though his passenger could perfectly well read them, the boatman volunteered their names as if this additional service would ensure a large gratuity.

'*Edgar*, sir, seventy-four guns . . . *Monarch*, seventy-four . . . *Glenelg*, transport . . . *Bedford* . . .'

Drinkwater stared up at each as they struggled past; occasionally someone stared back and once a midshipman in a bucking cutter alongside a frigate waved cheerfully. With their yard and stay tackles manned, the ships were taking in stores from hoys and ketches bouncing and ranging alongside them. One vessel was landing a defective gun – Drinkwater could see a trunnion missing from it – and several ships were working on their top-hamper, sending down their upper spars. And above every stern the squadronal ensigns of red, white or blue snapped in the breeze.

'*Royal George*, sir, first-rate. Tallest masts in the navy an' 'er main yard's the longest.'

Drinkwater stared at the great ship with her ascending tiers of stern galleries and her lofty rig. Above the ornate decoration of her taffrail, a huge blue ensign bowed the staff as it strained at its halliards.

'Dick Kempenfelt's flag, sir . . .'

'Yes,' Drinkwater replied, glancing up at the blue rectangle at the mizen truck, wondering if, at that moment, Kempenfelt was sitting at his desk mulling over the wisdom of recommending confirmation of the acting commission of the young man whose hired wherry even then bounced over a wave under his flagship's transom.

'Bin the flagship of Anson, 'Awke, Rodney an' Boscawen,' obliged the loquacious and informative wherryman. Then he leaned forward and gave Drinkwater a nudge with the air of a conspirator. Drinkwater turned, caught sight of a quid of tobacco as it rolled between caried teeth, and received a waft of foul breath.

'But she'm rotten, sir, fair rotten, they tell me.' He nodded, adding with malicious relish, 'They were to dock her way back, but it got put off.' He grinned again. 'Bit of luck you're on *Cyclops*, eh?' and the boatman laughed.

'I thought she was well built,' Drinkwater said, looking up at the great ship, for anything else seemed inconceivable. Upon her quarterdeck high above him, an officer was studying him through a telescope and Drinkwater thought him bored with his anchor watch. 'Didn't I hear she took ten years to build?'

'That's right, sir,' the boatman agreed enthusiastically, 'an' what 'appens to timber what's left out ten year?'

'Well, it weathers.'

'That's bollocks, sir, if you'll pardon me lingo,' and the man spat to leeward as if adding to the contempt of his dismissal. 'Beggin' your pardon, sir, but if that's what they teaches you young officers nowadays, then 'tis no wonder the fleet's rotten. Look sir, what happens wiv a fence when you puts it up, eh?'

Drinkwater had never in his life put up a fence, but he supposed the task might not be beyond him. 'Well you tar it, I imagine,' he ventured.

'You're a bright 'un, sir,' the boatman said. 'Of course you does. You tars it. You don't leave it out for ten year for the rain to soak it and the sun to split it, do you? No. But that's what they done wiv the *Royal George!*'

A week before Christmas, young Dicky White informed Drinkwater that his father had written and asked that his son be allowed to come home for Christmas. Drinkwater and White had become close friends and though Drinkwater's acting commission had distanced them, it had not destroyed their friendship. Even so, he knew that White possessed family interest and that his father's request would receive a favourable reply. The knowledge irked Drinkwater for he had no equivalent clout and, whatever his position *vis-à-vis* the midshipmen, he was the most junior officer in the gunroom. He felt a sudden certainty that the duty of Christmas would fall upon him. He stared for a moment out across Spithead to the grey shore of the Isle of Wight.

'I should like you to come with me and I have asked the first lieutenant,' White confided with a smile. 'You'll be glad to know he has no objection. Wallace has volunteered to remain on board.' White dropped his voice and added, 'There's a skeleton in the third lieutenant's locker, Nat. I've heard 'tis a gambling debt. I think he dare not set foot ashore. Either that, or an angry husband has a pair of pistols ready primed!'

The expression on White's face made Drinkwater laugh. 'I've heard nothing of the kind, Chalky. You have too much time in that mess of yours to let your imaginations run wild.' He grew serious, 'Look, my dear fellow, I'm vastly obliged to you for securing my release,' he paused, 'but ... oh dear, this is deuced awkward ...'

'You do not wish to accompany me to Norfolk?'

'I would dearly like to do so, but I have ... Damn it, Chalky, I have an invitation from ...'

30

'A lady!' White slapped his thigh in a highly precocious manner, his face broadening to a smile. 'Let me not stand in the way of love, Nat! I shall not say a word. I am so glad that I was the means of your furthering your suit! We shall leave together and we shall return to tell the first luff what a jolly time we had bagging pheasants!'

'Do you think we should go that far?' Drinkwater asked, laughing.

'Do you think we should not?' White retorted.

'Well, stap me, Chalky, if you aren't a veritable Cupid!'

Christmas of 1781 saw the streets of Portsmouth under snow. Even the warren of brothels and grog-shops that they passed through were lent an ethereal beauty by the dazzling whiteness of the snow. Set against an even tone of pearl-grey sky, the tumbled roofs, crooked chimneys and black windows seemed a haven of humanity rather than a nursery of vice and disease. The thin coils of smoke rising from fires of wood and sea-coal lent an air of happy domesticity to this illusion.

Soon they had left Portsmouth behind and found the road passable as it ascended the downs on the way towards Petersfield. White, with the air of a conspirator, had insisted he and Drinkwater leave the ship together. The conveyance Sir Robert White had provided for his son now departed from the post road sufficiently to put Drinkwater down within sight of the church tower of Farehurst. It was with a beating heart that he lugged his small portmanteau towards the vicarage, but anti-climax met him in the person of a small, careworn woman who opened the door and motioned him inside. She ushered him into what he took to be Mr Bower's study, for an ancient writing-table and a battered chair from which the majority of the stuffing had long since escaped, stood in the middle of the room. A litter of papers covered the table and two bookcases flanked the fireplace. An unlit fire was laid in the grate. Three odd upright chairs were set about the room, the pine boards of which were bare, and the windows were half-shuttered.

The woman opened these and waved him to a chair with a grunt. She avoided his eyes and pulled a grey shawl about her shoulders as if to emphasize the cold penury of the house. He did not sit, but moved to look at an engraving of Wells Cathedral above the overmantel, chafing his hands to stimulate circulation. Several books lay on the mantelshelf; idly he picked one up. It was a little anthology of poetry. On the flyleaf it bore the name *Eliz. Bower, her Book*. He flicked the

31

pages over until the name *Kempenfelt* caught his eye and he had just started reading the admiral's poem 'Burst, ye Emerald Gates' when the door opened.

Elizabeth stood just inside the room, her dark hair bound up in a ribbon, her brown eyes wide with surprise. 'Nathaniel!'

She took a half-step towards him and then faltered; he felt her eyes on his face and remembered his scar.

'You have been hurt!'

In a sudden, embarrassed reflex he touched it with his fingers. ''Tis nothing but a scratch. I had forgot it. I hope . . .'

She stepped closer and he clasped her outstretched hands. 'Oh, but it does,' she said smiling, 'it utterly ruins your looks. I am pleased to say no sensible woman will ever look at you again.'

'You guy me.'

'La, sir, you are clever too!'

'And you, Elizabeth, how are you?'

She sighed and her gaze fell away for a second, but then she brightened and looked at him, her face alive with that infectious animation that he sometimes thought he had almost imagined. 'Much the better for seeing you . . .'

'And your father?'

'Is old and worn out. He takes no thought for himself and is unwell, but he refuses to listen to my entreaties.' She paused, then tossed her head with a sniff. He drew her to him and felt her arms about him and smelt the fragrance of her hair as he brushed the top of her head with his lips. 'I am so very glad to have found you again,' he said.

She drew back and looked up at him, tears in her eyes. 'All I asked was that you should come back. How long do you have?'

'A sennight . . .'

After Mattins on Christmas morning, dinner in the vicarage was a merry meal. Having Drinkwater as a guest seemed to have given the Reverend Bower a new lease of life and his emaciated features bore a cheerful expression, notwithstanding the fact that he gently chided his house-keeper for failing to attend divine service.

'She doesn't understand,' he said resignedly, 'but when God has made you mute from birth, much must be incomprehensible. Nathaniel, my boy, do an old man a favour, slip out in about ten minutes with a glass of claret for her. She needs cheering, poor soul.'

After the modest meal of roast beef and oysters had been cleared away they exchanged gifts. Elizabeth had bought her father a book of sermons written by some divine of whom Drinkwater had never heard but who was, judging by old Bower's enthusiasm, a man of some theological consequence. So keen an appreciation of an intellectual present made Drinkwater's offering to old Bower seem insignificant, for he had been unable to think of anything other than a bottle of madeira he had bought from Lieutenant Wheeler. For his daughter, Bower had purchased a square of silk. It was the colour of flame and seemed to burst into the dingy room as she withdrew it from its wrapping. Elizabeth flung it about her shoulders and kissed her father, ruffling his white sidelocks with pleasure.

As unobtrusively as possible, Drinkwater slid Elizabeth's small parcel across the table. As she folded back the paper and opened the cardboard box it contained, her eyes widened with delight.

'Oh, my dear, it's beautiful!' She lifted the cameo out, held it in the palm of her hand and stared at the white marble profile of the Greek goddess on its field of pink coral. She looked up at him, her eyes shining, and it occurred to him that, though inadequate, his gift was sufficient to illuminate her dull existence. 'Look, Father . . .'

Elizabeth secured the vermilion silk with the cameo, leaned across and kissed him chastely on the cheek. 'Thank you, Nathaniel,' she said softly in his ear.

Drinkwater sat back and raised his glass. He was astonished when Elizabeth placed two parcels before him. 'I have no right to expect hospitality and generosity like this.'

'Tush, Nathaniel,' Elizabeth scolded mischievously, 'do you open them and save your speeches until you see what you have been saddled with.'

He opened the first. It contained a watch from the vicar. 'My dear sir! I am overwhelmed . . . I . . . I cannot . . .'

'I find the passage of time far too rapid to be reminded of it by a device that will outlive me. 'Tis a good time-keeper and I shall not long have need of such things.'

'Oh, Father, don't speak so!'

'Come, come, Elizabeth, I have white hairs beyond my term and I am not feared of death.'

'Sir, I am most grateful,' Drinkwater broke in, 'I do not deserve it . . .'

'Rubbish, my boy.' The old man waved aside Drinkwater's protest with a laugh. 'Let's have no more maudlin sentiment. I give you joy of the watch and wish you a happy Christmas. I shall find the madeira of considerably more consolation than a timepiece this winter.'

Drinkwater turned his attention to the second parcel. 'Is this from you, Elizabeth?'

She had clasped her lower lip between her teeth in apprehension and merely nodded. He opened the flat package. Inside, set in a framed border, was a water-colour painting. It showed a sheet of water enclosed by green shores which were surmounted by the grey bastion of a castle. In the foreground was a rakish schooner with British over Yankee colours. He recognized her with a jubilant exclamation. 'It's *Algonquin, Algonquin* off St Mawes! Elizabeth, it's truly lovely, and you did it?'

She nodded, delighted at his obvious pleasure.

'It's utterly delightful.' He looked at Bower. 'Sir, may I kiss your daughter?'

Bower nodded and clapped his hands with delight. 'Of course, my boy, of course!'

And afterwards he sat, warmed by wine, food and affection, regarding the skilfully executed painting of the American privateer schooner *Algonquin* lying in Falmouth harbour. He had been prize-master of her, and the occasion of her arrival in Falmouth had been that of his first meeting with Elizabeth.

A Commission as Lieutenant

Cyclops cruised in the Channel from early January until the end of April and was back in Spithead by mid-May when news came in of Admiral Rodney's victory over De Grasse off the West Indian islets called Les Saintes. Guns were fired and church bells rocked their steeples; peace, it was said, could not now be far away, for the country was weary of a war it could not win. It seemed the fleet would spend the final months of hostilities at anchor, but at the end of the month orders were passed to prepare for sea.

Admiral Lord Howe thrust into the North Sea with a dozen sail-of-the-line and attendant frigates to waylay the Dutch. The Dutch in their turn were at sea to raid the homeward Baltic convoy, but news of Howe's approach compelled them to abort their plans and Lord Howe had the satisfaction of bottling up the enemy in the Texelstroom. At the end of June he returned down Channel and his fleet was reinforced from Spithead. Twenty-one line-of-battle ships and a cloud of frigates stood on to the westwards, led by Vice-Admiral Barrington's squadron in the van and with Kempenfelt's blue squadron bringing up the rear. Rumour was rife that the combined fleets of France and Spain were at sea, as they had been three years earlier, but this time there would be no repeat of the débâcle that had occurred under the senile Hardy when the enemy fleets had swept up the Channel unchallenged. The Grand Fleet had the satisfaction of covering the Jamaica trade coming in under the escort of Sir Peter Parker and then stood south in anticipation of falling in with the enemy's main body. But the British were running short of water and reports were coming in that Cordoba, the Spanish

35

admiral, had turned south to bring Gibraltar finally to its knees. Lord Howe therefore ordered the Grand Fleet back to Spithead to take on water and provisions. At the end of August the great ships came into the lee of the Isle of Wight under a cloud of sail.

Some three hundred vessels lay between Portsmouth and Ryde, attended by the ubiquitous and numerous bum-boats, water-hoys, dockyard victualling craft, lighters, barges, wherries and punts, as well as the boats of the fleet. Despite the demands of the cruise and the sense of more work to be done as soon as the fleet was ready, the return to the anchorage brought a dulling to the keen edge of endeavour. The sense of urgency faded as day succeeded day and then the first week drifted into a fortnight.

Drinkwater had heard nothing of his commission being confirmed and began to despair of it, recalling Devaux's advice to petition the Trinity House for an examination for master. It was increasingly clear that he would receive no advancement without distinguishing himself, and since any opportunity of doing this seemed increasingly remote, his future looked decidedly bleak. His only consolation was a letter from Elizabeth, but even this irked him, for he had resolved to propose marriage to her when his affairs were on a better footing, and a lieutenant's commission would at least secure him half-pay if the war ended. Poor as it was, half-pay would be an improvement on her father's miserable stipend. His anxiety for her grew with the reflection that upon the old man's death she would not only be penniless but also roofless. He had almost lost her once before and could not face the prospect of doing so again, perhaps this time forever.

In the dreary days that followed, he fretted, unsettled by the proximity of the shore yet daily reminded of its blandishments; rooted by duty, but made restless by the lack of activity. This corrosive mood of embitterment settled on him as *Cyclops* swung at the extremity of her cable, and even the odd task that took him ashore failed to lighten his mood, since to go ashore but to be denied the freedom to go where he wished was simply an irksome imposition. Robbed of real liberty, Drinkwater had already acquired the true sailor's preference for his ship.

On a morning in late August, Drinkwater was returning from Portsmouth town whither he had been sent on behalf of the mess to make some purchases of wine, a decent cheese and some fat poultry. He was approaching the Sally Port and looking for Tregembo, the able seaman he had ordered to take back one load of mess stores, when a portly clerk bustled up to him.

'Excuse me, young sir . . .' The man attached himself to Drinkwater's sleeve.

'Yes? What is it?'

The clerk was breathless and anxious, wiped his face with a none-too-clean handkerchief and gaspingly explained his predicament. 'Oh sir, I just missed Acting Lieutenant Durham, sir, he's aide to Rear-Admiral Kempenfelt . . . There's his boat, confound it . . .' The little man pointed at a smart gig just then pulling offshore. Plunging his handkerchief back in his pocket, he drew a letter from his breast. It was sealed with the dockyard wafer.

'I wonder, sir, if I might trouble you to deliver this to the admiral aboard the *Royal George*. He is most urgently awaiting it.' Drinkwater's hesitation was momentary, but the clerk rushed on in explanation. 'There's a leak in the flagship, d'you see? The admiral and Captain Waghorne are very concerned about it. This is the order to dry-dock her and I was, I confess, supposed to have it ready for Mr Durham but . . .' The clerk wiped his hand across his mouth and Drinkwater sensed some awesome and official retribution awaiting this unfortunate drone of Admiralty. Suddenly his own lot did not seem so bad.

'But,' the clerk ran on, 'he is a most precipitate young man and had left before I had completed the copying . . .'

'Please don't concern yourself further,' Drinkwater interrupted impatiently. 'The flagship lies in my way. I only hesitate because I am waiting for some provisions and it may be ten or twenty minutes before I am ready to leave.'

Relief flushed the clerk's face and he pawed at Drinkwater in an effusion of gratitude. 'Oh, my dear sir, I require only your assurance that you will deliver the letter this afternoon, otherwise in your own good time, sir, in your own good time, to be sure.'

'Well you may rest assured of that.'

'And pray to whom am I indebted, sir?'

'Drinkwater, fourth of the *Cyclops* frigate.'

'Ah yes, Captain Hope. A most tenacious officer. Thank you, sir, thank you. I am vastly obliged to you, vastly obliged.' And the curious fellow backed away into the crowd, half bowing as he retreated. Drinkwater was left pondering the aptness of the adjective 'tenacious' as it applied to Hope.

A quarter of an hour later, *Cyclops*'s port cutter drew away from the beach and began the long pull to windward. Drinkwater settled himself in the stern-sheets, resting his feet on a large cheese.

Compared to the clerk, he was indeed fortunate, and it occurred to him that the encounter might be fortuitous, if not providential. The order in his pocket offered him an opportunity to present himself before Kempenfelt. The thought gave him a private satisfaction and his mind ran on to the order in his pocket, recollecting that other boat trip he had made in the chilling winter wind when the wherryman had given him lessons on ship-building and the erection of fences.

When they arrived alongside the flagship, Drinkwater ordered the cutter to lie off and wait, then scrambled up the huge ship's tumblehome and stepped into the gloom of the entry. The marine sentry came to attention at the sight of his blue coat whence the white collar patches had been removed but which betrayed their recent presence, and the duty midshipman, a young boy of perhaps eleven years of age, accosted him.

'May I enquire your ship and business?' the boy asked in a falsetto pipe that seemed incongruous against the dark and heaving background of the gun-deck.

'Drinkwater, fourth lieutenant of the *Cyclops*. I have a letter for Admiral Kempenfelt,' Drinkwater explained, adding, lest the boy take it from him and rob him of his opportunity, 'please be kind enough to conduct me to His Excellency's quarters.'

Drinkwater was shown into Kempenfelt's dining quarters which served, betwixt dinners, as an ante-room. At the table sat a man in a plain civilian coat. His pen moved industriously across a sheet of paper, stopping occasionally to recharge itself with ink from the well. Drinkwater observed that this action was so familiar to the admiral's secretary that he did not have to look up, but dipped his pen with unerring accuracy. Completing his task, the secretary sanded the paper, shook it and looked up over the top of a pair of half-moon spectacles. He had a shrewd face and his eyes did not miss the betraying patches of unweathered broadcloth on Drinkwater's lapels.

'Well, sir? State your business.'

'I bear a letter from the dockyard for His Excellency. I believe it was not ready when Lieutenant Durham left.' Without a word, the secretary held out his hand. Anxious to secure at least a glimpse of Kempenfelt, Drinkwater added conversationally, 'I understand the admiral is most anxiously awaiting it . . .'

'Then give it here, sir, and remove the anxiety from your mind,' the clerk retorted, his outstretched fingers making an impatient little flutter. At that moment the door to the great cabin opened and the light from the stern windows shone through, silhouetting a tall figure.

'Is Durham back with that order to dock yet, Scratch?'

'No, Sir Richard, but this young man has it.' Drinkwater relinquished the letter and the secretary applied his paper-knife while Kempenfelt regarded the stranger.

'Have I seen you before?' he asked, stepping out of the doorway so that Drinkwater could see his face properly.

'I think not, Sir Richard,' Drinkwater bowed, 'Drinkwater, acting fourth of the *Cyclops*.'

'Ah yes, Hope's hopeful.' Kempenfelt smiled. 'You've been wounded.'

'In the taking of *La Créole*, sir, in the Carolinas.'

'The Carolinas?' Kempenfelt's brow furrowed in recollection. 'Ah yes, I recall the business. A privateer, eh? A murderous skirmish, no doubt. Now Scratch,' went on the admiral, turning to his secretary who had read the note, 'what d'ye have there? Good news, I hope.' Kempenfelt held out his hand. 'Good day to you, Mr Drinkwater.'

Drinkwater retired crest-fallen, once again disappointed in the high aspirations of impatient youth.

'Our number, sir,' Midshipman White reported formally to Drinkwater, 'send a boat.'

Drinkwater raised the long watch glass and studied the *Royal George* and the flutter of bunting at her mizen yardarm. It was three days since he had taken aboard the order to dock and the great ship had remained stationary in her anchorage.

'Very well, Chalky, do you take the starboard cutter and see what they want, and while you're over there, try and find out why she hasn't been taken to dock. I took aboard an order for it and they seemed anxious to get her in.'

White obeyed the order with evident reluctance. The seductive smell of coffee and something elusive wafting up from below reminded them both that they had been on deck for some hours and were eager to break their fasts. A trip to the *Royal George* might delay White's breakfast indefinitely. Drinkwater watched amused as his young friend slouched off and called the duty boat's crew away. It was a fine, sunny morning and, were it not the latest of a now numberless succession of such days, Drinkwater might have taken more pleasure in it. He could not understand why the relief of the fortress of

Gibraltar had lost its urgency and supposed Admiral Cordoba had himself retired to Cadiz. Such matters had been much discussed in the gunroom of late and all concluded depressingly that the war was as good as over and that they sat at Spithead as mere bargaining counters for the diplomats.

Drinkwater fell to pacing the deck. Along the starboard gangway the sergeant of marines was parading his men for Lieutenant Wheeler's routine morning inspection prior to changing the sentries. Below, in the waist, the sail-maker had half the watch with needles and palms stitching a new main topsail. Hanks of sail-twine and lumps of beeswax were in evidence as the heavy canvas was stretched by means of hooks and lanyards to facilitate the difficult job of creating the sail. Old 'Sails' wandered round, looking over the shoulders of the seamen as they laboured, chatting quietly among themselves. Woe betide any man who drew less than ten stitches per needle-length, for he would receive a mouthful of abuse from the sail-maker. 'Such neat work would put a seamstress to envy,' Drinkwater recollected being told by Mr Blackmore, the sailing master, 'and so it should, for what seamstress has to build a dress capable of withstanding the forces aloft in a gale?' This seemed to clinch the superiority of a man-o'-war's sails over a duchess's gown, for though much reputation might ride on the latter, far more might rely on the even strength of those seams when worn aloft in a man-of-war.

Drinkwater smiled and looked forward. On the forecastle a party of men squatted on the deck, plying dark fids of *lignum vitae* as they spliced a large rope. Drinkwater had no idea where it was intended that the heavy hemp should go, for the work was endless, presided over by Blackmore and Devaux, whose men laboured away at the ceaseless task of maintaining the frigate's fabric. More men were scattered in the rigging, worming and parcelling, tarring and slushing.

Idly Drinkwater wondered at the cost of it all in terms of material. If such activity was going on in every one of the ships gathered together in that crowded roadstead, the financial resources behind them must be unimaginable: five, seven, perhaps ten or a dozen millions of sterling!

'Cutter's returning, sir,' the duty quartermaster reported, rescuing Drinkwater from his abstraction. White scrambled up the side and touched his hat-brim to the quarterdeck. 'Message for the captain,' he said, waving a letter, 'be back in a moment.'

40

White reappeared a few minutes later. 'The Commander-in-Chief wants a status report. Defects, powder, shot, victuals and water. Looks like we at least might be under sailing orders very soon. We've an hour to get it ready. The captain's to wait on Admiral Kempenfelt at nine.'

'I see.' Drinkwater greeted the news with mixed emotions. If they really were going to sea again, he resolved to write to Elizabeth immediately. It was pointless to prevaricate further. If she dismissed his suit he would no longer toss so aimlessly from horn to horn of this confoundedly disturbing dilemma!

'As for the other matter,' White rattled on, 'I had a long chat with a young shaver in her launch.' Drinkwater smiled inwardly. The 'young shaver' was probably a year or so younger than White himself who had matured marvellously since the mess bully Morris had been turned out of the ship. Perhaps it was the eleven-year-old that Drinkwater himself had met the other day. 'Apparently she *was* to dock and then a couple of dockyard officers came aboard and located a leak in the larboard side of the hold. They put the work in hand to caulk the seam from the inside and afterwards declared her fit for sea.'

'Did your young shaver venture an opinion as to how the ship's people felt about that?'

White frowned at the question. 'Well, he said that in his opinion the dockyard officers were a laggardly pair of old hens, but the ship was the finest in the Service. I considered challenging him on that, but declined on grounds of his youthful inexperience!'

'Very wise of you, Mr White,' Drinkwater observed drily. 'Besides, to maintain the honour of our thirty-six guns against his hundred-and-something would be to push matters to extreme measures.' Drinkwater stared across the water at the distant flagship which he could see in the interval between two third-rates. 'Your informant's opinion of the dockyard officers sounds like the repetition of someone else's, though. I've heard the ship is decayed, though what proportion is rumour and what is rot, is rather hard to judge.'

'Ah, but that's not all, sir,' said White, enjoying being the bearer of scuttlebutt. 'Yesterday evening the *Royal George*'s carpenter reported another leak, this time on the starboard side where the inlet valve draws water for the washdeck pumps!'

'What's that, d'ye say?' The master came on deck to catch part of their discussion. 'A leaking inlet valve, eh? Where d'ye say? Starboard

41

side? If it ain't enough to be pressed for another damned inventory of stores at short notice . . .'

'Morning, Mr Blackmore,' Drinkwater greeted the protesting master as he sought to tuck his unruly white locks under his hat. 'Rest easy. We were talking of the *Royal George*.'

'Well,' replied Blackmore, glancing at the flagship with relief, 'at the best it means the grommet sealing the valve's flange has become porous, but at worst the spirketting may be rotten, in which case the compression of the bolts will be ineffective and she'll leak.'

'Then she'll *have* to dock,' Drinkwater observed.

Blackmore shook his head. 'I doubt the inlet is more than half a fathom below the waterline. If we're in so confounded a hurry to sail, it's my guess they'll careen her. Now, I've work to do. If you've nothing better for this young imp, Mr Drinkwater, I've a host of errands for him!'

Drinkwater grinned at the expression of despair on White's face. It was the lot of a midshipman to tread the deck of a flagship one moment and rummage in the stygian gloom of a frigate's hold the next. 'You may have him, Mr Blackmore, and with my compliments.'

'Obliged, Drinkwater. Now, young shaver, you come with me . . .'

Smiling, Drinkwater watched the two of them go below. White's breakfast remained in doubt.

Lieutenant Wallace relieved Drinkwater at eight bells and he hurried below after colours. Lieutenant Devaux was lingering over his coffee and poured Drinkwater a cup as the messman brought in some toast and devilled kidneys.

'Compliments of the first lieutenant, sir,' the man mumbled in his ear.

'Thank you, sir,' said Drinkwater, catching Devaux's eye. His mouth watered in anticipation as he fisted knife and fork. 'This is a surprise. I thought I smelt something tasty, but I couldn't identify it and in any case assumed it to be for Captain Hope's table.'

'The single joy of our situation, Nathaniel, is the occasional amelioration of our tedious diet. Sometimes I think it worth it, but at others I do not. This morning is no exception, for the kidneys come with . . .', Devaux paused to sip his coffee, 'well, you will know about it.'

'The stores inventory?'

'I wish to God that's all it was, but dear old Kempenfelt wants to know how many musket balls the esteemed Wheeler has. "Enough", replies Wheeler, "to kill every Frenchman to be found in Spithead!" ' Devaux paused, laying down his empty cup and refilling it. 'In the absence of any true wit, one is constrained to laugh,' he added.

Drinkwater smiled as he chewed the kidneys. 'I had better lend a hand then. I gather Captain Hope has to see the admiral at nine, so there is little time.'

'Indeed not, but you had better shave and dress your hair. You must go with the captain.'

'I must?' Drinkwater asked, his mouth full.

'I shall not tempt fate, Nathaniel, but consider how you might clear a foul hawse, or send down the t'gallants, or get the mainyard a-port-last.'

'I am to be examined?' Drinkwater asked in astonishment, his eyes wide.

'You cannot expect a proficiency with that damned French skewer of yours to entitle you automatically to a commission in His Majesty's navy.'

'No, I suppose not.'

'So good luck. Eat up all those kidneys and prove yourself a devil to boot!' Devaux rose, smiling at his own wit, took his hat from the peg by the gunroom door and turned, suddenly serious. 'Don't forget to take your journals.' The door closed behind him and Drinkwater was abandoned to a lather of anxiety.

By a quarter to nine on the morning of 29 August 1782, Spithead was already crowded with the movement of boats and small craft. Among them coasting vessels worked through the congested roadstead. One of them, the fifty-ton *Lark,* laid herself neatly alongside the larboard waist of the *Royal George* and soon afterwards began to discharge hogsheads of rum into the first-rate, a task made somewhat easier for those hauling on the tackles by a slight larboard list. A few moments later a dockyard launch went alongside and the Master Plumber of the Dockyard seized the vertical manropes and laboriously hauled his bulk up the flagship's tumblehome. As soon as the yard boat had laid off, *Cyclops*'s gig ran in under the entry, just astern of the *Lark,* and Captain Hope, in undress uniform, went up the side to the screech of the side-party's pipes. He was followed by Acting Lieutenant Drinkwater, whose bundle of journals went up after him on a line.

As he trailed behind Hope through the gun-decks, leaning against

43

the flagship's increasing list, Drinkwater observed men coiling down the larboard batteries' gun tackles, for all the guns on that side had been run out through the opened ports. It was clear the *Royal George*'s company were in the process of careening her, as Blackmore had said they would. He also noted that the decks were even more crowded and noisy than those of *Cyclops*, the *Royal George* being similarly infested with what Blackmore collectively referred to as 'beach-vermin', but Drinkwater's anxious mind was dominated by the imminent and summary examination he must undergo and he thought no more of these facts.

Outside the admiral's cabin Hope paused and turned, bracing himself as if the ship were on the wind. 'Wait on the quarterdeck, Mr Drinkwater. You may be kicking your heels for some time. Be patient and muse on your profession. The admiral is a fast friend to those he knows, and particularly to men of merit. I have commended you most warmly, but I doubt not that he will want some confirmation of my opinion.'

'I understand, sir. And thank you.'

'Report to the officer of the watch then. Good luck. I shall send the gig back for you in due course.'

'Aye, aye, sir.'

Drinkwater touched his hat to Hope and turned for the companionway to the quarterdeck. The upper gun-deck which stretched forward from where he stood was a scene of utter chaos. The dutymen had crossed the deck from securing the larboard batteries and were running in the starboard guns to the extent of their breechings to induce an even greater list, upsetting the cosy nests that wives and families had established between the cannon. In consequence, there were squeals, shouts, oaths and every combination of noise that flustered women, exasperated men and miserable children could make.

As Drinkwater came up into the sunshine of the quarterdeck, he saw the officer of the watch and a warrant officer just in front of him.

'She's listed far enough, sir,' he heard the warrant officer say, presuming he must be the flagship's carpenter, 'and the water's just lapping the lower-deck gun-port sills.'

'Well get on with your work then, damn it,' the lieutenant responded tartly, 'and start the pumps.' He turned and caught sight of Drinkwater. 'Who the deuce are you?'

'Drinkwater, Acting Lieutenant of *Cyclops*, sir. I'm waiting on Admiral Kempenfelt.'

'Oh are you.' The lieutenant stared at the journals tucked under Drinkwater's arm and, seeming to sum up his situation, expelled his breath contemptuously. 'Well, keep out of the confounded way! I could do without a lot of snot-nosed infants hanging around my coat-tails this morning.'

'I shall of course keep out of your way, sir.' Drinkwater had no wish to further acquaint himself with the objectionable officer. He acknowledged the man had his own problems this morning and soon forgot him as he turned over in his own mind the answers to those questions he thought he might be asked. He presumed a small board of examination had been convened, for there were enough senior officers hereabouts to form a score of such boards, and the thought led him to wonder if he were not the only candidate. The lieutenant's comments seemed to indicate there might be others.

Drinkwater struggled uphill to the high starboard side and peered over in the vain hope of catching sight of the work that was causing all the trouble. The marine sentries on either quarter muttered an exchange and, as Drinkwater turned to cross the quarterdeck to the low side, a man wearing the plain blue coat of *Royal George*'s master came up from below and looked briefly about him. His face wore an expression of extreme apprehension and he too was muttering. He caught sight of the officer of the watch.

'Mr Hollingbury! Damn it, Mr Hollingbury . . .'

Lieutenant Hollingbury turned. 'What the devil do *you* want?'

'I must insist that you right the ship as I asked some moments ago. Right the ship upon the instant, sir! I insist upon it.'

'Insist? What the deuce d'you mean by insisting, Mister? *I* insist that you finish work on the damned cock. Have you finished work on the cock?'

'No, but . . .'

'Then attend to the matter. It is not pleasant standing here with such a heel . . .'

'Get the ship upright, you damned fool, there's water coming in over the lower-deck sills . . .'

'*What* did you say?' Hollingbury's face was suffused with anger and he advanced on the warrant officer. 'We haven't got her over this far to jack in before the task's done. I've ordered the pumps to be manned. Just attend to that damned cock, or I'll have the warrant off you, you impudent old bugger!'

The master turned away, his face white. He hesitated at the top of the companionway and his eyes met Drinkwater's. At that instant they both felt a slight trembling from below. 'She'll go over,' the master said, looking away from Drinkwater and down the companionway as though terrified of descending.

A sudden cold apprehension took possession of Drinkwater's guts. The master's prophecy was not an idle one. Instinctively he felt there was something very wrong with the great ship, though he could not rationalize the conviction of his sudden fear. For a moment he thought he might be succumbing to the panic that held the master rooted to the top of the companionway. Then he knew. The list was no greater than if the *Royal George* had been heeled to a squall of wind, but there was something unambiguously dead about the feel of her beneath his feet.

Then from below there came an ominous rumbling, followed by a series of thunderous crashes accompanied by cries of alarm, screams of pain and the high-pitched arsis of human terror.

Drinkwater ran across the deck and leaned out over the rail to catch sight of *Cyclops*'s boat.

'Gig, hoy!' he roared. '*Cyclops*, hoy!' He saw the face of Midshipman Catchpole in the stern look up at him. Drinkwater waved his arm. 'Stand clear of us astern! Stand clear!' He saw the boy wave in acknowledgement and then thought of Hope down below in the admiral's cabin. He made a dash for the companionway. The master had gone, but now an indiscriminate horde of men and women, seamen, marines, petty officers and officers, poured up from below, all shouting and screaming in abject panic. Then Hollingbury, his face distorted by fury at the rank disorder, barred his way. It occurred to Drinkwater that Hollingbury was one of those men who, even in the face of enormity, either deceive themselves as to their part in it or are too stupid to acknowledge that a crisis is occurring

'The ship is capsizing, sir!' Drinkwater hurled the words into the lieutenant's face. 'Capsizing! D'you understand?'

Hollingbury's expression changed as the import of Drinkwater's statement dawned upon him, though it seemed the concept still eluded him, as though it was beyond belief that the almost routine careening of a mighty man-of-war could so abruptly change to something beyond control. But the pandemonium emerging from below finally confirmed that the warning shouted in his very face by this insolent stranger might be true. Comprehension struck Hollingbury like a blow. The colour drained from the lieutenant's face and he spun round. 'My God!' His eyes fell upon the hogsheads of rum hauled out of *Lark* and lying on the deck. In a wild moment of misguided inspiration, he sought to extricate the ship. The only weights he could move rapidly on the low side of the *Royal George* were those rum barrels. 'Get those casks over the side! Heave 'em overboard! Look lively there, damn your eyes!'

A boatswain's mate saw the logic of the order and, driven by habit, wielded his starter. The men on deck and those who were pouring up from below, themselves habituated to obedience, did as they were bidden and rushed across the deck in a mass. But it was too late; their very movement contributed to disaster. The ship's lower deck ports were now pressed well down below the level of the sea. Water cascaded into the ship, settling her lower in the water, deadening her as Drinkwater had divined, drowning those still caught on the orlop and in the hold spaces, and adding the torrential roar of its flooding to the chaos below.

Drinkwater failed to reach the companionway. His momentary confrontation with Hollingbury had delayed him, but even had he succeeded, he would have been quite unable to defy the press of terrified people trying to reach the upper deck. Instead he lost his footing and fell as a gust of wind fluttered across Spithead to strike the high, exposed bilge and the top-hamper of her lofty rig. The gust laid the *Royal George* on her beam ends.

No longer able to support the weight of the remaining starboard guns, the rest of the breechings parted. On the lower gun-deck the huge thirty-two-pounders broke free and hurled their combined tonnage across the lower deck, joined on the decks above by the twenty-four- and twelve-pounders. Lying full length, Drinkwater felt the death throes of the great ship as she shook to a mounting succession of shudderings. He cast about for his journals as they slid down the deck, his heart beating with the onset of panic, abandoned them and clutched at a handhold.

Throughout the *Royal George*'s entire fabric a vast disintegration was taking place. It had started as the first guns broke adrift, careered across the decks and carried all before them, weakening stanchions, colliding with their twins on the opposite side of the gun-decks and knocking out the sills and lintels of the gun-ports piercing the larboard side. The increasing influx of water only settled the *Royal George* deeper. Had her capsizing moment been arrested, she might yet have righted herself sufficiently to be saved, but the rush of men to the

47

larboard waist was just enough to further increase the flow of water and, augmented by that fatal gust of wind, took her past the point of no return.

Finally, the parting breechings of the majority of the guns loosed an avalanche of cast iron in a precipitous descent. Gun after gun crashed into the ship's side, embedding themselves in softening timber, dislodging futtocks and transmitting tremulous shocks throughout the fabric of the hull. Such dislocations sprung more leaks far below, where the upward pressure of the water bore unnaturally upon her heavily listing hull and found the weaknesses of rot. The roundness of her underwater body caved inwards in a slow, unseen implosion that those far above, in terror of their lives, felt only as a great cataclysmic juddering.

Drinkwater, clinging to a train tackle ring-bolt, felt the tremor. Almost, it seemed, directly above his head, one of the half-dozen six-pounder guns that had lined the starboard rail of the quarterdeck strained at its breeching. He watched the strands of the heavy rope unravel ominously. The sight of it galvanized him with the reactive urgency of self-preservation. He began to scrabble upwards, fascinated by the fraying rope-yarns, as though they counted out the remaining seconds of his existence. He did not dare catch hold of the gun-carriage lest his weight accelerate the rope's parting, and stretched instead for the gun-tackle on the left-hand side of the carriage, the hauling part of which now dangled untidily downwards. Somewhere in the back of his mind was the image of the ship's starboard side at which he had glanced out of idle curiosity only a few moments earlier. If he could make the rail and get over it, he might yet escape!

His fingers closed on the gun-tackle, worked at it as his right foot, lodged on the eyebolt, raised him an inch, his fingers scrabbling for a better grip. Then he caught and grasped it and was about to grab it with his other hand when the gun breeching failed. The six-pounder ran away and he found himself pulled the last few feet up the violently canted deck as the descending gun unrove the gun-tackle. The truck hit his foot and he kicked at it just as his eyes caught sight of the proximity of the standing block to his fingers. He let go of the rope, kicked again, found a momentary foothold on the slewing and falling gun-carriage, and grabbed another rope which had dropped from a pin on the mizen rail. He slid back as it ran slack, then drew tight; he began to climb, frantic in his movements, gasping for breath, his objective in sight. With a final effort dredged from the inner resource of pure terror, he hauled himself up to the pinrail. Here there was no lack of handholds and, almost exhausted with the effort, his heart beating in his breast and his breath rasping painfully in his throat, he threw himself over it. Panting and shaking, he glanced back, almost vertically downwards. The mainyard, its extremity already in the water, had stabbed down across the deck of the *Lark*. What had happened to the crowd of people he had seen in the coasting vessel's waist a few moments ago, he had no idea, for only a few heads bobbed in the water, and he thought it unnaturally quiet.

He turned away, shuddering too much from exertion and visceral fear to be able to stand. Instead he crawled past the open ports of the starboard side whence came the loud sibilance of compressed air roaring upwards with columns of debris. He understood now why he could not hear anyone shouting or screaming. Every unsecured port on the starboard side stood open, venting a furious mist in which unidentifiable items flew upwards, to flutter down beside the ship. What had once been a woman's shawl or a baby's diaper, a book, a shoe or a man's hat, fell into the surrounding sea as flotsam. Drinkwater pulled himself together as he realized that, shallow though the water was, it was deep enough to swallow whole the vast bulk of the *Royal George*. He began to crawl aft.

Perhaps ten other men and a solitary woman who screamed and rent her hair in despair were visible on the starboard side. Another man, a marine by his tunic, was hauling himself out of an open port on the middle gun-deck, the water running off him. Drinkwater scrambled towards the woman, but she turned on him in a fury, her eyes wild with dementia, a torrent of abuse pouring from her. He turned aft, thinking again of Hope below in the admiral's state-cabin. Perhaps he could free the stern windows before it was too late, but the wreck beneath his feet trembled again and suddenly the venting roar died away and the circle of water about him approached.

He was on his feet now, running aft in search of *Cyclops*'s gig. He could see boats laying off, their oars immobile, the faces of their crews pale ovals as they watched the awesome sight of the *Royal George* foundering in the midst of the Grand Fleet, within sight of over three hundred vessels and the shore.

He had survived the immersion, being dragged painfully over the gig's transom and surrendered to the solicitous Appleby who had

49

chafed his naked and bruised body with brandy. He had been touched by the anxious concern of White and Devaux, and later mourned the loss of his journals.

He was never to know, though he might afterwards have guessed, that a few days later a sabre-winged fulmar, sweeping low over the wave crests somewhere to the westward, in the overfalls that run off St Alban's Head, had its roving eye caught by a patch of white. It banked steeply and rolled almost vertically as it made its curving turn, keeping the white patch in view as it swooped back on its interminably hungry reconnaissance. But the white paper was of no nutritional value to the fulmar and it levelled off and skimmed on westwards towards Portland Bill, its wings motionless as they had been all the time it had surveyed the sheet of paper.

The secretary's ink had run by then and no one could have read Kempenfelt's last signature, nor that the paper was a commission made out in the King's name for a certain insignificant Nathaniel Drinkwater.

The Flogging

The North Sea was a heaving mass of grey crests which broke in profusion, the pallid spume of their dissolution driving downwind.
Under close-reefed topsails and the clew of the foretopmast staysail,
Cyclops fought the inevitable drift to leeward, towards the shoals off
the inhospitable Dutch coast. Beneath the lowering sky, from which
neither sun nor moon obliged the patient Blackmore and his quadrant, the frigate lay battered by the fourth day of the gale. It was the
third day of cold rations, since it had proved impossible to maintain
the galley fire, and the only consolation to the shivering ship's
company was that they had loaded a fresh stock of beer at Sheerness.

Everything below decks was its usual compound of stink and
damp. Sea water squirted through the interstices of closed gun-ports
as the lee side buried itself, and the crew were employed at the pumps
for an hour and a half every watch. Men barely spoke to each other;
nothing beyond the barest detail of duty was discussed and every
man, irrespective of his station, sought only the meagre comfort of
his hammock or cot as he came below from the greater misery of the
deck.

Relieved by White, Midshipman Drinkwater made his bruised and
buffeted way below and clambered wearily into his hammock. The
dark of the orlop deck was punctured by the swaying lanterns which
imparted their weird and monstrous shadows as they oscillated at
different rates to the laden hammocks. From below came the swirl
and effluvia of the bilge, counterpoint to the creaks and groans of the
frigate's hull and the faint thrum of the gale roaring above through
the mast and rigging.

51

Despite his exhaustion, Drinkwater was unable to sleep. His active brain rebelled against the fatigue of his body. Dulled by the monotony of the gale and the necessity of ignoring his protesting and empty stomach, it now refused to let him drift into the seaman's one palliative for misery, the balm of exhausted sleep.

It hardly seemed possible that *Cyclops* was the same frigate that had fought under Rodney in the Moonlight Battle, or that the sullen faces of the seamen were those that had followed the young Midshipman Drinkwater through the bilge of the Yankee schooner *Algonquin* in a bid to avert confinement in a French fortress. But it was not the weather or the duty of a winter cruise in the North Sea which had induced this sleepless anxiety, it was the misery which prevailed aboard, so reminiscent of his first months in the frigate when the very cockpit to which an unkind fate had now returned him had been dominated by the vicious presence of the bugger Morris. Far from obtaining a commission, Drinkwater had found himself deprived of the privacy and privileges of the acting rank to which he had grown accustomed.

It was a cruel blow, made worse by the departure of Devaux. After the tragic loss of Captain Hope aboard the *Royal George*, Lieutenant Devaux had briefly commanded the ship for the passage to Sheerness. On arrival there, Devaux, whose eldest brother had blown out his own brains over a gambling debt, now learned the news, already months old, that his second brother had died in the trenches before Yorktown. Devaux thus found himself the 6th Earl of Dungarth in the Irish peerage, and this change in his circumstances induced Miss Charlotte Dixon, a young woman outstanding for her beauty and intelligence, to consent to become his countess. As Miss Dixon was not merely lovely and clever but also the sole daughter of a nabob, Dungarth was in some hopes of repairing his family's fortunes and swiftly relinquished the profession of a naval officer. To Drinkwater, Devaux's departure seemed like a double desertion, for the first lieutenant, poor though he might be, left to make an advantageous marriage, abandoning his lieutenant's commission without a second thought. Drinkwater, for whom such a qualification seemed an impossible attainment, was left to muse upon the inequities of life, with only the thin consolation of his correspondence with Elizabeth to help him come to terms with his return to the midshipmen's mess.

'I am sorry, my dear fellow,' Devaux had said on their last night in the gunroom as *Cyclops* lay within half a mile of the light-vessel at the

Nore. 'I should have liked to help you but my naval service is over. Perhaps we shall meet again, perhaps when there is peace you will come and stay with us . . .'

Perhaps . . . perhaps . . . How full of pathos that word seemed, and how Drinkwater envied Devaux the use of that plural pronoun.

Under orders though they were, their brief halt at Sheerness saw changes in the cockpit, as well as in the gunroom, but most of all a new commander read his commission to the ship's company.

Captain Smetherley, whose father supported the new government of Lord Rockingham, was twenty-six years old. Pleasant in disposition, he possessed an easy manner of command but had little practical experience to his name. He had been entered on a ship's books as a boy, had dodged the regulations and had been commissioned at sixteen with neither achievement nor examination to testify to his suitability. During his six months as a commander, he had been in charge of a sloop which had spent half that time at anchor in the Humber. With Captain Smetherley came an elderly first lieutenant named Callowell, a hard-drinking tarpaulin of the old school sent by a considerate Admiralty to offset the professional shortcomings of the new post-captain. Callowell was a man from the other end of the navy's social spectrum. Twice the age of his commander, a man with neither influence nor the dash that might have earned him merited promotion, he offered no threat to Smetherley in the matter of glory, but he was well known as a highly competent seaman and a tough sea-officer. Unfortunately, Callowell was also a harsh man. Cruelty and fault-finding were visited on all, irrespective of rank. Moreover, fellow-officers more favourably placed than himself who were disposed to assist the advancement of a competent, if disadvantaged officer, were turned away by Callowell's spite.

Within a few days, Drinkwater reflected, Callowell had made enemies of Appleby the surgeon, Lieutenant Wheeler of the marines and poor Lieutenant Wallace, and it was borne in upon Drinkwater how fine an influence Devaux had been on the frigate as a whole. He was greatly missed and, Drinkwater felt certain, he himself would not have been turned so precipitately out of the gunroom had Devaux remained aboard.

Smetherley's arrival had also, in Callowell's phrase, 'cleaned out the midshipmites' cockpit'. Only White and Drinkwater remained of the original midshipmen, and they were now joined by four young kill-devils to whose families Smetherley owed some obligation or who had solicited his favour. Both White and Drinkwater viewed this invasion with disquiet. It was clear that the four all knew each other, and while seasickness had demoralized them for the first few days, it was obvious from their slovenly indiscipline, their abuse of Jacob the messman, and their noise that they were going to prove troublesome.

Had they remained a week longer at anchor at Spithead, Drinkwater knew that White would have been able to leave the frigate, for he was daily in expectation of the order, but within a few days of the foundering of the *Royal George*, *Cyclops* had sailed for Sheerness. Rodney's defeat of De Grasse had revenged Graves's disgrace off the Virginia Capes, though it did not restore the Thirteen Colonies, and even as they tossed in the fury of the northern gale, Lord Howe and the Grand Fleet were relieving Gibraltar for the third and final time. As the unpopular conflict spluttered to its close, *Cyclops* had to maintain her vigil to see that neither Dutch nor French cruisers stole a march on the exhausted British nor tipped the delicate balance of negotiations in the peace talks that all seemed certain were about to bring matters to a conclusion. Perhaps, Drinkwater thought as he resolutely composed himself to grab a few hours' sleep, the war would at last be truly over. Providence had saved him from plunging to his death with all those other poor souls trapped aboard the *Royal George*; it must surely have preserved him for some purpose, and what purpose could there possibly be other than to allow him to return to Elizabeth?

Lieutenants Callowell and Wallace stood on the weather quarterdeck staring to windward. Callowell, his feet well spread and both hands gripping the rail against the heel of the frigate, was speaking to Wallace, his cloak beating about him in a sinister manner – like a bat's wings, Drinkwater thought, approaching them. He touched his hat to the two officers as he made his way aft to the taffrail to heave the log which the two quartermasters were preparing. It was almost eight bells, the end of the morning watch, and Drinkwater was tired and hungry. He nodded to the two petty officers, and the log-ship went over the side, drawing the knotted line off the spinning reel while Drinkwater regarded old Bower's watch.

'Now!' he called, and the line was nipped. 'Five knots?'

'And a half.'

'Very good. And how much leeway d'you reckon?' Drinkwater shouted above the roar of the gale, cocking an eye at the older quartermaster. The man had served as mate in a merchantman and knew his business.

"Bout eight degrees, I'd say.' Drinkwater and the second quartermaster nodded their assent.

'Very well. We'll make it so. You may hand the log.' And leaving them to wind in the hemp line, Drinkwater walked forward to move the pegs on the traverse board. The glass was turned, eight bells were struck and the forenoon took over from the morning watch. On deck men in sodden tarpaulins were stamping about, eager to be dismissed below, and those just emerged from the foetid berth-deck huddled in miserable groups in what shelter they could find, trying to delay the inevitable moment of a sousing for as long as possible. The petty officers made their reports and Drinkwater went aft to where Wallace and Callowell were still in conversation, staring out over the grey waste to windward.

'Beg pardon, sir . . .' Drinkwater shouted. The two officers looked over their shoulders, Callowell raising an interrogative eyebrow, though it was Wallace who was about to be relieved.

'Starboard watch mustered on deck. Permission for the larbowlines to go below, sir.'

Callowell looked at Drinkwater. From Wallace's look of embarrassment, Drinkwater knew trouble was brewing. He repeated his report and Callowell said in a voice raised above the wind, 'Mr Drinkwater, we are waiting . . .'

'Sir?'

'Waiting, damn you . . .'

'I'm sorry, Mr Callowell, but . . .'

'Mr Callowell is waiting for the courtesy of a "good morning",' Wallace said hurriedly.

Drinkwater had thought himself absolved from such an absurdity by the violence of the weather, the fact that he and Wallace had been on deck since four o'clock in the morning, and the salute he had given the two officers as he made his way aft to heave the log. He was about to swallow his pride, aware that to provoke Callowell with any form of justification was a waste of time, when Callowell denied him this small amelioration.

'As first lieutenant of this frigate, I expect my midshipmen to demonstrate the respect due to the senior officer below the commander. You, sir, can disabuse yourself of any advantages your late acting rank gave you, or any that might have been conferred by your

55

friendship with the last first lieutenant or the late Captain Hope. The fresh air of the foretopmasthead will do you the world of good, will it not, Mr Wallace?'

Wallace mumbled uncomfortably, but Callowell was not yet satisfied. 'But you shall first heave the log again and be pleased to use the glass, not your damned watch. She makes six knots.'

It was growing dark when Drinkwater was brought down from the masthead. The topgallant masts had been struck and he had lashed himself into the shelter available, passing the afternoon in a miserable, semi-conscious state, wracked by cold, cramps and hunger. He had been incapable of descending the mast unaided, and Tregembo and another seaman had sent him down on a gantline.

'There, zur,' the Cornishman had muttered, 'that bastard'll get a boarding-pike in his arse if ever we zees action.'

'Poor bugger can't hear you,' his companion said.

'Maybe not,' Tregembo said philosophically, 'but when he wakes up, he'll agree with me.'

On deck the pain of returning circulation woke Drinkwater to a full and agonizing consciousness that was too self-centred to admit even a single thought of revenge. He gasped with the pain, involuntary tears starting from his eyes, as poor White brought orders that were to further prolong his distress. From this state of half-recovery, Callowell demanded his immediate presence on the quarterdeck where, Drinkwater was told, it was time for him to stand his next watch. Had not Drinkwater been able to rely upon the loyal White to smuggle him victuals on deck and had he not eaten them equally unobserved, his collapse from cold and hunger would have proved fatal. As it was, he endured the ordeal.

Drinkwater was not the only victim of Callowell's harsh malice. Before the gale finally abated, several floggings of undue severity had been ordered out to the hands for trivial offences. Several of these would normally have been summarily dealt with by the frigate's regulating system, minor punishments being meted out by the boatswain and his mates. Devaux, had he even bothered to notice them, would have disdained to act. Callowell, on the other hand, possessed a knack of always observing these small incidents so that it seemed his presence actually caused them, and men shrank from him. The first lieutenant appeared indifferent to this shunning. Appleby named him *Ubique* Callowell, to the amusement of Wheeler, but it was Appleby

56

who first warned of serious discontent among the hands. His position as surgeon enabled him to divine more of the frigate's undercurrents than any gunroom officer and, as his business chiefly occupied him below decks, he was particularly sensitive to the moods of the people. In fact Callowell's behaviour only exacerbated a deteriorating situation. The ship's company had largely been aboard *Cyclops* since October 1779 and in all that time had not enjoyed a single day of liberty ashore. Nor had these long-suffering men been paid their wages. They had, however, had women aboard and had revelled in the excesses of unbridled lust, a pleasure paid for by their share of prize money but now requiring Appleby's mercurial specific against the lues. Some prize money, however, remained, and this excited an envious greed among those intemperate spendthrifts who were now paying painfully for past pleasures.

To compound matters, before leaving Spithead *Cyclops* had been obliged to pass twenty men to the *Bedford*, then under sailing orders, and had made up the deficiency from a draft embarked at the Nore where her new captain joined before she sailed to her cruising ground on the Broad Fourteens. The new crew members were duly taken aboard from the *Conquistador*, guardship at the Nore, the majority being 'Lord Mayor's men', those who made up the deficiencies in the parish quotas by the simple expedient of being released from the confinement ordered by the petty sessions.

Among the men from *Conquistador* were some skilled petty felons, men who owed neither His Britannic Majesty's Royal Navy in general nor their shipmates in the frigate *Cyclops* in particular any shred of loyal forbearance. Even before they had weighed from the anchorage off Sheerness, thieving had broken out on the berth-deck, but it was after the abatement of the gale that these men revealed the full extent of the two unsought contributions they had brought aboard.

The thieving was bad enough, but far worse was the gaol fever. The outbreak of typhus, a disease harboured in the parasites inhabiting these men's filthy garments, caused Appleby much labour and anxiety. The surgeon found the purser unwilling to issue slop-clothing until Callowell approved it and this the first lieutenant declined to do. Thus both thieving and disease permeated the ship, causing infinite distress and disorder among the men. The knowledge of a deadly infection striking indiscriminately only fuelled the pathetic desperation with which the miserable hands sought other diversions. With silver florins unspent upon the berth-deck, every form of card-sharping, knavery, pilfering and coercion flourished. Nor was this moral disintegration the sole province of the newly drafted men; on the contrary they were but the catalyst. Men who had been messmates, even friends, when confronted with sudden personal losses, turned on their equals to redeem them. As if this witches' cauldron were not enough, there were among the drafted men two devil-may-care light dragoons sentenced by a court martial to be dismissed from their regiment and sent as common seamen into the Royal Navy. They had received a flogging and had come to *Cyclops* with the notion that, since service in the navy was of a punitive nature, it was little deserving of respect. In their former corps, the 7th Queen's Own Light Dragoons, both men had been non-commissioned officers and they resented the treatment meted out to them by the boatswain's mates and, in particular, the midshipmen.

In the choice of his new midshipmen, Captain Smetherley had been unfortunate. Of the four who had come in his train, all were ignorant and incompetent, while the example of Callowell encouraged a viciousness sometimes natural in young men. Despite their youth they were usually more drunk than sober and they had discovered a means of amusing themselves by bullying and taunting the men until, answered back, they ordered the boatswain's mates to start the alleged offenders.

Such was the sorry state of affairs aboard *Cyclops*, and it augured ill after the fair and relatively humane regime of Hope and Devaux. The effect of the gale only exacerbated the deterioration in morale. What occurred in a few short days might have taken longer in a better climate or a pleasanter season, but it came as no surprise to those who regarded the new regime with distaste when trouble arose.

Two days after the gale had blown itself out and patches of watery sunshine and blue skies had replaced the grey wrack that had streamed above the very mast trucks, a sail was made out to the northward. The change in the weather had brought most of the officers on to the quarterdeck and the mood lightened still further as this news broke the monotony of their existence. The ship was standing to the northward, close-hauled on the larboard tack and carrying sails to the topgallants.

'Royals, sir?' Callowell asked Smetherley as he came on deck.

'As you see fit, Mr Callowell,' Smetherley said, falling to pacing the weather planking, hands clasped behind his back. Callowell turned to bawl his orders. *Cyclops* set her kites flying, the yards being run up when required and the sheets rove through the topgallant yardarms by the upper topmen. The pipes shrilled and the seamen leapt aloft, poking fun at the fumbling landsmen who were preparing to heave the halliards.

'A glass at the foremasthead, sir?' prompted Callowell.

'If you please, Mr Callowell,' assented Captain Smetherley with urbane assurance. Callowell turned to find Midshipman Baskerville at his elbow.

'Take a glass aloft and see what you make of him,' Callowell growled, and the midshipman passed Drinkwater with a smirk. He was the most loathsome of the captain's toadies, the leader of the quartet, related by blood to Smetherley and therefore unassailable. To Baskerville, Drinkwater was a passed-over nonentity, and while he was cautious of White, for he recognized him as one of his own, he did not scruple to use a high and usually insolent tone with Drinkwater. As Baskerville hauled himself into the foremast rigging, Drinkwater walked over to the lee rail where Blackmore was peering through his battered perspective glass, trying to gain a glimpse of the strange sail.

'Can you make him out yet, Mr Blackmore?'

'Not yet, but I'm thinking he'll be British, and sailing without convoy. Out of Hamburg at this season.' Blackmore was apt to be inscrutable at such moments and Drinkwater recollected that he had commanded a Baltic trader until ruined by war and knew the North Sea trade better than any other man on board. As the two men waited for the sail to be visible from the deck, neither witnessed the incident that provoked the coming trouble.

Amongst the men ordered into the lower rigging to see the royal yards run clear aloft was Roach. He had been rated landsman, as was customary, but as a former troop corporal of light dragoons, he was an active and an intelligent man. Whatever the shortcomings of their fellow landsmen, neither Roach nor his fellow-cavalryman Hollins lacked courage. Contemptuous of their new Service, they flung themselves into the rigging as though charging an enemy, disdaining to be associated with the drabber, duller men of the Sheerness draft. They were not yet of much use aloft but were clearly the raw material of which upper topmen were made, and their dare-devilment had already earned a grudging admiration from *Cyclops*'s people, especially those who had observed the state of their backs.

In descending the foremast rigging Roach, aware that to go

through the lubber's-hole was considered the coward's path, was about to fling himself over the edge of the top and into the futtock shrouds. The heels of his hessian boots, which he had found an indispensable weapon on the lower deck, trod on the up-reaching fingers of Midshipman Baskerville just then ascending the mast with his telescope. Hearing the youth's shout, Roach drew back into the top and, as the midshipman came over the edge, muttered a half-hearted apology. But he was grinning and this, combined with the sharp pain, provoked Baskerville.

'You bloody fool! You've made me drop the glass! What the devil d'you mean by wearing those festerin' boots, damn your eyes?'

'Doin' my duty, *sir*.' The dragoon drew out the last syllable so that it oozed from him like a sneer and he did it with the studied insolence of twenty years of barrack-room experience, deeply resenting the authority of the young oaf. Roach pressed his advantage. 'I apologized to you, *Mr* Baskerville.' Again there was that sibilant distortion in the title which set Baskerville fuming while Roach persisted in his grinning. But then another figure appeared in the top. It was a boatswain's mate.

'Mr Jackson,' Baskerville asked quickly, 'd'you see that man's grin?'

'Aye, I do.'

'Then mark it well, Jackson, mark it well and take the bugger's name!'

'Very well, sir. Here's your glass. You were fortunate I caught it.'

Baskerville almost snatched the telescope from Jackson's outstretched hand, then, without another word, swung himself into the topmast shrouds and scrambled upwards.

'And what have you done to upset Mr Baskerville, Roach?' the boatswain's mate asked.

'I trod on his fingers, Mr Jackson, and I apologized.'

Jackson shook his head. 'Tch, tch, tch. There's no fucking justice, is there? I wish you'd trodden on his fucking head, but you'll get a checked shirt for this, my lad, or my name's not Harry Jackson.'

Blackmore's prediction turned out to be accurate and the sail revealed herself as the brig *Margaret* of Newcastle, bound from Hamburg to London with timber and flax. At the frigate's signal she hove to and *Cyclops* rounded up under her lee quarter, backing her own maintopsail. Alongside Drinkwater, Blackmore muttered, 'Damn, you can smell the turpentine from here!'

Callowell leapt up on to the rail and raised a speaking-trumpet to his mouth. 'You're not in convoy, Mister. Any sign of enemy ships?'

'Aye,' responded a stout figure at the *Margaret*'s rail in the unmistakable accents of the Tyne, 'convoy dispersed by a ship-rigged Frenchman. He took twa vessels oot of tha ten of us. Be aboot twenty guns.'

'What of your escort?'

'A bomb-vessel. She couldn't work to windward before the Frenchman made off.'

'Where away?'

'Norderney!'

'Thank you, Captain! *Bon voyage!*' The patrician accent of Captain Smetherley replaced the abrupt Callowell. For once he had the situation in hand. 'Haul your maintopsail, Mr Callowell. Mr Blackmore, lay me a course for Norderney, if you please. Let's see if we can catch this damned Frog.'

'Lay *me*, be damned,' Blackmore muttered to Drinkwater and then, raising his voice, called out, 'Aye, aye, sir.'

Summary justice was a principle upon which Jonas Callowell dealt with all matters of discipline and good order. If an offence was committed, it was swiftly punished. When he received Baskerville's complaint he reported to Smetherley who lounged in his cabin, a glass of port in one hand.

'Damned rascal was insolent to the midshipman, insolence witnessed by Jackson, sir.'

'Jackson, Mr Callowell?'

'Bosun's mate.'

'Ahhh.' Smetherley took a mouthful of port and rolled it around his tongue, swallowed and smacked his lips. He looked up at Callowell with a frown. 'And you demand punishment?'

'Of course, sir. For the maintenance of discipline. Absolutely indispensable,' Callowell replied, a little astonished.

'Naturally, Mr Callowell, but the principle of mercy ... does it enter into the particulars of this case?'

'Not to my mind, sir,' said Callowell, who had never heard anything so damned stupid.

'Will two dozen suffice for insolence to a midshipman?'

'As you see fit, sir,' responded Callowell drily, but Smetherley, pouring another glass of port, needed to maintain the fiction of command and enjoyed a little light-hearted baiting of his first lieutenant.

'What, if you were in my position, would you give the man, Mr Callowell?'

'I'd smother the bugger with the captain's cloak, sir.'

'Three dozen, eh? Isn't that a trifle hard?'

'Not in my view, sir.'

'Mr Baskerville is a somewhat forward young man. His only redeeming feature, as far as I can see, is a rather lovely sister.' Smetherley pulled a face over the rim of his glass. 'But that would not concern you, Mr Callowell. Two dozen will suffice, I think.'

'As you see fit, sir,' Callowell repeated, leaving the cabin.

Roach was confined to the bilboes until the watch changed. When Appleby heard, he hurried to the gunroom where the first lieutenant was tossing off a pot of blackstrap.

'You cannot mean this, Mr Callowell?'

'Mean what?' asked Callowell, whose contempt for the surgeon's humanity was only exceeded by his dislike of the man himself whom he regarded as a meddling old wind-bag.

'Why flogging Roach, of course!'

'And why, pray, should I not flog Roach?' asked Callowell, lowering his tankard and staring at Appleby. 'Is he not guilty of insolence to an officer?'

'A very junior, inexperienced *under* officer,' Appleby expostulated testily, 'a mere insolent aspirant himself, without skill and wanting common manners to boot, but that is not the point . . .'

'Then for God's sake get to your damned point, Appleby!'

'How many's he getting?'

'Two dozen.'

'Two dozen! But that's twice the permitted limit for a post-captain to award!'

'Are you questioning the captain's authority, Mr Appleby? My word, you'd make a fine sight at the gratings yourself!'

'Damn it, Mr Callowell, you have no right . . .'

'Is that your point, Appleby?' Callowell broke in impatiently.

'No, no it isn't.' Appleby collected himself. 'Mr Callowell, Roach was given two hundred and fifty lashes after his court martial. I am empowered to prevent . . .'

'I've no doubt but that he deserved them,' broke in Callowell. 'As for your being empowered to do anything, Mr Appleby, I believe it is limited to advice. Well, thank you for your advice. It was my advice to Captain Smetherley that Roach be given *three* dozen . . .'

'I daresay it was, but heed me. The man's back is in no state to suffer further punishment. You'll kill the fellow.'

'So much the better. The man is no good to us, he will be nothing but trouble.'

'But . . .'

Callowell's emptied tankard crashed down upon the table and he rose to his feet, leaned across it and thrust his face into that of the surgeon. 'Listen, Appleby, do you cure the pox, the gaol fever, the itch, button scurvy and the clap, and when you can do all that you may come back here and teach me *my* duty. Now take your damnable cant back to where you belong and keep your fat arse out of the gunroom. It's for the commissioned officers, not bloody tradesmen. Get out!'

Appleby departed with what dignity he could muster, but word of the encounter percolated rapidly through the ship. The surgeon himself was far from capitulating. He approached Captain Smetherley and obtained a stay of execution of two days, until the Sunday following. It was unlikely to achieve anything other than to compel the inexperienced Smetherley to think again and, in the event, Appleby's compassion misfired badly. The delay only served to fuel resentment at Roach's sentence. Strict discipline made the life of the decent majority of the ship's company bearable, saving them from the predatory conduct of the worst elements of their own kind. But a virtual death sentence on a grown man of proven courage for insolence to a boy whose authority far exceeded his abilities and who had yet to prove his mettle to the hands, was a different matter.

Drinkwater was more aware of the state of things than the feckless wastrels who pounded Baskerville's back in congratulation as though he had won a great victory. He wished he had known of the matter before Baskerville had reported it to Callowell. Watching the scene, he determined matters could not go on and, now that they all appeared recovered from their seasickness, the moment seemed opportune. White was absent on deck and Drinkwater laid down the book he had been trying to read by the guttering illumination of the purser's dip.

'You sicken me, you really do.'

Silence fell on the rabble and the four faces turned towards him. 'Whom are you addressing?' Baskerville asked superciliously.

'All of you,' replied Drinkwater, staring up at their half-lit faces. In the gloom they possessed a diabolical appearance. 'You are a scandalous disgrace. It is likely that Roach will die, if not under punishment then as a consequence of it. If you had a shred of decency, Baskerville, you would go at once and withdraw the charge, say it was a mistake and apologize.'

'Why you contemptuous shit, Drinkwater,' said Baskerville, looking round at his friends. 'He needs a licking . . .'

'If one of you so much as lays a finger on me,' Drinkwater said, reaching up to where his French sword was slung by its scabbard rings on the deck beam overhead, 'I'll slit his gizzard.' He drew the blade with a rasp. 'Four to one is Frenchmen's odds, my fine bantam cocks, and you've yet to see action. Please, don't give me the excuse.' He paused. Irresolution was already visible in one or two faces and the light played on the wicked blade of the French sword. 'No, don't give me the excuse to defend myself, or I might take singular pleasure in it.'

Drinkwater rose. 'Brooke,' he said quietly, addressing the youngest of the midshipmen before him, 'go and fetch Jacob.' The boy hesitated and looked at Baskerville for permission, whereupon Drinkwater commanded, 'Go boy!' and Brooke scampered off in search of the messman. While he was gone, Drinkwater dragged his chest out, opened it and threw his belongings into it. A moment later the messman appeared, rubbing sleep from his eyes. 'Jacob, move my chest and hammock forrard. I shall sleep with the marines.'

'Aye, aye, sir.'

Drinkwater paused at the canvas curtain that served to screen off that portion of the orlop known as the cockpit. 'The stink of puppy-dogs in here is overpowering!'

By Sunday morning *Cyclops* had passed Norderney without sighting any enemy cruiser. The wind had dropped and there was a mist which persisted into the forenoon, resisting the sun's heat.

'Dense fog by nightfall,' Blackmore remarked.

After divine service the hands remained mustered to witness the punishment. The officers gathered about the captain; the marines lined the hammock nettings, their bayonets fixed. In the waist, over two hundred men were assembled. They murmured softly, like a swarm of bees. Triced up in the main shrouds, the grating awaited the prisoner.

Roach was escorted on deck by two boatswain's mates. He walked upright between them, his shirt loose and his breeches tucked into the offending boots. At the grating he took off his shirt, revealing the scabbed welts and blue bruising of his former punishment. The murmuring was replaced by a low rumbling.

'Silence!' commanded Callowell.

Smetherley stepped forward. 'Landsman Roach, I tolerate no insolence to my officers, commissioned or otherwise, aboard any ship under my command. You will receive two dozen lashes. Bosun's mates, do your duty!'

'Trice him up!' Callowell ordered, and Roach was thrust forward and his wrists seized and strapped to the grating. One of the men grabbed his hair and jerked his head back to shove a leather wad into his mouth.

'Shame!' called a voice from forward. It was answered by a chorus of anonymous 'Ayes!' from the crowd amidships. Wheeler drew his sword and commanded the marine drummer to beat his snare. Callowell bawled, 'Lay on!'

The two boatswain's mates, each with a cat-o'-nine-tails, began to administer the punishment, six lashes each in succession, while the drummer manfully maintained his roll and the men mouthed their disapproval. Roach spat the leather wad from his mouth and roared defiant curses until, at about the nineteenth stroke, he fell silent.

Drinkwater felt an utter revulsion at the spectacle. He sought distraction by observing the other officers. Appleby stood rigid, his portly frame wracked by sobs, the sheen of angry tears upon his ruddy cheeks. Blackmore gazed out over the heads of the crew, sure that the foremast catharpings could do with some attention. Wheeler stood like a statue, his drawn sword across his breast, his eyes flickering restlessly over the ship's company, waiting for the first sign of trouble. Callowell too watched the men, but with less apprehension than the marine officer. Blinded by the insensitivity of a life circumscribed by duty, he possessed no imagination, no compassion and few feelings for others. *Cyclops* was a man-of-war and sentiment of any kind was out of place upon her decks. To a man of Callowell's stamp, the emergence of personality among the people was an affront, and his cruelty stemmed from this conviction rather than any sadistic impulse. It was his lot to administer, and theirs to endure.

But next to Drinkwater, White stood stock still. 'Christ Almighty, I can see his ribs,' he whispered.

Servants of the Night

The fog Blackmore had predicted closed down during the afternoon. All day the becalmed *Cyclops* had drifted with the tide and, as the visibility deteriorated, the rattling blocks, slack cordage, slatting canvas and black hempen stays dripped moisture on to the wet decks. Below, the damp permeated everything. Shortly after sunset, when the light went out of the vapour surrounding them, Appleby reported the death of Roach. The news surprised nobody and *Cyclops*, shut in her world of sodden misery, seemed to hold her breath in anticipation.

Drinkwater was late being relieved at midnight. White rushed on deck breathless with apologies and anxious to avoid trouble.

'Couldn't sleep, Nat. Kept thinking of that poor devil's bones, then I must have dropped off...'

'Best not to think too much, Chalky,' Drinkwater put a hand on the younger midshipman's shoulder, 'you'll get over it.'

As he passed through the gun-deck on his way below, Drinkwater was half aware of movement forward. He hesitated. If trouble was brewing, he ought not to let it pass, but when he looked he could see nothing untoward and so passed on, bone-weary and eager for the small comfort of sleep. A light still showed through Appleby's door and Drinkwater went forward, ducking under the swaying hammocks, to wish him goodnight, for he knew the surgeon had been upset by the death of Roach. Drinkwater knocked. There was no reply and he cocked his ears. In the creaking darkness, assailed by the thousand sounds of the ship and of men snoring, he thought he heard an insistent grunt. Another, more identifiable, followed. He turned the handle, found it locked against him and forced the flimsy door with his shoulder. Appleby was trussed and gagged. His face was an unpleasant colour and his eyes started from their sockets.

Bending, Drinkwater released the gag and Appleby gasped for air while his rescuer turned his attention to the light-line binding wrists and ankles. Catching his breath, Appleby spat out, 'Mutiny, Nat! They meant me no harm. Wanted to know if I'd said Roach was unfit ... to receive punishment. That's my duty. My privilege ...'

'Who's their leader? The other dragoon?'

Appleby nodded. 'Yes. Hollins, his name is. I told them to desist.' Appleby rubbed his wrists, his face contorted with pain. 'I told 'em what'd been done to Roach was chicken-feed compared with what'd be done to them if they persisted, but they'd have none of it. So they trussed me. Apologized, but trussed me ... They're after Callowell. We've got to stop them, for they'll take Smetherley and Baskerville too! Before you know it, we'll all be involved!'

'Very well!' snapped Drinkwater, getting Appleby's ankles clear and rubbing them himself. 'Do you get Wheeler. Now!' He stood, remembering the noise in the gun-deck. 'There's no time to be lost,' he added, helping the surgeon get to his unsteady feet, then he turned and scrambled aft under the hammocks to the marines' berth. Grabbing his sword he savagely elbowed the hammock next to him. A grunt emanated from it.

'What the fuck ...?'

'Get your men up, Sergeant! Quietly!' he hissed insistently. 'Bayonets! And hurry! We've trouble!'

'Oh shit!' Waiting only for the appearance of the pale form of Sergeant Hagan's emerging limb, Drinkwater moved swiftly to the companionway leading to the berth-deck above. As he passed the cockpit, the light of the lantern at the foot of the companionway caught a face peering round the canvas curtain. 'Is something amiss?' It was Baskerville.

'No. Turn in! Keep out of the way!'

'Why've you got your sword?'

'Turn in!' Drinkwater could brook no delay for explanations. Crouching, he turned his back on Baskerville and cautiously ascended the companionway ladder. He could see no movement under the hammocks of the berth-deck and swung round the stanchion, heading for the gun-deck. As he poked his head above the upper coaming he realized he was not a second too soon. A pale, almost spectral group of barefooted men, perhaps a dozen of them,

67

in shirts and breeches, each clutching some form of weapon in their hands, were approaching the doors to the officers' cabins. Turning his head slowly, Drinkwater saw in the light of the after lantern that the marine sentry outside Captain Smetherley's door was nodding at his post.

There was no doubt that he was witnessing a combination of men bent on mutinous conduct, whatever the limitations of their intentions. Should he raise a general alarm or seek to defuse an explosive situation himself? He had no time to ponder and took consolation from the thought that Sergeant Hagan was behind him, for Appleby would not reach Wheeler in time. The men merged with the deep shadows round the guns, almost concealed behind the few hammocks that were slung in the gun-deck. To a casual observer the place was normal, a dark space the after end of which, abaft the companionway below, was lined with the cabins of the lieutenants and master, and which terminated with the captain's accommodation across the stern.

With sudden resolve Drinkwater flung himself over the hatch coaming and drew the hanger from its scabbard. The hiss of the steel rasped against the brass mounting, abruptly arresting the progress of the mutineers.

'Stand where you are!' His voice was low, yet carried through the gloom. 'Get forrard and out of my sight before I set eyes on one of you.'

'They killed Roach, Mister.' Hollins's voice came out of the darkness.

'And you've assaulted the surgeon. That's mutiny and you'll hang for it unless you obey me! Get forrard! Now!'

Drinkwater heard rather than saw the men behind him, smelt their presence and, glancing round, saw the dull gleam of drawn bayonets. 'We're right behind 'e, sir.' Sergeant Hagan's voice added to the menace of the stalemate.

'You don't frighten us with your boot-necked bullies ...' Hollins began, but Hagan cut him short.

'Shut your fuckin' mouth, Hollins, or you're a dead man.'

Drinkwater was aware of someone else puffing up on his left. 'What the devil's going on here?' asked Lieutenant Wheeler, a drawn hanger in his right hand.

'These men are being recalled to their duty, Mr Wheeler.'

'Is this a damned combination?'

'No, no,' Drinkwater said quickly, lowering his sword point, 'they were gambling, Mr Wheeler. A foolish occupation at this time of night,' Drinkwater jerked his head aft, 'but not as reprehensible as being asleep on sentry.'

Wheeler looked round at the nodding marine posted outside the captain's door. 'Sergeant Hagan!' he said in a low voice, pointing at the offending sentry.

'Now what about ... Stap me, they've gone!' In the few seconds allowed them, Hollins's men had melted away forward.

'Yes.' Much relieved, Drinkwater lowered his sword. Had they dispersed for the time being, or would they recombine? Perhaps tomorrow, or the next night? Would that something would happen, Drinkwater prayed, to distract them from the bloody death of their comrade.

'And what, Nathaniel,' Wheeler asked pointedly, after he had sent all his men except the sergeant below again, 'was all that about?'

'As far as I know, Mr Wheeler, those men were gambling dangerously.'

'With their lives, I gather, from what Appleby said,' Wheeler observed.

'With someone's,' Drinkwater replied.

'Make damned certain it ain't yours, my lad.'

'Or yours, sir.'

Drinkwater heard Wheeler sigh in the darkness. 'Damn you, Drinkwater,' he muttered, but even though he could not see the marine officer's face, Drinkwater knew there was no malice in Wheeler's voice. As if to confirm the matter, he felt a pat on the back. 'Better put that sword up.'

'Where's Appleby?' Drinkwater asked as he ran the French blade into its scabbard.

'In my cabin, recovering his wind. I gather the buggers ...'

Wheeler broke off and turned to the contrite marine whom the sergeant brought forward into the circle of lantern light at the head of the companionway. 'How in Hades' name did you sleep through all this?' he asked the unfortunate man.

'Dunno, sir. I'm very sorry, sir ...' The marine was trembling.

'You stink. Were you drinking before you were posted?'

'No, sir.'

An insistent cough came from Sergeant Hagan and the man admitted, 'Yes, sir.'

'You know what this means?'

'Aye, sir.'

'Post another sentinel, Sergeant, and put this ass in the bilboes. We'll deal with him later.'

He had just finished berating the sentry when Callowell's door suddenly opened. 'What's all this damned racket?'

In his hand Callowell held up a lantern. He peered about him, catching sight of the odd assembly of Wheeler, Drinkwater, Sergeant Hagan and the wretched marine at the head of the companionway. In the euphoria of his relief, Drinkwater almost burst out laughing at the ludicrous figure the first lieutenant cut in his night-shirt and tasselled night-cap. The spectacle clearly amused Wheeler also, for Drinkwater detected the catch in his voice as he replied, 'Damned sentry was dozing, Mr Callowell. Thanks to Mr Drinkwater's vigilance, he'll be punished.'

'What's that?' Wheeler repeated the explanation while Drinkwater caught the marine's eye. It was unfortunate that the marine should suffer the inevitable cat, but he had been asleep deeply enough not to be woken by the confrontation further forward.

'Damned certain he will be!' Callowell snorted, staring round him again. Appearing satisfied, he grunted and retired within his cabin. Wheeler and Drinkwater stood uncertainly for a moment, then Wheeler expelled his breath in a long, relieved sigh. 'Very well, Sergeant, carry on.'

'Aye, aye, sir.'

'Well,' said Wheeler in a low voice, 'as I said, poor old Appleby's hiding in my cabin where I've the remains of a bottle to crack.' Wheeler led aft, then paused, turned and giggled in Drinkwater's ear, 'Damn me if old Callowell don't remind me of Wee Willie Winkie!'

Neither of them saw the pale face of Baskerville retreat into the darkness of the berth-deck below.

Two days later, as *Cyclops* remained inert in the foggy calm, Drinkwater discovered a scrap of paper laid inside the lid of his sea-chest. On it were crudely spelt the words:

> *Yr Honor Mr Drinkwater,*
> *Yr humble Servants of the Night present ther Duty*
> *and Thank You fr yr indulgence.*
> *Ever yr Faithfull Friends.*

In the days that followed, Drinkwater was more content and the incident appeared to have relieved the tension in the frigate. He felt an occasional anxiety when he thought of Baskerville's face peering from the cockpit, but with Lieutenant Wheeler's support and every appearance of the suppression of mutinous sentiments, this lessened as time passed.

The fog persisted for several days, but eventually a cold breeze sprang up from the north-east and, under easy sail, *Cyclops* cast about between Helgoland and Borkum, still in search of an enemy sail. For her people, the wearying routine of the ship ground inexorably on. Occasional lighter moments were engineered when the weather served, and on the first afternoon of pallid sunshine, as the decks gradually dried after the fog, Lieutenant Wheeler determined to encourage some proficiency in fencing.

'How many times do I have to tell you, Nat? The merest pronation and pressure with the thumb and forefinger are all that are required. Look.' Wheeler removed his mask and demonstrated the point with his own foil.

Drinkwater and the marine officer occupied the starboard gangway during the afternoon watch. Both were stripped to shirt and breeches, despite the season, and their exertions had attracted a small crowd of off-duty sailors who sat on the forecastle guns or boats, or in the lower forward rigging, watching the two officers recommence the opening gambits of their bout.

Wheeler advanced, changing his line. Then, with a quick shift of footing, he executed a *balestra* and lunged at the midshipman. Drinkwater was not so easily fooled. He parried Wheeler's blade and riposted, catching the marine officer's shoulder. The hit was acknowledged and they came *en garde* again and resumed, with Wheeler quickly advancing. Drinkwater retreated, disengaged and drew his blade, then swiftly cut over Wheeler's *pointe*, dropped his own and lunged low at Wheeler's stomach.

Wheeler unmasked. 'By heaven, Nat, that was damnably good. To tell you the truth, I doubt there's much more I can teach you now you've digested my late point.'

Drinkwater tugged his own mask off. He was grinning as the two shook their left hands.

'Beg pardon, sir . . .' The former light dragoon Hollins approached Wheeler.

'What is it?' Wheeler ran his hand over his damp hair.

'Begging your pardon, sir, but have you ever considered introducing sabre parries for hand-to-hand fighting?'

'Well, cutlass drill incorporates some elements ...' Wheeler blustered, but Hollins could barely stifle a snort. He had seen the jolly tars exercising. It scarcely compared with the precise sabre drill of the Queen's Own Light Dragoons.

'May I, sir?' Hollins held out his hands to Drinkwater who relinquished foil and mask. Hollins flexed the blade, donned the mask, flicked a salute at Wheeler and came on to his guard. 'Cut at me, Mr Wheeler,' he said through the mesh of the mask, 'any point or direction.'

Wheeler advanced and cut at Hollins's head and the dragoon parried with his own blade held horizontally above his head. Wheeler cut swiftly at his flank and again the dragoon's blade interposed. For four breathless minutes, closely observed by the watchers, Wheeler whirled the foil from every conceivable direction. Hollins always met it steel to steel. Then, as the marine lieutenant flagged, Hollins counter-attacked and cut at Wheeler's cheek so that the mask flew off. The watching seamen burst into a spontaneous cheer until a voice cut them short.

'You there! With the mask!' It was Callowell who had come on deck. Disapproving of these sporting bouts, though unable to prevent them, Callowell had sought such an opportunity to curtail his subordinates' pleasure. He knew very well who the masked swordsman was, for the boots and cavalryman's breeches betrayed Roach's companion.

Hollins drew off his mask. Callowell strode over to him, wrenched the foil from his grip and rounded on Wheeler. 'Is this yours?'

'You know damned well it is. I lend it to Drinkwater,' Wheeler replied in a low, angry voice, darting glances at the surrounding seamen. Callowell was blind to the hint.

'Did you give this to this man?' Callowell asked Drinkwater, gesturing at Hollins.

'In a manner of speaking, sir.'

'You gave this weapon to a man serving His Majesty under sentence of a court martial? A known and convicted criminal?'

'It's only a practice foil ...'

'Never mind that, did you *give* it to him?' Callowell laid an implacable insistence upon the verb.

'Well, I lent it to him, sir. We were only practising ...'

72

'What is the trouble, Mr Callowell?' The captain's reedy voice interrupted Callowell's interrogation of the midshipman. He stood at the head of the companionway, pulling his cloak about him in the chill. Callowell stumped aft to report.

'Get forrard, Hollins, and keep out of sight,' Wheeler muttered, gathering up the fencing equipment and nodding to Drinkwater to precede him below.

'Mr Drinkwater!' Reluctantly Drinkwater laid aft to where Smetherley and Callowell stood beside the binnacle.

'Sir?' After the events and responsibilities of the last few days, Captain Smetherley's self-assured youth struck Drinkwater with peculiar force.

'Is it true that you gave a weapon to a seaman under punishment?'

'I lent a practice foil to a man for the purpose of a demonstration . . .'

'Did you, or did you not, give your weapon to this man . . . er . . .'

'Hollins, sir,' offered Callowell helpfully.

Drinkwater knew he had been boxed into a corner. 'I lent the foil I borrow from Lieutenant Wheeler to Hollins, yes, sir.'

'Well, Mr Drinkwater, that is a serious misjudgement on your part. I cannot see why the late Captain Hope had such faith in you. Such behaviour is as irresponsible as it is reprehensible and I shall consider what measures I shall take. As for this habit of appearing on the quarterdeck improperly dressed', Smetherley indicated Drinkwater's shirt, 'and uncovered', the captain gestured at Drinkwater's bare head, 'I shall cure that immediately. What is our latitude, Mr Callowell?'

'Fifty-four degrees north, sir.'

'Fifty-four north and November. Fore t'gallant masthead, Mr Drinkwater. Perhaps that will teach you to behave properly.'

The hours he spent aloft in this second mastheading were of almost unendurable agony. After the perspiration of the bout and the climb, the light wind quickly began to chill him and his nose, ears, fingers and feet were soon numbed, while his body went into uncontrollable fits of shivering. He had, as before, lashed himself securely out of a sense of self-preservation, but it was not long before he could not have cared less whether he lived or died, and then he was walking with Elizabeth through knee-length grass and would have been happy had there not been the anxiety that the fields through which they wandered hand-in-hand were limitless. The disquiet grew and grew, robbing him of any comfort until, looking at her, he found Elizabeth had gone and he held the frozen hand of a pallid and terrible Medusa and recognized the hideous pale succubus of his recurring dream.

But it was in fact Midshipman White, shaking him and calling him to wake up and wrap himself in the greygoe and tarpaulin he had hauled aloft. From that point, Drinkwater drifted in and out of semi-consciousness until Captain Smetherley ordered him on deck at midnight to stand his watch. The agony of returning movement wakened him and when he finally went below to his hammock a further four hours later, he was exhausted and fell asleep immediately.

The following morning, Appleby averred it was a miracle that he had survived, but Wheeler remarked that Drinkwater was 'an individual of considerable inner resource', a remark deliberately made in Callowell's hearing, though in the course of a half-private conversation between the marine officer and the surgeon.

At four bells in the forenoon watch, Captain Smetherley sent for Drinkwater. As he entered the cabin from the gloom of the orlop, his head and body still wracked by aches and pains from the previous evening, Drinkwater could see little of Smetherley but the captain's bust silhouetted against the stern windows. Beyond a watery sunlight danced wanly upon the wavetops and the bubbling wake as it drew out from under the hull. On the captain's left sat Lieutenant Callowell and also present, but standing, was Lieutenant Wheeler. The marine officer was in the panoply of full dress and his gorget reflected the light off the sea. As he entered the cabin, Drinkwater was aware that Wheeler was concluding an account of the fencing bout, prolonging it for Drinkwater's own benefit, that he might divine how matters lay. It seemed to Drinkwater that Smetherley might be beginning to perceive he was in danger of being made a fool of, for in his conclusion Wheeler was astute enough to placate Smetherley and to offer the captain some way out of his dilemma, without unduly arousing Callowell's further hostility.

'And so, sir, my excess of enthusiasm for the sport led to foolishness on my part, compromising Midshipman Drinkwater. Mr Callowell misunderstood the situation but, as a zealous officer, sought to prevent a, er . . .', Wheeler strove to find the means of explaining himself, '. . . a *contretemps*.'

Smetherley shifted uncomfortably in his seat and turned his attention to Callowell. 'Well, Mr Callowell?'

'The offence was committed, sir. A weapon was deliberately given to a man under punishment ... Mr Drinkwater's part in the affair is uncontestable: he admitted culpability in your hearing.'

'It was a foil, Callowell,' an exasperated Wheeler broke in, but Smetherley silenced him and Callowell pressed doggedly onwards.

'The weapon was deliberately given to a man under punishment by a man ...', Callowell paused and fastened his eyes upon Drinkwater who felt an instinctive fear of what the first lieutenant was about to say, 'by a man, sir, who has been seen engaged in conduct of a mutinous nature.'

Drinkwater felt himself go light-headed. Weakened as he was, his whole being fought the desire to faint and he clutched at the back of an adjacent chair while Wheeler took a half-step towards him out of concern before voicing his protest, but Smetherley's hand again restrained him.

'You talk in riddles, Mr Callowell.'

'Aye, sir, because I am unsure of the exact nature of the facts, not being a witness to the entire event, and I was apt to put a more charitable explanation upon matters until this present incident persuaded me that I had failed in my duty and should have reported my misgivings earlier.'

'Sir,' interjected Wheeler, ' this is a preposterous notion ...'

'Mr Wheeler, your partiality to a former messmate does you some credit, but let us hear what Mr Callowell has to say.' Smetherley was watching Drinkwater as the accused young man fought to master himself. 'I am marking the reaction of Mr Drinkwater with interest, and I wish to hear of what this event consisted. Mr Callowell, pray continue.'

'Well, sir, 'tis simple enough. The midshipman was outside my cabin the other night at the head of a number of other scum, known trouble-makers, sir, Hollins among 'em. Had not Lieutenant Wheeler arrived in the nick of time, at which this jackanapes put up his sword and whispered to the conspirators to disperse, you and I might not be sitting here now ...'

Drinkwater had mastered his nausea now and was filling with a contrary sense of burning outrage. He recalled Baskerville's face and knew for a certainty that the younger midshipman had concocted some malicious tale and let it be known to Callowell. He had little doubt that to Callowell, Drinkwater could be represented as a man nurturing an embitterment, though why that should act as incitement to mutiny seemed so perverse a sequence of cause and effect that it begged the motive of jealousy. Drinkwater's analysis was more accurate than he knew; it was also a shrewd summation of Callowell's own bitterness. Deprived of patronage himself, he habitually clipped the wings of any young rooster who seemed likely to get on. As for Baskerville, he was a nasty little toady, a boy for whom survival had been a matter of constant currying of favour and at which he had become expert. Baskerville was quite unable to see that, sooner or later, Callowell would select him for similar treatment.

For a moment there was silence in the cabin, then Drinkwater said in a low voice, 'That is a damned lie, Lieutenant Callowell, and since you have made it so publicly, I shall ask you to retract it, or I shall . . .'

'The only part of your statement that bears the slightest shred of truth, Callowell, is the fact that I arrived in time,' Wheeler broke in before Drinkwater could fling himself into deeper trouble. 'Mr Drinkwater had sent for me since he had the notion there was some trouble brewing after the death of Roach.'

'And was there?' Smetherley asked sharply.

'Oh yes,' Wheeler replied with cool assurance, 'and I, sir, was not surprised, neither in an emotional nor a practical sense . . .'

'Are you implying . . .?'

'I am implying nothing, sir,' Wheeler said with more force, 'I am merely stating that both Mr Drinkwater and myself in particular, as the officer commanding the marines, did our duty with an assiduity of which even Mr Callowell should have approved.'

'And you would have concealed this . . . this evident combination from me?'

Wheeler shook his head. 'I do not know where you received the idea of a mutinous combination, sir. Had it been such a thing, I doubt Mr Drinkwater would have survived his ordeal, since he confronted the disaffected men alone, and by the time I arrived he had cooled their ardour.'

'Well, what in God's name d'you think a party of men wanderin' around in the middle of the night is about, if it ain't murdering their officers?'

'Had they been intent on so doing, sir, Mr Drinkwater would not be here. He turned aside their anger very quickly . . .'

'What the devil d'you mean, "anger"?'

Wheeler sighed. 'Sir, in my opinion, and since you press me on the

76

matter, it was unwise to have flogged Roach on the word of Midshipman Baskerville.' Wheeler paused for a second and then an idea seemed to strike him, for he suddenly asked, 'Mr Callowell, did you see Mr Drinkwater with a drawn sword?'

'I knew he had drawn his sword . . .'

'But did you see him?'

'Well, I, er . . .' Callowell scratched his head.

'Or did Midshipman Baskerville tell you he had seen Mr Drinkwater with a drawn sword?'

'What the devil has Baskerville got to do with all this?' Smetherley asked, signs of boredom evident in the captain's face.

'He's a veritable imp of Satan, Captain Smetherley. I'm surprised you didn't know that . . .'

'But you lied to me, Wheeler,' Callowell said, 'you told me Drinkwater had called your attention to that marine we flogged for being asleep at his post.'

'That was not a lie, Mr Callowell, that was the perfect truth.'

'It wasn't all . . .'

But before Callowell had completed his new explanation or Smetherley had gathered his wits, a peremptory knock at the cabin door ushered in Midshipman White. 'Mr Wallace's compliments, sir, but we've a frigate under our lee and Mr Wallace thinks it's the man-o'-war we've been looking for!'

There was a moment's hiatus in the cabin, then Captain Smetherley shoved his chair back and rose to his feet. 'I shall have to give this matter further consideration, gentlemen. It seems we have more pressin' matters to hand. We shall resolve this later.'

The strange sail lay to until *Cyclops*, foaming downwind towards her, bared her iron teeth and broke out British colours at her peak. Having expected a friend and now realizing his rashness, the stranger crowded on sail and a chase began.

As they had left the captain's cabin with Smetherley's 'we shall resolve this later' ringing ominously in his ears, Drinkwater had expressed his gratitude to Wheeler.

'We are not yet off the lee shore, Nat, but by heaven I'll not see you ruined by that little bugger Baskerville, nor that oaf Callowell, neither. Just thank providential intervention for this fellow.' Wheeler jerked his head as though at the strange sail. 'Who, or whatever he is, he is a *deus ex machina*!'

Drinkwater's only shred of comfort was that his action station was now on the quarterdeck as signals midshipman and the captain's aide, a position that seemed to offer at least the opportunity of demonstrating his loyalty if an action resulted in the forthcoming hours. A cold resolution grew on him as time passed and the autumn day drew towards its close. He entertained little hope for the future, and the memory of his more recent mastheading filled him with a wild contempt for life itself.

A gibbous moon shone fitfully from behind the clouds, the pale shape of the stranger's towering canvas now dimming to a distant faintness, now revealed as a dramatic image. The two ships were close enough to remain in sight of each other throughout the night as both ran on to the northwards but, though *Cyclops* held her ground, she was unable to overhaul her quarry.

At about three o'clock in the morning the enemy attempted a ruse to throw off *Cyclops* and catch her pursuer at a disadvantage. Still some three points to starboard and about two miles distant, the enemy ship abruptly came to the wind, tacked and stood across *Cyclops*'s bow.

'Stand to your guns! Stand to your guns!' Callowell roared through his speaking-trumpet. The crew of the *Cyclops,* who had been clustered half-awake at their action stations for hours, were now summoned to full consciousness.

'What is it, Mr Callowell?' Smetherley asked, staggering forward and peering into the gloom. Quite unaware that the enemy was athwart his own hawse with his larboard broadside trained on *Cyclops* as she bore down upon his guns, like a bull upon the matador's sword, Smetherley rubbed the sleep from his eyes and relinquished the slight shelter and support of the mizen rigging.

'Up helm!' Callowell roared again. 'Up helm or we'll be raked!'

Callowell's order was too late. The flicker of the enemy cannon showed close ahead, just as the helmsmen began to drag the great tiller across the steerage below.

'Larboard battery! Fire as you bear!' Smetherley's voice cracked the night in its imperious shrillness. As the enemy shot tore into *Cyclops*, there was a brief pause and then a desultory fire was returned. The strange ship continued to turn off the wind to larboard and the two frigates ran down each other's sides on opposite courses, with *Cyclops* herself beginning her swing off the wind.

'Belay that order!' Smetherley now shouted, confusing the issue. 'Put your helm *down*, sir! *Down!*'

As the British frigate turned, she increasingly presented her vulnerable stern to the enemy, inviting further raking fire. Smetherley now sought to cross the enemy's rear, but the matter had been left far too late. The reversing helm dragged speed off the British frigate's progress and the brief moment in which *Cyclops* had her quarry at a disadvantage was lost. The larboard guns had yet to be reloaded, and the raking shots fired were far too few to achieve anything of significance. Then, as the enemy extended the range, the opportunity was lost.

Drinkwater reported his sighting of the enemy's ensign. 'French colours, sir.'

Smetherley's attention, however, was swiftly diverted to a more immediate concern.

'She'll not stay, sir,' Drinkwater heard Blackmore shout as *Cyclops* came up in the wind with a sluggish feel to her.

'God damn!' Smetherley swore as the ship steadied, heading into the wind's eye. With a crack and a kind of roaring noise that was compounded of parting ropes, flapping canvas and wood and iron descending in slow motion, the foretopmast went by the board. The extra pressure of the wind had parted forestays damaged by the enemy's opening shots and now, as *Cyclops* emerged into a patch of moonlight, the foredeck was littered with fallen spars and festooned with rigging and canvas from aloft. Some hung over the side, to tear at the frigate's forechains where men were already cutting away the wreckage.

Drinkwater dutifully returned his attention to the progress of the enemy. He thought the Frenchman would now escape entirely, but the enemy commander, having seen the predicament of the British frigate in the sudden moonlight, was not about to let an opportunity slip through his fingers.

'Enemy's wearing ship, sir!' Drinkwater reported.

'What's that?' Smetherley spun round, distracted from the mess on the forecastle and in the waist by Drinkwater's shout.

'He's wearing ship, sir.'

The patch of moonlight spread and they could plainly see the enemy cruiser's larboard broadside as she turned her stern through the wind.

'He's going to re-engage, sir,' Drinkwater remarked. Smetherley raised his glass and Drinkwater could hear him muttering. 'Call the master,' he said audibly after a moment.

Drinkwater went forward in search of Blackmore whom he found directing the work of clearing the mess forward and bringing the ship under command again.

'Captain wants you, Mr Blackmore,' he said.

Blackmore grunted, gave a final instruction and walked aft. 'Carpenter's reporting water in the well, sir,' he stated. 'That Frenchman's hulled us.'

'And he's coming back to finish off what he started, Mr Blackmore,' Smetherley said, pointing astern just as the moon disappeared again and they seemed suddenly plunged into an impenetrable gloom.

'Well, we're making a fine stern board at the moment, sir, he may misjudge matters.'

'I wish to re-engage,' Smetherley replied. Then, turning to Drinkwater, he ordered, 'Let the officers on the gun-decks know they're to open fire when their guns bear, the unengaged side to assist the other. D'you understand, Drinkwater?'

'Perfectly, sir.' Drinkwater ran off to find Wallace and cannoned into Callowell at the head of the companionway.

'Where's the master?'

'On the quarterdeck, sir, with Captain Smetherley. The Frenchman's running back towards us and I'm to let the officers on the gun-deck know.'

Callowell made off as Drinkwater descended into the greater darkness of the gun-deck. In contrast to the chaos above, a sinister order reigned below. Almost on the very spot where Drinkwater had turned aside the mutiny, all had changed. Gone were the grey lumps of the hammocks and the neat row of officers' cabins; gone were the white painted bulkheads shutting off the after end of the ship for the privacy of her commander and officers. Now a long, almost open space, intersected by stanchions, gratings, half-empty shot-garlands and the massive bulk of the two capstans, was lined by the gleaming black barrels of the frigate's main armament of guns. The fitful light of the protected battle-lanterns threw long shadows and conferred an ominous movement upon what was largely a motionless scene, with the gun-crews in readiness about their pieces and only the scampering of the ship's boys making any significant noise in the expectant gloom. It struck Drinkwater with peculiar force that these men had almost no knowledge of what was going on above their heads. He ran

80

forward in search of Wallace and found him peering out of a gun-port.

'Mr Wallace, sir.'

Wallace turned and straightened himself up as far as the deck-beams would allow. 'Ah, what news do you bring?'

'We've lost the foretopmast . . .'

'We thought something must have given way . . .'

'And the enemy's worn ship. You're to re-engage with whatever battery bears, the other side to assist.'

'Short range?'

'I would think so, sir.'

'Shot?'

'Whatever you think fit, sir,' said Drinkwater, only afterwards noting the significance of the phrase.

'Ball on ball, then. That should do for a start.' Wallace turned and shouted, 'Double-shot your guns, my lads! They're coming back for a taste of rusty iron!'

Suddenly the gun-deck was alive with movement, like a nest of rats stirred from their sleep, the gun-trucks rumbling on the planking and sending a trembling throughout the frigate.

'Good luck, sir.' Drinkwater hurried aft in search of the companionway and the upper-deck. Here too all had changed, for the distance between the two ships had closed and the enemy seemed to tower over them as he drove across their bows for a second time. But this was a more ponderous manoeuvre in contrast with the quick-witted desperation of the first. The enemy ship had shortened sail and, while *Cyclops*'s stern board had robbed the Frenchman of the chance to attack from leeward and rake the vulnerable stern of his quarry by throwing her maintopsail aback at the right moment, he might still inflict severe punishment on his former pursuer by lying to athwart *Cyclops*'s hawse.

However, now that the French ship was committed to raking from ahead, *Cyclops*'s stern could be thrown round so that her larboard broadside bore upon the Frenchman. Callowell and Blackmore were urging this on Smetherley who gave the impression of dithering before agreeing. By hauling the main braces and putting over the helm, *Cyclops* was now brought round by degrees so that as the enemy guns reopened fire, the British frigate's larboard guns roared out in reply.

But the French commander was a bold man and backed his own

maintopsail, drifting slowly down on to *Cyclops* and fighting his opponent gun for gun, matching discharge for discharge. A slow cloud of acrid powder-smoke rolled down upon them, musketry swept the deck like hail and, while heavy shot thumped into *Cyclops*'s hull, the lighter calibre ball from the Frenchman's quarterdeck guns, mixed with deadly canister and langridge, blasted holes through the hammock nettings and knocked men down like bloody ninepins in the cold light of the growing dawn.

The view each man had of the fight became obscured in the smoke. Drinkwater, obliged to be always at the captain's elbow, kept his eyes on the dull gleam of Smetherley's figure. The din of the guns and the sharp crack of musketry rendered him partially deaf so that he felt rather than heard the almost simultaneous discharge of a French broadside. It struck him as a wave of hot, stinking gas, accompanied by the whirring roar of a passing ball and the involuntary gasp as the thing winded him.

Two more such devastating detonations followed, acts calculated to have maximum effect before boarding, for Drinkwater heard Callowell, as if at a great distance although he could be seen through the smoke, screaming to repel boarders.

Drinkwater saw Smetherley draw his sword and, as he drew his own, he caught a glimpse beyond the captain of a looming hedge of cutlasses and boarding-pikes a moment before there came to him the jarring impact as the two frigates ground together. A moment later he was fighting for his life.

He thrust his right shoulder forward and parried a pike, recovered and hacked at the arm that held it. He missed, but the man was past him and lunging to the left where, out of the corner of his eye, Drinkwater saw a marine jabbing a bayonet. He was confronted next by an officer with fiercely gleaming eyes. Drinkwater beat the man's extended blade and, in something akin to disbelief, watched the blade drop from the officer's fingers. Dully he realized the man's wrist had been shattered and that the ferocity in the poor fellow's eyes was the shock of pain. A cutlass blade seemed to appear from nowhere, being drawn back to hack at him. Drinkwater swept his arm in a cutting arc which Hollins would have approved of and felt his blade bite into the cutlass-bearer's side as the weapon in turn slashed down. Somehow it missed him as the man dropped, knocking into Drinkwater with considerable force. Twisting away, Drinkwater slithered and fell. He felt a foot on his back and gasped for breath, filled with the vague idea that he would now be in further trouble for having deserted the captain. Then, the next instant, he was overcome by a desire to stay where he was, to give up this madness and succumb to the aching of his muscles. Who would notice? He might lie like a dog while the world took its course without him. It cared not for him; why should he care for it? He looked round and saw, twenty feet abaft him at the frigate's taffrail, a French officer fiddling with the ensign halliards. *Cyclops* was taken!

The thought filled him with an odd contentment. Smetherley and Callowell could go to hell, along with Baskerville and his miserable crew of insufferable cronies. But then he thought of poor White and of the things he had done for Drinkwater in tending him while he was enduring his two mastheadings; and Wheeler, who had helped him the previous morning; and poor old Blackmore and Appleby. Then the thought of captivity suddenly burst upon him as the French officer seemed to clear the halliards and begin to take down the British ensign. A second later Drinkwater was on his feet and rushing aft. The man looked round just as Drinkwater ran him through. Ice had settled in his heart now and his mind was strangely clear. He drew his blade from the dead weight of the fallen body, belayed the halliards and swung round. Looking forward he saw Captain Smetherley surrounded by three French seamen who were jabbing at him with pikes. Taking them in the rear, Drinkwater had dispatched two of them before the third fled and he confronted Smetherley who drew his breath in gasps.

'Recall, sir,' Drinkwater shouted, 'my loyalty's in question!' He was lightheaded now, not with the fainting fit which had almost overwhelmed him in Smetherley's cabin, but with a mad yet calculating coolness. Smetherley had regained his breath and, imbued with a bloody fighting lust and scarcely recognizing Drinkwater, flung himself at the rear of more Frenchmen who were pressing Wheeler's marines amid the heaving mass of men who struggled for possession of the forward quarterdeck. Drinkwater was left in sole possession of the space abaft the mizen and someone on the French frigate had noticed. A musket ball scored Drinkwater's shoulder, opening the seam of his coat and half turning him round with the force of its impact. As he stumbled, another French officer came over the rail, obviously intent on sweeping Drinkwater out of the way and finally hauling down the British colours.

Drinkwater met him with a savage swipe. The officer parried, but

83

only partially, and such was the force of Drinkwater's blow that his blade slid down the French officer's sword, cutting into the man's thigh, severing a tendon and causing him to drop to one knee. As his head slipped forward, Drinkwater thumped at the back of the man's skull with the pommel of his sword, felling him completely.

A moment later another man slumped at his feet and Drinkwater recognized the bloody wreck of Smetherley who had been cut down by three or four Frenchmen intent on taking him prisoner and securing the surrender of the frigate. 'Drinkwater!' Smetherley cried.

Drinkwater stepped across the captain's body and stood over him, slashing wildly left and right, holding off the attackers. Beyond his immediate surroundings, he was quite oblivious of anything else. Down below, the gunners still plied their deadly trade, the gunfire unabating as the guns' barrels warmed up and the great pieces fairly leapt with eagerness at each discharge.

He could not tell that the fire from the French frigate had slowed and then almost stopped as the battering of the British guns gradually overcame their opposition. Thus, as the French boarders gained ground on the upper deck of *Cyclops*, the fierce tenacity of the British gunnery from the deck below was pounding their ship to pieces. Drinkwater drove off those of the enemy immediately intent on securing Captain Smetherley, unaware that he himself had received several light flesh wounds.

As the French withdrew, Drinkwater regained his breath, aware of a general retreat and of an increasingly panic-stricken scrambling backwards of desperate men, pricked by Wheeler's marines' bayonets and hounded by British seamen. He had no idea what had caused this retrograde movement, but once started it seemed irreversible and soon Drinkwater saw the backs of the marines stabbing their way over the rail. Looking down, Drinkwater caught sight of Smetherley staring up at him, his eyes fixed and already clouding. The captain's white waistcoat was dark with blood and a great pool of it spread out round Drinkwater's feet. Then something splattered the pool of blood. Looking up, Drinkwater saw the French sharpshooter still in the mizen top. Without a pistol Drinkwater relinquished his charge and stepped to the larboard rail, put his foot on the truck of a quarterdeck gun and hoisted himself into the mizen rigging.

The French seamen were fighting like demons, contesting every inch of their own deck, but Wheeler was screaming at his marines, the majority of whom had ceased their advance or withdrawn to stand elevated in the *Cyclops*'s larboard hammock netting.

'Call off your men, Callowell!' Wheeler shouted at the top of his voice. 'I'll clear the deck!'

The marines discharged a volley at Wheeler's command. The musket balls were indiscriminate in finding their marks and several of the more advanced British seamen were caught in the fire, but the general effect threw the defenders back and into the brief interval the British poured, Drinkwater jumping down among them, unsatiated and eager for the appalling excitement of action.

A boy ran under his guard and stabbed a seaman next to him, then turned and made to jab at Drinkwater. Drinkwater drove the guard of his hanger into the boy's shoulder and knocked him down. Then he pronated his blade and lunged at a pig-tailed quartermaster defending the binnacle with a cutlass. Drinkwater's point drove through the quartermaster's windpipe and the wretched man died with a curious gasping whistle, clutching at his throat as he fell.

A tall, dark officer lay against the binnacle, his high collar decorated with gold, his broad shoulders bearing the bullion embellishments of epaulettes. A younger officer knelt by his side, then, sensing the looming presence of an enemy as the quartermaster crashed to the deck, stood and confronted Drinkwater, his hand holding a broken sword.

'Do you surrender, sir?' Drinkwater asked. To his astonishment the younger man nodded, dropped the broken weapon, bent and took from the feeble grasp of the fallen captain that officer's sword and offered it hilt foremost to Drinkwater.

'*Merci, M'sieur,*' Drinkwater managed, mercilessly adding with a jerking motion to the great white ensign overhead, '*et votre drapeau, s'il vous plaît.*'

The younger man looked down at the pallid face of his commander. The mortally wounded French captain opened his eyes, looked at Drinkwater, then closed them with a nod. A few moments later the oriflamme of Bourbon lilies fluttered to the deck just as the sun lifted over the lip of cloud that veiled the eastern horizon and flooded the scene with a sudden, dazzling light.

85

CHAPTER 5

Peace

They had been cheated of their prize, for within moments of her striking her colours, the French frigate *L'Arcadienne* took fire. It was necessary for *Cyclops* to be worked clear of her and to lie to and lick her own wounds while *L'Arcadienne* burned furiously, until, about an hour after noon, she exploded with a thunderous roar, flinging debris high into the air. This fell back into a circle of sea flattened by the detonation, over which hung a pall of smoke. When the smoke cleared, the French ship and most of her company had disappeared.

Among their own dead and wounded was old Blackmore. He took six days to die of a musket ball in the bowels, begging Drinkwater to take his belongings home to his wife and giving him his folio volumes of carefully observed notes and sketches, the fruit of a lifetime's interest. After the action, Lieutenant Callowell had taken command and was driven to the expedient of reappointing Mr Drinkwater to a temporary berth in the gunroom. Callowell remained indifferent to him, but no more was ever said of Drinkwater's participation in any mutiny and he suspected Wheeler's intervention. At all events, the incident was apparently closed and the shadow of it gradually passed.

After the terror of an action in which he had not distinguished himself but had been knocked unconscious, Midshipman Baskerville seemed less inclined to tell tales. Though he would not admit it, he was privately glad that Drinkwater never afterwards referred to the incident, though Wheeler spoke to him, leaving Baskerville in no doubt but that there were several officers who knew of his mendacity. After *Cyclops* was laid up in the Medway, Baskerville went ashore, never to return to sea, though in later years he spoke knowledgeably of naval affairs in the House of Commons, being returned as one of two members for a pocket borough. Captain Smetherley was granted an encomium in the *Intelligencer*, having died, it was stated, 'at his moment of triumph'. Moreover, the *Intelligencer* informed its readers, 'the Royal Navy had been thereby deprived of a gallant officer in the flower of his youth, and the Nation of a meritorious officer of whom it might otherwise have entertained expectations of long, gallant and distinguished service'.

The last weeks of the commission were strangely melancholic for all the officers, coloured by the dolorous prospect of half-pay. By contrast the hands were far more cheerful. The pressed men especially could scarcely refrain from desertion as they lay at the buoys in the Medway, with the smoking chimneys of Chatham a mere stone's throw distant. Only the promise of their pay, in some cases of four years' arrears, kept them at their duty as they sent down spars and ferried stores, guns, ammunition and sundry other items ashore. By the time they had finished, *Cyclops* was only a vestige of her former self, a dark and hollow hulk, stripped to her lower masts and with her jib-boom removed. She seemed much larger, for her thirty-two twelve-pounders and the chase and quarter guns had been laboriously hauled ashore, so lightening her considerably and causing her to ride high out of the water. Gone were the iron shot and powder, the cheese and butter, the kegs of beer and spirits, the hogsheads of salt pork, barricoes of water, bags of dried peas, sacks of hard grey flour, bales of wadding and oakum, blocks of pitch and barrels of tar. She bore little cordage, for most had been removed, from her huge spare cable to the reels of thin spun yarn. Only the lingering smell of these commodities served as a reminder of the warlike machine she had once been. All the myriad odds and ends that had made her existence possible, whose supply and issue had occupied the book-keeping skills of a small company of officers and petty officers over the long months of the commission, were removed for storage ashore. Shorewards went her anchors, lowered on to the mooring lighters from the dockyard by means of the only spar left crossed for the purpose, the main-topsail yard hoisted on the foremast in place of the foreyard. When the final load had gone, the large blocks were sent down and small whips left at the yard-arms. As almost the last task, the yard was cock-billed out of the way, leaving room for the next ship alongside.

In those last days, Lieutenant Callowell had received his promotion to commander, though he refused to leave the ship until she was reduced to the condition known as 'in ordinary'. He finally announced his decision to quit on the morning following the removal of the anchors. Early that forenoon, the marines were paraded for the penultimate time. Sergeant Hagan assembled his men with his usual precision, ensuring their appearance was immaculate. Their white cross-belts had been pipe-clayed to perfection, their breeches were like snow and their gaiters black as pitch. The older seamen watched with delight, knowing that the marines' imminent departure meant their own pay and discharge were soon to be forthcoming. As Hagan satisfied himself, the captain's gig was piped away and the sergeant fell out the entry guard who now joined the side-boys in *Cyclops*'s last show of pomp in the present commission.

A grey sky lowered over the river and a keen easterly wind brought the odour of saltmarsh across the ruffled surface of the Medway. The lieutenants and warrant officers assembled in undress uniforms, their swords hitched to their hips; the midshipmen fell in behind them. Wheeler, having inspected his men in Hagan's wake, placed himself at their head and, drawing his hanger, called them to attention. A deathly hush fell upon the upper deck. A moment later, Commander Callowell ascended the companionway. He wore a boat cloak over his uniform and as the wind whipped it about him, Wheeler threw out the order for his men to present arms.

The clatter of muskets and simultaneous stamp of feet were accompanied by the wicked gleam of pale sunlight upon bayonets. Wheeler's hanger went up to his lips and then swept downwards in the graceful arc of the salute. The assembled lieutenants brought their fingers up to the cocks of their hats.

'Gentlemen ...' Callowell remained a moment looking forward and responded to the salutes of his officers and the guard. Then, without another word, he walked to the rail and went over the side to the shrilling pipes of the boatswain's mates.

The silence lasted a moment more, then someone forward shouted out, 'Three cheers for "Bloody-Back" Callowell!' The air was split by a thunderous bellow. It was a cheer such as they had given *Resolution* in the gathering gloom at the beginning of Rodney's Moonlight Battle three years earlier. Drinkwater remembered the disquieting power of the noise and he watched now as they cheered and cheered, not for Callowell, but for themselves. They cheered for what they had made of *Cyclops*, for their collective triumphs and disappointments; they cheered at the alluring prospect of that spirit of unity being broken into the individual delights of discharge, grog shops and brothels.

As the gig pulled out clear of the ship's side, they could see the figure of Callowell humped in the stern-sheets. He did not look back.

That evening the gunroom held a valedictory dinner in the vacated captain's cabin. Wallace, as acting first lieutenant, presided in name only, for in reality it was Wheeler's evening. The midshipmen were guests, as were the senior warrant officers and senior mates, and the intention was to drink off the remaining wine in the possession of the gunroom officers, a quantity of the former having been taken out of *L'Arcadienne* before the fire had driven back the looters. Once the eating was dispensed with, the serious business of the evening commenced. Amidst the wreckage of chicken bones and suet dumplings, bumpers of increasing extravagance were drunk to toasts of increasing dubiety.

The whole evening was a marked contrast to Drinkwater's first formal dinner on board when Captain Hope had dined with Admiral Kempenfelt and he had been compelled to toast the company. He was a very different person from the ingenuous and inebriated youth who had risen unsteadily to his feet on that occasion. The harsh path of duty had matured him and his capacity for wine had much improved. Now he joined lustily in the singing of 'Spanish Ladies' and 'Hearts of Oak', and clapped enthusiastically when O'Malley, the Irish cook and the ship's fiddler, scraped the air of 'Nancy Dawson' on his ancient violin.

Finally Wheeler rose unsteadily to his feet. His handsome face was flushed, but his cravat remained neatly tied under his perspiring chin as he called the lubberly company to order.

'Gennelmen,' he began, 'gennelmen, we are gathered here tonight in the sight of Almighty God, the Devil and Mr Surgeon Appleby, to conclude a commission memorable for its being in an infamous war in which I believe all of us here executed our duty with honour, as behoves all true Britons.' He paused for the cheers that this peroration called forth from the company to die down. 'Tomorrow ... tomorrow we will be penniless beggars, but tonight we are as fit as fighting cocks to thrash Frenchmen, Dons and Yankees ...'

Wheeler paused again while more cheers accompanied Midshipman White's disappearance as he slid slowly beneath the table, his face sinking behind the cloth like a diminutive setting sun, to lie unheeded by his fellows whose upturned faces awaited more of Wheeler's pomposities. 'Gennelmen, I give you a toast: A short peace and a long war!'

The company cheered yet again and some staggered to their feet. They gulped their wine and thumped the table, calling for more.

'Silence! Silence!'

Hisses were taken up and some sort of order was re-established. 'It has been brought to my notice by the purser,' continued Wheeler, 'as Christian a gennelman as ever sat on a purser's stool mark you, that we are down to our last case of wine, which is . . . which is . . . which is what, m'dear fella?'

'Madeira.'

'Madeira, gennelmen, madeira . . .'

Wheeler collapsed into his chair amidst more cheers. The vacuum was filled by the last bottles being set out and the ponderous figure of Appleby rising to his feet. An attempt was made to shout him down. 'No speeches from the surgeon!'

'You're a guest! Sit down!'

But Appleby stood his ground. 'I shall not make a speech, gentlemen . . .' His voice was drowned in further cheers, but he remained standing when they died away. 'I shall simply ask you to raise your glasses to fallen comrades . . .'

A hush fell on the company and a scraping of chairs indicated a lugubrious assent to Appleby's sentiment. A shamefaced mumbling emanated from bowed heads as they recalled those who had started the commission and had not survived it – Hope, Blackmore and many others.

'And now . . .', resumed Appleby, and the mood lightened immediately.

'No speeches, damn your eyes!'

'Appleby, you farting old windbag, sit down!'

'And now,' Appleby went on, 'I ask you to raise your glasses in another toast . . .'

'For God's sake, Appleby, we've drunk to everything under heaven except your mother and father!'

'Gentlemen, gentlemen!' roared the surgeon, 'We have forgotten the most important after His Majesty's health . . .' Silence, apart from

90

White's brutish snoring under the table, again permeated the cabin. 'I prithee charge your glasses ... Now, gentlemen, I ask you to drink to this one-eyed frigate, gentlemen, this Cyclopean eye-of-the-fleet. Just as you are closing both of your limpid orbs in stupor, she is closing her noble eye on war. Gentlemen, be upstanding and drink to the ship! I give you "An eye of the fleet, His Britannic Majesty's frigate *Cyclops!*" '

There were punning shouts of 'Aye, aye!', much nudging of neighbours' ribs and more loud cheers which finally subsided into gurgling, dyspeptic mumblings and an involuntary fart from Wheeler. Suddenly the cabin door flew open and Sergeant Hagan entered wearing full dress uniform. Wheeler looked up blearily as the sergeant's boots crashed irreverently upon the deck and his right hand executed an extravagant salute circumscribed only by the deck beams above.

'Sah!'

'Eh? Whassa matter, ser'nt?' Wheeler struggled upright in his chair, affronted by the intrusion and vaguely aware that the sergeant's presence in parade dress augured some disagreeable occurrence elsewhere. Wheeler fixed the man with what he took to be a baleful stare, the vague disquiet of a summons to duty intruding upon his bemused brain.

'I have the honour to escort the officers' cheese, sah!' Hagan replied, looking straight into his commanding officer's single focused eye.

'Cheesh, ser'nt? Whadya mean cheesh?'

'Mr Dale's orders, sah!'

'Dale? You mean the carpenter?' Wheeler shook his head in incomprehension. 'You don't make yourself clear, ser'nt.'

'Permission to bring in the officers' cheese, sah!' Hagan persisted patiently in pursuance of his instructions, holding himself at rigid attention throughout this inane exchange.

Wheeler looked round the company and asked, 'We've had cheesh, haven't we, gennelmen? I'm certain we had cheesh ...'

But his query went unheeded, for there were more table thumpings and cries of 'Cheese! Cheese! We want cheese!'

Wheeler shook his head, shrugged and slumped back in his chair, waving his assent. 'Very well, Ser'nt Hagan. Please escort in the cheese!'

'Sah!' acknowledged Hagan and drew smartly aside. Two of the carpenter's mates entered bearing a salver on which reposed the cheese, daintily covered by a white damask napkin. At the lower end of the table, midshipmen drew apart to allow the worthy tarpaulins to deposit their load. They were grinning as they withdrew and Wheeler's numbed brain was beginning to sense a breach of propriety. He rose very unsteadily, leaning heavily upon the table. 'Sergeant!'

'Sah?'

'Whass that?' Wheeler nodded at the napkin-covered lump.

'The officers' cheese, sah!' repeated Hagan in the reasonable tone one uses to children, and executing another smart salute he retreated from the cabin, closing the door behind him.

Wheeler's misgivings were not shared by his fellow-diners who had just discovered that the remaining stock of wine amounted to at least one glass each. The demands for cheese were revived and with a flourish Drinkwater leaned forward and whipped off the napkin.

'God bless my soul!'

'Stap me vittals!'

'Rot me cods!'

'God's bones!'

'It's the festering main truck!'

'The what?'

'It's the god-damned truck from the mainmasthead!'

And there, amid the wreckage of what had passed for a banquet, sat the cap of the mainmast, pierced and fitted with its two sheaves for the flag halliards.

'Well, of all the confounded nerve ...'

'I'm damned if I understand ...' Wheeler passed a hand over his furrowed brow. Next to him Wallace had begun a slow *dégringolade* beneath the table.

'Hang on for your cheese, Wallace,' someone said.

'Dale's right,' Drinkwater said, 'I remember not believing him when he swore he had told me the truth back in seventy-nine.'

'Whadya mean?' Wheeler asked.

A chorus of slurred voices demanded an explanation. 'Mr Dale made it out of pusser's cheese,' Drinkwater explained. 'He carved it out of a cheese which had been supplied for the hands to eat ... it's cheese, d'you see? Cheese; it really is cheese!'

'Well I'm damned.' Wheeler sat back in his chair, looking fixedly at the object before him. 'Well, I'll be damned ...' and with that he slid slowly downwards, to join the company assembling beneath the table.

'Well, Nathaniel,' Appleby said, raising his glass and holding it up to the stumps of the candles in the candelabra, 'there are only a few of us worthy of remaining above the salt, it seems. Your health, sir.'

'And yours, Mr Appleby, and yours.'

'You don't care for any cheese, I take it?'

'Thank you, no.'

The next morning the marines turned out in order of route. Pulled ashore in the launch, bound for their billets at Chatham barracks, they left to ribald farewells from the high-spirited boats' crews. Wheeler departed with them, his pale face evidence of an aching head. Before he went down into the boat, he shook his fellow-officers' hands in farewell. To Drinkwater he said, 'Good luck, young shaver. Always remember what I have taught you: never flinch when you parry and always *riposte*.'

During the forenoon other officers left. Midshipman Baskerville and his gang were seen off without regret, but White, hung-over and emotional, took his departure with a catch in his voice.

'Damn it, Nat,' he said, wringing Drinkwater's hand, 'I'm deuced glad to be leaving, but sorry that we must part. You shall come and see us, eh? There's good shooting in Norfolk and there's always a bed at the Hall.'

'Of course, Chalky. We shall remain friends and I shall write as soon as I have determined what to do. You won't forget to deliver Blackmore's dunnage?'

'No, no. His house lies almost upon my direct route. I shall lodge at Colchester and make the detour to Harwich without undue delay.'

'Please pass my condolences to his widow. You have my letter.'

'Of course.'

'Well goodbye, old fellow. Good fortune and thank you for your solicitude when I was aloft. Appleby considered you saved my life.'

'Then we are quits,' White said, following his sea-chest over the rail with a gallant smile that seemed to cause him some agony. Drinkwater, suffering himself, grinned unsympathetically.

After the departure of the officers and their dunnage of sea-chests, bundles, portmanteaux, sword-cases, hat-boxes and quadrant-boxes, the frigate's remaining boats were sent in to the boat-pond and she was left with a dockyard punt of uncertain antiquity to attend her. At noon the ship was boarded by the paymaster and his clerks who brought with them an iron-bound chest with its escort of marines from the dockyard detachment. The men were mustered to the shrilling of the pipes in an excited crowd under the final authority of the boatswain and his mates. They turned out in all the splendid finery of their best shore-going outfits, sporting ribboned hats, decorated pea-jackets, elaborately worked belts of white sennet and trousers with extravagantly flared legs. Many held their shoes in their hands and those who had donned theirs walked with the exaggerated awkwardness of men quite unused to such things. As each man received his due reward, signing or marking the purser's and the surgeon's ledgers for the deductions he had accrued over the commission, he turned away with a wide grin, picked up his ditty-bag and went to the rail in quest of transport. Word had passed along the river, and boats and wherries arrived to lie expectantly off *Cyclops*'s quarters from where the unfortunate crew were confronted with the first joy of the shore, being subjected to the ravages of land-sharks who were demanding exorbitant charges to ferry them ashore.

In the wake of this exodus, the ship sank into a state of suspension, the silence along her decks eerie to those who had known them crowded with men and full of the buzz of human occupation.

Responsibility for the ship now fell upon the standing warrant officers, for Drinkwater's acting commission ceased the day *Cyclops* decommissioned, and in the absence of a master, the gunner was the senior. Drinkwater remained on board unofficially, his sole purpose in lingering to augment his knowledge and study, for he had received word from the Trinity House that he could attend for examination in a little over a fortnight and he was determined to secure at the very least a certificate as master as soon as possible. With the approval of the gunner, he therefore remained in the gunroom, and in that now echoing space once loud with Devaux and Wheeler's discourse, he unrolled Blackmore's charts and studied the legacy the old man had left him. Apart from a treatise on navigation, Drinkwater had found a dictionary and, to his surprise, some works of poetry. Somehow the memory of the sailing master and his didactic lectures on the mysteries of lunar distances did not square with the love-poems of Herrick and Rochester. Oddly, though, there seemed a strange, almost sinister message from beyond the grave implicit in a

94

slim anthology which contained a work by Richard Kempenfelt. He
read a couplet out loud:

Worlds and worlds round suns most distant roll,
And thought perplexes, but uplifts the soul . . .

This discovery briefly diverted his thoughts to Elizabeth and the
book of hers that he had found containing a hymn of the admiral's.
But it was the manuscript books which most fascinated Drinkwater
for, from his first appointment as second mate of a merchantman,
Blackmore had kept notebooks containing details of anchorages
and ports and the dangers of their approaches, of landfalls,
conspicuous features, leads through swatchways and gatways, and
the exhibited lights and daymarks of lighthouses and alarm vessels.
Interspersed with the carefully scribed text were exquisite drawings,
some washed in with water-colours, which turned these compendi-
ums into private rutters of sailing directions. It was a double surprise to find these talents in the old man, filling Drinkwater with a
profound regret that he had not done so earlier, that he had in some
way failed the dead man. The discovery of these things after
Blackmore's death laid a poignant burden upon him, a feeling of
lost opportunity.

To the inhabitants of the cockpit as a whole, Blackmore had been
a fussy old woman whose interest in versines, Napier's logarithms and
plane sailing were as obsessive as they were boring. Fortunately
Drinkwater had not found them so, and as a result had benefited from
Blackmore's patiently shared experience. He was too young to know
that such enthusiasm was enough for Blackmore and had decided the
dying man to leave his professional papers to his aptest pupil.

Drinkwater turned the pages of Blackmore's rutters. They
charted the dead man's life from the Gulf of Riga to the Dardanelles.
There were notes on anchorages on the coasts of Kurland and
Corsica, on ice in the Baltic and on the currents in the Strait of
Gibraltar. There were notes of the approaches to Stralsund and
some complex clearing marks off Ushant. There were observations
on Blackmore's native Harwich Harbour, and on the Rivers
Humber and Mersey, together with a neat chartlet of the Galuda
River in South Carolina. Drinkwater shuddered. He remembered
the Galuda too well, its mosquitoes, its dead and the manner of their
dying. He did not care to think of such things and dismissed them

from his mind. In an effort to concentrate, he wrote to Elizabeth, then bent himself to his studies.

Trinity House was an impressive building, situated on the rising ground of Tower Hill. Iron railings provided a forecourt to the stone façade, the ground floor of which comprised an arched entrance with Ionic columns supporting a plain entablature pierced by tall windows. These in turn were interspersed with ornate embellishments comprising the Corporation's arms and the medallions of King George III and Queen Charlotte, together with representations of nautical instruments and lighthouses. The Elder Brethren who formed the ruling court of this ancient body, as well as licensing pilots and buoying out the Thames Estuary, the Downs and Yarmouth Roads, and generally overseeing their own and private lighthouses, also examined the proficiency of candidates seeking warrants as masters or mates in the Royal Navy.

It was a contentious matter, for to command a brig-sloop or unrated ship of less than twenty guns, a lieutenant or commander was supposed to have passed an examination before the Elder Brethren of the Trinity House. Indeed, implicit in the very rank 'Master and Commander' was lodged an acknowledgement of navigational skill, allowing the holder the courtesy title of 'Captain', without the confirmed and irreversible rights attaching to that of 'Post-Captain'. Therein lay the rub. Despite the fact that the Brethren were mariners of experience, all having commanded ships, and in spite of the Corporation being empowered by Royal Charter, they were themselves merchant masters. Officers holding commissions from the King considered that to submit to such examination was an affront to their dignity. Thus the exigencies of service at sea and abroad, and the expediences of special cases, combined with the more powerful influences of blood and interest almost to negate the wise provision of this regulation. It was, therefore, unfortunately observed mostly in the breach. The resulting ineptitude of many commissioned officers as navigators had frequently caused danger to naval ships and ensured continuing employment for those men brought up in merchantmen, whose humbler path led them into the navy as masters and mates. These men had their certificates from the Trinity House and their warrants from the Navy Board but, competent though they might be, commissioned they were not.

Strictly according to regulation, a midshipman was not permitted to act as prize-master unless he had passed for master's mate and thus demonstrated his competence to bring his prize safely into port. A mixture of luck and expedience had secured Drinkwater his own warrant as master's mate when he had served briefly in the Corporation's yacht under Captain Poulter. At the time she had been flying the flag of Captain Anthony Calvert, an Elder Brother on his way to the westward from Plymouth, and Calvert had obtained a certificate for the young Midshipman Drinkwater. Despite this brief service in the Corporation's buoy-yacht, this was the first time Drinkwater had visited the elegant headquarters on Tower Hill, built by Samuel Wyatt.

Drinkwater was shown to a seat in an ante-room by a dark-suited clerk. An Indian carpet deadened all sound except the measured and mesmeric ticking of a tall long-case clock which showed the phases of the moon. On one wall a magnificently wrought painting by Thomas Butterworth depicted a ship being broken to pieces under beetling cliffs. Drinkwater rose and studied the picture more closely. It was of the *Ramillies* whose wrecking, Drinkwater recalled being told, was due to the errors made by her sailing master. The thought was uncomfortable and he turned, only to gaze into the forbidding stare of a pendulous bellied master-mariner whose portrait glared from under a full peruke wig. The mariner pointed to a chart on an adjacent table upon which were also a telescope and a quadrant. Beyond lay a distant view of an old ship, leaning to a gale.

'This way, sir.' The clerk's appearance made Drinkwater jump. Nervously gathering up his papers, he followed the man into an adjacent but larger chamber. Here more ancient sea-captains stared down at him, and a seductive view of a British factory somewhere, Drinkwater guessed, on the coast of India, occupied one entire wall. In the background, surrounded by green palm trees and some native huts, lay the grim embrasures of a dun-coloured fort above which British colours lifted languidly. In the foreground three Indiamen lay at anchor, with a fourth in the process of getting under weigh, while native boats plied between them. Between Drinkwater and the painting there was a long table upon which lay some books, charts, rules and dividers. Gingerly Drinkwater laid his papers alongside them on the gleaming mahogany.

A moment later a man in a plain blue coat with red cuffs, white breeches and hose, his hair powdered and tied in a queue, strode briskly into the room. Drinkwater recognized him as Captain Calvert.

'Mr Drinkwater, good morning. I recall our previous meeting. You caused me a deal of trouble.'

'I did sir?' Drinkwater's surprise was unfeigned. Such a beginning was unfortunate.

'The Navy Board wished you to sit a proper examination before they granted your warrant and referred the matter back to this House. I said you had passed a better examination than most of your ilk and the matter became a shuttlecock until they relented and issued you your warrant.'

'I had no idea, sir,' Drinkwater said. 'You must think me an ingrate for not thanking you properly.'

'Not at all. It was a point of principle between us and the gentlemen in the Strand.' Calvert waved Drinkwater's embarrassment aside and asked for his journals.

'I do not have them, sir,' he began as Calvert looked up sharply and withdrew his expectant hand. 'I was ordered to present myself for examination as lieutenant aboard the *Royal George* on the fatal morning she capsized, sir . . .' He paused and passed across the table a slim volume of manuscript. 'This is what I have done subsequently.'

'So you were one of the few to escape?'

'Yes, sir.'

'And would have passed for lieutenant otherwise?'

'I entertained that hope, yes, sir.'

'We are more exacting here, Mr Drinkwater. A master's certificate is not so easily come by.'

Calvert drew the book towards him and turned its pages with maddening slowness while Drinkwater sat, endeavouring to mask his nervousness. When he had finished, Calvert closed the book and looked up. 'Well, sir, you seem to have committed some knowledge to paper, let us determine to what extent you have retained it elsewhere.'

Drinkwater's mouth felt dry.

'How many methods are there to determine longitude?'

'Two, sir. By chronometer and by lunar distances.'

'And which would you employ?'

'The former, sir, though I have tried the latter.'

'And on what grounds do you favour the former method?'

'It is less complex and better suited to shipboard observations now that the necessary ephemerides are available.'

Calvert nodded. 'Very well. Pray, explain the principle of observation by chronometer.' Drinkwater launched himself into an explanation of the hour-angle problem, discoursing on polar distances and right ascensions. He had hardly finished before Calvert threw him a simple query about latitude. Drinkwater hesitated, sensing a trap, but then answered.

Without reacting, Calvert continued: 'You are asked by your commander to advise him of the best time for a cutting-out operation. On what would you base your response?'

Drinkwater's mind went obligingly blank. He had survived one such attempt by a French ship when *Cyclops* had been anchored in the Galuda. He remembered it only as a wild night of gun flashes, sword thrusts, shouts and mayhem.

'Come, come, Mr Drinkwater, this is not so difficult, surely?' Calvert prompted impatiently. 'Employ your imagination a little before you are dead with indecision.'

'I er, I should require a dark night . . . I should, er, make a study of any dangers to navigation and endeavour to supply sufficient details of these and any clearing marks which might aid the passage of boats . . . Oh, and I should seek to make such an attempt when the tides were most favourable, particularly for bringing the prize out.'

'Very well.' Calvert unfolded a chart and, turning it, pushed it across the table. He also indicated an almanac, a sheet of paper and a pencil. 'I wish to make such an attempt on a vessel lying in Camaret Road within the next week. When should I carry it out?'

Drinkwater bent to his task. Calvert presumed he knew the location of Camaret Road which was unfortunate, because he was not certain, but he soon found it near Brest and began the calculation that would give him a moonless night with the most favourable tide. It took him fifteen minutes to resolve the problem satisfactorily. An ebb tide out of the Iroise and a dark night gave him three possibilities and he chose the first on the grounds that if the operation failed or the weather was inclement, he would have two alternatives. Calvert expressed his approval and went on to ask him more questions, questions concerned with anchoring and sail-handling.

After further calculations, Calvert asked to be 'conducted verbally in a frigate from Plymouth Sound to St Mary's Road, Scilly'. It was a chink of daylight, for both men knew Drinkwater had made such a passage in the Trinity yacht all those months earlier. Drinkwater expatiated on the manoeuvre of weighing from Plymouth and standing out clear of the Draystone, of avoiding the Eddystone and the lethal, unmarked danger of the Wolf Rock, which he cleared by a bearing on the twin lights of the Lizard. Finally he recalled the leading marks for entering the shelter of St Mary's Road, keeping clear of the Spanish and Bartholomew Ledges.

Some questions followed about the stowage and storage of stores and cordage, an area of unfamiliarity to the candidate. Calvert asked, 'How would you stow kegs of spirits, Mr Drinkwater?'

Drinkwater havered. Did the significance of the question lie in the fact that the commodity concerned was spirituous? Or that it was in kegs? Clearly Calvert, a merchant master by trade, regarded it with some importance, as if a trick lay in its apparent simplicity. Then a magic formula occurred to Drinkwater, one he had heard Blackmore use frequently. Though he had never thought to employ it himself, being unsure of its precise meaning, its purpose struck him now. He ventured it in a blaze of comprehension. 'I should ensure they were wedged bung-up and bilge-free, sir.'

'Excellent. That will do very well, Mr Drinkwater. I desire you to wait in the ante-room. I shall fill out your certificate and you may present it to the Comptroller's clerks at Somerset House. I would not be too sanguine of an immediate appointment in a sixth-rate with the war ending, though.' Calvert smiled and held out his hand.

'I am not anticipating any such luck, Captain Calvert,' Drinkwater replied, taking Calvert's hand. 'I shall seek a berth in a merchant ship. I am anxious to marry and have been advised that opportunities in Liverpool are more likely.'

Calvert nodded. 'A fellow like you would be of considerable use in a slaver, no doubt of it. Well, good day to you. Pray wait a moment next door and I shall have my clerk bring you your paper.'

Drinkwater gathered up his documents as Calvert left the room. He returned to the ante-room and picked up his hat. He would go home to Barnet tonight, and see his mother and brother, then write again to Elizabeth with the news. He could afford to visit her before he went to Liverpool in search of a ship. Though greatly tempted, he forbore from winking at the pot-bellied mariner still gazing sternly down into the room. He was well pleased with himself and promised that before he made for Barnet, he would indulge himself with a meat-pie and a bottle in one of the eating houses nearby.

The clock ticked and the minutes drew into a quarter of an hour.

100

He supposed Calvert had been distracted on some important matter and settled himself to wait. After another quarter of an hour, he found himself incapable of sitting still and instead rose and began to study the wreck of the *Ramillies* under Bolt Head, but even this did not absorb him and he started to pace the carpet with mounting impatience.

At last, after what seemed an interminable delay, the clerk reappeared, but he bore no paper, only a summons that Drinkwater should wait a few moments more. After a further interval of ten minutes, Calvert reappeared.

'Mr Drinkwater,' Calvert said solemnly, so that Drinkwater imagined the very worst, 'the damndest coincidence, don't ye know . . .'

'You have the advantage of me, sir.'

'I have kept you kicking your heels, Mr Drinkwater, because news has just come in from Gravesend that the Buoy Warden requires the services of a mate in the *Argus*. It occurred to me that, were you so inclined and bearing in mind your intention to marry, the post might have fallen vacant at a providential moment.' Calvert paused, allowing Drinkwater to digest the fact that he was being made an offer of employment.

'The inordinate delay, I'm afraid, was occasioned by the urgent necessity to establish whether or not another officer, who had been half promised the next vacancy, still wished to take up our earlier offer. Happily, in view of the Peace, he has declined, and sails a week hence in a West Indiaman.' Calvert smiled. 'So there, sir. What d'ye say, eh?'

Drinkwater stammered his delighted acceptance.

Nathaniel Drinkwater and Elizabeth Bower were married in her father's parish church on a warm, late autumn day in 1783 during a short furlough taken by the groom. The Peace of Paris had been concluded two months earlier in September, and Drinkwater settled to his work in the service of the Trinity House, rising rapidly to mate. His wife stayed with her father for the first eighteen months of their marriage until his death in 1785. She then removed to London and took rooms in Whitechapel where she interested herself in a charitable institution. Drinkwater maintained a correspondence with Richard White, whose promotion to lieutenant and appointment to a frigate on the Halifax station he learned of in the summer of the following year.

Drinkwater also remained in contact with Lord Dungarth who on several occasions asked Drinkwater to dine with him in his modest town house. The two men were both interested in hydrographical surveying and Lord Dungarth had been asked by the Royal Society to evaluate the quality of charts then available to the Royal Navy and British merchant ships.

His Lordship moved in illustrious circles compared with the indigent and struggling Drinkwater, but he entertained his guest without condescension, increasingly appreciating his judgement and acknowledging his professional skills. As for Drinkwater himself, he gradually forgot his naval aspirations.

PART TWO

High Water

Without careful and patient observation, the culmination
of the tide is a moment so fleeting that it is soon gone,
leaving only the mark of its passing as it falls.

The White Lady

The passing of the *Vestal's* paddles had thrust Drinkwater astern, tumbling him in the pitiless whirling of the water so that the pressure in his ears seemed like lances thrust into his skull, and the ache of his held breath had translated itself into a mighty agony in his lungs. Within the strange compass of this pain appeared to teem a plague of memories, each passing in such swift succession that they seemed agents of his destruction, tormenting him to stop holding his breath and let his lungs inhale . . .

There was a vague lightening in the darkness and as it grew the memories faded. As his ribs faltered and could no longer contain the desire to breathe in, he struck upwards and the light was suddenly all about him. He was overwhelmed by it and gasped with the shock. The pain in his lungs seemed far worse now, as he broke the sea's surface and sucked in great gulps of air.

As mate of the *Vestal*, Mr Forester had run up from the boat-deck to the bridge the moment he heard the cries of alarm and knew something was wrong. Poulter turned from the bridge wing above the starboard sponson, his face ashen.

'I have run over the boat . . . The telegraph failed . . . The engines could not answer . . .' Poulter's voice barely carried over the noise of the wind and the thrashing of the paddles.

'I will clear away the other boat,' said Forester, casting a quick look in their wake where, for a brief second, he thought he could see something bobbing, but then the counter lifted and a wave intervened.

'I could not stop the ship . . .', Poulter went on as Forester turned and saw Potts staring at the captain. It was clear neither man could quite believe what had just happened. Forester hesitated for a moment, then said, 'We must stop, sir. Stop and turn round.'

'Yes . . . Yes, of course.' Poulter made a visible effort to shake off the effects of shock and Forester moved swiftly to the charthouse and, quickly opening the log-slate, scribbled against the time: *Telegraph failure. Unable to stop engines. Ran down port cutter.*

Then he leapt for the bridge ladder, shouting orders as he went. 'Call away the starboard cutter!' he yelled. 'Boatswain, post a man in the foretop with orders to keep a lookout! We've run the port boat down!'

Notwithstanding the badly shaken Captain Poulter, Forester consoled himself with the thought that they had successfully rescued men from the water before. As for Captain Poulter, the *Vestal*'s master pulled himself together with the need to react to the emergency. He quickly passed word that the men on the foredeck should remain as additional lookouts. Then he ordered a chain of men to pass his orders verbally to the first engineer. Having slowed his ship, Poulter began to turn her, to comb her wayward wake and relocate his lost boat, all the time hoping that the people in her had clung together and had not been the victims of *Vestal*'s huge and lethal paddles.

Such arrangements took time to effect, but within fifteen minutes Poulter had brought his ship's head round and had closed the estimated location of the disaster. Calling down for dead slow speed, he scanned the sea ahead of the ship. Up at the base of the bowsprit and aloft in the rigging, his men were doing likewise. One of the men at the knightheads called out and pointed at the very instant he saw something himself. He was joined by the seaman in the foretop. Poulter focused on the object as *Vestal* neared it.

It was a dark, hard-edged shape, like a porpoise's fin, which he recognized instantly as a section of the boat, the bow he thought, where the gunwales and the stem were joined with a knee. Then he saw a head bobbing near it, and another . . . Poulter's spirits rose in proportion. It was always damnably difficult to see men in the water and, he thought, the men in the boat could not have been dispersed very much. If only Captain Drinkwater had not been so old and the boat had not run under the ship. Perhaps they would be lucky . . .

Drinkwater was reduced to a terrified primal being, intent only on staying afloat and aware of the feebleness of his body. He was

106

wounded and hurt, wracked with agonies whose location and origins were confused but which seemed in their combined burden to be preventing him from swimming. The realization overwhelmed him with anxiety. He had a strong desire to live, to see his wife and children again. He was shivering with cold, weighed down by his waterlogged clothes but, energized by the air he now drew raspingly into his lungs, he renewed his fight to live.

In terror he found he could no longer swim. His body seemed leaden, unable to obey the urgent impulses of his brain. He went under again, swallowing mouthfuls of water as he floundered, before panic brought him thrashing back to the surface, his arms flailing in a sudden reflexive flurry of energy. Then, quite suddenly, both ending the panic and bringing to his conscious mind a simultaneous sensation of sharp pain and a glorious relief, his right arm struck an oar. A second later he had the thing under his armpits and was hanging over it, gasping for breath and vomiting sea water and bile from a burning throat.

The sensation of relief was all too brief, swept aside by a more sobering, conscious and logical thought. They would never recover him. He was going to die and he recalled the presentient feeling of doom he had experienced when lost once before in a boat in an Arctic fog. It had been cold, bone-numbingly cold so that he had shivered uncontrollably then as he shivered now. He had no right to live, not any more. He was an old and wicked man. He had killed his friends and betrayed Elizabeth. He had lain with Arabella Stuart in that brief liaison that had drawn from him an intense but guilty passion. Why had Arabella so affected him and turned his head? Was it because it had always been turned since he had set eyes on Hortense, whose haunting beauty had plagued him throughout his life, an exciting alternative to Elizabeth's loyal constancy? And what was love? And why was it that what he had was not enough? Was it ever enough, or were men just wicked, inevitably, innately evil? But he had not loved Arabella, not as he loved Elizabeth. Their parting had not affected him beyond causing him a brief, if poignant regret. Yet his hunger for her at the time had been irresistible. Was that all? Was the sole purpose of their encounter nothing more than that? The waywardness of it struck at the certainties he had clung to all his life. Surely, surely . . .

And as he sucked the air into his aching lungs he recalled Elizabeth and tried to seize her image, as if holding it in his mind's eye would

107

revive hope and lead him to understand what was happening to him. Were all men left to die and obliged to relinquish life in this terrible desolation? Was it not therefore better to be cut in two by an iron shot and to be snuffed out like a candle? And then he knew, and felt the conviction with the absolute certainty of profound insight. He had been tempted, and had succumbed to the flirtatious loveliness of the American beauty, because the remorse he had afterwards suffered had saved him from the greater, irreversible sin of insensate entanglement with Hortense.

It made sense with a simplicity directly attributable to providential intervention, and in the moment that he realized it, he felt a great burden lifting from him. This relief came with an easing of his breathing and the final eructation of his cramped and aching stomach. He raised his head as he lay wallowing over the oar, and looked up. He could see the ship again! She had turned round and grew larger as she came towards him. As she drew near, he could see a man up in the knightheads pointing ahead of the ship.

Drinkwater raised an arm and waved. He tried to shout, but nothing came from his mouth except a feeble croak. It would be all right! They could see him. He was not going to drown. He was redeemed, forgiven. He began to laugh with a feeble, manic sound through chattering teeth.

The forward lookouts aboard *Vestal* had not seen Captain Drinkwater. They had caught sight of two of the oarsmen and Captain Drew, who clung to the bow section of the port cutter in which was lashed an empty barricoe for added buoyancy. They lay some two hundred yards beyond Captain Drinkwater, who again passed unseen beneath the plunging bow of the *Vestal*.

Drinkwater looked up again. *Vestal*'s bowsprit rose over him like a great lance. He saw the rigging supporting it, the twin shrouds, the white painted chain bobstay which angled down to the iron spike of the dolphin-striker that passed half a fathom above his head. Then came the white lady who, following the iron spike as the ship drove her bow into a wave, seemed to sweep down towards him with malevolent intent. A cold terror seized his heart as the ship breasted the wave and rose, lifting the figurehead so that the white lady seemed suddenly to fly above him higher and higher, retreating as she did in the dream.

Then the forefoot of the *Vestal*'s bow thrust itself at him, striking the oar and wrenching it from his grasp. The foaming bow wave separated him from it and swept him down the ship's port side. He tried to shout again but suddenly the sponson threw its shadow and the paddle-wheel drove him down and he was fighting for his life with Edouard Santhonax in an alley in Sheerness, breathless after his run, and aware that he had allowed himself to be caught at a disadvantage, the consequences of which were as inevitable as they were dreadful. As the Frenchman's sword blade struck down in the *molinello*, he felt the thing bite into his shoulder with the same awful finality as he had experienced all those years ago.

Two paddle floats hit him in succession in passing and sent him deeper into the swirling depths of the turbulent sea. The roaring in his ears was the thunder of a great battle, the endless, ear-splitting concussion of hundreds of guns. It was inconceivable, terrible, awful. He glimpsed Camperdown and Copenhagen and Trafalgar. He glimpsed the darkness of a night action and saw, as he came near the surface in the swirling water of the paddle race, the pallid faces of the dead.

There were so many of them! Faces he had forgotten, faces of men he had never known though he had had a hand in their killing – of a French privateer officer, of a Danish captain called Dahlgaard, of an American named Tucker, of an anonymous officer of the French hussars, of Edouard Santhonax, of old Tregembo whom he had dispatched with a pistol shot, of James Quilhampton whose death he had mourned more than all the others. They seemed to mock him as he felt his body spin over and over, and the constriction in his breast seemed now to be worse than ever and somehow attached to the laughter of these fiends who trailed behind the white lady and struck with the cold, deep into his soul.

Tales of the Dead

'Nathaniel, what is it?'

Elizabeth looked up from her needlework as she sat by the fire. Her husband was staring through the half-opened shutter, out across the lawn in front of Gantley Hall where, judging by the draught that whirled about her feet and the noise in the chimney, a biting easterly wind was blowing. The rising moon cast a pale glow on his face, a chilling contrast to the warm candle-light and the glow of the fire. She watched his abstracted profile over her spectacles for a moment, then bent to her work with a sigh. He was not with her in the warm security of their home; his restless spirit was still at sea and his poor, divided heart revealed itself in these long intervals of abstraction. Then she heard the chink of decanter on glass and the low gurgle of poured wine.

'You drink too much,' she said without looking up.

'Eh? What's that?'

'I said, you drink too much. That is the fourth glass you have had since dinner. It does not improve your conversation,' she added drily.

'You are becoming a scold,' he retorted.

She ignored the provocation and looked up at him. 'What is troubling you?'

'Troubling me? Why nothing, of course.'

'Why then are you looking out of that window as though expecting to see something? Is the garden full of ghosts?'

'How did you know?' he asked, and their eyes met.

'There is something troubling you, isn't there?'

He shook his head. 'Only the weather, my dear,' he said dismissively, closing the shutter and crossing the room to sit opposite her. He stretched his legs out towards the fire.

'And the ghosts?'

He sighed. 'Oh, at moments like this I recall Quilhampton . . . And one or two others . . .'

'Why at moments like this?' she asked, lowering her needlepoint and looking at him directly over her spectacles. She saw him shrug.

'I don't know. They say old men forget, and 'tis largely true to be sure, but there are some memories one cannot erase. Nor perhaps should you when you have borne responsibility.'

Elizabeth smiled. 'It is the burden of that responsibility that prevents you from accepting things as they are, my dear,' she said gently. 'If, as you say you believe, Providence guides us in our lives, then Providence must bear the burden of what it creates. After all, you yourself are what you are only partly by your own making.'

Drinkwater smiled over his glass. 'Yes, you are right.' He leaned forward and patted her knee. 'You are always a fount of good sense, Elizabeth.'

'And you drink too much.'

'Do I?' Drinkwater looked at his empty glass. He placed it on an adjacent table. 'Perhaps I do. A little.'

'What o'clock is it?' Elizabeth asked.

Drinkwater lugged out his watch and consulted it. 'Almost ten,' he said, looking up at her. 'What is it?'

'Oh nothing. I was just thinking you have had that watch a long time.'

He gave a short laugh. 'Yes, so long that I forget it was your father's.'

'It was, I think, the only thing of any real value he had.'

'Except yourself,' he said.

'Thank you, kind sir.' Elizabeth stifled a yawn. 'I shall not linger tonight,' she said, laying down her work. 'Susan will have put the bedpan in an hour since.'

'Then I shall not make up the fire . . .'

Drinkwater was interrupted by a loud and urgent knocking at the door. 'What the devil . . .?' Their eyes met.

'Were you expecting someone?' Elizabeth asked, a sudden suspicion kindled in her.

'No, not at all,' Drinkwater answered, shaking his head and rising stiffly. He hobbled awkwardly towards the hall door muttering about his 'damned rheumaticks'.

111

Elizabeth sat and listened. She heard the front door open and felt the sudden in-draught of cold air that sent the dying fire leaping into a brief, flaring activity. She heard, too, a man's insistent voice and her husband's lower response. Cold air ceased to run into the room and she heard the door close. The exchange of voices continued and then her husband came back into the room.

'What is it, Nathaniel?'

'There's a vessel in trouble in the bay. I have Mr Vane in the hall. He has his trap outside. I shall have to go and see what can be done.'

Elizabeth sighed. 'Very well. But please ask poor Mr Vane in for a glass while you put on something suitable for such a night.'

Drinkwater turned back to open the door and waved for the visitor to enter. 'Remiss of me, Vane, come in. My wife will look after you while I fetch a coat.'

'My boots, Captain . . .'

'Oh, damn your boots, man. Come you in.'

'Thank you, sir.' Vane was a large man who always looked uncomfortable indoors, despite the quality of his coat and cravat. He entered the drawing-room with his customary awkwardness. 'Mistress Drinkwater.' He bowed his head, turning his low beaver in his hands.

'I should like to say it was pleasant to see you, Mr Vane, and in a sense it is,' Elizabeth said, as she rose smiling, 'but at this hour and in such circumstances . . .'

'Aye, ma'am. There's a ship in trouble. I saw the rockets go off just as I was going up with Ruth and, as you know, the Captain likes to know . . .'

'Oh, yes,' Elizabeth said, handing a glass to her unexpected visitor, 'the Captain likes to know. Here, take this for your trouble.'

'I didn't ought to . . .'

'You may need it before the night's out.'

Vane's huge fist closed round the glass and he smiled shyly at his benefactress, for Elizabeth had established him as the tenant in Gantley Hall's only farm. Vane had been driven off land that his family had worked for years by an extension of the Enclosures Act. He had come to Elizabeth's notice while eking out a living as a groom in Woodbridge where, for a while, she and Louise Quilhampton, the dead James's mother, had run a small school. Louise had heard of his plight and the incumbent of Lower Ufford had stood as guarantor of his character when Elizabeth, in the absence of her husband at sea,

had come to grips with the management of the small farm they had
bought with the estate. She had liked his slow patience and the ability
the man possessed to accomplish an enormous amount without
apparent effort. It was in such stark contrast to her own erratic
attempts to accomplish matters that she had regarded the arrival of
Mr and Mrs Vane as providential, an opinion shared by her fatalistic
husband. Vane was supported by his energetic wife. Ruth Vane was a
plain woman of sound good sense who managed a brood of children
with the same efficiency as her geese and hens. On his rare visits to
Home Farm, 'The Captain' as Drinkwater was always referred to
between them, voiced his approval. 'Mistress Vane runs as tight an
establishment as the boatswain of a flag-ship, and that bear of a
husband of hers puts me in mind of a lieutenant I once knew ...'
Elizabeth smiled at him now.

'Please sit down. Do you know what manner of ship is in distress,
Mr Vane?'

'No, ma'am. But I've the trap outside. We can soon run down to
the shingle and take a look.'

A moment later Drinkwater re-entered the room in his hessian
boots and cloak. He bore in his hands his cocked hat.

'You will need gloves, my dear.'

'I have them, and my glass.' Drinkwater patted his hip. 'Come,
Vane. Let's be off.'

Vane put his glass down and a moment later Elizabeth stood alone
in the room. She turned, made up the fire and resumed her needlework.

'Can't see a damned thing!'

Drinkwater spoke above the roar of the wind which blew directly
onshore and was much stronger than he had anticipated. They stood
on the low shingle escarpment which stretched away to the north-east
and south-west in a pale crescent under the full moon, its successive
ridges marking the recent high tides. The shallow indentation of
Hollesley Bay, 'Ho'sley' to the local people, was an anchorage in west-
erly winds, but in the present south-easterly gale, washed as it was at
this time in the moon's life by strong tides, it could become a death-
trap.

'Well, Vane, there are no more rockets going up ...'

'No, sir.'

'And that's all you saw?'

'Aye. I didn't waste time coming down to take a look, remembering your orders, like.'

'Quite right.' Drinkwater swept the desolate tumbling waters of the bay with his glass once more, then shut it with a snap. 'Well, 'tis possible she was farther out and may have got into Harwich.' He waved his glass to the southward.

'Aye, Captain, that may well be the case.'

Drinkwater remained a moment longer, his cloak flapping round him like a dark flag, and then he turned to Vane. 'Well, Harry, we've done our best. If any poor devil is out there, there's precious little we can do for 'em. Let's to bed!'

'Right, Captain.'

And with that the two men turned and stumped up the shingle beach towards the waiting trap, the stones crunching under their boots.

Susan Tregembo woke them the next morning with the news. There had been a wreck in the night, a lugger, it was thought, though not much of her had been washed up and rumour said she had knocked her bottom out on the Cutler shoal in the dark, though how anyone knew this only compounded the mystery. This conjecture had been brought by Michael Howland who worked for Henry Vane and whom Vane had sent down on one of the plough horses to ride the tide-line between Shingle Street and Bawdsey soon after dawn.

'Have they found any of the poor devils?' asked Drinkwater, sitting up in bed, eyeing the coffee pot that Susan seemed reluctant to settle in its usual station.

'Yes, Captain, and there's a note for you.' She set the tray down and handed Drinkwater a folded paper. He reached for his spectacles and recognized Vane's rounded hand.

Home Farm
About 6

Sir,

I have had from my Lad Howland some Sad News that Four Bodies came Ashore between the Towers at Shingle Street. He is much Frighted, but I am gone to get Them. One he says is of a Woman. Will you send to the Justices or What ought I to Do?

Y'r Serv't
Hen. Vane.

114

Having dismissed Susan with orders for his horse to be saddled, Drinkwater pulled on his breeches, dressed and drank his coffee. Twenty minutes later, after a quick breakfast, he was in the saddle, urging the horse past the gaunt ruins of the old priory which rose, ivy-covered, in the grounds to the rear of the Hall. He had no time for such antiquities this morning, for on horseback Drinkwater was as awkward as Vane in a drawing-room. He loathed riding, not merely because at his age the posture of sitting astride pained 'his rheumaticks' sorely, but because he had no expertise in the saddle. A passion for horses had killed his father, and his brother Edward had loved the damned beasts, but Nathaniel had disappointed his parent in having no natural aptitude for them, and an early fall had so knocked him about that his mother had insisted that Ned might ride because he enjoyed it, but Nat should not if he did not wish to. Nat had never wanted to since, but there had been a wild and tempestuous ride from Tilsit to Memel . . .

'By God!' he muttered, bobbing up and down as his nag trotted and his hat threatened to go by the board, and remembering how Edouard Santhonax had tried to prevent Drinkwater bringing *Patrician* back from the Baltic with the news of the secret treaty between Tsar Alexander and Napoleon, and how he had fought Santhonax in the Dutch frigate *Zaandam*. 'That mad dash all ended here in Ho'sley Bay!'

He had killed Santhonax in the fight, revenging himself upon the Frenchman who had so savagely mauled his shoulder ten years before in an alley in Sheerness. And he had thereby widowed Santhonax's wife, Hortense . . .

But enough of that. Such thoughts plagued younger men than himself, though he had seen Hortense a year ago when she had come to him like Nicodemus, by night. Damn the woman for a witch! She had inveigled out of him a pension on the grounds that she had performed a service to the British government. Drinkwater had been obliged to pay the thing himself. One day Elizabeth must find out and then there would be the devil to pay and no pitch hot enough, by God!

He found Vane and his two men with a small cart from the farm. They had already loaded two of the bodies and were handling the third as Drinkwater approached. Drinkwater forced his horse down the shingle towards the breakers that still crashed with a mighty roar. But the wind had dropped, and although the air was full of the salty tang of spray, it was now no more than a strong breeze.

A few pieces of black painted wood were strewn about the beach, and a large grating around which some small kegs had been quickly lashed told how the four had come ashore.

'When Michael found 'em, they were all tied to that,' Vane explained, coming up to Drinkwater's horse and pointing to the extemporized life-saver.

'They are all dead, I presume,' Drinkwater queried.

'Come and see, Captain.'

Drinkwater dismounted and Vane took his horse's reins as they walked across the shingle. The third body had just been put on to the cart and the men were returning for the fourth. By the feet, he could see it was that of a woman, though a shawl had been thrown over her face. Drinkwater bent and drew back the shroud.

Underneath, the vacant face of Hortense Santhonax stared unseeing at the sky. She was as white as the lady in his dream.

'Why do they have to come here?' Elizabeth asked, as she watched Vane's men carry the corpses into the lower barn.

'We shall bury them in the priory,' Drinkwater said shortly, his face grim.

'It is very sad . . .'

'I can only think they must have been trying to run into the Ore, though to do so in a south-easterly wind would have been sheer foolhardiness . . .' He was thinking out loud and Elizabeth held her peace. If she was bewildered by her husband's idea of burying the victims of the storm within the grounds, his next remark astonished her.

'I want the woman brought up to the house. Susan shall lay her out . . .'

'But I have sent for old Mrs Farrell. She always . . .'

'No,' Drinkwater said sharply, 'Farrell may do the men, but Susan shall see to the woman.'

'But why . . .?'

'Because I say so.'

Elizabeth looked sharply at her husband and was about to remonstrate when she caught sight of the expression on his face as he turned away. On rare occasions, he still considered himself upon a quarterdeck and she was usually quick to disabuse him of the idea, but there was something different about this.

Elizabeth held her peace until the late morning, when the woman's

116

body had been brought up to the Hall. Vane's men were busy sawing up planks for the coffins and Drinkwater was drafting a statement to send into Woodbridge after it had been attested to by Vane. Elizabeth went into the parlour where Susan was laying out the wretched woman.

'Oh, ma'am, you didn't ought to ...'

'It's all right, Susan, I'm no stranger to death. I had to do this for my father ...'

Susan seemed about to say more but held her peace and worked at loosening the woman's clothes.

'She was very beautiful,' Elizabeth remarked sadly.

'But for this,' said Susan, lifting a heavy tress of hair which had once been a glorious auburn but which now contained strands of grey. She exposed the right side of the dead woman's head.

'Dear God!' A coarse scar ran in heavy seams of fused flesh from under the profusion of hair, over the line of the jaw and down her neck. The right ear was missing. 'The poor woman.'

'Looks like a burn,' said Susan, rolling a pledget into the mouth and forcing the jaw closed. 'Mistress, I have to move her to reach her lower parts.'

'Let me help.'

' 'Tisn't necessary, Mistress, really 'tisn't.'

'It is quite all right ...'

Elizabeth sensed Susan's resentment at her interference. It was unlike the woman, with whom she had enjoyed a long and amicable relationship. Elizabeth began to sense something odd about the whole business and said, 'I wonder who she is? She is well dressed for travelling. This habit is exquisite ...'

'Mistress, I ...'

'What on earth is the matter, Susan?'

''Tis the Captain, Mistress ...'

'The Captain?' quizzed Elizabeth, frowning. 'What on earth has he to do with this matter?'

Susan shook her head and said, 'If you wish to help, Mistress, take her camisole off. 'Twill be there if 'tis anywhere.'

'Susan! What in heaven's name are you talking about? What will be there?'

'It would have been better had you not known, my dear.'

Elizabeth spun round to see her husband standing just inside the parlour door. Both she and Susan sought to interpose themselves

117

between Drinkwater and the pale form lying half exposed upon the table.

'Well, Susan?' Drinkwater addressed the housekeeper.

'Nothing yet, sir, but I haven't had time to . . .'

'Nathaniel, what is all this about?'

'*Who* is all this about, my dear, would be more correct.'

'You know her, do you not?' Elizabeth's question was suddenly sharply charged with horrible suspicions.

'I do, yes. Or rather, I knew her. Once.'

'Shall I go, sir?' Susan asked anxiously, aware of the gleam in her mistress's eyes.

'That is not necessary,' Drinkwater said flatly. 'I have entrusted you to search her and you know enough to have your curiosity aroused. Such titillation only causes gossip. You would be prudent not to make too much of what you hear, and to speak about it only between yourselves.' He smiled, a thin, wan smile, so that Elizabeth's initial suspicion was at once confirmed. Yet she also felt strangely moved. There was much about the life her husband had led that she knew nothing of, but she sensed that if he had deceived her with this once lovely creature, there would have been more than common infidelity about it.

'She is, or was until last night, a sort of spy,' Drinkwater began, addressing Elizabeth. 'She peddled information and acted as a go-between. Her presence aboard a wrecked lugger in Ho'sley Bay argues strongly that she intended coming here . . .'

'Here? To see you?' Elizabeth asked.

'Yes.' Drinkwater sighed. 'It is a long and complicated story, but many, many years ago she was among a group of *émigrés* we rescued off a beach in western France. Some time afterwards, while resident in England, she turned her coat and married a dashing French officer named Edouard Santhonax. It was he who gave me the sword-cut in the shoulder.' Drinkwater touched the place, and Elizabeth opened her mouth in astonishment.

'Later, he was sent out to the Red Sea where, by chance, I was party to the seizure of his frigate which I afterwards commanded . . .'

'The *Melusine*?' asked Elizabeth, recalling the sequence of her husband's ships.

Drinkwater shook his head. 'No, it was some time after that . . .'

'The *Antigone*?'

Drinkwater nodded. 'But her husband and I were to cross paths

118

again. It is odd, but I fought him not far . . . no perhaps', he said wonderingly, 'on the very spot where she drowned. Just offshore here, some few miles off the Ness at Orford. I killed him in the fight . . .'

'Then you made a widow of her.' Elizabeth looked at the face now bound up with a bandage.

'Yes.'

'That is terrible.'

'I do not deny it. But had I not done so, there is little doubt but that he would have made a widow of you.'

Elizabeth considered the matter. 'How very strange.'

'That is not all.'

'You mean you . . .'

'I have seen her since,' Drinkwater broke in, 'the last time less than a year ago, in April . . .'

'Nathaniel!'

'She came aboard *Andromeda* while we were anchored off Calais. She laid before me information concerning the intention of some French officers to liberate Napoleon after he was sent into exile.' He paused and gave a wry smile. 'It may sound extraordinary, but one might say the world owes the present peace, at least in part, to Hortense Santhonax . . .'

They looked at the corpse with a curious fascination, the silence broken suddenly by a faint escape of gas from the body which moved slightly, startling them.

'Oh, Lord!' giggled Susan nervously, pressing a hand to her breast.

Drinkwater's expression remained grim. 'Come, Susan, search the lining of her habit.'

'Do you look for papers, Nathaniel?' Elizabeth asked.

'It occurs to me that she might have been carrying them, yes.'

'But the war is over.'

'Yet she intended to come here. Unless she came on her own account, she must have had a purpose.'

'Why should she come upon her own account?'

'My dear, this is neither the time nor the place . . .'

'Then let us discuss it elsewhere.' Elizabeth was suddenly brusque. 'Susan is busy and we should leave her to her task.'

Drinkwater shrugged and let his wife hustle him out of the parlour and into the drawing-room.

'Well, sir,' she said sharply, turning on him. 'You have something to tell me, I think. If she was coming here on her own account, and I cannot think, with the war over, that any other reason would move her, I wish to know it. Besides, you said just now that the last time you saw her was in April last. How many times had you seen her previous to that? Do you expect me to believe all this was related to Lord Dungarth's department? Tell me the truth, Nathaniel. And now, before you have a drink, sir.'

'Sit down, Bess, and rest easy.' Drinkwater smiled and eased himself into a chair, leaning forward to rake the fire and throw some billets of wood on it. 'I met her before our encounter last April in the house of a Jew named Liepmann, near Hamburg, and yes, it was all in some way connected with Lord Dungarth and the business of his Secret Department. After his death it fell to me, as you know, to carry on some of his work. Hortense had moved in high places. It was said she was the mistress of Talleyrand, until the Prince of Benevento ousted her in favour of the Duchess of Courland. Did you see her scar? She was badly burned at the great ball given by the Austrian Ambassador in Paris on the occasion of the marriage of the Archduchess Marie-Louise to Napoleon. There was a fire, d'you see ...'

'The poor woman.'

'Yes, she was much to be pitied.'

'And you pitied her?'

'A little, yes.'

'To the extent of ...' Elizabeth faltered.

'Of what? Come, say it ... You cannot, eh?' Drinkwater was smiling and stood up, crossing the room to pour two glasses of madeira as he spoke. 'Yes, I pitied her but not as you imagine. It would not be true to say I did not consider lying with her, she was extraordinarily beautiful and possessed a very great power over men.' Drinkwater handed Elizabeth a glass. 'I shall tell you frankly that I once embraced her.'

Drinkwater paused, sipping his wine as his wife held hers untouched, regarding him with a curious, suspended look, as if both fearful and eager to hear what he had to say.

'I pitied her certainly, for when I saw her last, she was much reduced in her circumstances. She asked me to arrange a pension, but', he shrugged, 'it was impossible that any minister would listen to me and I did not possess the influence of John Devaux.'

'So you made her a grant yourself of fifty pounds per annum.'

'You know!'

'I knew you were supporting someone. We have the wreckage of others here, Susan and Billie Cue ... I knew from an irregularity in our accounts that you had provided for someone else. It never occurred to me that it was a Frenchwoman.'

Drinkwater sighed. 'I had not wished you to know, lest the explanation be too painful, but I give you my word that nothing beyond that embrace ever passed between us.'

'Your bankers are indiscreet, Nathaniel,' Elizabeth said with a smile. 'But', she went on, her face sobering, 'she cannot surely have been coming here to see you about that, unless she wished for more. D'you think that was it?'

Drinkwater shook his head emphatically. 'No. She would never have asked for more. She wanted the means to live quietly, that is all. No,' Drinkwater frowned, 'it is very odd, but I was thinking of her only last night, wondering how she was surviving under the restored Bourbons ...'

'She was your ghost?'

Drinkwater nodded. 'Yes, damned odd. She had, like almost all of her generation, sided with Bonaparte. Obscurity would have been best for her, but that may not have been possible for such a creature under the restored Bourbons. It strikes me therefore that there must have been two possible reasons for her coming here now. One might have been to solicit accommodation hereabouts, to appeal to our charity. The other, to bring me some intelligence.'

'And to sell it, perhaps?'

Drinkwater shrugged. 'Perhaps. Perhaps it was to do both, to sell the latter to gain the former. She would have been safe enough in England, heaven knows ...' He frowned. 'But ...'

'But?'

'I don't know, but neither seems quite in keeping with so hazardous an undertaking as making passage in a lugger in such unpropitious circumstances ... And yet ...'

'Go on.'

'It is just possible that news of sufficient importance might make the game worth the candle, and it would be entirely in keeping with her character to persuade the commander of an unemployed lugger-privateer to make the attempt.' He stood and refilled his glass.

'I see.' Elizabeth held out her own glass. 'She was an uncommon woman.'

Drinkwater nodded and poured more madeira. 'Not as uncommon as you, my darling, but remarkable, none the less.'

'Then we had better let her turbulent spirit go, and put her earthly remains within the old sanctuary.'

Drinkwater bent and kissed his wife's head. 'I ought to see if Susan has found anything.'

But all Susan had found were twenty golden sovereigns sewn into the lining of Hortense's skirt. Drinkwater gave five to Susan, three each to Vane's men who had helped recover the bodies, five to Vane for the elm boards and his own trouble, and the remaining four to the clergyman who buried her under the great flint arch of the ancient priory.

In the days that followed, it occurred to Drinkwater that Hortense might have been motivated by some intrigue involving the delegates at the Congress of Vienna. But the idea of his being able to influence anything of such consequence was ridiculous. He was now no more than an ageing post-captain, superannuated on the half-pay of his rank, one of hundreds of such officers. The notion that he might cut any ice with the government was preposterous!

There was, nevertheless, something that still troubled him, and it seemed to offer the most likely explanation for Hortense taking so great a risk as to try and contact him in such weather. And ten days later it was Elizabeth herself who confirmed his worst fears. Vane had just ridden in from Woodbridge and had seen the mail go through with the news being shouted from the box.

Napoleon had escaped from Elba on 26 February. Hortense's body had been washed ashore on the 21st.

The Letter

Drinkwater, in common with every other superannuated officer in the British navy that spring, wrote to the Admiralty offering his services. He ended his letter with a *postscriptum*.

> *If Their Lordships have no immediate Command for me, I would be Honoured to act in a Voluntary Capacity to Facilitate the Embarkation of the Army destined for Flanders from Harwich, if that was the Government's Purpose, or in any Other Capacity having regard for the Urgency of the Occasion. Should such Employment not be Consonant with the Board's wishes, I desire that Their Lordships consider that my Cutter-Yacht, Manned at my Private Expense, be made available for any Service which may Arise out of the Present Emergency. She would Prove suitable for a Dispatch Vessel, could mount Four Swivel Guns and is in Commission, in Perfect Readiness for Sea. I should be Happy to provide a Berth for Lieutenant G.F.C.Frey if Their Lordships so wished and that Officer could be placed upon Full Pay.*

Drinkwater had acquired his cutter-yacht from a builder at Woodbridge who had laid her down as a 'speculation'. Drinkwater was certain this so-called speculation might have proved profitable had not the war ended the previous year and with it the immediate conditions favouring prosperous 'free trade'. Though in the event the peace was to prove but a temporary hiatus, the cessation of smuggling meant that the cutter was up for sale, and Captain Drinkwater's arrival in search of a pleasure yacht was regarded by the builders as providential. She was bought in the late summer of 1814 for the sum of seventy guineas, which amounted to the interest paid on some investments Drinkwater had made with the house of Solomon and Dyer. Drinkwater and his friend Lieutenant Frey had commissioned her in a short cruise out to the Sunk alarm vessel that autumn. Thereafter, they had contented themselves with a single pleasant jaunt upon the River Ore, entertaining their wives and making poor Harry Vane hopelessly sick, though they had ventured no further than the extremity of the river's bar.

Throughout the winter, the cutter had lain on a mooring in a creek which ran inland from the mouth of the Ore, a short ride from Gantley Hall. After his experience 'at sea', Vane refused to ship in her a second time, but he used her as a static gun-punt and, with the help of his cocker spaniel, loaded all their tables with succulent waterfowl for Christmas.

Notwithstanding the superstitious notion that to use the name again might bring bad luck, Drinkwater had named the cutter *Kestrel* as a tribute to his old friend James Quilhampton who, like Drinkwater himself years before, had commanded a man-o'-war cutter of the same name. Lieutenant Frey, who had served with both Drinkwater and Quilhampton, had acquiesced, for he had married Quilhampton's widow Catriona. Frey, reduced to genteel penury on a lieutenant's half-pay, now occupied himself as a portraitist and had within a short time earned himself a reputation in the locality, being much in demand and receiving commissions from officers of both the sea and land services, many of whom wanted their exploits at sea or in the peninsula recorded with their likenesses. He therefore executed battle scenes as well as formal portraits. As a consequence of his assiduous industry, he had a busy studio and had rescued both himself and his wife from the threat of poverty.

Despite this activity, Frey was not averse to joining Drinkwater in offering his own services to the Admiralty, and when Drinkwater received a letter *requesting and requiring* him to submit his cutter for survey at Harwich *as soon as may be convenient*, he sent word to Frey. Their Lordships had fallen in with Drinkwater's suggestion that, provided he gave his services as a volunteer, Lieutenant Frey should notionally command the cutter, which would be taken up for hire provided she satisfied the surveyor resident at the naval yard at Harwich.

Neither Catriona nor Elizabeth greeted the news with enthusiasm, but Drinkwater's explanation that he doubted *Kestrel* would do much more than act as tender to the transports slightly mollified his own wife. Catriona, having lost her first husband, was less easily consoled, for she had conceived the notion that she might as certainly lose her second husband as she had the first in a vessel of the same name. Poor Frey, who was devoted to her, was clearly torn between the prospect of playing a part in the new campaign with the inducement of professional preferment or of continuing his work as a provincial artist. However, during March, a string of sittings were cancelled due to the flood of army officers returning to the colours, and this recession in trade and the prospect of full pay overcame Catriona's misgivings with the potent argument, traditionally attractive to a MacEwan, of sound economic sense.

Drinkwater took on two unemployed seamen at his own expense and, having laid in some stores, wood and water, sailed from the Ore to arrive at Harwich on 6 April. He presented himself the following morning to the naval commissioner of transports at the Three Cups, a local public house, where his deposition that the vessel was newly built dispensed with the inconvenience of a survey. Captain Scanderbeg, the commissioner, though senior to Drinkwater, had previously been employed ashore and was too hard-pressed to make an issue of such matters.

'Sir,' he had agreed civilly, 'if you say she is new-built and sound, I shall not detain you. The documents for a demise charter will be prepared by this evening.'

At sunset on 7 April 1815, the yacht *Kestrel* became a hired cutter on government service. However, the matter of an armament proved more difficult until the eager Frey discovered eight swivel guns which had been taken out of a merchantman then undergoing repairs at the naval yard. With a little judicious lubrication of palms and throats, he inveigled four of the small pieces out of the hands of the vessel's master, along with a supply of powder and shot. More powder and some additional bird-shot were a matter of requisition, to be supplied by the artillery officer in the Harwich Redoubt, a place already known to Drinkwater.

'Were we here at any other time, in any other circumstances, Frey, we should have found our path strewn with every obstacle known to the ingenious mind of man, but this', Drinkwater gestured at the bustle of the port as they stood on *Kestrel's* deck, 'almost beggars belief!'

Harwich Harbour was largely a roadstead with no wharfage beyond the slips of the naval yard. The town, dominated by the spire

125

of its church of St Nicholas, the patron of sailors, stood upon a small, low peninsula, surrounded by river, sea and saltmarsh, and commanded the entrance to the haven formed by the confluence of the rivers Stour and Orwell with the guns of its newly built redoubt. A notable battle had been fought in the town's narrow streets in 1803 when the Impress Service decided to round up the greater part of its male population for His Majesty's service. The local inhabitants were, however, versed almost to a man in the ways of the sea, and the over-eager regulating officers soon discovered that they had miscalculated and found themselves imprisoned with their prisoners, while the doughty wives of their victims waved their gutting knives in the streets outside. In fear of their lives, the press-gang eventually released their unwilling recruits and retreated with a few 'volunteers', men whose absence from the town meant they avoided unplanned matrimony or a summoning before the misnamed justices for the illegal acquisition of game. It was after this, known locally as 'the Battle of Harwich', that Scanderbeg had arrived to tighten up the public service.

Though for long a packet station, whose inn-keepers and publicans were notorious for fleecing travellers for the bare necessities of a night's lodging and whose civil officers understood that a certain necessary urgency might prevail in matters of official communication, the little town was unused to coping with the unprecedented military influx which now assailed it. Every inn and every lodging-house seemed stuffed with redcoats. Stands of arms littered the paved walkways of the narrow streets, horses were tethered in lines upon the green, and an ancillary village of canvas tents lay between the old gatehouse of Harwich and the adjacent twin town of Dovercourt. The remnants of the hospital, used for the accommodation of thousands of soldiers dying of the Walcheren fever but six years earlier, had been revived to harbour battalions of infantry, troops of cavalry and batteries of artillery.

The only consistent military organization obvious to a casual observer was a determined effort on the part of officers and men alike to assume attitudes of ease as close as possible to a source of liquor. True, the occasional horseman rode in from Colchester on a lathering horse, calling out for directions to the adjutant of a regiment of foot, or desiring to be directed immediately to the lodgings of Colonel So-and-so, but soon afterwards, a shrewd observer might have noted, the immediacy had gone out of the young aide's quest

126

and he would be seen quaffing a glass or two, or attempting the intimate, if temporary, acquaintance of an absent fisherman's wife or daughter. And all this inactive activity was accompanied by a vast and querulous noise which spilled into the streets from open doors, and accompanied everyone abroad in the narrow lanes and narrower alleyways which divided up the town.

As for Colonel So-and-so, he had gone to ground in a room in the Three Cups or the Drum and Monkey, with or without a local moll, but assuredly clasping a bottle or two. The only industry clearly under weigh was that of the seamen, whom the soldiers had temporarily displaced from the role of the town's habitual drunks. These men laboured off the beach which flanked the eastern side of the town, ferrying a steady dribble of infantrymen and their equipment in flat lighters out to the transports waiting at anchor on the Shelf whose blue pendants lifted languidly in the light airs from the west.

'The army embarks,' intoned Frey, getting out his sketching block. 'Tis odd that the gentlemen who wish for their likenesses to be shown against great sieges never ask me to paint such confusion, yet it seems to be the means by which the army goes to war.'

'Indeed it is and I find it rather frightening,' Drinkwater added. 'Do you suppose the French proceed in the same way?'

'I suppose', Frey said, laughing, 'that they do it with a good deal more noise, better food and more humour . . .'

'Why more humour?' Drinkwater asked, mildly puzzled.

'They must be more inured to it than our fellows,' Frey answered, with that simple logic which so characterized his level-headed good sense. 'If you do something idiotic many times, you must laugh at it in due course, surely?'

Drinkwater shrugged. 'It is a point of view I had not considered before. Perhaps you are right.'

'Men laugh in action, at the point of death, and men laugh on the gallows, so I suppose it is quite natural, some sort of reflex to ease the mind.'

'Or mask it from common sense,' Drinkwater added.

'Yes, probably. I confess I should not like to be landed on a foreign beach and march to meet an enemy who might kill me. At least if I die on a ship, I am among friends.'

'I suppose these lobsters consider their battalions constituted of friends.'

'I still pity them,' said Frey, finishing off his rapid sketch of the

Harwich waterfront. He looked up at Drinkwater. 'Do we have any orders, sir?'

'Well, I have received nothing, Mr Frey, but as lieutenant-in-command, perhaps you should solicit some from the commissioner, Captain Scanderbeg. He has his office in the Three Cups, in Church Street, adjacent to the church.'

'There is one other thing, sir.'

'What is that?'

'We need a small-arms chest. You and I have our swords and I have a single pistol . . .'

'I have a brace of them, but certainly we have nothing for the men. Do you ask Scanderbeg.'

'Very well.' Frey picked up his hat and called for the boat.

Drinkwater was certain that the reopening of hostilities would in due course result in the speedy recommissioning of many frigates and ships-of-the-line and the resumption of the blockade of French ports. It was possible, though by no means probable, that he would be called upon to take command of one of the latter, but he could not sit idly at home while events on the Continent took so exciting a turn in the hope that Their Lordships might remember him. They knew where he was if they required him.

The news of Napoleon's escape had been accompanied by several wild rumours, not the least of which was his sudden death, but the appearance of the quondam Emperor at the head of his troops in Paris and that of Louis XVIII in Ghent put paid to all wishful thinking. The Bourbons had returned to France and behaved as though the Revolution had never occurred, and the French populace had welcomed their Emperor back again. Misgivings they might have had, but the lesser of two evils was clearly preferred. King Louis had wisely removed himself over the frontier.

The hurried reassembly of the Allied armies was put in hand. The delegates at Vienna declared Napoleon Bonaparte to be outside all laws, broke up their conferences, balls and assignations, and returned to their chancelleries, palaces or headquarters. Everywhere Europe was astir again, jerked out of its euphoric assumption of peace, for the devil rode out once more at the head of his legions. It was impossible for a man of Drinkwater's character and history to sit idly by while the world teetered on such uncertainties. Until such time as Their Lordships had a ship for him, the proximity of Gantley Hall to the natural harbour of Harwich compelled him to take part in the urgent movement of the army across to the Belgian coast. Serving as a volunteer was a time-honoured course of action, and placing Frey in command of *Kestrel* gave the younger man the chance, if the war dragged on, of attaining the rank of commander and perhaps post-captain, thus securing a comfortable living for the remainder of his days.

For Drinkwater, in the fifty-third year of his life, the status of volunteer aboard his own yacht was most congenial. Frey delighted in the notion of command, and Drinkwater could relax, as he did now, watching with some amusement the movement of the flat lighters shipping out the horses of a regiment of light dragoons. The seamen assigned to the duty clearly had some difficulty in making the troopers understand the necessity of the animals remaining tranquil on the short passage across the shallows to the transports, and even more in communicating this requirement to the horses themselves. A good deal of shouting seemed essential to the task, which made the horses more nervous, and Drinkwater saw two seamen knocked into the sea and one wretched horse go overboard, to swim wild-eyed in the frothing tide that ebbed to seaward, pursued by a boat whose coxswain failed to understand that the more he holloaed and whistled at it, the more determined the horse became to escape. Drinkwater had some sympathy with the poor beast when its hooves found the bottom and it dragged itself up the beach by the Angel Battery, to be caught at last by some infantrymen lounging about there.

Drinkwater was surrounded by such vignettes and totally absorbed in them, so that he started as Frey, returning in the yacht's boat, ran alongside, almost under his nose. He was even more astonished to see Elizabeth sitting in the stern alongside the lieutenant.

'Elizabeth! What on earth brings you here? Not bad news, I hope?'

He helped her over the side and kissed her, and as he did so, she whispered, 'I have something very private for you,' with such insistence and so significant a stare of her brown eyes, that he took alarm. 'How did you get here?' he asked, frowning.

'We lashed poor Billy Cue on the box of the barouche . . . I left him at the Three Cups where a young woman promised to help him.' Poor Billy had had both legs shot off and, while immensely strong in the trunk and arms, was otherwise like a baby. Drinkwater had provided for him years earlier, and he had proved a useful member of the household, propelling himself about on a low board mounted on castors. Dismissing Billy from his thoughts, Drinkwater tried to gloss over Elizabeth's intrusion.

Turning to Frey he asked, 'Did you find any orders for us?'

'No, sir, but remarkably, I have been told that we are to receive a draft of six seamen and that we are to draw stores and victuals from the Victualling Board officers at the Duke's Head. And I am to bring off an arms chest. Apparently the Impress Service maintain extra arms here in the Redoubt, ever since there was some trouble with the local populace. I've the matter in hand.'

'Good Lord, Captain Scanderbeg has not been idle. We shall be remarkably tight then. See to it, if you please. I daresay orders will follow . . .' But Elizabeth was plucking with annoying urgency at his sleeve. He turned and ushered her below.

'What the devil is it, Elizabeth?' he asked as soon as they were in the saloon. Putting her finger to her lips, she drew him aside into the small cabin Drinkwater had had partitioned off.

'Nathaniel, I have been out of my wits hoping you had not precipitately sailed off to glory,' she said hurriedly in a low, mocking tone. 'Something remarkable and rather macabre has occurred.'

'Go on,' he said with growing impatience, as she appeared to fumble with her riding habit.

'You recall that when we buried Hortense, we laid her out in her small clothes?'

'Yes.' Drinkwater frowned as Elizabeth held out a pair of fine kid gauntlets.

'After you had gone, a sheepish Susan came to see me, to say that she had not disposed of Hortense's outer garments but had cleaned them and put them aside. I suppose she had some idea of retaining them herself, for they were very fine, or of disposing of them at some pecuniary advantage . . .'

'Yes, yes, I understand, but what has this . . .?'

'Please be silent a moment,' Elizabeth retorted sharply. 'She had been considering what to do, I think, probably troubled by her conscience, and, in drawing these beautiful gloves through her hands thus,' Elizabeth demonstrated the abstracted action, running the long cuffs of soft grey leather through her fingers, 'she encountered a stiffness which aroused her curiosity.'

Elizabeth took one glove and turned the cuff. A satin lining of pale blue had been snipped open, revealing a secret hiding-place.

'And inside she found what? Nothing?' Drinkwater asked.

'On the contrary. She found this.' Elizabeth now drew from her breast, with something of the air of a conjuror, a tightly folded and sealed letter. 'It has your name upon it.'

Drinkwater took the letter and turned it over. It bore his name without title in a hand he did not know.

'In view of what you had told us both when Hortense was being laid out, Susan came to see me and made a clean breast of the matter. I made light of it, thanked her, and told her that of course she might have what she wished of Madame Santhonax's effects. I promised her the gloves when I returned. I brought them merely to make you understand why the letter took so long to find. I suppose it was fortunate that we did find it . . . Nathaniel, are you quite well?'

Drinkwater looked up. He had broken the seal of the letter and had read its contents. A cold fear clutched at his heart. On his face, now grown pale, beads of perspiration stood out. Before he had gathered his wits, he murmured, 'My God Bess, this could ruin us.'

Elizabeth frowned. 'What do you mean?' she asked, both her husband's fright and his ghastly expression alarming her. Drinkwater laid the letter down on the shelf formed by a stringer and reached inside a locker for a bottle and two glasses. Elizabeth picked up the letter and read it. Drinkwater filled the glasses and turned to hold one out to Elizabeth. 'I don't understand,' she said, looking up from the letter. 'What is there in this to so alarm you?'

'She would have explained, of course,' Drinkwater said, half to himself, 'that was her purpose in coming and in such circumstances.' He drank deeply, adding, 'the damned fool'.

'That is hardly fair . . .'

'No, no,' he said, shaking his head, 'not her. *Him.*'

'Him? What *him*? Nathaniel, if you are going to speak of ruin, please don't use riddles . . .'

Drinkwater shook himself out of his introspection. 'I am sorry, Bess, it's something of a shock. This', he took the letter gently from her unresisting hand and folded it, 'is from my brother Edward. You know a little of his circumstances. He left this country many, many years ago and, after some time, obtained a position along with many other foreigners in the Russian Army. I had some dealings with him during my service in the Baltic . . .'

'Was he connected in some way with Lord Dungarth's Secret Department?'

'Yes, loosely. Certainly he sought to gain credit by assisting me and, by implication, Lord Dungarth. I suppose, from what this says,' he tapped the letter, 'he reached Paris when the Allies occupied the city last year. I would judge that there he met the ever-resourceful Hortense, and at some stage in what I deduce to be an *affaire*, he may have revealed his true identity.' Drinkwater paused. 'Indeed,' he went on with a profound sigh, looking at Elizabeth directly, 'it seems only too probable that he revealed everything.'

'And that everything constitutes our ruin, I assume?'

'Yes.'

'But why?'

'Because when he left this country, he was wanted for murder.'

'*Murder?*' Elizabeth faltered, her face draining of colour and an edge entering her voice. 'And you, of course, being you, helped him escape.'

'I was a damned fool . . .'

'But she is dead and this letter . . . I wish I had never opened the glove, but I thought it something important, that you should know of it and that . . .' Elizabeth faltered, and then added with sudden conviction, 'It doesn't matter though, does it? The letter asks that you should go to Calais to meet the person who signs himself "O". You have merely to ignore it, to pretend it never arrived . . . I mean, how are you so sure that it *is* from Edward?' And with that Elizabeth snatched the offending paper back and tore it swiftly into pieces. Drinkwater looked on with a chillingly wan smile.

'But it did arrive, Bess. You know it, I know it, Susan Tregembo knows it. Even Frey must be aware that something is up.'

'But you don't *know* it was from Edward. You are guessing, aren't you?' Elizabeth pressed. 'It is signed *O*. Of what significance is that?'

'Only that Edward's assumed name, the name by which Lord Dungarth knew him, was *Ostroff*. In Russian it means island, a small piece of land surrounded by a hostile sea.'

'You are certain?'

'I am as certain as I can be. In fact I think I recognize the hand now', he added, 'from the way my, no, *our* surname is formed.'

There was a brief silence as they regarded the fragments of paper littering the cabin deck. It was broken by Elizabeth. 'Well, you are surely not suggesting you go to Calais?'

'If my brother is in Calais now, then he is stranded there, a Russian officer in a French port which has become Bonapartist again. He might be murdered there, which would be retribution of a sort, but

132

otherwise there is nothing to stop him crossing the Channel by hiring a boat or bribing a fisherman. If I can at least try to reach him, I may discover his intentions. Perhaps, after all these years, we have nothing to fear, but I cannot live the rest of my life knowing that I abandoned my brother, feckless devil though he is and possessing as he does the power to ruin us all.'

'And what shall you do if you do meet him? Shoot him?'

Drinkwater laughed. 'Would you prefer I drowned him?'

'I wish to God you had never had anything to do with him . . .'

'And what would you have done when your own kith and kin came to you in the extremity of desperation . . .?'

Elizabeth bit her lower lip and shook her head. 'I don't know. But murder . . .'

'Well, I am not exculpating him,' Drinkwater said with a sigh, 'but he caught his mistress in bed with another man. You yourself found the merest suspicion of such conduct betwixt Hortense and myself a thing deeply disturbing. An intemperate man like Ned, in the high, indulgent passion of his youth, was scarcely to be expected to react other than as he did.'

Elizabeth considered the matter for a moment, then it seemed that she braced herself as she made up her mind. 'You shall go to Calais. And I shall come with you.'

'No. *I* shall go to Calais,' Drinkwater said with sudden decisiveness. 'Edward, through Hortense, knows where we reside. *You* shall go home and stand guard. If Edward comes to you, send Vane to leave word at the Three Cups in Harwich. The letter shall state that the mare has produced a fine black foal and you thought I should know. Remember that. Occupy Ned, and I will return as soon as possible. Mercifully, I can leave Frey in command and absent myself without occasioning any trouble. My only concern at this moment is to detach myself from this place. Come, we must go ashore at once. Take those damned gloves to Susan. I wish her joy of them. Let us lay this confounded ghost once and for all!' And taking his wife in his arms, he crushed her to him. 'Now, put on a happy smile and look as if you are pleased to see me while I escort you ashore.'

Having seen Elizabeth off, with a smiling Billie Cue lashed happily upon the box, Drinkwater ducked into the Three Cups. He had met Lieutenant Sparkman in its taproom some eighteen months before when Sparkman, an inspector of Sea-Fencibles, had reported the arrival of a strange Neapolitan officer on the Essex coast and lit a train of powder that had led to the fight with the *Odin* and the death of James Quilhampton in the Vikkenfiord. A woman bobbed in front of him, her stays open to reveal her breasts, offering him a drink. He did not remember Annie Davis, though she had delighted Sparkman all those months ago and, more recently, had put a smile on Billie Cue's face, though it had cost him a small fortune. Now Drinkwater swept past her and made for the back room where Captain Scanderbeg held court.

'Ah, Captain Drinkwater, pray do sit down.' Scanderbeg sat back in his chair and lifted a pewter mug interrogatively. 'A drink?'

Drinkwater shook his head. 'Thank you, no.'

Scanderbeg was in his shirt-sleeves, the table before him littered with papers, some of which had found their way unintentionally to the floor while others were more purposefully arranged in a wicker basket at his feet next to which was coiled a small spaniel. A ravaged quill pen stuck out of a large ink-well and a pen-knife lay beside them.

'I have ordered a small draft of men for you . . .'

'So I hear and thank you for that, but it is not the cause of my visit. Captain Scanderbeg, I can see you are a busy and, if I mistake not, a harassed man . . .'

'By God, sir, I have never known such a thing as this damnable embarkation. I was Regulating Captain here a year ago and was resurrected for the present emergency in *this* blasted incarnation.' Scanderbeg tapped his breast as though this revealed his change of status. 'I tell you, sir, governments know not what they do when they declare war with such alacrity! Would you believe that I had a pipsqueak captain of light dragoons in here this very forenoon complaining, *complaining* mark you, that my men, the seamen that is, were taking insufficient care of his blasted horses. When I asked to which ship they were assigned, the *Adventure*, *Philarea* or *Salus*, he said he did not know, so I asked which troop he meant, the first or second and so forth, that I might divine the men responsible. He said, "Oh, I don't mean troop horses, damme! I mean me own chargers, sir!" I asked how many of these festering chargers he had and he said four, two of which had cost him four hundred guineas. Four hundred guineas! God, sir, I hope the poxy French shoot the fucking things out from under his arse! I told him that if he had nothing better to do than complain, he had time enough to see to the matter himself and that a couple of hundred guineas to the tars embarking the cavalry mounts would see each of his damned chargers piggy-backed out on the backs of a score of mermaids! Bloody popinjay!'

Drinkwater could not help but grin at Scanderbeg's predicament, despite the urgency of his business, and wondered if the horse he had seen in the water earlier had been one of the importunate young dragoon officer's mounts.

'He threatened to report me to General Vandeleur,' Scanderbeg railled on, 'and I said he might do as he damned well pleased. When the regiment had all embarked, I discovered their field forge and far-riers still sitting in the horse lines out by the barrack field. No one had passed word to them to mount up, or whatever the festering cavalry do when they want to move off! I tell you, Drinkwater, the French will make mince-meat of 'em! Thank God for the North Sea and the Channel. Aye and the navy!' And with that Scanderbeg tossed off the contents of his pot and slammed it down on the table. He shook his head and blew through his cheeks. 'I beg your pardon, Captain, but . . .' he shrugged. 'What can I do for you?'

'I think, Captain Scanderbeg, 'tis more what I can do for you. I can relieve you of one anxiety at least.'

'That, sir, would be the first word of co-operation I have received a sennight since!' Scanderbeg brightened visibly. 'You are going to tell me you have some orders.'

'Indeed I am. How did you know?'

'Too long in the tooth, Captain Drinkwater, not to know that I would be the last to be told. Well?'

'I am pushing over to reconnoitre Calais and Boulogne. If the French have any of their corvettes ready for sea, they might wreak havoc among our transports . . .'

'By heaven, sir, you're right! Well, well, go to it, sir, and if there is anything further you require, I shall do my limited best.'

'Thank you. I hope your post don't become too irksome.'

'I could *almost* wish for a frigate with her bowsprit struck over the Black Rocks,' Scanderbeg riposted with a smile, and Drinkwater left with the impression of an indomitable man who would, despite the odds and to the discomfiture of many, get the army embarked in time.

Walking back down Church Street he encountered a troop of horse artillery. The five field-guns and single howitzer gleamed in the sunshine. The bay horses that pulled them were handsome in their harness, and the soldiers that rode postillion were sitting chatting, while the young officer commanding them, having made a few

135

remarks to his bombardier, turned in his saddle, caught sight of Drinkwater and saluted.

'Good day, sir. Captain Mercer of G Troop Royal Horse Artillery, at your service. Are you perhaps the naval commissioner?'

Drinkwater returned the salute and shook his head. 'Alas, no, Captain Mercer, the officer you want is Captain Scanderbeg. He is quartered next to the church in the Three Cups.'

'Thank you, sir.'

'Captain Mercer ...'

'Sir?'

'Make sure you don't leave anything behind ... the odd gun or limber, for example. I fancy your colleagues in the light cavalry have sorely tried his patience this morning.'

Mercer grinned. 'What would you expect of Vandeleur's brigade, sir?' he remarked.

'I have no idea, Captain, but a little more than they appear capable of, it seems. I just hope the French are as accommodating as Captain Scanderbeg. Good day to you.'

Drinkwater passed on, quite ridiculously light-headed. He had Scanderbeg to thank for bringing the problem of Edward into a more reasonable perspective. Moreover, he had released himself from any obligation to the commissioner. And he would be going to sea. Suddenly that, at least, was compensation enough. And with the thought buoying him up, he hailed the boat.

Calais

The following morning proved foggy and while it delayed the trans-ports from leaving port, the hired cutter *Kestrel* lay wallowing damply off the Head of the Falls, having slipped out of Harwich the previous evening. Hardly had Frey's men lugged the stores and arms chest aboard than Drinkwater passed orders to sail. Once her mainsail was hoisted, and provided the weather remained reasonable, she was an easy vessel to handle. Though Drinkwater and Frey stood watch and watch, it was possible to divide their crew into idlers, available throughout the daytime, with the pressed men in three watches. It was scarcely a punishing regime and, superficially at least, bore a resemblance to the yachting excursions Drinkwater and Frey had indolently planned during their winter evenings together.

Drinkwater's notion of reconnoitring Calais was a sound one; indeed he expected to encounter at least a gun-brig from Chatham keeping an eye on the port. More difficult would be penetrating the place, not an easy task for a British naval officer during so uncertain a political period, but the greatest problem he confronted lay in the means by which he might locate Edward. The letter had given him few clues, and Elizabeth had screwed it up and torn it into so many pieces that his attempt to reconstruct it proved futile. It did not matter. It was intended merely to validate Hortense's appearance. He recalled it as a simple enough message, to the effect that *an old friend* who was *now very intimate with the bearer* wished to be *embarked at Calais and looked forward to renewing a close acquaintanceship.* There were key words containing a hidden significance which Drinkwater, with his eye for such things combined with a conscientious anxiety, had soon noticed. The *old friend* gave away a little, but in truth there were few now left in the world who could claim an 'old' friendship with him. Besides, this relationship was emphasized by the words *close acquaintanceship*. As to intimacy with the bearer, Drinkwater did not need to read between the lines there: Hortense, though mutilated by boiling lead, had still been beautiful, and Ned was past fifty. The only real mystery was how the two had met, and he had no way of divining that fact without asking directly. Of one thing he was certain, Hortense had risked a great deal in her attempt to contact her benefactor. He recalled Lord Dungarth's prophetic remark when they had let her go years earlier, that they would save themselves a deal of trouble if they had shot her. Well, well, Drinkwater mused, they had not shot her, and their combined infirmity of purpose had led to his present predicament. The fact that brother Edward had become Hortense's lover was an exquisitely painful irony, he thought, turning his mind back to the problem of contacting a fugitive Russian officer in a hostile port.

It did not suit Drinkwater to leave matters to fall out as they might. That something would turn up was a maxim that in his experience rarely functioned, except for other people, of course. It seemed he had but two choices, to do the thing himself or to get someone else to do it, and neither recommended itself. He did not wish to go ashore and if he did, what could he achieve? He could hardly wander round Calais in his uniform and to do so in his civilian garb invited arrest and a firing squad. And even if he were to risk going ashore, he could scarcely knock on doors and ask, in his barbaric and imperfect French, if a Russian officer who was really an Englishman had been seen hanging about. The whole matter bordered on the preposterous!

The alternative was to contact a fishing-boat. French fishermen were no different from their English counterparts and would do anything for money. Fortunately he had sufficient funds with him and could buy access to the network of gossip that would exist among the drinking dens, *cafés* and *bistros* that these men frequented when ashore. The fishermen of the Dover Strait, irrespective of nationality, had been carrying odd persons back and forth across the Channel for a generation, and they would almost certainly know of anyone who was seeking a passage. Besides, by now Edward might well have bitten the bullet and arranged his own passage. In fact, it was more likely that he would turn up at Gantley Hall to alarm Elizabeth than that he would be standing obligingly on the beach at

Calais. Too long a period had elapsed since Hortense had left in her lugger for an impatient man such as Edward to remain long in idle impotence.

For the whole of 10 April, *Kestrel* lay inert, washing up and down in the tide, her decks wet with the condensation that dripped from her sails and rigging. Drinkwater took the opportunity of calling his tiny crew aft. He had appointed his own two paid hands as boatswain and carpenter, and they had some notion of who they were working for, but the half-dozen pressed men had no idea.

'My lads,' Drinkwater began, looking over the smallest crew he had ever commanded, smaller even than that allocated to him when, as a midshipman, he had been sent away as prize-master of the Yankee schooner *Algonquin*. 'For those of you just shipped aboard, I am Captain Nathaniel Drinkwater. I am the owner of this cutter and she is on charter to the Government for special service. She is commanded by Lieutenant Frey here and he is acting under my orders, both of us being in His Majesty's service. Our orders in the first instance require us to take a look into Calais. Much will depend thereafter on what we discover. What I shall rely upon you for is a prompt and willing response to orders. That is all.'

He watched them disperse. The pressed men were quite clearly seamen and did not seem unduly resentful at their billet. Perhaps they were meditating desertion at the first opportunity. Oddly, Drinkwater did not find the thought particularly uncomfortable. At a pinch he and Frey could sail *Kestrel* home themselves.

On the morning of the 11th, a breeze sprang up out of the north-west quarter and, though it soon dropped again, there was sufficient to keep steerage way on the cutter as she ghosted south-east towards Calais. It was Drinkwater's first real passage in her and it was clear she had been built for speed, for with the quartering wind and her long boom guyed out to port, she ran down wind with ease. Frey seemed content to lean against the long tiller as the white wake ran out from under the counter, leaving Drinkwater to pace along the windward side, from the heavy sister-blocks of the lower running backstay to the starboard channel. The small swivel guns, one of which was mounted on either bow, with the second pair aft covering the cutter's short waist, pointed skywards. Their iron crutches could be lodged in the same holes drilled for belaying pins, and Drinkwater mentally selected three other positions which might prove useful if they ran into any trouble. Of one thing he was relatively certain: if there was any kind of wind, even a light air, he judged they had an excellent chance of out-running even a French *chasse marée*.

None the less, considerations of this kind were mere temporary distractions and, when the French coast hove in sight, Drinkwater realized he was no nearer a solution as to how to contact Edward than he had been when they had sailed. Contacting fishermen seemed the best option, though how he might guarantee that remained an unresolved problem. For some minutes he stood amidships, his glass steadied against the heavy shrouds, watching the low white cliffs fall away as the coast stretched eastwards towards Calais. A strong tide ran along the shore and it would carry them up to the jetties. Drinkwater decided to progress by degrees, and the first of these would be to determine the state of the port. He closed his Dollond glass with a snap, pocketed it and walked aft.

'Now, Mr Frey,' he said formally, looking upwards, 'we have British colours at the peak.'

'Aye, sir.'

'I mean to run up along the coast and approach Calais from the west. The tide will be in our favour and I want to push up between the jetties. Make as though you intend to enter the port. Load all the guns with well-wadded powder. No shot. Be prepared for the French to fire on us, but I want a demonstration made.'

'You're going to tempt anyone bold enough to try their luck against us, are you, sir?'

'I think we might have the legs of even a French corvette, don't you?' Drinkwater replied, dissembling with a grin.

'I'd be damned disappointed if we didn't, to be honest, sir,' Frey replied, smiling back.

'Very well. We will then haul off for the night and heave to offshore. Tomorrow morning we shall do the same again. After that I shall decide what further we can achieve.'

'Very well, sir, I understand.'

Drinkwater was tempted to say, 'No you don't', but confined his reaction to a confirming nod. 'I gather from the smell that you have found one among the pressed men capable of acting as cook,' Drinkwater remarked, sniffing appreciatively, for their table thus far had been unappealing.

Frey nodded. 'One of 'em volunteered, sir. Name of Jago.'

'Well that's fortunate. Let's hope we deserve such luck.'

*

It was early evening and the wind had steadied to a light breeze as they wore ship off Cap Blanc Nez and began to run along the coast towards the spires of Calais. The cutter heeled a little, slipping through the water with astonishing grace and speed. Had Drinkwater not been so preoccupied, he might have appreciated the sublimity of the moment, but he was denied that consolation, and it was left to Frey's sensibilities as he leaned against the tiller, his eye occasionally wandering upwards to the peak of the gaff where the large red ensign lifted in the breeze. The flooding tide added to their speed and this augmentation made them appear to scud along the shoreline, persuading Frey that the subject would make a delightful painting.

Drinkwater, for his part, watched the approaching port with unease. Just inshore and slightly ahead of *Kestrel* a pair of small luggers were running parallel with them, making for home. They appeared unconcerned by the proximity of the British cutter, so fluid was the political situation. Drinkwater wondered if they might not provide the contacts he required. He turned and walked aft.

'I assume the swivels are ready?' Drinkwater asked.

'Aye, sir. As you required.'

'Very well. Now edge down on those fishermen, Mr Frey, if you please. I want them to get a clear look at us.'

'Aye, aye, sir.' Frey leaned on the tiller and *Kestrel*'s bowsprit swung round as she turned a point to starboard, lining itself up on a church spire.

'Friendly waves to the Frogs now, lads, if you please,' Drinkwater said as they caught up with the rearmost lugger. The two French boats were trailed by screeching gulls who dipped and fought over the scraps of entrails lobbed overboard by the men industriously cleaning their catch before they reached port. The heavily treated brown canvas of their sails and the festoons of nets half-hanging over their rails gave them a raffish appearance, and the low sunlight flashed on the gutting knives and the silver skins of the fish as the fishermen worked with deft and practised ease. Aft, the skippers stood at their tillers, with a boy to trim the sheets, regarding the overtaking British cutter with little more than a mild curiosity as she surged alongside them.

Drinkwater stood beside the lower running backstay and raised his hat. Along the deck his crew waved. Impulsively the lad alongside the aftermost lugger responded, but the skipper merely jerked his head and those of the fishermen amidships who looked up did so only for a second, before bending to their task again.

'Happy-looking lot,' someone remarked as the first lugger dropped astern and they overtook the second. She was closer and Frey altered to port again to avoid actually running her down. Drinkwater read the name across her transom: *Trois Frères*. They received a similar reception from her. 'Very fraternal,' Frey remarked.

'Never mind, Mr Frey. Word of an insolent British cutter in the offing will circulate the waterfront before dark and they have at least saved us from the attentions of those gentlemen.'

Drinkwater indicated a small hill which overlooked the final approach to the entrance. It mounted a battery, and at least two officers, conspicuous in their bell-topped shakos, could be seen regarding them through telescopes.

'Stand by those swivels then,' Drinkwater said, and Frey called to his men to blow on their matches.

'I want you to tack in the very entrance and fire both guns to loo'ard as you do so.'

Frey called his men to stand by the sheets and runners. They were drawing close to the jetties now, and were being watched by at least one man who stood at the extremity of the seaward jetty beneath the lighthouse.

The stream of the tide bypassed the entrance itself but ran fast across it, swirling dangerously round the abutment of the seaward jetty now opening on their port bow. 'Watch the tidal set on that jetty, Mr Frey.'

'Aye sir, I have it . . .' Frey grunted with the effort.

'Ready about and down helm!' Frey called, and *Kestrel* turned on her heel and came up into the wind with a great shaking of her sails. The wind was getting up as the men ran away with the starboard runner falls and let fly those to port. The two crumps of the swivel guns echoed back from the wooden piles of the jetty, then *Kestrel* lay over on the starboard tack and stood to the westward. On *Kestrel*'s port quarter the two French luggers sailed blithely into Calais and on her starboard beam the piles of the extremity of the seaward jetty suddenly loomed above them. Drinkwater looked up. The man was still there, staring at them, with the lighthouse rising behind him.

Drinkwater raised his hat again and, with a grin, called out '*Bonsoir, M'sieur!*' But the man made no move of acknowledgement beyond spitting to leeward. 'An expectorating Bonapartist,' Drinkwater remarked, jamming his hat back on his head.

Frey gave a laugh of nervous relief. He had nearly been caught out by the tide carrying him against the jetty-head. Panache was one thing, but it had seemed for one anxious moment dangerously close to disaster!

As if to chastise them for their impudence, two shot plunged into the sea off their port beam. Looking astern, Frey and Drinkwater caught sight of the smoke dispersing from the muzzles of the cannon in the battery.

'Well, I think we have made our presence known, Mr Frey,' Drinkwater said.

They stood away to the north-west as darkness closed in and when they had hauled sufficiently offshore, Frey hove to. Leaving the deck to the boatswain, the two officers went below to dine.

'Well, I don't know what we will achieve tomorrow, but I think we should be off Blanc Nez again by about five o'clock . . .'

'That will give us the tide in our favour again,' Frey added enthusiastically, sipping at his wine as Jago came in with a steaming suet pudding. 'By God, Jago, that looks good!'

'*Bon appetit*, they says hereabouts I think, sir.'

Drinkwater looked up sharply. 'You don't speak French do you, Jago?'

'*Mais oui, M'sieur*. I speak it well enough to pass among the French without their suspecting I am English.'

'And how did you acquire that skill, may I ask?'

'Well, sir, 'tis how I learned to cook, too. You see, sir, I was a boy shippin' out of Maldon in ninety-eight with my old pa. We was, er, fishin' like,' he winked, looking at Drinkwater and then at Frey, 'if you gets my meanin', sir . . .'

'You mean you were smuggling?'

'Good God, no sir. I was a mere lad . . .'

'Then your father was smuggling.'

'Not quite, sir. We was actually fishing off the Kentish Knock when up comes this big cutter, flying British colours, and lies to just upwind and floats a boat down to us. Imagine our surprise when over the side comes this Frog officer, all beplumed and covered in gold. He wants the skipper, that's me dad, to take a packet into Maldon and to hand it over to a man at an address he gave him. I think he gave Pa some fancy passwords and such like. To make sure of it, he took me out of the boat and carried me off with him . . .' Jago shrugged. 'Sommat happened to the boat, I remember she was leakin' awful and there was some bad weather blew up next day. Anyway there I was dumped

143

on a small farm near Abbeville. The farmer was an invalid soldier and I learned the place was often used by strange men who were passin' back and forth across the Channel. They avoided bein' seen in Calais or Boulogne but weren't far away when the time came for 'em to ship out. That's how I speak French, sir.'

'Fascinating, Jago. You must have been released at the Peace then.'

'That's right, sir. One day I was put aboard the Dover packet with three golden sovereigns in me pocket and told to go home. Me old widdered mother thought me the answer to her prayers.'

'You seem to be the answer to ours,' Frey said, picking up knife and fork.

'Oh yes, sorry, sirs. Don't you let me spoil your suppers.'

'What an odd tale,' Frey said with his mouth full.

'Yes, indeed.'

They were off Blanc Nez at dawn, and to the southward, running up from Boulogne, was a brig-sloop. 'British or French, I wonder?' Drinkwater asked as he came on deck in answer to Frey's summons.

'It doesn't much matter, sir, since we don't have the signal book aboard. If you've no objection, I suggest we run straight up and keep ahead of him.'

'Very well. With the wind the way it is this morning, if he's French we can escape to windward,' Drinkwater replied, for the breeze had veered a point or two into the north-north-west. 'We should have the legs of him.'

A few moments later it was clear that the brig-sloop had seen them and had decided to give chase, for she was setting studding sails with a speed that bespoke British nationality. However, they were already running along the sandy shore to the west of Calais, impelled by the hurrying tide, the hands busy loading the swivels and joking amongst themselves. A few moments later, as the sun rose above a low bank of cloud over the fields of France, the red ensign went aloft once more.

This morning there were no fishing-boats to mask them, nor did the earliness of the hour render them invisible to the vigilant eyes of the French gunners. As they ranged up towards the entrance of Calais harbour, shot plunged into the sea around them, raising tall columns of water on either beam.

But the speed of the tide under them combined with the swiftness of the cutter to frustrate the French artillery. The nearest they got to hitting *Kestrel* was to soak her decks with water. There were some early

144

morning net fishermen on the seaward jetty whose gear dropped over into the water, but they took scant notice of the British cutter. Years of war and blockade had inured them to such things and they were quite indifferent to the presence of a British ship so close to home.

When they had tacked off the breakwaters and stood back to the westwards, they found that the French gunners in the battery had shifted their attention to the brig-sloop. As they went about, the commander of the brig-sloop, seeing that the cutter was not French and running for shelter in to Calais, also tacked, frustrating the French gunners. Both vessels now stood clear of the coast, with *Kestrel* overhauling the brig.

Drinkwater closed his glass with a snap. '*Adder*, mounting eighteen guns,' he announced. As they surged up under the brig's quarter, Drinkwater saw her young commander at the starboard hance raise his speaking-trumpet.

'Cutter, 'hoy, what ship? You are not answering the private signal!'

Frey looked at Drinkwater and Drinkwater said simply, 'You are in command, Mr Frey.'

Frey handed the tiller over to the boatswain and went to the rail, cupping his hands about his mouth.

'Hired cutter *Kestrel*, Lieutenant Frey commanding, under special orders. We have no signal books but I have Captain Drinkwater aboard,' Frey added, to avoid being taken under the sloop-commander's orders. 'Have you seen any French men-of-war?'

'Who d'ye say is on board?'

'Captain Nathaniel Drinkwater . . .'

'Ask him who his commander is,' Drinkwater prompted.

'. . . Who desires to know who commands the *Adder*.'

'I am John Wykeham. As to your question, there are three corvettes in Boulogne, but heave to, if you please, I have something to communicate to Captain Drinkwater.'

'You had better do as he asks, Mr Frey.'

'Very well, Captain Wykeham. I shall come to the wind in your lee.'

Half an hour later the young Commander Wykeham clambered aboard *Kestrel* and looked curiously about him. Frey met him with a salute. The two men were of an age.

'May I introduce you to Captain Drinkwater, sir . . .'

The two men shook hands. 'I thought I was to be the only cruiser on the station, sir,' Wykeham said.

145

'Is that what you came to say?' Drinkwater asked.

'Not at all, it is just that your presence is something of a surprise, sir. And, forgive me for saying so, but your cutter is somewhat lightly armed for so advanced a post.'

Drinkwater smiled. 'She is a private yacht, sir, on hire for Government service, but come below, Commander Wykeham, and let us discuss what troubles you over a glass.'

Once in the tiny cabin with charged glasses, Wykeham asked, 'Your special Government service, sir . . .'

'Yes?'

'Does it have anything to do with a Russian officer?'

Drinkwater was quite unable to disguise his astonishment. After mastering his surprise he replied, 'Well, as a matter of fact, yes. Do you know of such a person?'

'I have a Russian officer on board. He came off to me by fishing-boat the day before yesterday. Speaks broken English, but excellent French, a language in which I have some ability. I gather he was caught in Paris by the return of Bonaparte and failed to get out in time. *Cherchez la femme*, I think. How did you know about him?'

'I had a message about him,' Drinkwater said obscurely, adding to mollify the obvious curiosity in the young commander's eyes, 'I have long had dealings of this sort with the enemy coast.'

'Ah, I see.'

Drinkwater smiled. 'I doubt whether you do, but your discretion does you credit. What is this fellow's name?'

'He claims to be a colonel, Colonel Ostroff. An officer of cossacks, or irregular horse. Is he your man?'

'I rather think he might be,' Drinkwater replied, his heart beating uncomfortably, 'but tell me something of the circumstances by which he made contact with you.'

Wykeham shrugged. 'I have been poking my nose in and out of Calais and Boulogne this past fortnight. My orders are to ensure no French men-o'-war escape to harry our shipping crossing to Ostend and if anything of force emerges either to engage or, if of superior force, to run across to Deal, make a signal to that effect, then chase until help arrives. Well, the evening before last, we were approached by a fishing-boat with which we had had some contact a few days earlier. Actually we paid good English gold for some *langoustines*, and I thought the avaricious buggers had come back for more, until, that is, they fished this Russkie lobster out of the hold. Green as grass he was,' Wykeham recollected, laughing. 'He asked for a passage to England, said he would pay his way and that he had been cut off in Paris and had only escaped to the coast by the skin of his teeth. Muttered something about bearing diplomatic papers.' Wykeham shrugged. 'I had no reason not to rescue the poor devil, so I took him aboard. He was anxious to be landed, but I told him he would have to wait. He was most indignant, but now fortunately you have arrived.'

'Well,' said Drinkwater, 'I can take him off your hands and leave the station to you.'

'That would be very satisfactory,' said Wykeham, rising, 'I shall send him over directly.'

Drinkwater followed Wykeham on deck and stood apprehensively as the brig's boat bobbed back over the waves and ran alongside. Fishing out his glass he levelled it and watched a figure, dressed in a sober coat and beaver, clamber down into it, whereupon the boat shoved off and headed back towards them. Drinkwater's heart thumped uncomfortably in his breast. He had a dreadful feeling of chickens coming home to roost, and his knees knocked, making him foolishly vulnerable to an indiscretion. He made an effort to pull himself together, but found himself in the grip of a visceral terror he had never before experienced.

Colonel Ostroff

Paralysis gripped Drinkwater as he watched the boat approach. He was robbed of the capacity to think, and stood like a loon, as though his brother's return automatically meant the ruin he had so greatly feared. He might, he thought afterwards, have acted in such a way as to bring ruin upon himself had not he recalled, quite inconsequentially to begin with, that this supposed stranger allegedly spoke poor English. He did, however, speak good French and that fact called for an interpreter. The presence of Jago would act as a brake upon any precipitate action the impetuous Edward might take. Drinkwater turned and called forward, 'Pass word for Jago to lay aft!'

Then he said to Frey, 'Send this man below with Jago, I'll interview him in the cabin. You may set course for Harwich.'

'Aye, aye, sir.'

Drinkwater hurried below, seated himself in the cabin and endeavoured to compose himself. A few moments later, with a clattering of feet on the narrow companionway, Jago led the newcomer into the cabin.

'Pray sit down, sir,' Drinkwater said coldly, waving to the bench settee that ran along the forward bulkhead as Jago rendered the invitation into French. Time had not been entirely kind to his brother and there was a moment when Drinkwater thought they might have got the wrong man. A wide scar ran across his cheek and bit deep into the left side of the nose. Unlike his elder brother, Edward seemed to have lost much hair.

'Ask him his name, Jago.' The exchange revealed the stranger to be

Colonel the Count d'Ostroff, of the Guard Cossacks, lately in Paris on the staff of Prince Vorontzoff.

'He asks for a pail, sir. Feeling sick.'

'You'd better get one.'

The gloom of the cabin after the daylight on deck clearly caused 'Ostroff' some difficulty in seeing his interlocutor, but the moment Jago had gone, he leaned forward and peered into Drinkwater's face. 'It is Captain Drinkwater, isn't it?' he asked with a low urgency.

'I am Captain Nathaniel Drinkwater, yes.'

'Don't you recognize me?' A touch of alarm infected the man's voice, which betrayed a trace of accent.

'Yes ...'

'Nat, I must talk to you.' 'Ostroff' swallowed hard, his face pallid, his eyes intense.

'Help me at least by maintaining this fiction until we reach Harwich,' Drinkwater said coolly.

'No! You cannot leave the French coast ...'

'I understand', Drinkwater said in a loud voice, overriding his brother as Jago and the bucket noisily descended the companionway, 'that you speak a little English.'

But the Colonel had no time to confirm or deny this. Instead he grabbed the bucket from Jago's hand and vomited copiously into it. As his head emerged he turned it to one side and, between gasps for breath, let out a stream of French. The only words Drinkwater recognized, and which seemed to be repeated with emphasis, were '*très important*'.

'He says, sir, that it is very important that you do not leave the coast. He says there are three people ashore who must be taken aboard before they are killed.'

'Did he ask Commander Wykeham of the *Adder* to bring them off?' The question was relayed and the Colonel nodded his head. 'And what did Commander Wykeham say?'

Drinkwater waited. It was a foolish question, he realized, but Edward was equal to the occasion, even though he was suffering. 'He, that's Commander Wykeham, did not seem to understand, he says, sir. That's why he, the Colonel here ... Do I call him the Colonel or the Count, sir?'

'Let's stick to Colonel, Jago.'

'Very good, sir. Well, that's why the Colonel came across to us so obligingly, sir. Thought we'd be an easier touch.'

'Yes, thank you, Jago.' Drinkwater caught Edward's eye and sighed. 'Who are these three fugitives? Victims of the change of government?'

The Colonel nodded and set the bucket down beside him. 'I speak good English,' he said, looking at Jago, 'I can speak directly to your captain, thank you.'

Jago turned from one officer to the other with an astonished expression on his face. 'Well, God bless my soul,' Drinkwater said hurriedly. 'I think you may go then, Jago. I'm obliged for your help.'

'Will you be all right, sir?' asked Jago, looking suspiciously at the Colonel.

'I think even I can defend myself against a seasick man, Jago, thank you.'

Jago withdrew with an obvious and extravagant reluctance. As he disappeared, Drinkwater held up his hand. 'The rules of engagement', he said in a low voice, 'are that you call me "Captain" and I refer to you as "Colonel". Now, I have news for you, your mistress is dead.' Edward's mouth fell open, then he retched again, a pitiful picture of personal misery of the most intense kind. Drinkwater felt a sudden wave of sympathy for his visitor, that instinct of protection of the older for the younger. Averting his face, he pressed on. 'It is only by the greatest good fortune for you that she died almost on my doorstep, otherwise you would have had to consign yourself to the ministrations of Commander Wykeham ...'

'*Mon Dieu* ... *La pauvre* Hortense ... How did it ...? I mean ...' Edward raised his unhappy, sweating face from the wooden bucket, all thoughts of Commander Wykeham far from his mind. A pathetic tear ran down his furrowed cheek and Drinkwater guessed he was near the end of his tether.

'You sent her off at a terrible risk ...'

'No! It was she who insisted on sailing in that damned *chasse marée*, insisted it would be all right, that she could contact you ... The bloody skipper promised he knew the English coast like the back of his hand.'

'Well, that's as may be. The lugger was dashed to pieces upon a shoal,' Drinkwater persisted. 'Hortense was washed up dead on the beach not far from my home, between the Martello towers at Shingle Street. We found her the next morning. She has been buried ... Well, never mind about that now. I am sorry, I had no idea you knew her.'

Edward shook his head and wiped his eyes. 'Damnation, Nat ...'

150

'Stop that!' Drinkwater snapped, 'Don't let your damned guard down! Not yet!' He veered away from the personal. There would be time to rake over their respective lives later. 'These confounded fugitives, I have no wish to appear inhuman, but what the devil have they to do with me?'

'If the Bonapartists get hold of them they will probably be shot.'

Drinkwater sighed. 'A lot of people have been shot in the last twenty-odd years, Colonel. I had the dubious honour of escorting King Louis back to his country a year ago. It seems our labours were in vain. From what I hear, the Bourbons did little to endear themselves to their subjects and those who support them deserve little sympathy . . .'

'These are not Bourbon courtiers, Captain,' Edward said, pulling himself together and speaking rapidly. 'They are the Baroness de Sarrasin and her two children, aged nine and ten. The Baroness was born into a liberal but impoverished noble family. She was very young during the worst excesses of the Revolution and, being a woman living in the remote countryside, escaped the worst. Later she married an officer in the army. He too was of noble blood, an *émigré* who returned when Napoleon invited the nobility back to France to join the army. He served Bonaparte with distinction and was created a Baron of the Empire, but last year he was on Marshal Marmont's staff and . . .' Edward shrugged.

'And?' Drinkwater prompted.

'You do not know what Marmont did?'

'Should I?'

'Marmont surrendered his entire Army Corps before Paris, precipitating the fall of Napoleon. The Baroness's husband was implicated in the capitulation and she is consequentially tainted as a result of *his* involvement. The loyalties of all members of the family have, as I believe you know, been confused and inconstant.'

'As *I* know?' Drinkwater queried with a frown. 'How should I know about this Baroness de Sarrasin and her family?'

'Since her husband's disgrace she has reverted to using her maiden name. The officer she married was named Montholon . . .'

Drinkwater frowned. 'Montholon! But that was Hortense's maiden name. So, he is Hortense's brother?'

'*Was* her brother. He was mysteriously killed while out riding soon after Napoleon reached Paris. The Baroness and her children were hidden by friends. You have to help her!'

'*Have to?* Is she your lifeline now?'

Edward shook his head. 'For God's sake,' he said, dropping his voice still further, 'I am neither an ingrate nor a monster. I have the chance to make some sort of reparation for the past. I need your help. If you cannot do it for me, pray do it for Hortense's sake. She said you were fond of her, that you had duelled with each other for years . . .'

'Did she?' Drinkwater said flatly. 'Duelled, eh? Is that how she put it? Well, I suppose 'tis as good a metaphor as any. Tell me how you met her. That strikes me as the oddest coincidence of all.'

'It is easily explained. Hortense was a friend of Madame Ney's. The Marshal had made something of a reputation in Russia and Prince Vorontzoff wished to meet him. I was on the Prince's staff and we attended one of Madame Ney's *soirées* . . .'

'Where you met Hortense, and thereafter matters took their natural course.' Drinkwater's tone was rueful.

'Quite so.'

'But how', Drinkwater went on, 'did you make the connection with me?'

'It was our intention to marry . . .'

'You and Hortense proposed to marry!'

Edward nodded. 'Yes. Does that surprise you?'

Drinkwater shook his head. 'No,' he said, giving a low, ironic laugh, 'no, not in the least. Pray continue.'

Edward shrugged. 'The war was over and I obtained my discharge from the Russian army. Paris was most congenial, and my long acquaintanceship and service with the Russian *ton* had taught me French. I thought in French and now hardly ever utter a word in English, though Prince Vorontozoff knew me to speak it and, as I was in his confidence, he occasionally conversed in it with me.'

'Did he know you to be an Englishman?'

Edward nodded. 'Yes, there are many foreign officers in the Russian service, though most are Germans. I gave out that I came from a family of merchants who had lived abroad for some time.'

'And by the time you met Hortense, you had proved yourself to the Russians.'

'It was difficult after Tilsit, but Prince Vorontzoff was wholly opposed to the alliance with Napoleon. He retired to the country and I went with him. He had Arab bloodstock and you will recall my interest in horses.'

Drinkwater nodded. 'But you have not told me how you linked Hortense with me.'

'Well, I wished to marry her and settle in Paris. I had provided for myself quite well.' Edward grinned. 'There were some rich pickings between Moscow and Paris, but that is by the by. Hortense struck me as being alone, despite her intimacy with Madame Ney. Baroness de Sarrasin was suspicious of her, due to the disgrace of her first husband, and it was clear she was the recipient of charity. The fall of Napoleon did not divide France, it fragmented the country. Many of the Marshals accepted the restoration of the Bourbons in return for the retention of their positions, titles and fortunes. Be that as it may, Hortense accepted me. In confidence, she told me she received a small competence from a source in England for services to the British government. I assumed this was to prove to me that her loyalties were sound. I also assumed she meant a pension and she might have lied, but she didn't, she said no, it was from a man she held in the highest esteem, though fate had made him an enemy. I thought, of course, that she had been this mysterious benefactor's mistress and that the enmity had grown up after some intimacy, but she denied this vehemently. Sheer curiosity led me to ask the name of her benefactor and sheer innocence led her to reply with our ... your surname.'

'God's bones, I had no idea ...'

'You see, the fact that she was an intimate of the Neys, and I knew she was the widow of a disgraced officer, Edouard Santhonax, yet had a pension for services to Great Britain, led me to conclude that her past was as complex as my own, beset by divided loyalties and so forth.' Edward rubbed a hand over his sweating chin. 'I suppose it gave us something in common; we were both what used to be called, with disparagement, "adventurers".'

'So you told her you were my brother?' Drinkwater asked, frowning.

'Yes, eventually. When Napoleon escaped from Elba and Paris was in an uproar. Friendships that seemed to cement the new order of the restored Bourbons dissolved overnight. Everyone seemed compromised, some more than others. There will have been no shortage of informers to jostle the petitioners at Napoleon's new court. Ney rode south to bring back Bonaparte in an iron cage and promptly went over to his old master. As for me, I was now a Russian living in a city which was set fair to turn hostile, and Hortense was among the tainted. In addition the Baroness arrived, her husband dead, her own fortunes overturned. She was now in the same position as her once despised sister-in-law. Hortense was fond of her brother's children. She had had none of her own . . .'

'I never thought of her as a matron . . .'

'She was not all ambition, you know, but she was brave and resourceful.'

'She suggested you contacted me, I suppose.'

Edward nodded. 'Yes. She regarded you as a person of some influence. I had no idea whether you were an admiral, but from our last meeting I recalled you were engaged in matters usually outside the competence of a common captain in the Royal Navy. Hortense knew that you and a certain peer were involved in clandestine activities, so naturally you seemed the only person we could turn to. This was as clear to me as to her, but over this fortuitous circumstance lay the foolish actions of my youth. I had compromised you fatally. I had to tell her we were related, and why I could not come directly. She was astonished, of course,' he said with a wan smile, 'and at first refused to believe that I could possibly be your brother. I think she thought the claim an extravagant attempt on my part to impress her, but she eventually saw the folly of that and I was able to persuade her by revealing the few facts I knew about you.' He sighed, then added, 'She knew you a long time ago, I gather.'

'I rescued her from the revolutionaries – oh, years ago – just as it appears I must do again with this Baroness of yours.'

'Nat . . .' Edward leaned forward, his face earnest, his voice very low. Grasping his brother's wrist he said, 'I have not forgotten the great debt I owe you for helping me escape the gallows . . .'

'You escaped justice, by God!'

'Maybe. But the rescue of the Baroness and her children is something in reparation.'

'A noble expiation', Drinkwater said with heavy irony, 'which you have already alluded to, but somewhat dependent upon the charity of your over-burdened kin.'

'And I have lost Hortense . . .'

'Perhaps we have both lost her.'

Edward frowned. 'You were never her lover . . .'

'Is that a question or a statement? But no, I never was,' Drinkwater said hurriedly. He paused a moment, then asked, 'Hortense was not the only woman in your life. Have you not left a wife in Russia?'

154

Edward shook his head. 'A mistress, yes, in fact two, both married. But I am not the complete smell-smock you think me.'

Drinkwater smiled. ' "Smell-smock", now there's an expression that betrays how long it is since you spoke English.' He sighed. 'Well, it is good to see you again. Our last meeting in Tilsit was, you will recall, dangerous enough . . .'

'Look, Nat . . .'

'For God's sake, do not relax your guard! Stop calling me that, or 'twill slip out!' Drinkwater snapped. 'I have a great deal . . .'

'I realize what you have done . . . Look, I have no intention of being anything other than a Russian officer. I can arrive in England as a Russian officer protecting the Baroness. I can spend the rest of my life speaking French. I can retire as the Baroness's protector, if she wishes, and live somewhere quietly. God knows I've endured my own share of frozen bivouacs! This might not quite equate to your cumulative privations, but I do not think there is a soul alive who would recognize Ned Drinkwater, do you?'

Drinkwater looked at his brother. 'How did you get that?' he asked, indicating his own nose. 'A sabre cut?'

Edward nodded. 'On the field of Borodino. A cuirassier of the 9th Regiment. They carried the Raevsky redoubt at the point of the sword. It was my misfortune to have borne a message into the place about thirty seconds before they arrived!'

Drinkwater rose and drew out a bottle and glasses from the locker. 'You will not know that it was Hortense's husband who tried to frustrate my return from Tilsit with the intelligence you obtained for us.'

'That is not possible!'

'And I killed him,' Drinkwater added.

'*Mon Dieu!*' Edward sat back, clearly astonished.

'I think', Drinkwater said slowly, handing Edward a glass, 'that your services at Tilsit might buy you immunity for your crime.'

Edward shrugged. 'Perhaps, but I should not wish to put the matter to the test. It would still cloud your own reputation. Aiding and abetting . . .'

'Yes, yes,' Drinkwater interrupted testily, 'those two words haunt me to this day.' He tossed off his own glass and rose to stand swaying in the cabin as *Kestrel* stood out to sea.

'I can stay Russian,' Edward almost pleaded. Drinkwater paused and the two men stared at each other in the shadowy cabin. 'What damned curious lives we have led,' Edward added reflectively.

155

'What damned curious times we have lived through,' Drinkwater replied.

'D'you remember what Mother used to say?'

'No, what in particular?'

'That "a friend is a friend at all times, but a brother is born for adversity".'

'Am I supposed to find that consoling? If so I find it confoundedly cold comfort. We are about to stick our heads into a noose, Colonel. By demonstrating so conspicuously outside Calais last night and this morning, in order that somehow you should be made aware of our presence, we have alerted the authorities very effectively. Now we must turn back and make a landing. I presume this Baroness and her children are in Calais itself?'

'No, at a small farm outside. You will need to get ashore to the east of the port if you don't wish to pass through Calais itself.'

'I certainly have no wish to do that. On an open beach, in an onshore wind, with a single small boat. You certainly were born for adversity, Colonel.' And with that Drinkwater left his brother with the bottle, the bucket and his thoughts, making his way on deck to try to put his own in order.

The Landing

Kestrel stood offshore until the coast of France had dropped over the horizon astern, then they altered course to the east-north-east and ran parallel with the shoreline before turning south again. Just as twilight occluded the day, they saw the faint glim of light at Calais and, allowing for the set of the tide, laid their course for a point some five miles east of the town. In the interim, Drinkwater had told Frey the bare essentials of the operation. The Russian officer, Colonel Ostroff, was responsible for aiding the escape of a French baroness and her two children. They were currently in a farmhouse outside Calais and a small party was to be landed on the beach that night. Frey's orders were to haul offshore and to wait. Ostroff had assured Drinkwater that they could reach the farmhouse, withdraw the fugitives and escape to the beach before daylight. The shore party was to consist of Drinkwater, Ostroff and Jago, for the latter's knowledge of the local dialect might prove useful.

Both Drinkwater and Frey knew that the operation hinged entirely upon their getting safely ashore and pulling the much larger party out again. It was one thing to land three men through the surf, men who might flounder ashore wet but in reasonable safety, but quite another to re-embark those three men after a night's march with the added encumbrance of a woman and two children. However, any alternative plan seemed too risky, and it was a business Drinkwater had some knowledge of. He therefore gave Frey careful instructions, and the entire crew of the cutter were made aware of the night's business.

As they ran in towards the coast again, they all ate a hearty meal of boiled ham, onions and carrots, accompanied by the last of the fresh bread. Ostroff and Drinkwater prepared a brace of pistols each which, with their swords, were neatly parcelled up with powder, ball and shot, and wrapped in oil-cloth. Drinkwater pulled grey trousers on over his boots but wore his old undress uniform coat and a plain bicorne hat. Ostroff remained in his dark civilian habit and Jago was loaned a blue coat.

There would be a quarter moon after midnight, though the night sky was cloudy and the blustery northerly breeze was chilly enough to drive people indoors after dark. The breeze would, however, also create a heavy surf on the beach, and Drinkwater tried to warn his brother of the problems they might encounter. It was an hour after dark before they finally closed with the coast, the boatswain plying the lead amidships. The proximity of the shore was announced by a steepening of the sea and the appearance of the pale strand with its fringe of rollers above which the spray smoked pallidly in the fitful starlight. Frey brought the cutter to, the boat was launched and the three men tumbled into it, Drinkwater amidships at the oars, Jago forward and Ostroff aft. Each man carried his oil-cloth bundle over his back on a line. The two oars were secured by lanyards so that they should not be lost, and in Jago's charge the boat's painter was secured to a long length of line flaked out on the cutter's deck, a line made up of several lengths which the cutter had provided and which included the unrove halliards from the main and jib topsails.

As soon as the boat had shoved off, Frey dropped the cutter's head-sails, scandalized her mainsail and let go her anchor, to hold *Kestrel* just long enough to let the boat, under the impetus of wind and sea, drift and be paddled towards the beach. Drinkwater gently back-watered, keeping the boat's head to sea, while Jago watched the line as the men on board *Kestrel* paid it out. The boat bobbed into the surf where it fell first one way and then the other, the drag on the line and a deft working of the oars by Drinkwater amidships keeping her from completely broaching to, though she rolled abominably and Edward shifted awkwardly, clearly unhappy with the violent motion and the occasional slop of water into her.

'Sit still, damn it!' Drinkwater commanded sharply. Suddenly, some twenty yards from the thundering surf, the boat jerked. The line was not long enough. Then, after a few moments, the vessel fell violently into the trough of a wave, evidence that a further length had been bent aboard *Kestrel* and was being paid out. Now they entered the last and most dangerous phase of their uncomfortable transit.

Drinkwater leaned back and turned his head. 'Be ready, Jago.' He had to shout to make himself heard as the waves now peaked and fell in breakers all about them. Rising high, the boat suddenly dropped and Drinkwater anticipated a bone-jarring crash as the keel struck the sand, but the next second, at a steep angle and lurching to one side as she went, she seemed to climb like a rocket as a roller ran ashore under her.

'Now!'

Jago jerked the boat's painter with all his might and they felt the bow tugged round as those aboard *Kestrel* ceased paying out and belayed the long line. They shot up and down, the spray filling the air about them, their hands, gripping the gunwales, soaked by water splashing into the boat.

'Over you go!' Drinkwater shouted at Edward, who sat hunched and immobile in the stern. The violent movement of the boat almost threw them out of its own accord, then he was gone, suddenly leaping and turning all at the same moment, so that a few seconds later Drinkwater saw the dark shape of him floundering ashore against the pale sand and the final wash of the breakers as they surged exhausted up the beach.

Now it was his turn. He shipped the oars and moved aft, taking his weight and bracing himself with his hands on the gunwales. He crouched on the stern thwart, facing the beach. In fact he felt his muscles cracking with the effort; he was too damned old for this sort of thing! In fact he was a bloody fool! He looked up. Edward was standing not thirty yards away, watching the boat as it sawed at the painter and rose up and crashed down in the very midst of the breakers. Drinkwater cleared his head and concentrated, seeking a moment as the boat descended when he should not have too much water beneath him. Sensing the time was right, he jumped over the stern, landed heavily up to his knees in water and ran forward as fast as he could, almost toppling as he went. He felt his brother grab him and he paused, panting.

'Damn you and your confounded Baroness,' he gasped without rancour. Edward chuckled and both men turned and watched for Jago to follow. 'You managed that very well,' Drinkwater said.

'It is just as well that I learned a few Cossack riding tricks,' Edward muttered shortly. 'Ah, here he comes.' Jago was caught by an incoming breaker which washed up around him, soaking him to the waist, but now they were ashore, their bundles dry and none of them much the worse for the experience.

'It'll be a damned sight more difficult leaving,' Drinkwater remarked, as they turned and walked directly up the wide slope of the beach. Half way up the sand they stopped and stood in a group. Drinkwater reckoned that with the night-glass, Frey would be able to see that they had made it and, sure enough, the boat was suddenly gone, plucked back to *Kestrel* by the long line. Before they struck inland Drinkwater took a last look seaward. He could just make out the dark shape where the cutter's scandalized mainsail stood out against the sky. The tide was making and had two hours yet to rise.

'Come on,' he said, and turned inland. They needed to find the coast road and a landmark to which they could return and which would lead them back to the right part of the vast beach which ran for miles, from Calais to Ostend and beyond, to Breskens and the great estuary of the Schelde, away to the east-north-east.

They found some pollarded willows which would serve their purpose, then Edward went ahead to discover the road. He said something in French which Jago repeated to Drinkwater. 'He says, sir, that it is as well he is an officer of light cavalry. An officer of light cavalry has to have an eye for the country.'

'I see,' said Drinkwater as, after employing this instinct for a few moments, Edward led them towards the track. Soon afterwards, with the sea lying to their right, they were tramping along the paved coast road in silence, with only the sound of the wind rustling the grass and brushwood in counterpoint to the deeper thunder of the surf on the shore.

They walked thus for about an hour. A few cows in meadows to the left of the *chaussée* looked up at them and lowed in mild surprise, but they might otherwise have been traversing an uninhabited country. Finally, however, they came upon a cluster of low buildings which revealed themselves as a small village strung out along the road and through which they walked as quietly as possible. They had almost succeeded when, at the far end, they disturbed a dog which began to bark insistently, straining at the extremity of its retaining chain. As they hurried on, the dog was joined by a clamorous honking of alarmed geese.

Ahead of him, Drinkwater heard Edward swear in French, then a window went up and behind him, with commendable presence of mind, Jago shouted something. It cannot have been very complimentary, for the disturbed villager yelled a reply to which Edward

160

quickly responded. The riposte made the window slam with a bang. Drinkwater forbore to enquire the nature of the exchange and hurried on. Once clear of the village the deserted *chaussée* stretched ahead of them again until it disappeared in a low stand of trees.

When they were well away from the village, Edward turned and made a remark to Jago. The seaman laughed and Drinkwater recognized Jago's response of '*Merci, M'sieur*'. They were the only words he had been able to interpret for himself.

'What did you say to that fellow, Jago?' Drinkwater asked.

'Only that he should strangle his fucking dog before I did, beggin' yer pardon, sir. Then he said honest folk should be in bed and the Colonel replied that honest folk should be marching to join the Emperor's eagles, not lying in bed next to their fat wives.'

'That was well done,' Drinkwater said admiringly. Such an exchange was scarcely going to arouse suspicions that foreigners were abroad.

'There is a turning somewhere ahead,' Edward said quietly in English. 'I am relying upon our finding it, for it leads directly to the farm we want, though it may still be some way off, for I never went east of it before.'

They marched on in silence and less than half an hour later discovered the turning, no more than a track joining the paved road. However, if Drinkwater had anticipated that the location of the track would bring them near their goal, he was mistaken, for they seemed to tramp inland for miles over slowly rising ground. Drinkwater began to tire. Like most seamen, while he could do without sleep for many hours and endure conditions of extreme discomfort, walking was anathema to him. The sodden state of his boots and stockings, the chafing of wet trousers and the chill of the spring night only compounded his discomfort, and already blisters were forming on his feet. Added to these multiple inconveniences, Edward set a fast pace, moving with such heartening confidence that, though Drinkwater was content to let him lead on, privately he cursed him. He began, too, to feel a mounting concern at the length of the return journey. The night was already far advanced and he fretted over the state of the tide and the conditions they would find on the beach when they returned to it.

At last, however, the shape of a building hardened ahead of them. As an enormous orange quarter moon lifted above a low bank of cloud to the east, they arrived on the outskirts of the farm within which the mysterious Baroness had taken refuge.

161

Edward left Drinkwater and Jago in the lee of a stone wall and proceeded alone to give notice of their arrival. As he vanished, another dog began to bark. The noise, unnaturally loud, seemed to fill the night with its alarum, but both men hunkered down and closed their eyes, speaking not a word but bearing their aches and pains in silence. It occurred to Drinkwater that he had got ashore almost dry-shod compared with Jago. The poor man must be in an extremity of discomfort.

'Are you all right, Jago?' he whispered.

'A little damp, sir, but nothing to moan about.'

'Very well,' Drinkwater replied, marvelling at the virtue of English understatement and settling himself to wait. He almost drifted off to sleep, but a few minutes later Edward returned and called them in. Drinkwater rose with excruciating pains in his legs and back. The warm sickly smell of cattle assailed them as they clambered over the wall and then passed through a gate in a second wall. Crossing a yard slimy with mud and cattle excrement, they entered the large kitchen of a low-ceilinged stone house. The room was warmed by a banked fire and dominated by a large, scrubbed table. Edward was speaking rapidly to an elderly man who wore a nightgown and a cap whose tassel bobbed as he nodded. Behind him, similarly attired, was a buxom woman pouring warm buttermilk into three stoneware mugs. To this she added a dash of spirits before shoving them across the table. Drinkwater muttered his formal '*Merci*', but Jago was more loquacious and the farmer's wife nodded appreciatively while her husband continued to engage Edward in what appeared to be a violent argument.

'A little bargaining and complaining, sir,' explained Jago over the rim of his steaming mug, divining Drinkwater's incomprehension. Suddenly the door behind them opened. The sharp inrush of cold night air was accompanied by the terrifying appearance of a large bearded figure, wrapped about in a coat and wearing oversize boots. Turning at this intrusion, Drinkwater's tired brain registered extreme alarm, and he was about to reach for a pistol when Edward's response persuaded him it was unnecessary.

'Ah, Khudoznik, there you are ...' Edward caught his brother's eye. 'My man Khudoznik. He is a Cossack.'

Drinkwater recognized the type, and the faint smell that came with him, from his time at Tilsit. 'You might have mentioned him,' Drinkwater retorted, looking at the Russian who stared back. Then they were distracted by the swish of skirts. The Baroness, a pretty but pale and frightened blonde woman with her two children, all in cloaks, appeared from the door guarding the stairs and seemed to fill the kitchen with a nervous fluster. She looked anxiously at the strangers, darted an even more suspicious glance at the silent Cossack and, though Edward stepped forward to embrace her and reassure her, continued to regard them all with deep concern.

Edward briefly indicated Drinkwater, referring to him as '*Le Capitaine Anglais*'. The woman half acknowledged Drinkwater's bow, then swung round and gabbled at Edward, but he was up to the occasion.

'*Silence, Juliette!*' He turned to the children. '*Allons, mes petits! Allons!*' He passed a handful of coin to the farmer and indicated the door. Drinkwater emerged into the stink of the yard once more. Five minutes later they were heading north along the track which was now bathed in pale moonlight.

Inevitably, the return journey took longer. Neither the Baroness nor her children were capable of moving at the speed of the four men. The girl whimpered incessantly until, without a word, Edward took her hand from her mother's and, clasping it in his own, led her on. After a few hundred yards she tripped over a flint in the track, pitched to her knees and began to wail.

Edward's palm covered her mouth as he picked her up. Whispering into her ear, he scarcely slackened his pace, giving the Baroness no time to commiserate with her unhappy daughter. The girl clung to his neck. The boy tramped doggedly on. Drinkwater had heard Edward say something encouraging to him in which the words '*soldat*' and '*marche*' were accompanied by '*mon brave*'. After a while Jago fell in alongside the lad and, from time to time, spoke briefly in French. The boy responded, and Drinkwater judged from his tone of voice that the lad was not uninfluenced by the adventure of the night. He himself was left to offer the Baroness his arm. She accepted at first, but they had dropped somewhat behind when the girl fell and, having relinquished it in order to catch up, she did not seek his support again, politely declining further assistance. Despite this she made a greater effort to keep up, though Drinkwater thought she found the plodding presence of the Cossack at the rear of the little column intimidating.

Drinkwater now began to consider how on earth they were going

163

to get the frightened trio and the Russian into the boat and soon decided that the method he had chosen would prove inadequate. He had mentioned this possibility to Frey who, with the change of tide, would have his own work cut out in remaining as near as possible to the landing place without dragging his anchor. The tide would be on the ebb now and, if they were much delayed, Frey might have to haul *Kestrel* off into deeper water. Drinkwater tried to console himself with the thought that they were making quite good progress, all things considered, though he wondered how long Edward could carry the girl. The wind had dropped a little too, he thought, and that was all to the good.

When they gained the *chaussée*, they turned right and, reaching the low stand of trees, they paused for a short break. Something seemed to be bothering Edward, for while the others caught their breath under the trees, he went out into the middle of the road, scuffing the dust with his right boot. Drinkwater pushed himself off from the tree trunk against which he had been leaning and approached his brother.

'Is something amiss?' he asked in a low voice.

'Yes,' said Edward, pointing at the ground. 'Since we were here last, some horses have passed through.'

'Cavalry horses?'

'Yes. Quite a lot of them too, I would say.'

'Going which way?'

'East. The wrong way for us.'

'God's bones!' Drinkwater considered the matter a moment. 'We shall be all right if we remain behind them, though, surely?'

'Let us hope so,' Edward responded grimly, 'but if I were you, I'd get your arms ready before we move off.'

'I'll tell Jago, but we don't want to alarm our friends.'

'They're alarmed already.'

'Your Cossack might prove useful. Is he armed?'

'He has a pistol.'

'How long has he been in your service?'

'Some seven years now. He attached himself to me after the battle of Eylau. Khudoznik is a nick-name meaning "artist". 'Tis a tribute to his abilities at foraging.'

'He will be quite unfamiliar with the sea, I imagine.'

'That, brother, is why I did not tell you of him before.'

164

The Fugitives

Before they set off again, Edward warned them to walk at the edge of the *chaussée* in single file and to drop into the grass beside the road at his signal. If they hesitated, he emphasized, they would be lost. Drinkwater was aware that he impressed this point upon the Baroness and that she nodded in acknowledgement, her face clear in the moonlight.

Drinkwater looked up at the sky. The cloud had almost gone, leaving only low banks gathered on the horizon. 'Of all the damnedest luck,' he muttered to himself. Then they set off again.

It seemed to the anxious and weary Drinkwater that they marched in a dream. The ribbon of road, set for the most part along a raised eminence and flooded by moonlight, appeared to make them hugely conspicuous and quite unavoidable. Their gait was tired and they stumbled frequently, the Baroness immediately in front of Drinkwater falling full length at one point. He helped her up, but she shook him off and, as their eyes met, he could see by the line of her mouth that she was biting back tears of hurt, rage and humiliation.

They walked like automata, their brains numbed by fear and exhaustion. Robbed of all professional instinct ashore, Drinkwater had abdicated responsibility to Edward whose military experience was, he realized with something of a shock, clearly extensive. Watching their rear, his brother would also, from time to time, run on ahead on some private reconnaissance. Once he stopped them and they crouched in the grass, unaware of what had troubled their leader, but after a few terrifying minutes which woke

165

them all from their personal catalepsies with thundering hearts, Edward waved them on again and they resumed the bone-weary-ing plod-plod of the march. In a curious sense the return appeared to be both longer and shorter than the outward journey. Though they seemed to have been traversing the high-road for half a life-time, quite suddenly they were approaching the huddle of build-ings that formed the farm on the outskirts of the village and where the exchange of repartee had amused them earlier. Matters seemed less risible now.

Looking anxiously ahead, with apprehensions about the geese and dog uppermost in their minds, they had almost forgotten their rear when the Cossack suddenly ran forward to join Edward. The two men abruptly crouched down. At the peremptory wave of Edward's arm, the rest of the party dropped into the grass again, sliding down the shallow embankment into the damp shadows. Raising his head, Drinkwater caught a glimpse of his brother staring back the way they had come. Then he heard a whisper in French, loosely translated by Jago. 'Keep absolutely still, sir. There's someone coming up astern.'

As he lay down and closed his eyes, Drinkwater felt the beat of the horse's hooves through the ground. He remained motionless as the noise peaked. The regular snort of the horse, the jingle of harness and the clatter of accoutrements seemed almost on top of them. Then the odorous wind of the passing of man and beast swept over them and was gone. Drinkwater looked up. The single horseman had not noticed them.

Edward wormed his way back down the line to where Drinkwater lay. 'That was a hussar orderly,' he whispered. 'My guess is that he had orders for the body of horse which passed along this road earlier. They may be in the village ahead or they may have passed on, but we cannot take any chances. I am going forward to have a look. You remain here with Khudoznik.'

'Very well, but remember we do not have much time. The tide . . .' But Edward was gone and Drinkwater felt a sudden deep misgiving. He turned and wriggled forward to warn the Baroness through Jago. 'Explain to her that our ship is not far away.'

'Aye, aye, sir.' Jago did as he was bid, then came back to Drinkwater.

'Beg pardon, sir.'

'What is it?'

'The lady says, "nor is the dawn", sir.'
'No.'

They must all have slept or dozed. Drinkwater was vaguely aware of the girl and the Baroness moving away at one point. Realizing the personal nature of their intended isolation, he made no move to remonstrate. He was too stiff and chilled. The next thing he knew, it was growing light. Seized by a sudden alarm, he realized they could wait no longer. It was clear that the village was full of French cavalry and that, presumably, Edward had remained concealed somewhere to keep them under observation and watch for when they moved on. But suppose something had happened to Edward? Suppose he had been taken prisoner?

Drinkwater was now fully awake, his mind racing, his concern for Frey's predicament paramount. Edward was a plausible bugger, he spoke excellent French and would probably come to little harm. As for himself, the Baroness and her children, their soiled presence on a coastal road in northern France would be far less easily accounted for. As for the Cossack, what reasonable explanation would any French officer accept on *his* score? After all, Drinkwater himself wore a sword, had a pair of pistols stuck uncomfortably in his belt and wore the uniform coat of a British post-captain. Cautiously he wriggled up the slope. The road remained empty as far as he could see, but the roofs of the village seemed much nearer now and there were wisps of smoke rising above them. People were on the move, and whether they were villagers stoking their stoves or hussars lighting bivouac fires was immaterial. They effectively blocked Drinkwater's escape route.

Where the hell was Edward? Drinkwater cast aside the peevish reliance on his brother. Whatever had happened to him, it was clear that Drinkwater himself must now take matters into his own hands. There was only one thing to do.

'Jago!' he hissed. There was a movement in the grass and the seaman's bleary-eyed face appeared, looked round and realized it was daylight. 'We are going to have to go down to the beach and walk along it, below the line of this road. There's no other way of getting round the village. The Colonel seems to have disappeared. Tell the Baroness to get ready to move. And be quick about it.'

'Aye, aye, sir.'

Drinkwater rose to his feet and jerked his head at the Cossack. The man understood, looked round and peered in the direction of the

167

village. Then he shook his head. Drinkwater shrugged with massive exaggeration, though it understated his irritation at finding himself saddled with the man. The Russian indicated the village and Drinkwater turned away. If the damned fool went into the village it might distract the French cavalry, but it might also precipitate a search for more odd characters wandering about the roads.

Drinkwater's head was just below the level of the *chaussée*. He raised it cautiously and stared north. The rough scrub gave way to sand dunes about half a mile away. They would have to move quickly, before the whole damned world and his wife were awake! '*Allons!*' he said, breaking cover.

Despite the danger of leaving their place of concealment, he felt better once they began to move. Their cramped and chilled bodies protested at the demands of walking, but by degrees the activity proved beneficial. Low willows broke the landscape and periodic halts in their shadows revealed that they were free from pursuit. The first stop also revealed the lonely figure of Khudoznik following them. Once they had passed the dunes, Drinkwater considered they would be relatively safe and he tried to pick a route which would place an intervening dune between themselves and the village, regretting, in a brief and bitter moment of irony, that he did not have a light cavalry officer's eye for the country. He would have removed much anxiety from his mind had he done so, for in fact the village was already hidden behind a shallow rise, protected from the icy blasts off the North Sea. Obscured by this low undulation, they reached the dunes without being detected.

Their going slowed as they dragged through the fine sand and Drinkwater ordered a halt, turning back for fifty yards to see if he could observe anything of Edward. The line of the road formed the horizon and was clear against the lightening sky, hard-edged and quite empty. It promised to be a fine spring day and the air was already full of the multiple scents of the earth. Of Edward there was no sign but when he reached the others it was clear the Baroness was in a frenzy of anxiety.

'The lady wants to know where Colonel Ostroff is, sir. She says she won't move without him.'

'Tell the lady Colonel Ostroff is reconnoitring the enemy and that she is to come on with us.'

He waited while this exchange took place. It was clear from the

Baroness's expression and attitude that she did not take orders from English sea-officers. Jago's interpretation confirmed this. 'She says, sir, that she wants to go back.'

'Very well.' Drinkwater passed the woman and scooped up the girl. 'Tell her,' he said over his shoulder as he strode away, 'she may do as she damned well pleases.' The girl writhed in his arms and a blow from her fist struck him across the nose just as her foot drove into his groin so sharply that he swore at her with ungallant ferocity. She froze in his arms, staring at him with such horror that he felt sick with hunger, pain and fear. He had no business to be here; he was too old for such quixotic adventures; such things were part of his youth. He stumbled on, fighting the nausea that her assault had caused. A few minutes later he had to pause again and looked back. Jago was following him with the Cossack. A hundred yards behind, the Baroness and her son had been arguing, but now they began to follow. Turning again, he stumbled on, the sand dragging at his feet. Then, looking up, he caught sight of the hard grey line of the sea-horizon.

'Now, Frey,' Drinkwater muttered as he paused and waited for the party to close ranks, 'it all depends upon you.'

As the expanse of sea opened before them, Drinkwater saw the cutter. Behind him he heard Jago telling the Baroness, for whom the sight of the limitless ocean was a profound shock, that their ship was in sight. So insubstantial a vessel as the little *Kestrel* scarcely mollified the poor woman, who had difficulty seeing it in the twilight. Reduced by anxiety and exertion, she fainted. As for the Russian, he stood staring uncomprehendingly at the seascape before him.

'*Attendez-vous votre mère!*' Drinkwater snapped at the young boy as he set the wailing and struggling girl down and turned to Jago. 'Get some brushwood, anything to make a fire to attract Lieutenant Frey's attention!'

The cutter was some four or five miles to the north-east of them, presumably lying offshore not far from the point at which they had been landed. It was clear Frey had had to get under weigh and had been unable to remain at anchor all night so close inshore, but Drinkwater had anticipated that. Although *Kestrel* was apparently some way off, the tide, ebbing along the coast to the westward, would help Frey reach them, and the distance along the coast which he would have to cover was not as far as it looked. If only they could make themselves seen, they had a reasonable chance yet. Fire without smoke was what they required, for it was a certainty that Frey would be on the look-out for them.

Ignoring the groans from the unfortunate Baroness, Drinkwater bent to the task of building a fire as Jago brought in driftwood and detritus from the last spring high-tide line. The Cossack, seeing what they were doing, turned from the sea and joined Jago in the hunt for fuel. As Drinkwater worked at building the pile of combustible material, splitting kindling and laying a trail of gunpowder from his pistols into the heart of it, he was aware of the boy standing beside him.

'*M'sieur,*' the lad demanded. '*M'sieur . . .*'

Drinkwater looked up and then, cutting short the boy's protests about the honour of his mother, explained in his poor French, '*M'sieur, regardez le bateau.*' He pointed at the distant cutter, then at the heap of wood before him. '*Je désire faire un feu, eh? Comprenez?*' He turned again to the cutter and made the gesture of a telescope to his eye. '*Le bateau regarde la côte. Eh bien! Embarquez!*' Drinkwater made a gesture that embraced them all.

The boy looked at him coldly.

Drinkwater inclined his head with a smile and reached for his pistol just as Jago arrived with more fuel. 'Explain to the boy', he said, as he went on building the fire, 'that I heartily esteem his mother, she is a brave and courageous woman and his sensibilities do him credit, but we have no time to argue and scant time for courtesies. Tell him also, that many, many years ago, I rescued his father from a French beach near Cherbourg and that he may trust me to do my utmost for him and his family. *And*, when you have done all that, tell him to convey this to his mother and sister and ask them to do exactly as I say in the next hour. Impress upon him that I require their absolute trust and obedience. And tell him that if he is not satisfied, I shall be happy to exchange pistol shots with him when we reach England.'

Drinkwater looked up at the boy and smiled as Jago rattled off his translation. The expression on the boy's face metamorphosed several times and then he drew himself up and gave a short bow before withdrawing towards his mother and sobbing sister.

'What is your name, my boy?' Drinkwater called in English, and Jago obligingly translated.

'Charles.'

'Well, Charles, *bonne chance!*' Bending to the powder trail, Drinkwater pronated his wrist so that the pan and frizzen of the pistol

170

lay over the tiny black heap, and pulled the trigger. There was a crack and flash, then a flaring as the powder caught and carried the sputtering fire into the heart of the pyramid of wood. A moment later a wild crackling was accompanied by small but growing flames licking up through the pile.

'Don't let us down, Frey, don't let us down,' Drinkwater intoned, raising his eyes to the distant *Kestrel*.

The fire flared up wonderfully, throwing out a welcome heat that drew the Baroness and her daughter towards it. Jago kept them away from the seaward side as Drinkwater stared at the cutter for the first sign that they had seen the fire and knew it for the beacon it was. He walked down the beach, detaching himself from it in the hope that they might see his figure.

For a long time, it seemed, nothing happened. *Kestrel* lay with her bowsprit to the north-north-east, stemming the tide, hove to on the starboard tack and standing offshore slightly, trying to maintain station. It was the worst aspect from which to attract attention. The fire began to die down, though Jago revived it with more driftwood. It died down a second time and Drinkwater was about to give up when he saw *Kestrel* swing round and curtsey to the incoming sea as she tacked and paid right off the wind which had now veered more to the eastwards. He hardly dared hope for what he so earnestly desired, but a few moments later she was headed south-westwards and Drinkwater saw a red spot mount upwards to the peak of the gaff.

'British colours!' he muttered to himself, and then he turned and walked back up the beach to the huddle of fugitives, unable to conceal his satisfaction.

'They have seen us,' he announced. And as they watched, sunlight flooded the scene, turning the grey sea to a kindlier colour and chasing away the fears of the night.

Escape

Drinkwater hurriedly kicked the fire out. '*Allons!*' he said and began to lead off down the beach. The sight of *Kestrel* running along the coast towards them relieved him sufficiently to spare a thought for Edward. If his brother had encountered trouble, there was little he could do to help. If not, then Edward must by now, with the coming of the sunrise, have realized that the party could not lie alongside the high road and that Drinkwater would quite naturally gravitate towards the sea. In either case, Edward's salvation lay in his own hands. At the worst they could cruise offshore until, somehow, he re-established contact.

The five of them had reached the damp sand which marked the most recent high water and stood waiting patiently while *Kestrel* worked down towards them, looking increasingly substantial as she approached beyond the line of breakers. Drinkwater took Jago to one side as they assessed the size of the incoming waves.

'This isn't going to be easy, Jago.'

'No, sir.'

'They're frightened and they're hungry. Trying to get them to clamber into the boat is going to prove impossible, so I want you to take the girl and I'll take the Baroness. We will lift them over the gunwale and I want you to go off first. I'll follow with the boy. Don't come back for me. Stay aboard . . .'

'But sir . . .'

'Jago, you're a good fellow and you've done more than necessary tonight, but don't disobey orders.'

'Aye, aye, sir.' Jago paused, then asked, 'What about that bearded fellow, sir? Who is he?'

'He's Colonel Ostroff's Cossack servant and God knows how we are going to get him into the boat. Perhaps we shall just put a line round him and drag him out to the yacht.' Drinkwater turned and looked along the beach. The vast expanse of strand stretched for miles and remained deserted. 'So far, so good,' he said, 'but I don't know how long our luck will last.'

'No, sir.'

'Now go and pick up the girl, for the boat's coming.'

Frey had not wasted time. He had towed the boat astern and now sent it in on its line, a single man at the oars as instructed, to work it inshore across the tide. Drinkwater ran back up the beach and saw a figure sitting at *Kestrel*'s cross-trees. Watching the bobbing and rolling approach of the boat he waited until she was in the breakers and then flung up his hands and waved his arms frantically above his head. The figure in the cutter's rigging waved back and, somewhere out of sight of Drinkwater, beyond the curling wave-crests, they ceased paying out the line and the boat jerked responsively. The tide had taken the thing down the coast a little but the wind was just sufficiently onshore to drive it into the shallows with a little assistance from the oarsman. Hurrying back to the waiting fugitives, Drinkwater nodded to Jago. The seaman turned to the boy and commanded him to stay put, then he scooped up the girl and began to wade into the sea.

'*Madame, s'il vous plâit ...*' and without further ceremony, Drinkwater lifted the Baroness and followed Jago, leaving the Cossack to shift for himself. At once a wave almost knocked him over. The woman screamed as she took the brunt of it, stiffening in his arms. The sudden shock of the cold water and the spasm of the Baroness caused him to stumble and he fought to keep his balance as he lugged the greater weight of her sodden clothing. The mangled muscles of his wounded shoulder cracked painfully, but he managed to keep his footing. Jago, ahead of him, was now up to his armpits in the water but was able to lift the terrified girl above his head and deliver her roughly into the keeping of the oarsman.

Drinkwater struggled forward, the water alternately washing him back and forth, tugging at his legs one second, then climbing his body to thrust at his chest. It swirled about his burden so that he half-floated, half-floundered, while the frightened woman clutched him and averted her face. Jago was splashing back towards him, giving him an arm as he shuffled, bracing himself as every successive wave washed up to him. Then he was in the breakers, close to the boat, and Jago and he had the woman between them. The boat seemed to come close, then a wave rolled in and the boat soared into the sky. Drinkwater felt the insupportable weight of the wave knock him over. He fell backwards, oddly cushioned by the water, but with the gasping Baroness fighting free and both of them lying in the receding wave, undignified in their extreme discomfiture as they fought for their footing.

Jago had also been knocked down, but the two men, soaked and now shivering, grabbed the Baroness and helped her to her feet. In the wake of the steep breaker, the sea fell away and in the brief lull Drinkwater was yelling: 'Now, Jago! Now!'

The two men struggled together, clasped their arms beneath the protesting woman's rump and hove her up. The boat loomed again, then fell and was suddenly, obligingly close to them, offering them an instant of opportunity. They pitched the woman in with a huge, unceremonious heave as the oarsman trimmed the craft. The Baroness cried out with the impact and the hurt, while a moment later Drinkwater was flat on his back, fighting for breath as he dashed the water from his eyes. Ten yards away the transom of the boat flew up into the air with Jago clinging to it, kicking with his feet.

The oarsman was pointing and shouting, but Drinkwater, struggling to his feet, waved for them to get out, shrieking the order and then turning to make his sodden way back to the shore and the others. Wiping his eyes, he hoped that the ordeal of the Baroness had not completely unnerved her son.

As he waded through the shallows, he saw the young boy watching the departing boat as the line from *Kestrel* plucked it out into deeper water. Alongside him, his face obscured by his beard, Khudoznik stared expressionlessly. Drinkwater tried to smile reassuringly, but the smile froze on his lips, for beyond the boy, a line of horsemen spread out across the sand.

They were some way off and Drinkwater spun round to try and gauge how long it would be before the boat came in again. It would take some time to get the Baroness and her daughter aboard *Kestrel* and perhaps they had not yet seen the approaching cavalry in their preoccupation. *Kestrel* was, after all, only a yacht and had but a handful of men as her crew who would be occupied in dispositions they had made on the assumption that this evacuation would take place in the dark, uninterrupted by the intervention of any enemy.

He ran a little way up the beach in an attempt to gain some elevation to see what was happening, but *Kestrel's* waterline remained out of sight behind the cresting breakers, though a dark cluster of men amidships could be seen actively engrossed in some task. He looked over his shoulder. The cavalry were quite distinct now, advancing at a gallop, and he felt the knot of panic wring his guts. His pistols were soaked and empty, his sword his only defence. He hurried back to the boy who, in turning to follow him, had seen the cavalry. So had the Russian.

'*M'sieur, regardez!*'

Drinkwater nodded at the boy. 'Where in the name of Hades is that boat?' he muttered, hurrying back. Suddenly he saw the transom on top of a wave and Jago's face above it waving the oars as he backwatered furiously.

'Come on, son!' Drinkwater cried, holding out his fist and splashing forward, waving at Khudoznik to follow. He felt the boy's hand take his and the two of them splashed forward, first up to their knees in the water and then, suddenly, to their waists, then their breasts.

Faint cries came from behind. Drinkwater thanked heaven for fine soft sand – horses could get through the stuff no quicker than humans – but his moment of congratulation was short-lived. Out of the corner of his eye Drinkwater could see that off to the right, half a dozen horsemen had ridden directly down to the firm wet sand and were thundering towards them at full gallop. Jago drifted closer and Drinkwater thrust the boy forward.

'Tell him to hold on, Jago! Don't try and get us aboard!'

'Aye, aye, sir.'

The boy understood. The two of them splashed and kicked and grasped the gunwale of the boat and then they succumbed to the feeling of being drawn through the water as the line was hauled in. After what seemed an eternity Drinkwater felt them bump alongside *Kestrel*. He called for a rope with a bowline to be dropped down and, passing his arm round the boy's waist, got him to put his head and shoulders through the bight as he spat water and kicked with his feet.

'*Courage, mon brave!*' he shouted in his ear. The boy was shivering uncontrollably but above him he could see the white face of his mother. Blood ran down her cheek from a gash on her forehead but she had extended her hand in a gesture of supplication and she wore an expression of such eloquent encouragement and bravery that Drinkwater fought back his emotions. 'Haul away!' he bellowed harshly as he waited his own turn, watching the boy's spindle shanks lifted out of the sea above his own bobbing head.

'Welcome back, sir,' Frey called down to him. 'Where's the Colonel?'

'We lost contact,' Drinkwater said, but then Frey looked away as the first ball flew overhead.

'Here, sir!' The bowline dropped alongside Drinkwater. He let go of the boat and struggled into the loop. The next second the line was cutting excruciatingly into his back and under his armpits as he was drawn high out of the sea. For a moment he stared at the cutter's wildly pitching deck and the great quadrilateral of her slatting mainsail, then as he descended he span slowly round. The beach looked suddenly very close and there in the surf was the Cossack Khudoznik running alongside a single horseman and pursued by a semi-circle of hussars.

One hussar had lost his shako and another was already dead on the sand. A second fell as Khudoznik ran in among the horse's legs, grabbed a boot and swiftly detached it from the stirrup, pitching the trooper off his horse which he then mounted with consummate agility. Alongside him the single horseman tossed aside his pistols and drew a sword. It was Edward.

A moment later Drinkwater was lowered to the deck.

'That's the Colonel, sir!' shouted Frey, pointing.

'I know!' Drinkwater turned to find Jago alongside. 'Get the Baroness and her brats below, Jago. Mr Frey, clear the left flank with one of the swivels. But Frey was already pointing the after port swivel, and its sharp bark sprayed the beach with small shot.

Drinkwater threw his legs over the cutter's rail and dropped back into the boat. The swivel had struck one of the hussars from the saddle and hit a horse. Miraculously it had left both Edward and Khudoznik unscathed, but the following shot from the forward swivel was less partial. Edward's horse foundered beneath him and he threw himself clear as it staggered and sank to its knees with a piercing whinny. Khudoznik had whipped the pistols from the saddle holsters and was laying about him when a second shot from the after gun drove the hussars back. By now a frantic Drinkwater, his teeth chattering, was paddling backstroke towards the beach, shouting at Edward.

'Run into the sea, Ned! For God's sake don't stay there!'

A hussar bolder than the others, an officer by the look of his fur shabraque, spurred forward, intent on sabring the fugitive, but Edward still had his sword and cut wildly with it so that the officer's horse reared. At the same moment Khudoznik drove his own mount directly at the attacker. Just as Edward avoided the low thrust made by the hussar officer under his mount's neck, horse and rider crashed to the sand under the impact of the Cossack's terrified horse. With its bit sawing into its mouth, it reared above the dismounted hussar and its wildly pawing hooves struck the unfortunate man.

Edward staggered back and saw for the first time that it was Khudoznik looming above him. He shouted at him in Russian, but the next second the Cossack lurched sideways as a carbine ball struck him in the side of the skull. Khudoznik slipped from the saddle and landed heavily on the wet sand. Edward took a single glance at him, then turned and ran into the sea.

No more than ten yards separated them now, then Drinkwater felt the boat strike the bottom with a jarring thud that made his own teeth snap together. Edward seemed to tower over him before the next wave passed under the boat and then he had his arms over the transom and Drinkwater was jerking the painter and saw it rise dripping from the water as the hands aboard *Kestrel* lay back on it. As they began to draw out through the surf followed by a few balls from the hussars' carbines, Drinkwater met his brother's eyes as Edward gasped for breath.

'Where the hell did you get to?' Drinkwater asked.

'The devil . . .' Edward retorted, but his explanation was cut short. Drinkwater felt the ball strike the boat through the body of his brother. Over Edward's shoulder, he saw a hussar lower his carbine and reload.

Now that the boat was clear of their field of fire, the swivels aboard *Kestrel* opened up again behind them, the shot buzzing past overhead as Drinkwater lunged aft to grab Edward.

'Hold on, Ned! Hold on!' A thick red stream ran astern of the boat.

'Too late, Nat. My back's shot through.' He looked up and Drinkwater saw the last flicker of the departing soul. 'No trouble . . . to you now . . .' he gasped as he relinquished his grasp upon the boat and upon life itself. Drinkwater tenaciously clung on to his brother as he was once more pulled alongside *Kestrel*. Ned was dead before they reached the cutter's side, but they dragged his body aboard and laid him in the scuppers.

'Are you all right, sir?' Frey asked as Drinkwater almost fell over

Kestrel's low gunwale on to the deck, while a last carbine ball whined overhead.

'Yes, yes.' He looked down at Edward. The eyes were already glazed, opaque. 'Poor fellow', he sighed, as he bent down and closed the lids. Then he stood and looked at Frey. 'Do you get under weigh now, Mr Frey.'

'Those devils have given up now,' Frey said matter-of-factly, jerking his head at the shore. Drinkwater turned to see the hussars tugging their mounts' heads round and turning away. Several of the horses had bodies slung over their saddles. One, that of the Cossack nicknamed Khudoznik, lay exposed by the retreating tide.

'You need to dry yourself, sir,' Frey advised, 'you look blue with cold.'

'What's that? Oh . . . oh, yes, I suppose I am a trifle . . .' Drinkwater realized he was chilled to the marrow and quite done in. He stared again at Edward's body, reluctant to leave it. 'We'll take him home and bury him,' he said to Frey, as he moved on shaky legs towards the companionway.

'It's a long way from Russia,' Frey remarked.

'Yes. But perhaps that does not matter too much.'

The Chase

'Out of the frying pan, Mr Frey,' Drinkwater said, lowering the glass. Astern of them, the sharply angled sail of a lugger broke the line of the horizon with a jagged irregularity as the French *chasse marée* came up, carrying the wind with her. Seven miles further north *Kestrel* experienced nothing more than a light breeze. 'Almost the only circumstances', Drinkwater muttered angrily, 'which could place us at a real disadvantage.'

Frey turned from his place by the tiller as Drinkwater looked aloft, but they had every stitch of canvas set and no amount of tweaking at the sheets would improve their speed. Drinkwater cast about him. 'They must have slipped past *Adder*. At any other time we might have expected a British cruiser in the offing but all we have in sight at the moment are a couple of fishermen ...'

He raised his glass again. It was damnably uncanny. The lugger was carrying the wind with her, sweeping up from the south, and would be quite close before they felt the benefit of it themselves. He looked at Frey. A brief glance was enough to tell him that he was seething at their ill-fortune. He would be dog-tired now after a sleepless night, as were the rest of them, Drinkwater himself included. Poor Frey, *Kestrel* was a pathetic enough command; to lose her to the enemy like this would be a worse blow to his pride than the loss of the yacht to Drinkwater!

Perhaps there was something they might do, though.

'I'm going below for a few moments, Mr Frey.'

'Aye, aye, sir.'

In the cabin the Baroness and her daughter were fast asleep, wrapped in blankets while their outer garments dried in the rigging above. The boy Charles lay on the settee awake, his face pale with seasickness, his eyes huge and tired. Drinkwater smiled, trying to convey reassurance to the young lad. He smiled wanly back at him. 'That's the spirit,' Drinkwater said, helping himself to some cheese, biscuits and wine as he drew out a chart and studied it. 'Help yourself,' he offered, indicating the wine and biscuits and hoping the lad would remain below and not get wind of their pursuer.

After about ten minutes of plying dividers and rules, Drinkwater stuffed the chart away, pulled his hat down over his head and went up on deck. Striding aft he relieved Frey.

'Go and try to get some sleep, there's a good fellow. You need it and we may have work to do in an hour or two.'

'I don't give much for our chances, sir. At the very least he'll have twice our numbers, and we made enough of a display of ourselves outside Calais to call down the vengeance of heaven. I don't suppose the deaths of half a dozen cavalrymen endeared us to them either.'

'Very well put, Mr Frey. Now do as I ask while I try and devise a stratagem.'

'Do you think . . .?'

'Don't ask me.'

Reluctantly Frey handed over the tiller and the course. Drinkwater leaned his weight against the heavy wooden bar. 'I'm going to alter a little to the westwards. Now do you go below for an hour. I shall call you well before things get too lively. Stand half the men down too.'

Frey went forward and some of the men on deck drifted below. *Kestrel* was just feeling the wind picking up and began to slip through the water with increasing speed, as though she felt a tremor of fear at the approach of the large, three-masted lugger coming up astern.

Drinkwater steadied the cutter on her new course and settled himself to concentrate upon his task. The satisfactions in steering were profound. The sense of being in control of something almost living struck him and he recalled that he had forgotten so much of what had once been familiar as he had risen to the lonely peak of command. He made a resolution not to look astern for half an hour. It was difficult at first, but the glances of the others on deck, increasing in frequency and length, told him the lugger was gaining on them so that, when the thirty minutes had passed, he turned, expecting to see the lugger's bowsprit almost over their stern. Though she was still some way off, two miles distant perhaps, she was no longer alone.

180

Now he could see a second lugger behind her, five miles away or maybe more, but close enough to spell disaster if his half-germinated plan miscarried. He resolved to wait twenty minutes before he looked again and set himself to reworking the hurried and imperfect calculations he had made below.

He now discovered a greater anxiety, that of wishing to see the chart, to re-measure the distances and make the tidal estimates again. It was easy enough to make a silly error, to rely upon a misunderstanding only to find that the stratagem, which was shaky enough as it was, would misfire and carry them to disaster. And then, with a forceful irony, a thought struck him. *Kestrel* was his own property and he might do with her as he pleased. He would not have to answer at his peril and so was free of one constraint at least, thank heavens!

He began to stare ahead and study the surface of the sea, to try and discern the almost invisible signs of the shoals, where the tide ran in a different direction and at a slower speed. The mewing gulls had a good view of these natural seamarks and he looked up to see the herring gulls gliding alongside, their cruel yellow beaks and beady eyes evidence of their predatory instincts. But they were lazy hunters; he was looking for more active birds fishing on the edge of the bank ahead.

He saw the first tern almost immediately, flying along with a sprat or some small fry silver in its red beak, and then another diving to starboard of them, under the foot of the mainsail. He craned his neck and stared intently over the port bow. As he did so a man forward rose and peered ahead, aware of Drinkwater's concern. A moment later more terns could be seen and then his experienced eye made out the troubled water along the submarine ledge.

'Sommat ahead, sir, looks like a bank . . .'

'It's the Longsand! Take a cast of the lead.'

Alongside the rushing hull the sea ran dark and grey, dulled by the cloud sweeping up and over the blue of the sky. The sounding lead yielded seven fathoms and then suddenly it was only three and they passed through a strip of white foam, dead in the water like the cast from a mill race seen some few hundred yards downstream. As suddenly as it had appeared, the white filigree was gone and the water was brown and smooth, as though whale oil had been cast upon it. Drinkwater knew they were running over the Longsand Head. He counted the seconds as *Kestrel* raced on, her pace seemingly swifter through the dead water on top of the bank.

'By the mark, two!'

Drinkwater felt the keen thrill of exhilaration, his heart fluttering, the adrenalin pouring into his bloodstream. At any moment their keel might strike the sand, and at this speed the impact must toss the mast overboard, but he held on, pitching the risk against the result, until the man in the chains called out 'Three ... By the deep four ... By the mark five!' and they were over the bank and ahead of them they could just see the low stump of the brick tower daymark on the Naze of Essex. Drinkwater, his knees knocking uncomfortably, altered course a touch and looked astern. His plan had almost worked, but the big lugger had seen the trap just in time and bore away, to run north, round the extremity of the bank, losing ground to the escaping cutter. It was not so very remarkable, for the commander of so large a lugger would know these waters far better than Drinkwater, who was relying upon knowledge learned thirty years earlier in the buoy-yachts of the Trinity House. Nevertheless, they had increased their lead and every mile brought them nearer the English coast and the presence of a British man-o'-war out of Harwich to the north-west of them.

The wind had steadied now, a topsail breeze which, in the lee of the Longsand, drove *Kestrel* homewards with inspiriting speed. Drinkwater forgot his exhaustion in the joy of handling the little cutter and for a few moments scarcely thought about her pursuers until the anxious looks of the men on deck again drew his attention to them. He turned and looked over his shoulder.

The two enemy luggers were closer together now and were setting more sail, clear evidence that they were determined to overhaul *Kestrel* before she made it into Harwich harbour.

'They must know of the quality of our passengers,' he muttered grimly, for this was surely no mere retribution for the death of a handful of hussars or British insolence in the entrance to Calais. And then he recalled the man who had watched them from the extremity of the Calais jetty, and wondered who or what he was and whether he had anything to do with this determined pursuit.

Drinkwater had hoped that he might lure the larger of the two luggers over the Longsand so that she ran aground, and in doing so he had let *Kestrel* sag off to the west a little. With the flood tide now running into the Thames estuary from the north, he had to regain that deliberately sacrificed northing, sailing across the tide while the French luggers already had that advantage from their forced diversion round the seawards extremity of the shoal. There was, however, a further obstacle behind which he would feel safe. If he could lure the luggers on to the Stone Banks, to the east of the Naze, he could shoot north into Harwich through the Medusa Channel.

The idea filled him with fresh hope and he laid a course for the Sunk alarm vessel, lying to her great chain mooring and flying the red ensign of the Trinity House. She lay ahead, with her bow canted slightly across the tide under the influence of the strong southerly breeze. She was a fortuitous seamark and one which the Frenchmen might even attack if they were frustrated in their pursuit of *Kestrel*.

For another twenty minutes they ran on, the luggers still gaining slowly, though now heeled under a vast press of canvas. As the range closed, Drinkwater called the crew to their stations for action and Frey, blear-eyed and looking far worse than if he had never slept, staggered out on deck, followed by the boy Charles.

'Send the lad below,' Drinkwater began, but it was too late. The boy had seen the luggers and glimpsed the large tricolours, and his face betrayed his fear.

'It's to be a damned close-run thing, Frey. We might make it into the Medusa Channel, we might not, but I think you had better . . .'

'You keep the helm, sir, now you have it. I'll send two men aft to trim sheets, then I'll fight the ship,' and without another word Frey swung away to see to the loading of the swivels and the mustering of the men with their small arms.

Drinkwater leaned on the tiller and, as Jago and a man named Cornford came aft, he ordered a little weight taken in on the mainsheet. *Kestrel* dashed through the water and a gleam of sun came through the clouds to turn to silver the spray driving away from the lee bow, making a brief rainbow with its appearance. Looking astern, terns dipped unconcernedly in their wake, while a fulmar quartered the sea in a single swoop. The fulmar caught Drinkwater's eye, swept down and upwards, away across the dark, predatory shape of the luggers' sails, absorbed only in its ceaseless quest for food and quite unaware of the grim game of life and death being played by the men in the three vessels below.

The nearer and larger of the two luggers was driving a bow wave before her that rose almost under her gammon iron. Her sails were stiff as boards and, even at the distance of a mile, Drinkwater could see the three great yards which spread her sails bending under the strain. If only, he thought, if only one would carry away . . .

But they stood, as did the lighter topsail yards above them, and the Frenchman loomed ever larger as the distance between them shrank and their courses converged. Drinkwater stared forward again and saw the tall lantern mast of the Sunk alarm vessel also growing in size as they rapidly closed the distance. He was aiming *Kestrel*'s bowsprit for the bow of the anchored vessel, hoping to draw his pursuer in close enough for him to lose his nerve and bear away again as the tide swept them down on to the alarm vessel. It was an old trick, learned, like so much else he had used recently, in the buoy-yachts a lifetime ago, to determine the position of the alarm vessel's anchor by sailing up-tide of her, when any prudent mariner would pass down-tide, under her stern.

Forward, Frey turned and stared aft, suddenly alert to the danger into which they stood. Seeing Drinkwater confidently aware of how close they were going to pass the alarm vessel, he relaxed and made some remark to the hands who looked aft and laughed. But Drinkwater was too tense even to notice. Every muscle he could command was strained with the business of holding *Kestrel* on her course without deviation, gauging the exact strength of the lateral shift of the racing hull under the influence of the tide, yet making allowances for the quartering sea which created a gentle see-sawing yaw. He could see the hull of the Sunk now and the men lining her rail as the three vessels closed, and at that moment, the first gun was fired. The shot passed across *Kestrel*'s deck, right under the boom and out over the port side, to be lost somewhere in the choppy seas on their port beam.

'God's bones!' Drinkwater blasphemed, as the wind of the shot's passing distracted him. The next second he was aware of a ragged cheer from the crew of the alarm vessel and the rush of a red hull and slimy green weed along a waterline that passed in a blur as the cutter dashed across the tide and was suddenly under the Sunk's high bow. Then there seemed a number of cries of alarm, of crashes and the thud of another gun, of a great rushing to starboard and more shots, of pistols and the starboard swivels all barking at once in a moment of packed incident in which he took no part, rooted as he was to the heavy tiller. All he saw as they tore past the alarm vessel was the great iron chain of the Sunk stretching down to the anchor in the seabed below them. Then they had run beyond the Sunk's bow and he relaxed, looking round to watch the strength of the tide as it bore them sideways and as the apparent motion made the alarm vessel seem to cross their own stern. He looked round for their nearer pursuer. She had been unable to pass up-tide of the alarm vessel and had been compelled to haul her wind and duck under the Sunk's stern. In doing so she had passed so close that she had exposed herself to one of the alarm vessel's carronades, mounted as a warning gun but loaded with an extempore charge of debris. The discharge of old nails and broken glass tore through the lugger's straining foresail as she bore up too much. As a consequence, her stern brushed the alarm vessel's hull and her mizen snagged it. Her after rigging was torn away, dragging the whole mizen, mast, sail and yard with it. As she broke away from the Sunk, the lugger left white canvas fluttering from the stern of the alarm vessel and with it her tricoloured ensign. Of the second lugger, all that could be seen was the peak of her sails to the south-east as she reached across the wind, anxiously watching the fate of her consort.

'Harden in those sheets!' Drinkwater roared, pushing the tiller with all his might. 'Stand by to tack ship!'

Instantly Frey divined Drinkwater's intentions. 'Prepare those starboard swivels! Get those port swivels mounted over here!'

Kestrel dipped into the wind with a flogging of her sails and paid off on the other tack. Runners were set up and let go, the sheets shifted and slackened as *Kestrel* spun to port, swung off the wind and ran back towards her late tormentor. Confusion reigned on the deck of the *chasse marée* as *Kestrel* passed on the opposite tack, spattering her with small-arms fire and raking her with the swivels.

'Here, Jago!' Drinkwater tossed the seaman one of his pistols and Jago aimed and fired it into the throng of men struggling to bring their lugger under command again. Seeing the pitiful sight and the execution done to the lugger's decks, Drinkwater noted the mainsail had ripped badly so that she was almost immobilized.

'How I wish we had one decent gun,' he lamented to himself, but Frey had had all four swivels discharge into the enemy as they passed and the carnage was bad enough. The second lugger was a mile away now, and stood steadily south-eastwards. Drinkwater pursued her for a while and had the satisfaction of chasing her from the field before he turned back towards their erstwhile enemy. The larger *chasse marée* was a sorry sight, her mainsail down on deck. And though the main topsail was being hoisted and she might yet run off before the wind, it appeared she was *hors de combat*. Inspiration struck Drinkwater, 'Where's young Charles, Jago?'

Jago called out in French and Drinkwater saw the lad raise his head

185

from beside the boat on her chocks amidships where he had been huddled, watching the action.

'Tell him to find out this fellow's name, Jago, and then ask if he surrenders.' Drinkwater raised his voice. 'The rest of you prepare to fire and to scandalize the mainsail and heave to.'

As they came dancing up under the overcast and pointed their little guns at the lugger, the boy called upon her to surrender. The response was a torrent of French at which the lad stiffened and Jago merely laughed.

'Well, damn you, what does the bugger say?' Drinkwater prompted Jago, who addressed a few words to Charles.

'*Elle est la* Mathilde Drouot *de Calais, M'sieur. Le maître est mort, et . . .*' The boy shrugged and looked appealingly at Jago.

'She's the *Mathilde Drouot* of Calais, sir, the master is killed and her mate says he is compelled to surrender to pig-butchers. He has had five men killed besides the master, and eight wounded. One is very bad and he asked if we had a surgeon.'

Drinkwater pulled a face. 'That is unfortunate, I had no idea the swivels were so effective . . .'

Jago shook his head. 'I don't think it was our swivels, sir. I reckon it was the men on the alarm vessel firing broken glass bottles at 'em from a large-bore carronade mounted on the quarter.'

'I see. We may take the prize, but not the credit.'

'Aye, I reckon so, sir. 'Tis against the laws of war, the Frog yonder says, sir.'

Drinkwater ignored the objection. 'Tell the *Mathilde Drouot* to pitch all his ramrods overboard, then head for Harwich. Tell him to stay in close contact under my guns. If he tries to make a run for it, I shall sweep his decks with glass bottles myself. I think we have a few down below, don't we, Mr Frey?'

'A few, sir, but not many.'

'Then let us hope the matter is not put to the test, eh?'

Captain Scanderbeg was somewhat ruffled to be woken early next morning by a lieutenant demanding accommodation for prisoners-of-war in the town bridewell.

'And who, sir, are you, pray?' he asked, emerging dishevelled from his chamber in the Three Cups.

'Lieutenant Frey, sir, of the hired cutter *Kestrel*. I have some twenty-seven prisoners and several need a surgeon, sir.'

186

Scanderbeg frowned. '*Kestrel*, she's Captain Drinkwater's yacht, ain't she?'

'Yes, sir, under my command. We fought an engagement off the Sunk yesterday afternoon and took a French National lugger, sir. We anchored last night on the southern end of the Shelf and . . .'

'And here you are disturbing me, Lieutenant . . .'

'Frey, sir.'

Scanderbeg sighed, then said mildly, 'I recall you now. Well, damn you, sir, you shall wait until I have shaved and broken my fast and then perhaps we shall find somewhere for your confounded prisoners. Don't you know I have an army to embark?'

'So I see, sir,' said Frey politely, withdrawing. 'I do beg your pardon. I had no idea it took quite so long.'

Scanderbeg stared at the retreating young man, then he scratched his head and burst out laughing. 'By God, sir, neither did I!'

PART THREE

Ebb Tide

It is said that of all deaths, drowning is the least unpleasant.

The Oar

Captain Poulter leaned over the railing at the port extremity of his bridge. His agitation was extreme, though he fought to conceal it as he waited patiently for the wreckage of the boat to be recovered, along with the survivors clinging on to it.

He counted the bobbing heads; two remained missing. One was almost certainly old Sir Nathaniel and he half-hoped the other might be Drew, but he could see the Elder Brother now and realized the other was Mr Quier, *Vestal*'s second mate.

Poulter willed Forester to hasten the recovery, though he knew full well that the mate and his boat's crew were doing their utmost. When at last the matter was concluded, he shouted for half speed ahead.

'We have everyone except Sir Nathaniel and Peter Quier, sir,' Forester reported when he eventually came up on the bridge.

'Yes, I know.' The two men looked at each other. They were both thinking their luck had run out, but neither wished to voice the apprehension. 'We must keep on searching, Mr Forester.'

'Aye, aye, sir.'

'Quier has a chance, I suppose . . .'

'Let us hope so.'

Drinkwater was not so cold now and thought he had stopped shivering. It did not seem to matter that the water rose above his head. There was a simple inevitability about things; an acceptance. All would be well, and all would be well . . .

It was almost a disappointment when, without effort, almost in spite of himself, he encountered the oar again and found that he was breathing, his head clear of the water with the arch of the sky above him. But now it hurt to breathe; almost as much as it hurt not to . . .

Last Casts of the Dice

Edward was buried next to Hortense in the grounds of the old priory and with him Drinkwater consigned a great anxiety. Once he might have relied upon the protection of Lord Dungarth, but after the Earl's death, had Ostroff's true identity or past crime of murder been exposed, along with his own part in Edward's escape, he scarcely dared to think what would have happened to Elizabeth and the children. That Edward had rendered signal service to the British Crown at Tilsit might not have weighed in his favour so long after the event, and now, in any case, the war had finally ended and with it those expedient measures behind which wrongs were obscured.

Nine weeks after the return of *Kestrel* from the French coast, England learned of the débâcle of Waterloo, the quondam Emperor's flight to the west coast of France and his surrender to Captain Maitland of the *Bellerophon*. Thereafter, the presence of Napoleon aboard ship in Torbay attracted widespread interest before he was transferred into the *Northumberland* and carried south, to exile on distant St Helena. In the months that followed, Elizabeth persuaded her husband to fill in those gaps in his personal history that the loss of his early diaries during the sinking of the *Royal George* had caused by writing down his memoirs. She considered her husband's service to be of some interest to their children and, while she expected him to be deliberately reticent concerning some of the incidents in his life, she knew sufficient to want his sacrifices, and by implication her own, not to go unknown by their family. There was also a more practical consideration, and in initiating her husband's task, Elizabeth demonstrated the depth of her own understanding.

For Drinkwater the process brought back many memories. So daily an accompaniment of his life had the war become that the absence of it seemed to remove the main purpose of existence itself, and yet he learned that for Elizabeth and his household, the war had been but a distant backdrop to their own lives, lives which were more intimately connected with the ebb and flow of the seasons than the tides, of ploughing and planting, of reaping and harrowing, of tending livestock and mending fences, of buying and selling, of butter-making and fruit-bottling. Drinkwater was at first suspicious of Elizabeth's motives, suspecting her of wanting him occupied and not interfering in the business of the estate, but he quickly realized that he was guilty of a mean misjudgement. Elizabeth was only too acutely aware that the end of the war and the end of active service would confront Drinkwater himself with numerous regrets and frustrations, and that while he might say he wished to be left in peace, indeed he might desire it most sincerely, nevertheless such a desire would in time wane and, in the manner of all ageing men, he would wish for the excitements of youth and maturity. A period of reflection and evaluation would, she astutely hoped, reconcile him to a gentler, less tempestuous life.

In the first year of peace, Drinkwater bent to his task and found that it did indeed ease his transition from active command to the life of a country gentleman. He had no knowledge of either livestock or agriculture and eschewed the company of farming men, not out of snobbery but out of ignorance of their ways and their conversation. They were as great an oddity to him as was he to them. There were fewer expressions more accurate or appropriate than that of being a fish out of water. Rather than try, as many of his naval contemporaries did, to join the squirearchy, he retained the habit of command, was content with his own company and, when in need of male companionship, sought that of his friend Frey. Frey's expectation of advancement had terminated with the sudden end of the war and he had returned to painting, enjoying a continuing success. A solicitous husband, he nevertheless slipped away from time to time to laze afloat aboard *Kestrel* for a day or two. It seemed impossible that on these very decks had once lain the body of a mysterious Russian officer, or that they had carried off the Baroness and her children from the teeth of a French hussar detachment in the very yacht that lay at anchor beneath the hanging woods on the River Orwell.

Drinkwater received an occasional letter, written in painful and stilted English, from the young Charles Montholon. He had acquired a certain importance because his uncle, General Montholon, had been appointed to the small suite which accompanied to St Helena the man the British cabinet had meanly insisted was to be known as 'General Bonaparte'. This tenuous connection had, despite the young man's fugitive situation during the Hundred Days, encouraged an ambition to join the French army on the assumption that the glories of the past might be replicated in the future. Drinkwater sincerely hoped they would not; a world riven by battles of Napoleonic proportions was not one that he wished his own son to inhabit, but reading Charles Montholon's correspondence, it occurred to Drinkwater that his own generation had lived their lives in an extraordinary period which, seen through the younger man's eyes, was already vested with a vast and romantic significance. Not the least thread in the fabric of this great myth was the distant exile of the dispossessed emperor.

While Napoleon languished on his rock, Drinkwater completed his journals and enjoyed his quiet excursions under sail. Occasionally he and Frey would undertake a little surveying of the bar of the River Ore, or Drinkwater would submit a report on some matter of minor hydrographical detail. These, finding their way to the Court of Trinity House, in due course resulted in his being invited to become a Younger Brother of the Corporation and this, in turn, led him to accompany a party of Elder Brethren in the Corporation's yacht on an inspection of the lights in the Dover Strait. Thus, one night in the summer of 1820, anchored in The Downs close to the *Severn*, a fifty-gun guardship attached to the Sentinel Service, Drinkwater found himself at dinner with a Captain McCullough, commander of the *Severn*, who had been invited to join the Brethren at dinner.

The after cabin of the Trinity yacht was as sumptuous as it was small, boasting the miniature appointments of a first-rate. The meal began with the customary stilted exchanges of men with an unfamiliar guest in their midst. McCullough, who had joined Drinkwater and the two embarked Elder Brethren, Captain Isaac Robinson and Captain James Moring, by way of his own gig, was quizzed about his naval career and his present service.

'I made the mistake', he admitted, smiling ironically, 'of suggesting that the revival of smuggling might be countered by several detachments of naval officers and men posted along the coasts most exposed to the evil. Their Lordships took me at my word and offered me the appointment of organizing the task. The command of *Severn* came, as it were, as a by-blow of their decision, for she acts as storeship and headquarters of the force.'

'And as a visible deterrent, I daresay,' observed Captain Moring, who had recently relinquished command of an East Indiaman.

'I believe that to be the case, yes.'

'How many men do you command?' asked Captain Robinson.

'The whole force amounts to only about eighty men who occupy the old Martello towers along the shore. Each division, of which there are three in Kent, is commanded by a lieutenant, with midshipmen and master's mates in charge of the local detachments. A similar arrangement pertains to the westward in Sussex. Each post has a pulling galley at its disposal, so we are an amphibious force.'

'You take your posts at night, I imagine,' Drinkwater said, 'and enjoy some success thereby.'

'As an active counter-action to the nefarious doings of the free-trading fraternity, we have enjoyed a certain advantage, yes, though this has not been achieved without loss.'

'You suffer deaths and injuries then?' Drinkwater asked.

'Oh yes, severely on occasion. The smugglers are a ruthless lot and will stop at nothing in their attempts to run their damnable cargoes.'

'Well, I confess that the odd bottle of contraband brandy has passed my lips in the past, but with the peace and the present difficulties the country faces, the losses to the revenue must be stopped,' Captain Moring put in.

'Indeed,' went on McCullough, nodding, 'and the problem lies in the widespread condonation that exists, partly due to the laxities practised during the late war, but also due to the material advantage accruing to the individual in avoiding duty.'

There was a brief and awkward silence, then Captain Robinson raised his glass and remarked, 'Well, sir, I give you the Sentinel Service ...' and they drank a toast to McCullough's brainchild.

'Perhaps,' Drinkwater added, 'one might consign the magistracy to some minor purgatory. I gather that when the Preventive Waterguard were formed, what, twenty years ago now, they often threw out of court actions brought against well-known smugglers.'

'That is true,' went on McCullough, warming to his subject with the enthusiasm of the zealot, 'for the justices were usually the chief bene-ficiaries and how else does a man get rich in England but by cheating the revenue? But they are less able to try the trick on naval men, and besides, there was some mitigation during the war when continental trade was made difficult and it was in our interest to encourage it. The paradox no longer exists, therefore the matter is simpler in its argument. Its resolution, however, remains as difficult as ever.'

'The risks are high for those caught,' said Moring.

'Indeed. I should not wish to face transportation or the gallows, but the profits are encouraging enough and the risks of apprehension, despite our best efforts, are probably not so terrifying.'

'No,' put in Drinkwater. 'And it is not entirely to be wondered at that fellows made bold by the experiences of war and who find no employment in peace, yet see about them evidence of wealth and luxury, should turn to such methods to support their families.'

'That is true, sir,' replied McCullough, 'and there is a certain irony in seeing victims of the press remaining at sea for their private gain . . .'

'That is not so very ironic, McCullough,' Drinkwater responded, 'when you take into account the fact that the men who oppose you and the revenue officers are by birth and situation bred to the sea and find it the only way to earn their daily crust. I am certainly not sympathetic to their law-breaking, merely to their situation. It seems to me that an amelioration of their circumstances would remove many of the motives that drive them to break the law.'

'You mean measures should be taken by government', Robinson asked incredulously, 'to *regulate* society?'

'I think that is a necessary function of good government, yes.'

'Government regulation gave us the confounded income tax,' protested Moring.

'Well,' said Drinkwater, 'I think the present government can give us little . . .'

'You are a reformer, sir!' said Moring accusingly.

Drinkwater smiled. 'Perhaps, yes. There can be very little wrong in promoting the welfare of others. I seem to recall something of the sort in the gospels . . .'

'Damned dangerous notions . . .'

'Revolutionary . . .'

'Come, gentlemen, keep a sense of proportion,' argued Drinkwater. 'We cannot entirely ignore events either over the strait or, for that matter, on the other side of the Atlantic . . .'

'I doubt our present Master', remarked Moring, referring to the Corporation's senior officer who, as Lord Liverpool, was also the Prime Minister, 'would agree with you.'

'I hope, sir,' said Drinkwater, with an edge to his voice, 'that you are not implying disloyalty on my part by my expressing my free and candid opinion? One may surely disagree with the opinions of another without the risk of retribution? After all, it is a hallmark of civilization.'

There was a moment's awkward silence, then McCullough said, 'The present state of the country is a matter for concern, I admit, but this should not condone law-breaking.'

'I do not condone law-breaking, Captain McCullough. I have already said so. The present woes of our country, with trouble in our unrepresented industrial towns, unemployment in our countryside and difficulties in trade, are matters close to all our hearts,' Drinkwater persisted. 'My case is simply that the solution lies either with government or in revolution, for there are limits to the toleration of even the most passive and compliant people. I have spent my life in fighting to contain the latter and see that the wise solution must therefore lie with the former. Was Lord Liverpool here this evening, I am certain he would agree with me that something must be done. But the problem seems to lie in what exactly one does to ameliorate dissatisfactions. One can hope something will turn up, but this seems to me damned foolish and most unreliable. The unhappy experience of France is that one cannot throw over the cart without losing the contents and that to do so runs the risk of bringing down a tyranny greater than the one formerly endured. On the other hand simply to obstruct all progress upon the principle of exclusion seems to me to be both dangerous and foolish.'

'What policy of what you are pleased to call *improvement*', sneered Moring, 'do you advocate then, Drinkwater?'

'Since you ask,' Drinkwater replied, smiling wryly, 'a policy of slow but steady reform, a policy which would be perceptible to men of every condition, but which would allow due controls to be exerted. It is my experience that neither coercion nor bribery produce loyalty, though both may produce results, whereas some moderating policy would be wiser than sending in light dragoons to cut up political meetings that can have no voice other than in open fields.'

'Well, I ain't so damned sure,' said Moring, motioning the steward to refill his glass as he dabbed at his mouth with a napkin.

'Of course you're not,' Drinkwater said quickly, 'for it is your certainties you must sacrifice . . .'

'Gamble with, more like,' put in Robinson.

197

'Indeed. But you have spent your professional life gambling, Captain Robinson, pitting your wits against wind and sea, bringing your cargoes safely home against considerable odds, wouldn't you say?'

Robinson nodded with lugubrious acquiescence, apparently defeated by this line of argument.

Moring was less easily subdued. 'But that doesn't alter the fact that by conferring liberties upon the masses, disorder and chaos might result,' he persisted.

'True, but so they might if we leave Parliament unreformed and half the veterans from the Peninsula wandering our streets as beggars, and half the pressed seamen returned to common lands they find enclosed, or consigned to those stinking factories that are no better than the worst men-of-war commissioned under Lord Sandwich's regime in the American War. God forbid that the English disease of snobbery should set a real revolution alight! Imagine what the men who raped and pillaged their way through Badajoz might do to London!'

'But Drinkwater, to enable a government to function in the way you so passionately advocate, it must needs garner its revenue,' argued McCullough, a note of vexed desperation in his voice.

'Unquestionably, McCullough. Gentlemen, I apologize for ruining your evening,' said Drinkwater, temporizing, 'I am in no wise opposed to Captain McCullough's Sentinel Service and had we not drunk to it already I should have proposed a toast to it now . . .'

But Drinkwater was interrupted by a loud knocking at the door and the sudden appearance of the yacht's second mate.

'Begging your pardon, gentlemen, but there's a message come for Captain McCullough. Your tender's just arrived, sir, with word of a movement along the coast, and they're awaiting orders.'

McCullough rose, a somewhat relieved expression crossing his face. 'I'll be up directly,' he said to the second mate and, turning to the others, apologized. 'Gentlemen, forgive me. It has been a most stimulating evening, but I must leave at once. My tender, the *Flying Fish*, was not expected to return until tomorrow, so this news means something considerable is under weigh . . .'

Robinson waved aside McCullough's explanation. 'Now, Drinkwater, here's an opportunity for us all to do our duty! Will you accept our services as volunteers, McCullough? You will? Good man! Gentlemen, to our duty . . .'

And with that Robinson rose and went to his small cabin, muttering about priming pistols. 'Will you have us, sir?' Drinkwater asked, rising slowly to his feet. 'Antique and libertarian as we may seem, we are not wholly without experience in these matters.'

McCullough shrugged. '*Your* reputation is solid, sir, but I am not so certain how strong a *trade*-wind blows . . .'

'Come, sir,' Moring snapped as he leapt to his feet, 'that remark is of dubious propriety. Let us show *you* how strong a trade-wind may blow, damn it!'

And so the uncongenial occasion broke up in petty rivalry, and Drinkwater went reluctantly to shift his coat and shoes, and buckle on his hanger.

It was a moonless night of pitchy darkness and a light but steady southerly wind, a night made for the running of tubs on to the beaches of Dungeness, and the *Flying Fish* slipped south-westwards under a press of canvas. The comparison with *Kestrel*, thought Drinkwater, as he squatted on one of the tender's six carronade slides, ended with the similarity of the tender's rig. Thereafter all was different, for *Flying Fish* was stuffed with men, and the dull and sinister gleam of cutlasses being made ready was accompanied by the snick of pistol frizzens as the men prepared for action. What precise intelligence initiated this purposeful response, Drinkwater had only the haziest notion. Treachery and envy loosened tongues the world over, and word of mouth was a deadly weapon when employed deliberately. But patient observation, infiltration and careful analysis of facts could, as Drinkwater well knew from his brief tenure of command of the Admiralty's Secret Department, yield strong inferences of intended doings.

In truth his curiosity was little aroused by the matter; he felt he had exhausted his own interest in such affairs years ago. It was, like the command of *Kestrel*, something he was quite content to give up to a younger and more eager man. Every dog had his day, ran the old saw, and he had had his. If the evening's evidence was anything to go by, he was out of step with the temper of the times. Younger men, men like Moring, Robinson and McCullough, had made their own world and he was too rooted in the past to do more than offer his unwanted comments upon it. Nevertheless, it seemed that with the past something good had been lost. He supposed his perception was inevitable and that the hard-won experience and wisdom of existence was perpetually squandered as part of the excessive bounty of nature. These men would learn in their turn, but it seemed an odd way for providence to proceed.

Such considerations were terminated by McCullough summoning them all aft. Stiffly Drinkwater rose and joined the others about the tiller. A master's mate had gone forward to brief the hands, and Drinkwater stood listening to McCullough while watching the pale, bubbling line of the wake draw out from under the *Flying Fish*'s low counter, creating a dull gleam of phosphorescence at the cutwater of the boat towing astern.

'Two of our pulling galleys reported a long-boat from Rye run across to France a couple of nights ago,' McCullough was saying. 'Information has reached us that the contraband cargo will be transferred to three fishing-boats which will return independently to their home ports. The long-boat will come in empty, apart, I expect, from a few fish.

'The rendezvous is to be made on the Varne Bank, near the buoy of the Varne. It is my intention that we shall interrupt this. I want prisoners and I want evidence. From you, gentlemen,' McCullough said, turning to his three volunteers, 'I want witnesses, not heroics.'

As Moring spluttered his protest, Drinkwater smiled in the darkness. At least Elizabeth would approve of him being a witness; he was otherwise less certain of her enthusiasm for his joining this mad jape.

'And now, gentlemen,' McCullough concluded, 'I must insist upon the most perfect silence.'

For another hour they squatted about the deck, wrapped in their cloaks against the night's damp. The low cloud was breaking a little, but a veil persisted over the upper atmosphere, blurring the few stars visible and preserving the darkness.

But it was never entirely dark at sea; the eyes could always discern something, and intelligence filled in details, so that it was possible, while one remained awake, to half-see, half-sense what was going on. The quiet shuffling between bow and helm, accompanied as it was by whispers, told of the transmission of information from the lookouts, and in due course McCullough himself, discernible from the shape of his cocked hat and a tiny gleam on the brass of his night glass, went forward himself and remained there for some time. Drinkwater had, in fact, almost dozed off when something like a voltaic shock ran along the deck as men touched their neighbours' shoulders and the company rose to its feet.

After the long wait, the speed with which events now accelerated was astonishing. The preservation of surprise had compelled McCullough to keep his hand hidden until the last moment and now he demonstrated the skill of both his interception and his seamanship, for though their course had been altered several times in the final moments, it seemed that *Flying Fish* suddenly ran in among several craft to the accompaniment of shouts of alarm and bumps of her intruding hull.

The drilling of her company was impeccable. On a single order, her mainsail was scandalized and the gaff dropped, the staysail fluttered to the deck with the thrum of hanks on the stay, and men seemed to drop over the side as they invaded the rafted boats which, until that moment, had been busy with the transfer of casks and bundles of contraband.

For a brief moment, it seemed to the observing Drinkwater that the deterrent waving of dimly perceived cutlass blades would subdue the smugglers, but suddenly riot broke out. Cries of surprise rose in reactive alarm, the clash of blade meeting blade filled the night, and the grunt of effort and the flash and report of the first pistol opened an action of primitive ferocity. Beside Drinkwater, Moring was jumping about the deck with the undignified and frustrated enthusiasm of a schoolboy witnessing his first prize-fight, while all about them the scene of struggle had a contrived, almost theatrical appearance, for the pistol flashes threw up sharp images in the darkness and these stayed on the retina, accompanied by a more general perception of men stumbling about in the surrounding boats, grappling and hacking at each other in a grim and terrible struggle for mastery.

This state of affairs had been going on for no more than two or three minutes with neither side apparently prevailing, though shouts of execration filled the air along with the cries of the hurt and the occasional bellowed order or demand for surrender. Suddenly matters took a turn for the worse.

The ship-keeper, left at the helm of the *Flying Fish*, added his own voice to the general uproar. 'To me! Help! Astern here!'

Drinkwater turned to see the flash of a pistol and the ship-keeper fall dead. A moment later a group of smugglers came over the *Flying Fish*'s stern and rushed the deck. He lugged out his hanger just in time, shouting the alarm to Moring and Robinson, and struck with a swift cut at the nearest attacker.

He felt the sword-blade bite and slashed at a face. It pulled back

201

and, in the gloom, the pale oval passed briefly across the dim light from the *Flying Fish*'s shrouded binnacle. For a moment, Drinkwater thought he recognized the man but he swiftly dismissed the thought as a figure loomed to his left and he thrust hard, driving his very fist into another man's belly as his sword-blade ran his victim through.

Drinkwater felt something strike his own shoulder as he twisted his wrist to wrench the sword-blade clear and half staggered, barking his shin painfully against a carronade slide as he broke free of his dying assailant. After the first moment of shock and the reactive thunder of his accelerating heart, he found the cool analytical anodyne to this horrible work. He seemed to be able to see better, despite the darkness, and he breathed with a violent and stertorous effort, snorting through distorted nostrils as he hacked at the invaders, slashing with a terrible effect, and twisting his wrist with a savage energy that tore at the very tendons with its violence. He was a butcher of such ferocity that he had cleared the deck and fought his way to the very stern over which the last of his opponents jumped, when he heard Robinson cry out, 'Turn, sir! Turn!'

It was the smuggler he had first seen and whom he thought he had struck down, the man whose face had been briefly illuminated by the binnacle light. Now he recognized him, and by some strange telepathy, he himself was recognized.

'Jago!'

'Stand aside, Captain, or I'll not answer . . .'

'You damned fool!'

'Stand aside, I say!'

For a moment they confronted each other in silence as Drinkwater raised his sword. His madness cooled and then, through teeth clenched ready for reaction, he muttered, 'Go over the side, man, or I must strike you . . . Go!'

But Jago did not jump. Instead, the sword of another ran him through from the rear and he stood transfixed, staring at Drinkwater as he fell, first to his knees and then full length, snapping the sword-blade and revealing his executioner as Captain Moring, a broken sword in his hand.

'That, sir,' Moring said, his eyes agleam, 'is how strong a trade-wind may blow!'

The Knight Commander

Drinkwater drew off his gloves, threw them on to the table and took the glass stopper from the decanter.

'There are some strange ironies in life, are there not, my dear?' he asked, pouring two glasses and handing one to Elizabeth. 'To be thus honoured as an act of spite against a foreign power for something done years ago seems too ridiculous.'

Accepting the glass, Elizabeth sank into a chair, kicked off her shoes and wriggled her toes ecstatically. 'Thank you, *Sir* Nathaniel,' she said, smiling up at him.

'I hope that is a jest and does not become a custom,' Drinkwater replied, sitting opposite and raising his glass in a silent toast to his wife.

'Is that a command, Sir Nathaniel?'

'It most decidedly is, my dear, or else I shall have to call you *Milady* and refer to you as *Her Ladyship* . . .'

'*Leddyship*, surely, my dear.'

'Well at least we agree about that being fatuous.'

'I was referred to in that way sufficiently today to last me the remainder of my life. But tell me', Elizabeth said, after sipping her wine, 'what you mean by annoying foreign powers. It all sounds rather serious and sinister, this matter of spite.'

'It's also damned ironic, but I had no idea until that fellow, what was his name, the cove who looked after us at the levée . . .?'

'Ponsonby, I think.'

'That's the fellow! Must have spent half his life bowing and scraping! What a damned tedious time he seems to have had of it too . . .'

'Took us both for a pair of country tree-sparrows and I'm not surprised, this gown must be at least three years out of fashion . . .'

'You looked perfect, my dear, even the King said so.'

Elizabeth clucked a laugh. 'Bless him,' she purred, 'he reminded me of a rather over-grown midshipman in his enthusiasm. He seemed to have a soft spot for you too.'

'Yes, odd that. I think 'tis because we both commanded the frigate *Andromeda* at one time or another and he still believes I took the *Suvorov* when I commanded her. Well,' Drinkwater said with a sigh, ''tis too late to disabuse him now that I'm dubbed knight for my trouble.'

'Knight Commander of the Bath,' his wife corrected, laughing, 'that is surely better than being an *Elder* Brother of the Trinity House.' She made a face. 'But you haven't told me of this spiteful snub to France.'

'Not France, my dear. Russia is the target of the Government's displeasure. The diplomatic vacillations of St Petersburg have, as Ponsonby put it, to be "disapproved of" and this disapproval has to be signalled by subtle means . . .'

'La, sir, and you are a "subtle means", are you? Well,' she burst out laughing, ''tis as ludicrous as being a Knight of the Bath or an Elder Brother . . .'

'And I never commanded a ship-of-the-line,' he laughed with her, adding ruefully, 'nor hoisted a flag, though I managed a broad pendant but once.'

'My dear Nathaniel, the King is not quite the fool he looks. Your services were more subtle than the means by which your knighthood is to be used against the Russians, and the King knows sufficient of you to be aware that of all the post-captains on the list your name is the most deserving . . .'

'Oh come, my dear, that simply isn't true.' Drinkwater spluttered a modest protest only slightly tinged with hypocrisy.

'Well I think so, anyway.'

'I approve of your partiality.' Drinkwater smiled and looked about the room. They had hardly changed a thing since the house had been left to him as a legacy by Lord Dungarth. It had apparently been the only asset in Dungarth's estate that had not been sold to satisfy his creditors. It was a modest place, set in a terrace in Lord North Street, and it had been Dungarth's intention that Drinkwater should use it when he succeeded the Earl as head of the Admiralty's Secret Department. In the event Drinkwater's tenure of that office had been short-lived and the house had merely become a convenience for Drinkwater and Elizabeth when they were in London. They had discussed selling it now that the war was over and they had purchased Gantley Hall, but Elizabeth, knowing the modest but secure state of their finances, had demurred. Now, with her husband's knighthood, it had proved a wise decision. She was already contemplating a visit or two to a dress-making establishment near Bond Street in anticipation of the coming season.

'I thought His Majesty paid you a singular compliment in speaking to you for so long,' she said, echoing his mood of satisfaction.

Drinkwater laughed. 'Whatever King William's shortcomings,' he said, 'he does not lack the loquacity or enthusiasm of an old sailor.'

'They say he knew Nelson.'

'They say he doted on Nelson,' Drinkwater added, 'and certainly he admired Nelson greatly, but poor Pineapple Poll had not a shred of Nelson's qualities . . .'

Drinkwater refilled their glasses and they sat in silence for a while. He thought of the glittering occasion from which they had just returned, the brilliance of the ladies' dresses and the uniforms of the men, the sparkling of the glass chandeliers and mirrors, the powdered immobility of the bewigged servants and the ducking, bobbing obsequiousness of the professional courtiers.

Among such surroundings, the pop-eyed, red-faced, white-haired King seemed almost homely, dressed as he had been in his admiral's uniform, leading in Queen Adelaide who had, after years of open scandal, replaced Mrs Jordan, the actress. The King's eyes had actually lit up when he caught sight of Drinkwater's uniform, and after the ceremony of the investiture, he had asked how high Drinkwater's name stood upon the list of post-captains.

'I am not certain, Your Majesty,' Drinkwater had confessed.

'Not certain! Not certain, sir! Why damme, you must be the only officer in the service who don't know, 'pon my soul! Confess it, sir, confess it!'

'Willingly, sir, but it is perhaps too late to expect an honour greater than that done me today.'

'Well said, sir! Well said!' The King had turned to Elizabeth. ''Pon my soul, ma'am, your husband makes a damned fine diplomat, don't he, eh?'

Elizabeth dropped a curtsey. 'Your Majesty is too kind.'

'Perhaps he ain't always quite so diplomatic, eh?' The King laughed.

'Well, let that be, eh? But permit me to say, ma'am, that he is a lucky man in having you beside him, a damned lucky man. I speak plain, Ma'am, as an old sailor.' The King looked at Drinkwater. 'Charming, sir, charming. I hope you won't keep her in the country all the year.'

'As Your Majesty commands.'

The King had dropped his voice. 'I purposed your knighthood years ago, Sir Nathaniel, d'ye recall it?'

'Of course, sir, you were most kind in writing to me . . .'

'Stuff and nonsense. You might have confounded Boney, and saved Wellington and all those brave fellows the trouble of Waterloo. Damned funny thing, providence; pulls one up, sets another down, don't you know . . . Ah, Lady Callender . . .'

'What are you laughing about?'

Elizabeth's question brought him back to the present. 'Oh, the King's notion that I might have saved Wellington the trouble of fighting Waterloo. It was absolute nonsense, of course. I could only have done that had the Congress at Vienna decided to send Napoleon to the Azores rather than Elba. His Majesty has, it seems, a rather loose grasp of detail.'

'But he recollected that promise to make you a knight.'

'Remarkably yes, but I think it had more to do with taking a revenge upon the Admiralty, of putting Their Lordships in their places, than with upsetting the Russians, as Ponsonby suggested.'

'Why so? *Had* Their Lordships at the Admiralty upset him?'

'Indeed, yes. They had, you may recall, prevented him from commanding anything after *Andromeda* on account of the harshness with which he ruled his ship . . . except, of course, the squadron that took King Louis back to France, and then he had Blackwood to hold his hand. I think he felt the humiliation keenly, though I have equally little doubt but that Their Lordships acted correctly.'

'I had forgotten . . .'

'We have so much to forget, Elizabeth. Our lives have been rich in incident, I often think.'

'Well, my dear, you have all that heart could desire now,' Elizabeth said.

'Indeed I have. I can think of nothing else except a lasting peace that our children may enjoy.'

'I do not think even *your* knighthood will annoy the Russians to the extent of spoiling that, Nathaniel,' Elizabeth said, laughing.

'Indeed I hope not,' her husband agreed. 'Here's to you, Lady Drinkwater, and the luck of Midshipman Drinkwater who found you in an apple orchard.'

'And to you, my darling Sir Nathaniel.'

'May I speak?'

'Of course, sir,' said Frey, glaring at the immobile Drinkwater as he stood in a futile attempt to look impressively relaxed. Frey's attention shifted from his model to his canvas as he worked for some moments, his face intense, his eyes flickering constantly from his image to his subject. Periodically he paused to recharge his brush from his palette or mix more colour.

'This reminds me of standing on deck for hours in bad weather, or in chase of the enemy. One is obliged to be there but one has nothing to do, relying upon others to work the ship. Consequently one passes into a state of suspended animation.'

'Yet,' Frey said, placing his brush between his teeth while he turned to his side table to replenish his dipper with turpentine, 'yet you always seemed to be aware of something going wrong, or some detail needing attention, I recall.'

'Oh yes, I was not asleep, though I have once or twice fallen asleep on my feet. But under the cataleptic conditions I speak of, I had, as it were, retreated into myself. All my professional instincts were alert but my mind was passive, not actively engaged in the process of actually thinking.'

'And you are not thinking now?' asked Frey almost absently, as he worked at the coils of bullion that fell from Drinkwater's shoulders.

'Well I'm thinking *now*, of course,' Drinkwater said, with a hint of exasperation which he instantly suppressed, 'but a moment ago I felt almost disembodied, as though I was recalled from elsewhere.'

'Ah, then your soul was about to take flight from your body . . .'

'And how the deuce d'you know that?'

'I don't know it. I just think it might be an explanation,' Frey said simply, looking at Drinkwater but not catching his eye and immediately returning to his canvas.

'You don't think it might be that I was just about to fall asleep?'

'You said yourself', said Frey, working his brush vigorously, 'that it reminded you of how you felt when you stood on deck. Presumably you weren't about to go to sleep then? In fact I supposed it to be a natural state to enable you to remain thus for many hours.' He paused, then added, 'My remark about the soul may have been a little facetious.'

'You wish to concentrate upon your work. I shall remain quiet.'

Frey straightened up, relaxed and looked directly at his sitter. 'Not at all, sir. Please don't misunderstand . . .'

'My dear Frey, I am not deliberately misunderstanding you. But I have never thought you had the capacity for facetiousness. I think you believed what you said, but you have no means of justifying it on scientific principles and so you abandon it rather than have me ravage it with my sceptical ridicule.'

Frey smiled. 'You were always very perceptive, Sir Nathaniel, it was one of the more unnerving things about serving under you.'

'Was I?' Drinkwater asked, his curiosity aroused. 'Well, well. I suppose as you are engaged in painting my portrait it would not be inappropriate to quiz you a little on your subject.'

Frey laughed. 'Not at all inappropriate, Sir Nathaniel, but immodest in the extreme.'

'Nevertheless,' persisted Drinkwater with a grin, 'my curiosity quite naturally overwhelms my modesty.'

'Well that is not unusual, but it is rather disappointing in so unusual a character as yourself, sir.'

'Ah, now you are just baiting me and I'm not certain I should rise to it.'

'Perhaps that is truly my intention.' Frey resumed work, dipping his brush in the turpentine, filling it with a dark colour and applying it to his canvas with those quick, almost indecently furtive glances at his subject that Drinkwater found strangely unnerving.

'What? To put me off pursuing this line of conversation?'

'Just so, sir. To embarrass you into silence.'

'Do your sitters always want to talk?'

Frey shrugged. 'Some do and some don't. Most that do soon get bored. I am apt to reply monosyllabically or occasionally not at all, and then, depending upon my sitter's station and person, I am obliged to apologize.'

'But I can quite understand the concentration necessary to execute . . . By the by, why does an artist "execute" a portrait?'

'I really have no idea, sir.'

'Anyway, the concentration necessary to do your work must of necessity abstract you from gossip.' Drinkwater paused, then went on, 'So some of your sitters are difficult?'

'Many regard me as no more than a servant or at best a clever craftsman. The example of successful artists like Sir Joshua Reynolds counts for little here in the country, and wherever the gentry pay, they believe they own . . .'

'There is more than a hint of bitterness in your voice, Frey.' Drinkwater sighed. 'I am sorry I did not do more for your advancement in the Service. I can see it must irk you to be painting me in sash and star . . .'

'That is not what I meant, Sir Nathaniel!' Frey protested, lowering brush and palette, and emerging fully from behind his easel, no longer looking at Drinkwater as a subject for his brush.

'I know, I know, my dear fellow, of course it isn't what you meant, but I know it is what you feel and it is perfectly natural . . .'

'No, sir, you read me wrongly. I am aware that you did what you could for those of us who regarded ourselves as being of your "family", but the death of poor James Quilhampton, though providing me with the opportunity of happiness with Catriona, set an incongruously high price upon so-called advancement. Believe me, I have no regrets. Indeed, sir, you will not know that, upon your recommendation, I was asked to accompany Buchan's Arctic voyage in 1818. I rejected the appointment because I did not wish Catriona to be left alone again; she had suffered too much in the past.'

'I had no idea you might have gone north with Buchan,' Drinkwater said. 'Well, well. But you are a kind fellow, Frey, I have long thought you such.'

'No more than the next man, sir,' Frey said, colouring, and then he looked down at his palette, refilled his brush and resumed work.

For a moment the two men's private thoughts occupied them and silence returned to the studio. Drinkwater thought of his own Arctic voyage and the strange missionary named Singleton whom he had left among the Innuit people. And then, as he was stirred by an uncomfortable memory, the door opened and Catriona entered bearing a tray. Instinctively Drinkwater moved, before realizing the enormity of his crime.

'My dear Frey, I beg your pardon.'

Frey laid down his gear, wiped his hands on a rag and smiled at his wife. 'Please do break the pose, Sir Nathaniel. Let us enjoy Catriona's chocolate while it is hot.'

'He will keep you sitting there until your blood runs cold, Sir Nathaniel,' she said knowingly, guying her husband, her tawny eyebrows raised in disapproval. 'A've told him about the circulation of the blood, but he takes no notice of good Scottish science.'

'Thank you, my dear,' Drinkwater said, smiling and taking the cup and saucer. 'I am sure this will restore my circulation satisfactorily.'

Drinkwater looked at Catriona's pleasant, open face. She was no beauty, but he had seen a portrait of her by her husband which had the curious effect of both looking like her to the life yet investing her with a quite haunting loveliness. Elizabeth, who had also seen the painting, had remarked upon it, attributing this synthesis to a combination of Frey's technical skill and his personal devotion.

'It is', Elizabeth had explained in their carriage going home, 'what makes of a commonplace portrait, a work of art.'

He thought of that now as Catriona placed Frey's cup of chocolate upon his work table, and he saw the small gesture of gratitude Frey made as they smiled at each other. He envied them this completeness. His own contentment with Elizabeth was quite different. He acknowledged his own deficiencies and was reminded of the uncomfortable thought that had entered his head with Catriona's appearance.

'Will you take tea with us, Sir Nathaniel, when he has finished with you?'

'That is most kind, my dear. If I am not an inconvenience.'

'You will be most welcome.' She stood beside her husband, looking from the portrait to Drinkwater who, by agreement, was not to see the work until Frey judged it complete.

'I shall finish all but the detail of the background today,' Frey said.

'I shall be glad. When I am under such scrutiny I feel like an object.'

'That is what he sees you as,' Catriona threw in. 'However,' she added, putting her head to one side and looking at the portrait, 'I think you will be tolerably pleased.' And with that pronouncement she gathered up her skirts and swept from the room.

Frey and Drinkwater exchanged glances, the former's eyes twinkling. 'She is my harshest critic.'

'And yet the picture you painted of her is outstanding.'

'Oh that. She will not let me hang it. Since that day I showed it to you and Lady Drinkwater, it has stood facing the wall. I think when I am dead, Catriona will burn it,' he said, laughing and gathering up his brushes and palette again. 'They are strange creatures, women . . .'

210

And yet, thought Drinkwater, resuming his seat and the pose, you understand them infinitely better than I do myself.

'A little more to the left, sir ... No, no, just the trunk of the body ...'

Again they fell silent. Drinkwater knew the uncomfortable thought could not be excluded from his mind, and that it must needs be uttered. He had never enjoyed complete intimacy with any other human being, not even Elizabeth, for there had always been that vast gulf created by his profession, his long absences and his ignorance of most of her life ashore. There had been the brief and torrid physical passion with the American widow, a moment of intimate joy so exquisite that its aftermath was a long and lingering guilt. The effect was to have prohibited a more destructive lust with Hortense Santhonax, for she had infected him with another sickness, that of discontent and wild longing. He had, by chance, captured a portrait of her when he took her husband's ship *Antigone* in the Red Sea, and it had lain like a guilty, reproachful secret in the bottom of his sea-chest for years until he had burnt it. It was ironic that she, perhaps the most beautiful of the women whom he had known, now lay under the ruined flint arch of the priory at Gantley Hall, alongside his wild and ungovernable brother Ned.

But perhaps men, at least that majority of men in his situation and from which Frey was excluded, never got close to women. It demanded the most noble sacrifice upon Elizabeth's part for her to comprehend all the complex workings of his seaman's mind. God knew she was a marvel and had done her best! That he was unable to understand her in her entirety was, he concluded, one of those imperfections in life that were profoundly regrettable, but equally profoundly unavoidable. The enigma resided in the eternal question as to why mankind troubled itself with the unattainable. He sighed. Providence had regulated the matter very ill, but that is why many men, he supposed, were often easier in the company of their own sex. He had been close to young Quilhampton and had counted him a friend. After James's death, for which he still held himself accountable, he had grown very friendly with Frey. That last escapade upon the coast of France had left them with more than the bond of shared experience, and he thought that the thing had coalesced when Frey had said that if Drinkwater handled *Kestrel*, he himself would fight her. In that odd moment of decision, they had become one, divining each other's thoughts as they engaged in their horrible profession of execution.

211

And so, in the circumambulatory nature of thoughts, he was returned to the central theme of his anxiety and unconsciously uttered a deep sigh.

'You seem to be in some distress, Sir Nathaniel. Is it the pose?'

'What?'

'Are you all right, sir?'

'No, if I am honest, I am far from being all right . . .'

Frey lowered his brush and stepped forward. 'Please relax, sir,' he said, alarmed. 'Pray invigorate yourself!'

Drinkwater smiled. 'No, no, my dear fellow, do not concern yourself. I am merely troubled by conscience. Invigorating myself at such a moment might prove fatal!'

Frey gave his sitter a steady, contentious look; what they had between them come to call, with reference to Catriona, 'a Scotch glare'.

'No, really. I am quite content to sit still a little longer.'

Frey stepped back behind the easel and resumed work. 'I cannot imagine why your conscience should trouble you, sir. I have not known another person with your sense of duty.'

'That is kind of you, Frey, but it may be the essence of the problem. Duty is a cold calling. It induces men to murder, giving them licence without consolation. Have you any idea how many men I have killed?'

'Well no, sir.' Frey looked up, astonished at the candour of the question.

'No,' replied Drinkwater bleakly, 'neither have I.'

'But . . .' Frey began, but Drinkwater pressed on.

'One remembers only a few of them and they were almost all friends! James, for example . . .'

'You did not kill James!' Frey protested.

'There were others, Frey . . .'

'I cannot believe . . .'

'You do not have to. It is only I who need to know. And I don't . . .'

'But you once said to me that you did not believe in God, Sir Nathaniel, that matters were moved by great but providential forces. Providence has been good to you. This portrait, for example,' Frey said, stepping back and waving his brush at the canvas, 'is evidence of that. Surely the reward is to be enjoyed . . . To be appreciated . . .'

'You are probably right, my dear fellow. I was always a prey to the blue-devils. We drag these deadweights through our lives, and the megrims have been a private curse of mine for many years.'

'You have been lonely, sir,' Frey said reasonably. 'Perhaps it is the penalty for bearing responsibility.' He paused and worked for a moment of furious concentration. 'Perhaps it is the fee you must pay to achieve what you have achieved, a kind of blood-money.'

Drinkwater grinned and nodded. 'You are a great consolation, Frey, and I thank you for it. Alas,' he added sardonically, 'I think there may yet be unnamed tortures still awaiting me.'

'Apart from your rheumaticks, d'you mean?' Frey replied, returning the smile, pleased to see the lugubrious mood lifting.

'Oh yes, far worse than mere rheumaticks.'

For a further fifteen minutes, silence fell companionably between them and then Frey stepped back, laid down his brushes and palette, and picked up a rag. Vigorously wiping his hands he said, 'There, that is all I shall need you for. I think perhaps you had better pass verdict, Sir Nathaniel. Though I say so myself,' he added, grinning with self-satisfaction, 'I do believe 'tis you to the life.'

The Rescue

The spectral faces of the dead came near him now, touching him with their cold breath. If he expected vengeful reproaches, there was only a feeling of acceptance, that all things came to this, and that this was all there was and would ever be. His mind filled with regrets and great sadnesses, too complex and profound for him to recognize in their particulars, and in these too he felt touched by the unity of creation, reached through the uniqueness of his own existence.

In his dying, providence made one last demand upon him.

There was someone near him, someone tugging at the oar with a frantic desperation which seemed quite unnecessary.

'Oh, God!' the man spluttered, thrashing wildly. 'Oh, thank God!'

Dimly it was borne in upon Drinkwater that clinging with him on the oar was Mr Quier.

'Sir Nathaniel . . . 'Tis you . . .' The oar sank beneath their combined weight. 'It's me, Sir Nathaniel . . . Quier, sir, Second Mate . . .'

Odd that he should have known two men whose names began with that curious letter of the alphabet. Odder still that he should make the comparison now, in this extremity, a last habitual shred of rational thought. But he was feeling much warmer and he had seen Quilhampton a little while ago, he was sure of it. Or perhaps it was Frey . . . Frey and Catriona, yes, that was it, the presence of Catriona had confused him.

'The oar', he said with a slow deliberation, 'will not sustain us both . . .'

Drinkwater felt the oar suddenly buoyant again, relieved of the young man's weight. Mr Quier, it appeared, had relinquished it and kicked away.

This was wrong. It was not what he had meant by his remark, but it was so difficult to talk, for his jaw was stiffened against the task. With a tremendous effort of will, Drinkwater hailed Quier.

'Mr Quier, don't let go, I beseech you!'

Quier headed back, gasping and spitting water, fighting his sodden clothing in his effort to stay afloat. He suddenly grasped the oar loom again with a desperate lunge just as Drinkwater let go.

'Hold on, my boy,' he whispered, 'they're sure to find you ...'

It was Mr Forester who saw the man in the water waving. He shouted the news to Captain Poulter without taking his eyes off the distant speck as, every few seconds, it disappeared behind a wave only to reappear bobbing over the passing crest.

'Six points off the port bow, sir! Man waving!'

Poulter called out, 'Hard a-port! Stop port paddle!' He heard with relief the order passed below via the chain of men and was gratified when *Vestal* swung in a tight turn. Poulter was sodden with the perspiration of anxiety, yet his mouth was bone dry and he felt a stickiness at the corners of his lips.

'Come on, come on,' he muttered as he willed the ship to turn faster.

'Three points ... Two!' *Vestal* came round with ponderous slowness.

''Midships! Steadeeee ...'

'Coming right ahead!' Forester bellowed, his voice cracking with urgency.

'Meet her!' Poulter ordered. 'Steady as she goes!'

'Steady as she goes, sir. East by south, a quarter south, sir.'

'Aye, aye. Make it so. Both paddles, dead slow ahead!'

Vestal responded and Poulter, seeing Forester's arm pointing right ahead, ordered Potts to bring the ship's head back to starboard a few degrees, to open the bearing of the man in the water whom he himself could see now.

'Steer east by south a half south.' He turned aft from the bridge wing to check the men were still at their stations, ready to lower the boat once more. Reassured, he noted they were only awaiting the word of command. Poulter swung forward again and watched as they approached the man in the water. Poulter could see it was Quier, the second mate, who maintained himself by means of his arms hanging over the loom of one of the smashed boat's oars.

'Thank God for small mercies,' Poulter breathed to himself, then, raising his voice, he ordered: 'Stop engines! Half astern!'

Beneath him, hidden under the box and sponson, the paddle-wheels churned into reverse. Slowly Quier drifted into full view almost alongside them, some twenty yards away on the port beam. As *Vestal* came to a stop, he looked up at them. He was quite exhausted, his face a white mask devoid of any emotion, bereft of either relief or joy. Quier's expression reminded Poulter of a blank sheet of paper on which he might write 'Lost at sea', 'Drowned' or 'Rescued'.

'Stop her!' he called out, then, leaning over the rail, shouted, 'Boat away!'

So close was Quier that it seemed almost superfluous to lower the boat. It looked as if he might be hooked neatly with the long boat-hook and hove on board like a gaffed fish, but Poulter knew the second officer's life was not saved yet, that considerable effort had still to be expended by the boat's crew to haul the helpless, sodden man out of the sea and into the boat. Poulter turned to the able-seaman stationed on the port bridge wing as lookout.

'Run down to the officers' steward and tell him to bring hot blankets from the boiler room up to the boat-deck right away.'

'Aye, aye, sir.' The man abandoned his post for a moment and disappeared below. Poulter envied the sailor the opportunity to run about, for he found such moments of inactivity irksome in the extreme. He was impatient now. Locating a man was so damnably difficult and the weather was not going to last. The glass was already falling and the sky to the westwards looked increasingly threatening.

Poulter frowned; where there was one, there might also be another. Carefully he scanned the heaving surface of the grey-blue sea surrounding the ship for a further sign of life, but could see nothing. He made himself repeat the process twice, working outwards in a circle of ever-increasing diameter, surveying the scene slowly so that he reckoned to cover every few square feet as the sea writhed and undulated beneath his patient scrutiny. He held in his head a mental chart of the search pattern he had carried out. Although he knew how, from a single central point, a combination of wind, tide and the frantic efforts men might make under duress could spread the debris from a capsized boat, he was as certain as he could be that *Vestal* had quartered the area in which they might reasonably expect to find the upset crew. Indeed, they had not been unsuccessful, for with Quier they had now found everyone but Sir Nathaniel Drinkwater.

216

Sadly, the evidence, or lack of it, seemed conclusive, and by now Poulter privately held out no hope for the elderly captain. The shock alone must have dispatched him long since. Poulter's ruminations were brought to an end as a cheer went up from the men waiting at the davit falls on the boat-deck. Quier was being taken aboard the boat, and a moment later the crew had their oars out again and were vigorously plying them as they pulled back towards the waiting ship. Putting the tiller hard over, the coxswain skilfully spun the boat in under the suspended blocks and his crew hooked on to the falls. Seldom had Poulter seen it done smarter. The boat fairly flew upwards as the falls were hove in, plucking her out of the water.

'Mr Forester!'

'Sir?'

'I don't suppose Quier knows anything of Captain Drinkwater, but ask.'

'Aye, aye, sir!'

Potts was waiting at the wheel as Poulter called out, 'Steady as you go! Half speed ahead!' *Vestal* gathered way and recommenced her search. The lookout had returned from his errand and a moment later Forester joined Poulter on the bridge.

'Sir! Don't go too far away, Quier says Drinkwater was with him a little while ago and that he insisted on leaving the oar to Quier. Apparently it would not support them both.'

'Does Quier think . . .?'

Forester shook his head. 'I don't think Quier can think of anything very much, sir. He has no idea how long he has been in the water and certainly not of how long he has been hanging on to that oar. But it seems Drinkwater was definitely alive not so very long ago.'

'Very well.' With a sinking heart Poulter was convinced he already knew the worst: old man or not, Captain Drinkwater had been lost at sea in an unfortunate accident. 'We shall continue the search, Mr Forester,' he said formally. 'Tell the lookouts to remain sharp-eyed. We don't give up until there is no hope at all, d'you understand?'

'Yes, of course, sir.'

Two hundred yards away, one cable's length or one-tenth of a nautical mile distant from the *Vestal*, Captain Sir Nathaniel Drinkwater caught a last glimpse of the ship. It was a dark mark upon his fading perception, no more. It meant nothing to him, for he was dis-embodied and might have been at Gantley Hall, walking on the soft,

217

rabbit-cropped grass that he always thought of as a luxurious carpet. Elizabeth was there too, and somewhere about the ruins of the priory were the laughing voices of Richard and Charlotte Amelia. He remembered that he hardly knew their children and tried to tell Elizabeth how much he regretted the fact, but somehow he was unable to, although she was beside him and he could see her face quite clearly in the swiftly gathering dusk. He was certain he was holding her hand, but the children had gone.

They had often walked beneath the ruined arch of the priory in the long years they were granted together. Gantley Hall was a modest house, but the ivy-covered remnant in the grounds gave the place a fashionably Gothick aura and had proved a fitting resting-place for Hortense and Edward, two spirits who had never, it seemed to Drinkwater, had anywhere to call their own.

Frey had been right, as Frey so often was, in saying that providence had been good to him.

Providence had been kind to his family too. Charlotte Amelia had married, and had had children, though he could not recall her married name. It bothered him and it bothered him too that he could not remember how many children she had had, or what their names were. Had not one died? Yes, the little boy, the third child. He could ask Elizabeth, but she would think him an old fool for not knowing about his grandchildren. And what had happened to Richard? He had not married, had he?

It was almost dark now and they had turned back towards the house. He felt Elizabeth's hand dissolve from his own and she moved on ahead of him. He wanted to ask her the answers to these terrible questions. She would know and it no longer mattered what she would think of him for having forgotten. Elizabeth would help him, he felt sure, but she was walking away from him and growing smaller and smaller with the distance that seemed to grow inexorably between them . . .

He tried to call her name . . .

'There is no need for you to be on the bridge, Mr Quier,' Poulter said as the Second Officer appeared, wrapped in warm blankets. He was deathly pale and still shaking with cold. 'You should go below; you will catch your death of cold, sir!'

'I'm all right, sir, it's Sir Nathaniel, sir . . .'

'What about him?'

'We were together, sir. Right up to the end.'

Poulter frowned. 'Mr Quier, while we lay alongside you getting you inboard, I searched the surrounding sea meticulously. I could see nothing.'

'But he gave me the oar, sir. Insisted I had it, though he was clinging to it first. He saved my life, sir.'

'Mr Quier,' Poulter said kindly, 'you are still feeling the effects of your ordeal. You had been in the water for well over an hour. Pray go below and remain there until later. I do assure you we shall continue to look for him, but I fear we are already too late. Console yourself. In due time you will simply recall Sir Nathaniel's last act as one of great selflessness.'

'I thought perhaps the gulls might have found him and have given us a clue,' Poulter said, 'but the wind is getting up again and we will have a full gale by the end of the afternoon.' He raised his voice. 'Hard a-starboard and steady on sou' sou' west.'

Vestal rolled heavily as she turned and the three men on the bridge wing steadied themselves by grasping the rail, their faces stung by a light shower that skittered across the sea.

'I think, Captain Poulter, that we must regretfully conclude that Sir Nathaniel has drowned.' Captain Drew turned and looked aft, raising his eyes to the ensign. 'We had better half-mast the colours.'

'I'll see to it, sir,' Forester said, and he crossed the bridge to where one of the lookouts still stared out over the heaving grey waste of the Atlantic Ocean.

'I shall give it another hour, sir,' Poulter said firmly.

'You are wasting your time. Stand the additional lookouts down now, Captain Poulter,' Drew said, watching Forester dispatch the able-seaman aft to tend the ensign halliards. 'I think we have done all that we can.'

'I command the ship, Captain Drew, and I ran the boat down, God forgive me. The responsibility is mine . . .'

'Forester told me the telegraph chain parted. It is what is to be expected from so newfangled a contraption. It was not your fault and I shall not say that it was, if that is what is concerning you.' Drew's tone was testy. 'He was an old man, Captain Poulter. Infirm. Rheumaticky. The shock of immersion has killed him long since. Quier's notions of the passage of time have been distorted by his ordeal. Sir Nathaniel could not possibly have survived for very long.'

'That is probable, Captain Drew, but it would have been better if, after so many distinguished years' service, he had died in his bed.'

219

Drew gave Poulter a long look, sensing the reproach in his voice. 'You do not think we should have attempted the landing, eh? Is that it?'

Poulter sighed. 'I have observed that such so-called misfortunes often follow a single mistake or misjudgement. The fault seems compounded by fate. An error swiftly becomes a disaster.'

'And you think', Drew persisted, 'that we should not have made the attempt?'

'I shall always regret that I did not dissuade you, sir, yes.'

'And you therefore blame me?' Drew asked indignantly.

'I said, sir,' Poulter replied quietly, 'that I shall always regret that I failed to dissuade you from leaving the ship and making the attempt.'

'That verges on the insolent, Captain Poulter,' Drew said, stiffening.

'As you wish, Captain Drew . . .'

For a moment Drew seemed about to leave the bridge, then he hesitated and thought better of it. Poulter turned away and stared about him again, dismissing Drew from his mind. There would inevitably be some unpleasantness in the aftermath of this unfortunate affair, but no good would come of moping over it while there was still a task to be done, no matter how hopeless. There was a definite bite to the wind now and the rain came again in a longer squall that hissed across the sea. The day was dissolving in a monotonous grey that belied the high summer of the season. He had almost forgotten Captain Drew when the Elder Brother cleared his throat, reclaiming Poulter's attention.

'Let us say no more of the matter now, Captain Poulter,' Drew said. 'Sir Nathaniel died doing his duty and he was a sea-officer of impeccable rectitude.'

'Indeed he was, sir,' Poulter said coolly. 'Let us hope his widow finds that a sufficient consolation.'

Two miles away Nathaniel Drinkwater gave up the ghost. The faults and follies of his life, the joys and sorrows, finally faded from his consciousness. In his last moments he felt an overwhelming panic, but then the pain ebbed from his body and he became subsumed by a light of such blinding intensity that it seemed he must cry out for fear of it, and yet it did not seem uncomfortable, nor the end so very terrible.

The Yellow Admiral

The arrival of mail at Gantley Hall was sufficiently unusual to arouse a certain curiosity upon the morning of 20 July 1843. The post-boy was met by Billy Cue who had heard the horse and skidded out on his board to see if his services were required. The legless Billy had acquired his name from the line-of-battle ship *Belliqueux,* aboard which he had been conceived, but he had long since converted himself from the sea-urchin he had been born to a general handyman in the Drinkwater household. Susan Tregembo had originally put him to work scrubbing the flags in her kitchen, a task for which she felt him fitted, but Billy's good nature was undaunted by this practical approach and, by degrees, he made himself indispensable. He had grown into a good-looking man and was said to cut a dash among the more soft-hearted of the local farm girls, so that, upon the death of her husband, it was rumoured that Susan Tregembo allowed Billy into more than her kitchen.

He made up for his lack of mobility by skating about on a board fitted with castors, driven by his powerful arms which wielded a short pair of crutches. With these contrivances, he was able to get around with remarkable agility. He had also acquired a considerable skill as a carpenter, working on a bench set one foot above the level of his work-shop floor. Here he had made a number of stools, steps and low tables, and these permitted him to carry out a multitude of tasks, the most remarkable of which was the care and grooming of Drinkwater's horses. Though Drinkwater was no lover of horse-flesh, the demands of household and farm had required the maintenance of four or five patient beasts who could pull a small carriage or trap, or act as hack when their master or mistress required a mount. Thus, while he might black boots, scrub floors and polish silver, it was in the stables of Gantley Hall that Billy Cue reigned as king.

'You are an ingenious fellow, Billy,' Captain Drinkwater had said when he had first seen the arrangement his protégé had made in one of the stalls to enable him to curry-comb the horses.

'Got the notion from the graving dock in Portsmouth, sir. A set of catwalks at shoulder height lets me get right up to the beasts,' Billy had said from his elevated station.

'Are you fond of horses then, Billy?' Drinkwater had asked.

'Aye, sir, mightily,' Billy had replied, his eyes shining enthusiastically.

'But you've never ridden one?'

'Not with me stumps, sir, no.'

'Then you had better make such use of the trap as you wish. 'Tis no good having a first-class groom who cannot get about the countryside.'

Billy's gratitude had resulted in daily offers of the trap being at Elizabeth's command and an increase in errands into Woodbridge or even Ipswich, notwithstanding the most inclement weather, while any horse arriving at Gantley Hall drew an immediate reaction from Billy. Thus, when the post-boy arrived on that fateful morning, it was Billy who took delivery of the letters and brought them to Susan.

'Two letters,' he announced, 'one from the Admiralty and one from, er ...' He scrutinized the post-mark, but was unable to make head or tail of it and Susan swiftly took both from him with a little snort of irritation, indicating that Billy was trespassing upon preserves forbidden him by the proprieties of life. Susan cast her own eyes over the superscriptions and sniffed.

'Her Ladyship's gone for a walk,' Billy offered helpfully. 'The usual place, d'you want me to ...?

'You mind your horses, my lad,' Susan scolded, 'I'll see to these,' and gathering her skirts up, she swept from the kitchen, leaving a grinning Billy in her wake.

'You're a curious woman, Susie,' he muttered, chuckling to himself as he watched her run off in pursuit of her mistress. She had never ceased nagging him as if he were a boy when they met about their duties, which was a strange and incomprehensible contradiction to her behaviour towards him as a man.

Susan Tregembo was a woman for whom idleness was a sin and for whom keeping busy had at first been a necessary solace and later became a habit. But though she manifested an unconscious irritation when she discovered idleness in others, those who knew her well

222

forgave her brusque manner, for much of her activity was directed at the comfort of others, and in her devotion to 'the Captain' and his wife she was selfless. Neither had been bred to servants and they never took this devotion for granted, least of all Elizabeth who, in her heart of hearts, would many a time in the loneliness of her isolation have welcomed Susan as an equal. But her husband's rank made such things impossible and with his successes, culminating in his retirement and knighthood, had come the irreversible constraints of social conformity. For Susan, the matter was never in doubt. Elizabeth was of the quality because she possessed all the natural advantages of birth and education. Her Ladyship's penurious upbringing, her struggle to cope with the demands of running the household of a poor country parson and of maintaining some semblance of social standing in the face of the ill-concealed condescension of almost all with whom she was obliged to come into contact, was not a matter that troubled Susan. She had married a man who had claimed that his future lay with Nathaniel Drinkwater, and she had fallen into step with his decision. It never occurred to Susan Tregembo that the same Nathaniel Drinkwater had had a hand in her husband's death. As she tripped across the grass towards the great ruined arch of the priory where she knew her mistress would be found, she was only conscious of being, in her own way, a fortunate creature, rescued from the harsh life of the waterfront with all its pitfalls and temptations by 'the Captain' and his lovely wife.

On warm summer mornings, it was Elizabeth's invariable habit to take a short walk in the grounds of the Hall. Since she had learned that on the east coast of Suffolk any change in the weather would not arrive until about an hour before noon, a fine morning beckoned. The grounds of the Hall were not extensive, bounded by a road, a stream and the farmland rented to Henry Vane, but they included the jagged ruins of the old priory and these, broken down though they were, anchored her to her ecclesiastical past, reminding her of her father more than her maker. Chiefly, however, they performed the function of a private retreat where she was able to escape the demands of the house and sit in the warm, windless sunshine, content with a book, her correspondence, or simply her own thoughts. Her husband had been much in her mind of late. She had had difficulty reconciling herself to his absences on account of the Trinity House. She thought him too old for such duties and the jokes about his appointment as an 'Elder' Brother had seemed somewhat too near the mark for wit. Though he

223

cited the appointments of octogenarian admirals to posts of the highest importance during the late war, claiming that the responsibilities of Barham and St Vincent far outweighed those of a mere 'Trinity Brother', her husband's assurances failed to mollify Elizabeth. She had long nurtured a chilling conviction that Nathaniel would not be spared to die in his bed like any common country gentleman, and for several days past she had slept uneasily, troubled by dreams.

In the daylight she had chided herself for a fool, rationalizing the irrational with the reflection that she simply missed him, that she herself was old and that with age came the ineluctable fear of the future. And as she sat beneath the great arch, its flint edge jagged on one side, overgrown with ivy and populated by the buzzing of bees, its inner curve smooth with the masonry of its elegant coping, she was mesmerized by a single cloud which, pushed by a light breeze, moved against the sky and made it look as though the masonry was toppling upon her.

She was almost asleep when she heard the rustle of Susan approaching through the bushes which, she noted, needed trimming back to clear the path. Susan's appearance started a fluttering in Elizabeth's heart which increased as she saw the hastening nature of her housekeeper's approach and the letters in her hand.

'What is it, Susan?' Elizabeth asked anxiously, sitting up and pulling her spectacles from her reticule.

'Billy's just brought in two letters, your Ladyship, one's from the Admiralty . . .'

'The Admiralty?' Elizabeth frowned. 'What on earth does the Admiralty want?' She looked up at Susan as she took the two letters and then read the superscriptions.

'The other is to you, ma'am.'

'So I see. I suppose I had better open that first. Thank you, Susan.'

'Thank you, ma'am.' Susan bobbed a curtsey and retreated, looking back as she passed through the bushes to where Elizabeth was opening the first letter. She read it with a cold and terrible certainty clutching at her heart. Unconsciously she rose to her feet as though the act might put back the clock and arrest the news. Captain Drew had been sparing of the details, wrapping the event up in the contrived platitudes of the day, expressing his deepest regrets and ending with a solicitous wish that Lady Drinkwater could take consolation from the fact that her husband had died gallantly for the sake of others. Exactly what Captain Drew meant by this assertion was not quite clear, nor did his phraseology soothe Elizabeth in any way. Distraught as she was,

224

Elizabeth was not beyond detecting in Captain Drew's words both condescension and a poor command of self-expression.

But as she sat again, her tears coming readily, her down-turned mouth muttering, 'Oh, no, oh no, it should not have been like this', she thought something stirred beyond the arch. It was a man, but her tears half-blinded her. For a moment or two the certainty that it was her husband grew swiftly upon her, but the shadow lengthened and turned into Mr Frey.

'Lady Drinkwater, good morning. I do hope I didn't startle you. Forgive me for taking the liberty of entering through the farm . . . My dear Lady Drinkwater, what is the matter?'

'He's dead,' she said, looking up at the younger man. 'My husband's dead, drowned in a boating accident, at sea . . .' She held out Drew's letter for Frey to read.

'My dear, I'm so sorry . . .'

Overcome, Frey sat beside her and hurriedly whipped out his handkerchief, reading the letter with a trembling hand. After he had digested its contents he looked at Elizabeth. She shook her head. 'It had to happen,' she said as she began to cry inconsolably, 'but why at sea? Why not here, amongst his family?'

Frey put his arm round her and, when her sobbing had subsided to a weeping, she rose and he assisted her into the house.

It was Henry Vane who, much later, walking through from the farm to offer his condolences, found the second letter lying on the grass. Frey was still with Elizabeth and had sent Billy Cue into Woodbridge to summon Catriona and bring her out in the trap to stay with Elizabeth overnight. Vane presented himself and the lost letter.

'It seems to be from the Admiralty,' Vane said, handing it to Frey who, having taken a look at the embossed wafer, agreed.

'Thank you, Henry. I think it can be of little consequence now, but I suppose I should let Her Ladyship know.'

'How is she?' asked Vane, his open face betraying his concern.

'Inconsolable at the moment.'

'Would you present my condolences?'

Frey shook his head. 'No, no, my dear sir, you are of the family and have as much right as me to be here, come in, come in.'

Frey announced Vane and left him with Elizabeth for a few moments, joining them after an interval. Vane sat alongside her, holding her hand, and Frey noticed she seemed more composed.

'There was a second letter, Elizabeth,' Frey said softly. 'Vane found

225

it; you must have dropped it.' He held it out towards her. 'It has an Admiralty seal.'

'Please open it. It cannot be of much importance now.' She smiled up at him and he slit the wafer and unfolded the letter. For a moment he studied it and then, lowering it, he said with a sigh, 'Sir Nathaniel attained flag rank on the 14th. He has been gazetted rear-admiral, Lady Drinkwater.'

'They are rather late, are they not?' Elizabeth said, with a hint of returning spirit.

'I think Sir Nathaniel would rather have died a post-captain than a yellow admiral,' Frey said with his engaging smile.

Elizabeth reached out her other hand and took Frey's. 'I am sure you are right, my dear,' she said, shaking her head, 'and I am sure he would rather have died at sea than in his bed, painful though that is for me to acknowledge. Do you not think so?'

Frey nodded and gently squeezed Elizabeth's hand. 'I rather think I do, my dear.'

It took some months for Elizabeth to feel her loss less acutely, but her husband's absences during the long term of their marriage had, despite their last years of intimacy, in some ways prepared her for widowhood.

'It seems to me', Catriona had once said to her, after the untimely death of her own first husband and before she had married Frey, 'that a sea-officer's wife lives in an unnaturally prolonged state of temporary widowhood in preparation for the actual event.' It was a sentiment with which Elizabeth perforce agreed. She was an old woman and her lot, compared with Catriona's for instance, had been a far easier one.

If she regretted anything, it was that she had not known her husband well until both of them were advanced in age. Now, that sweet pleasure, and it seemed very sweet in retrospect, was forever denied her. It was at this point that she recalled the task she had given him: that of recording his memoirs. About twelve weeks after the news of Drinkwater's death had arrived at Gantley Hall; after his body which had been washed up on the beach of Croyde Bay was sent home in its lead coffin; after the visits of their children and the renewed weeping that accompanied the funeral rites; and after Sir Nathaniel Drinkwater had been laid with due pomp and ceremony beside his brother Edward and the mysterious Hortense, it occurred to Elizabeth to go through her husband's papers more thoroughly than she had at first done.

She was familiar with most of what she found, though she had not read the pages of penned memories earlier, merely flicked through them. Nor did she now intend to read them in their entirety, but her eye was caught by this phrase or that, and as she dipped into them so the hours passed and she felt a curious contact with him as she sat in silence. Regretfully reaching the end of the document which had no real conclusion, but simply mentioned his continuing connection with the sea through the Trinity House, she was about to lay it down when a loose leaf of paper, folded in half and stuck in amid the rest, fluttered to the floor. She bent and picked it up, unfolding it as she did so.

It seemed to be a draft, separate from the main body of the memoirs and written with less certainty, for it contained several erasures and corrections. At the top right-hand corner was scribbled a date. With a fluttering heart, she noted it had been written on the eve of his departure to join the *Vestal*, and it struck her that he might have had some premonition of his death. It was not so curious a fancy, she thought, given his age and the exertions of the duty he was about to undertake. She had to wipe her eyes before the script swam into focus.

In Concluding these ~~Memoirs~~ Recollections, Drinkwater had written, *I am ~~almost~~ Compelled almost, to Review my Life, to Weigh the Balance of Profit and Loss, not in terms of Success, for Providence, as Frey reminded me, has been Materially Kind to me, but in terms of Usefulness. My Actions will have caused Grief in Quarters /quite unknown to me, and in Quarters known to me but not to Those whom I have Offended and this Troubles me. Such a Pricking of Conscience may be but an Indulgence, perhaps a Punishment in Itself, for those whom I dispatched from Life had no such Period for ~~Contemplation~~ Reflection or Regret.*

Yet I was Compelled by Duty and I am left Wondering whether I am thereby Exculpated and whether Anyone takes Ultimate Responsibility? The King, perhaps? In whose Name and under whose Authority a Sea-Officer conducts himself and Who was Mad? Or is All Ordered by Providence? And is it therefore beyond our Comprehension?

If it were so, it would be a great burden lifted from my Soul.

~~I think that~~ ~~It seems that~~ ~~I can only conclude~~

In the end, the Complex <u>must</u> be rendered Simple, and our Understanding kept Imperfect.

Elizabeth laid the sheet of paper in her lap and stared out of the window. Grey clouds were sweeping in from the west and she would need a candle if she intended reading any more, but there was nothing else to read. Her husband had found a kind of peace, she thought, rising. As Frey said, providence had been very kind to him.

Author's Note

In this, the fourteenth and last in a series of novels which form the 'biography' of Nathaniel Drinkwater, I have taken some liberties with the patience of my readers. For this I must crave an indulgence. For twenty years I have accompanied Drinkwater and, from time to time, our lives have enjoyed curious parallels. His capture of the *Santa Teresa* and heady anticipation of prize money coincided with my own part in the salvage of a cargo ship in the North Sea which, at first sight, seemed to hold the promise of a small fortune; his incarceration in an attic office at the Admiralty happened when I myself relinquished sea-going command in exchange for an office desk. It was no accident that he assisted me in escaping my confinement, just as I engineered his own. There have been other, more technical comparisons, but they would be tedious to enumerate and, in this last novel, he has, at least at the time of writing, preceded me over the final threshold.

In the invention of Drinkwater and his adventures, I have worked through an obsessive fascination with the period in which he lived. Beyond the basic concept and a handful of historical facts, I started each story with no particular idea of what exactly would happen to the main protagonist. For me the process of writing was to find out, and to that extent Drinkwater's life was not entirely my own conscious creation. I have consequently derived much fun from the stimulation which this form of exploration produces, but one thing I resolved upon, that where what appeared to be expedient invention threw up a train of events, I must follow the train of cause and effect to its conclusion. To this end, this fourteenth book concludes several yarns, bringing together storylines begun in the earlier novels. It is for this that I ask my readers' indulgence, in the hope that they, like me, wanted to know what happened to Hortense, or Edward or Mr Frey, or why for years poor Nathaniel endured the recurring and horrible nightmare of the white lady.

As to the manner of Drinkwater's death, it is expected nowadays that a novelist must most assiduously research his subject. Some years ago, I came across an account by an eighteenth-century seaman who had only narrowly escaped drowning. It was powerfully written and made an impression on me, thus sowing the seed of an idea. Furthermore, by a series of personal misadventures, I have myself been three times helpless in the sea. On one of these rather desperate occasions, I did not expect to live.

For those who wish to know upon what historical hook the substance of this last tale is hung, the Trinity House Steamer *Vestal* did indeed run her own boat down on 14 July 1843 after abandoning an attempt to land at the foot of the cliffs at Hartland Point. Also drawn from life are Captain McCullough and the Sentinel Service, a little known part of the Royal Navy's rich history. As for the two troopers aboard *Cyclops* in 1780, it is matter of fact that in that year two men were dismissed from the 7th Queen's Own Light Dragoons and sent to serve in the Royal Navy as a punishment. Moreover, cheese issued by the royal dockyards was often of such age and consistency that sailors fashioned it into boxes and worked it like wood, and there is a record of a cheese being fashioned into a mast-truck, fitted with flag halliard sheaves and shipped atop a warship's mast where it remained for the duration of her commission. Such are the happy gleanings of assiduous research!

As for more seminal inspiration, whilst still a teenager I came across six battered volumes of William James's monumental *Naval History of Great Britain*, which records in meticulous and largely accurate detail every action fought by the Royal Navy during the wars of the French Revolution and Empire. I parted with my pocket money of half-a-crown, a sum which now sounds as archaic as the age of the books themselves, though they had been published a century before my own birth. Astonishingly, most of the pages were uncut. This purchase was to create a lifelong interest in maritime history and to result ultimately in the 'biography' of Nathaniel Drinkwater.

I am aware that when coming to the end of a much-enjoyed book, the reader is often assailed by a sense of regret. Something of the same *tristesse* hangs over me now as I tap out the last words of the saga.

I have immensely enjoyed writing the series, but every voyage has its ending and Drinkwater exceeded his allotted three score years and ten to die not ignobly. To those of my readers who have shared something of this enjoyment, may I simply express my gratitude. Your support meant the whole tale could be told, and while your precise image of Nathaniel Drinkwater may differ slightly from my own, the substance of his invention is common to us both.